THE SUMMER PACT

THE
SUMMER
PACT

A NOVEL

EMILY
GIFFIN

BALLANTINE BOOKS

NEW YORK

Copyright © 2024 by Emily Giffin

Published in the United States by Ballantine Books, an imprint of Random House, a division of Penguin Random House LLC, New York.

BALLANTINE BOOKS & colophon are registered trademarks of Penguin Random House LLC.

Hardback ISBN 9780593600290
Ebook ISBN 9780593600306

Printed in the United States of America on acid-free paper

randomhousebooks.com

2 4 6 8 9 7 5 3 1

First Edition

Book design by Jo Anne Metsch

This one is for Kate,
my trusted assistant and treasured friend.

The Summer Pact explores love and loss, touching on issues surrounding alcohol abuse, mental health, and suicide. More than 700,000 lives are lost due to suicide every year, and it is the fourth leading cause of death among fifteen-to-twenty-nine-year-olds. Please read with care. If you or your loved ones are in distress, call the 988 Suicide & Crisis Lifeline for free, confidential 24/7 support.

THE SUMMER PACT

HANNAH

OFTEN WONDER WHAT makes our coming-of-age friendships so powerful. I know the usual theories. . . . That they fill the void of adolescent loneliness. That they give us a sense of belonging. That they shape our adult identities. All these things are true, but when it comes right down to it, I think it's a simple matter of who was there by our side, bearing witness to our loss of innocence.

For me, that moment came late, during the spring of my fourth year in college. As my classmates and I studied for final exams and counted down the days to graduation, emotions ran high. We were excited about the future but weren't quite ready to part ways and face full-fledged adulthood. At least I wasn't. I couldn't imagine life without the people who brought meaning to mine: Summer, Lainey, and Tyson. My best friends.

The four of us had met in the basement lounge of our dorm our first year, just days after we arrived at the University of Virginia. It was a Thursday night, the kickoff to the weekend, but none of us was in the mood to go out. Summer was studying at a corner table, her face buried in *The Odyssey* as she furiously highlighted passages. Lainey and I sat at separate tables near her. We had books open, too, but were spending more time on our phones. Tyson was kicked back on a sofa, watching a baseball game on the muted television.

We were the only four people in the room, and for a long time, nobody spoke or made eye contact. Summer was the first to break the ice, putting her book down, standing up from her table, and walking over to the sofa. She sat down beside Tyson and asked who he was rooting for.

"The Yankees," he said.

I watched them out of the corner of my eye, admiring Tyson's profile. With a strong jawline, high cheekbones, and flawless golden brown skin, he was decidedly handsome.

"Are you from New York?" she asked.

"No, D.C. But I hate the Orioles," he replied matter-of-factly, not giving her much to work with.

"So you're a Nats fan?"

"Sadly, yes," he said.

"I hear you," Summer said. "I'm a Cubs fan."

"Ah, a Chicago girl," Tyson said.

"Well, I'm from the 'burbs. Naperville." She smiled. "But, yeah, I'm a lifelong Cubs fan."

"Well. At least you guys have won a couple titles," Tyson said.

"Yeah. In 1907 and 1908!" She laughed.

"Hey, it's better than none," he said. "I'm Tyson, by the way."

"I'm Summer," she said, then looked over her shoulder at Lainey and me, repeating her introduction.

"I'm Lainey. And I know nothing about baseball!" Lainey's smile and energy lit up the room.

"I'm Hannah," I said, feeling a wave of my usual social anxiety.

"Where are you guys from?" Summer asked us.

"I'm from Atlanta," I said.

"Encinitas," Lainey said. "Near San Diego."

"Wow. That's *far*," Summer said. "How'd you end up at UVA?"

"I needed a change of scenery. And somehow, I got in!" She gave us another magnetic smile, her light brown eyes sparkling. "What about you guys? Why Virginia?"

Tyson cited in-state tuition; I told them my father and grandfather were both alums; and Summer said she had been recruited to run track and cross-country. Tyson looked intrigued, then promptly launched into rapid-fire questions about Summer's events and PRs. She answered modestly, but her times were incredible. As we marveled at her 4:36 mile, Lainey quipped that she only ran when being chased.

"Do you find yourself being chased often?" Tyson deadpanned.

"Oh, you'd be surprised," she said with a smirk and a toss of her long brown curls.

She was clearly flirting, but it seemed more playful than strategic, and despite how pretty she was, she didn't seem full of herself.

Summer went on to ask about our majors, sharing that she was pre-med.

Tyson said he was debating between English Literature and Religion and would likely go to law school. Lainey said she was thinking about studio art or drama.

"Were you into theater in high school?" Summer asked her.

"I dabbled," Lainey said. "But I'd rather be a screen actor than do stage stuff."

"Very cool," Summer said, shifting her gaze to me. "What about you, Hannah?"

I told her I was undecided.

"What do you think you might want to do?" Summer pressed. "Jobwise?"

My mind went embarrassingly blank, as it always did with this line of questioning. "I don't know. Maybe interior design . . . or something in education."

Summer nodded, remarking that teaching was such an admirable profession, as I decided that I liked her. I *really* liked her. She had such a down-to-earth, genuine vibe, exactly the way I'd always imagined people from Illinois—and all the *I* states, for that matter. She even *looked* wholesome, right down to her freckles and strawberry-blond pigtails.

"Yeah. Plus I love kids," I said, thinking that what I wanted more than any career was to get married and have babies and be the kind of stay-at-home mother who bakes cookies and does crafts.

But that wasn't something you could really admit, so I changed the subject, asking if they planned to rush in the spring. For me, Greek life was an absolute given. Many of my high school friends were already in the process of pledging at Georgia, Alabama, and Auburn, where rush took place before classes began. My mother was obsessed with what they were all doing and was already feverishly gathering letters of recommendation from anyone she knew who had any sort of connection to what she called the "top-tier sororities" at Virginia.

Summer shook her head, explaining that as a student-athlete, she wouldn't have time. That made sense, but I was surprised when Lainey declared that she would rather "poke her eyes out with a hot stick than audition for friendship."

"I feel you," Tyson said. "My dad was an Alpha and really wants me to follow in his footsteps, but I kind of want to do my own thing. We'll see."

I listened intently, intrigued by their answers. For the first time, it occurred to me that there might be an alternative path to a college social life than joining a sorority. It also crossed my mind that Summer, Lainey, and Tyson might become my people. I had the strange feeling they would be.

We kept talking, covering a myriad of topics, including our families and siblings (Summer had an older brother, while Lainey, Tyson, and I were only children); our high schools (Tyson and I had gone to small private schools while Summer and Lainey went to large public schools); and our relationship status (we were all single).

Before I knew it, it was after midnight, and we had bonded in that magical way you hope will happen when you get to college. Summer said she really needed to get to bed—she had early morning practice—so we exchanged numbers and set up a group text thread. The following night we met for dinner, and in no time we'd become a foursome.

As organic as our friendship felt at the time, I look back now and see how unlikely it was. Beyond the utter randomness of our meeting in that lounge, we came from such different worlds. Lainey was raised by a single mother in a hipster surf town; Tyson's parents were part of the D.C. elite, his father a high-powered attorney and his mother a federal judge; Summer was the quintessential Midwesterner with a sporty, apple-pie family; and I was the sole Southerner, growing up saying "yes, ma'am" and "no, sir," going to church on Sundays, and wearing bows in my hair.

Somehow, we all clicked, though, like pieces of a puzzle, each of us bringing something different to the group. Tyson was the deep thinker; Lainey the free spirit; Summer our bright star and leader. I was never quite sure what my role was, and I sometimes wondered what they saw in me. I told myself that every friend group needed a cheerleader, and I had always been a good one. I took pride in that.

I attended all of Summer's home meets, encouraged Lainey to pursue her love of acting, and supported Tyson's social justice efforts on campus.

Incidentally, and much to my mother's dismay, I never ended up joining a sorority. I discovered that when it came to friendship, I preferred quality over quantity—and that my gut was right: Summer, Lainey, and Tyson *were* my people.

THE NEXT FOUR years flew by, and suddenly we were on the brink of going our separate ways. Tyson was headed to Yale Law School; Lainey had taken a PR gig in New York City to support herself while auditioning; and I was returning home to work in a furniture showroom at the Atlanta Decorative Arts Center.

Only Summer's plans were somewhat up in the air. With a 4.0 in a grueling biochemistry major and a near-perfect MCAT score, she had already been accepted to several top medical schools, including Ohio State, Northwestern, and Michigan. But she'd been waitlisted at Harvard—her dream school—and was nervously awaiting a final answer. In addition to her academic stress, she was weeks away from competing in the ACC and NCAA championships, consumed with worry about a lingering ankle injury. During her college career, she had set two school records and become an All-American three times over, but she had yet to win a title. It was a monkey on her back.

The night before her final *ever* college exam, the two of us sat together on the Rotunda steps, a few yards from her historic room on the Lawn, where only the most outstanding members of our class were granted permission to live. Nursing a Red Bull, she was a basket case of nerves. As I listened to her vent about her microeconomics class, I resisted the urge to say *I told you so*. Everyone at UVA knew that course was a GPA killer—and there had been no need for a biochem major to take it.

Instead, I told her what I'd been telling her for four years, ahead of countless races and tests. That she was going to kick ass.

She shook her head, tugged on her ponytail, and said, "Not this time, Hannah. I seriously think I might fail."

"That's ridiculous. Worst-case scenario, you get your first B," I said, then reminded her that she had already gotten into three amazing med schools.

"Yes. But they're not *Harvard*," she said.

I sighed, feeling the slightest edge of irritation, then got to my feet, brushing off the back of my cutoff shorts. "All right," I said. "I'll let you get back to it."

She looked up at me and said, "Where are you headed?"

"To dinner with Lainey and Tyson. Then to that lacrosse party."

A fleeting look of FOMO crossed her face before she said, "Don't you have an exam on Friday?"

"Yeah. But it'll be easy."

"Ugh. I'm jealous."

"Of my mediocrity?" I joked.

She smiled back at me, then told me to have fun.

LATE THE NEXT morning, I woke up with a mini-hangover, regretting that last wine cooler. I checked my phone and saw a missed call and text from Summer: OMG. I'm so screwed. Call me.

I started to call her back, but a wave of nausea overcame me, and I put my head back down on my pillow. Our usual song and dance could wait.

About an hour later, I woke up and called Summer back. She

didn't answer, so I left a message, showered, and walked to Bodo's, our favorite bagel shop. I bought two egg sandwiches, then headed to the Lawn and knocked on her door. There was no answer, so I turned to go, but then decided to leave a sandwich on her desk, along with a congratulatory note. Regardless of how she'd done on her final, she was finished with college exams. It was a milestone. Knowing she usually kept her room unlocked, I twisted the knob and pushed the door open.

In what became the worst moment of my life, I looked up and saw Summer, my beautiful best friend, hanging from a ceiling light fixture. Her neck was tied with the orange silk scarf I'd given her for her twenty-first birthday. Her legs were bare and dangling. Her green eyes were open but vacant.

I screamed for help, then called 911. With the operator still on the line, I dropped my phone to the floor and scrambled onto a chair next to Summer. I reached up, frantically clawing at that tight silk knot. All the while, I silently prayed to God, begging Him to save her.

Deep down I knew I was too late, but I refused to believe it. It was beyond comprehension. She was too healthy and fast and strong. She had *just* texted me. She was going to graduate with us next week. She was going to med school. She was going to be a doctor and *save* lives. Not die young.

At some point, the quiet boy who lived in the room next door appeared in the doorway. *Holy Mother of God,* I heard him whisper before grabbing a pair of scissors from Summer's desk. He handed them to me, and as I used them to sever the scarf, he wrapped his arms around Summer, lowering her to the hardwood floor, where he immediately began CPR.

From there, my memory becomes jumbled, though certain details will be etched in my brain forever. I remember the moment the paramedics arrived and took over, and my wave of foolish hope as I listened to their calm voices and beeping gadgets and the static from their walkie-talkies. There could still be a miracle, I told myself, as I called Tyson, then Lainey, leaving them hyperventilating voicemails. I remember the small crowd that gathered silently on the steps of the Rotunda, staring toward Summer's room. I remember the sight of Tyson sprinting across the Lawn, stumbling into my arms, gasping for breath. I remember the university security guard who held him back, telling him he couldn't go any farther. I remember his guttural sobs as he fell to his knees. I remember the sight of that black zippered bag and the panic I felt knowing that Summer's body was trapped inside the darkness. I remember the sound of the gurney bumping along the brick walkway as Tyson and I trailed behind, clinging to each other. I remember the ambulance—the thud of doors closing and the unceremonious way it pulled out of the lot. Most of all, I remember the deafening silence that followed.

SUMMER DIDN'T LEAVE a note. She had called Tyson and Lainey—after she called me—but they hadn't picked up, either, and she hadn't left voicemails for any of us. The only real clue we had was that final text to me.

I dutifully and shamefully shared it with Summer's parents when they came to collect their daughter's body, along with her belongings, but I couldn't bring myself to admit that I'd waited over an hour to return Summer's call. When they asked if I had any idea what she had been referring to in her text, the only thing I could come up with was that she hadn't done well on her exam. I told myself that couldn't be it, though; nobody was that much of a perfectionist. Not even Summer.

Meanwhile, the tragic news tore across campus like a wildfire in

a windstorm. Everyone knew the cause of Summer's death, but nobody knew why she did it. Tyson, Lainey, and I didn't entertain
those questions or conversations, but the speculation still trickled
its way back to us. Some thought it was run-of-the-mill depression.
Others blamed it on Summer's ankle injury and the stress of being
a college athlete. Still others wondered if there was a boy or a
breakup to blame. Then came the rumors that Summer had been
caught cheating on her micro exam. Several classmates claimed that
they had seen their professor tap Summer on the shoulder before
they both left the room.

After nearly seventy-two hours, the university released an official
statement. It was eloquent, expressing the community's great sorrow, along with its deepest condolences to Summer's family, friends,
and teammates. But it provided no answers. If Summer's parents
were given additional information, they chose not to share it with us.

To this day, Tyson insists that Summer would never cheat. That
she was too honest and ethical. But I came to believe that it was the
only explanation that made sense. At that point, UVA still had a
strict, single-strike honor code, so if Summer had been found guilty,
her punishment would have been expulsion. She would not have
received a diploma. Her school running records would have been
expunged. She would not have gone to Harvard—or any other medical school. In Summer's mind, her life would have been over before
she took it.

THE FOLLOWING YEAR was a never-ending nightmare. Guilt and
grief consumed me. I couldn't go anywhere or do anything without
triggering a memory of something Summer loved. Starbucks. Gua-
camole. Country music. Baseball. Board games. Black Labs. Eighties

rom-coms. Nineties sitcoms. Four-leaf clovers. The color pink. Anything related to running or Chicago or our beloved university.

At least once a day, I had the urge to call and talk to Summer. In those moments, I'd often reach out to Tyson or Lainey instead, but they were both so busy. The first year of law school was grueling, and Lainey was caught up in a whirlwind of auditions and parties in the city that never sleeps.

Meanwhile, I felt like I had regressed to my old life in Atlanta. I went to all the same places I'd gone in high school and hung out with all the same people. Even my job felt depressingly familiar, as I spent forty hours a week peddling overpriced furniture and lighting fixtures to the usual suspects, including many of my mother's wealthy Buckhead friends.

And then there was my mother herself. For four years, I'd managed to escape some of her daily scrutiny. The distance had been heavenly. But she picked up right where she'd left off with her backhanded compliments and relentless critique of my clothes, hair, figure, makeup, skin, and posture.

She was especially obsessed with my love life—or rather my *lack* of a love life—and bombarded me with unsolicited advice, which she called "suggestions." I tried to tell her that I wasn't in the frame of mind to date—I was too sad—but she persisted, and I continued to jump through her hoops. It was an exhausting cycle.

AS WE APPROACHED the one-year anniversary of Summer's death, I texted Lainey and Tyson, asking if the three of us could schedule a visit. They agreed it was a good idea—that it had been way too long. Lainey suggested some California sunshine. She said her mother would be out of town that weekend, and we could stay at her little house near the beach. It sounded wonderful—or as wonderful as things could be without Summer.

A few weeks later, we all flew to San Diego, then drove to Encinitas. On our first afternoon together, we didn't talk much about Summer. We just strolled along Coast Highway 101, a lively street flanked by hipster bars and funky boutiques, as Lainey pointed out her old haunts.

"Hey! We should get matching tattoos!" she said, as we passed the sketchy-looking shop that had inked the small Libra scale on the inside of her left ankle. "We could get Summer's initials."

"My mother would kill me," I blurted out.

"You're twenty-*three*, *Hannah*," Lainey said. "You don't need her approval anymore."

"I know," I said. "But I kind of hate tattoos, too."

"Thanks a lot," Lainey said with a laugh.

"I hate them for *me*," I said. "I love yours for *you*."

"Yeah, yeah," she said, smiling.

Tyson chewed his lip, deep in thought. After a few seconds, he said, "I feel like we should do *something*, though. In Summer's memory."

"Like what?" Lainey asked.

"I don't know yet," Tyson said. "It'll come to me."

LATER THAT NIGHT, after we made dinner and cleaned up the kitchen, we opened a second bottle of wine. The mood was somber, then downright dark.

"Have either of you ever . . . had any sort of suicidal thoughts?" Tyson asked us at one point.

I winced hearing the word—one I could no longer bear to say aloud—then shook my head.

"No. Never," Lainey said. "What about you?"

Tyson hesitated just long enough to concern me, then said, "I've wanted to disappear, but not *die*."

"Disappear? Where?" Lainey asked.

"Disappear from anywhere ... *everywhere* ..."

"Um. That's called 'death'," Lainey said.

"No. It's not the same thing. It's not about wanting to *die*. It's about wanting to escape pain," Tyson said. "Do you know the David Foster Wallace quote? Where he likens suicide to jumping from a burning building?"

Lainey and I said no.

"It's not that the person doesn't fear falling—because he *does*—it's just that falling feels less terrible than burning," Tyson said, paraphrasing the quote.

"*Damn*," Lainey whispered. "When you say it like that, I sort of get it. Almost."

"Me too," I said, wishing for the millionth time that I had called Summer the second I got her text. Gone straight to her room. *Saved* her.

The wave of guilt and regret was followed by a familiar aftershock of confusion and anger. Why had the toughest person I'd ever known given up so suddenly, with no warning whatsoever?

"Promise me you would never—" I said to Tyson.

"See? That's the point," Tyson said. "I don't think that's a promise anyone can make. Unless you've been standing in that burning building, you just don't know what you'd do."

"But promise you would at least *talk* to us—" I stopped in mid-sentence.

As I looked into Tyson's eyes, I could see a lightbulb going off. "That's it! That's the promise we need to make.... If we ever feel like we've hit rock bottom—whether for a specific reason or no reason whatsoever—we have to promise to talk."

"Yes," I said, nodding emphatically. "Not only talk. But come together. Like this."

"Yes," Tyson said. "Just like this."

"No matter where we are or what we have going on," Lainey added.

Tyson nodded, then pulled a spiral notebook and ballpoint pen out of his backpack, turning to a blank page.

"What are you doing?" Lainey asked.

"I'm drawing up a contract," he said, clicking the pen and starting to write furiously.

After a few minutes, he stopped, looked down at the page, and said, "There. Finished."

"What does it say?" Lainey asked.

He cleared his throat and read aloud: *In the days, months, and years to come, should we, the undersigned, find ourselves in a crisis, depression, or moment of deep sorrow or darkness, we hereby solemnly swear to reach out to one another before taking any drastic steps or making any permanent decisions. We make this pact in Summer's name and memory.*

"Wow," I breathed. "That's perfect."

Tyson nodded, then said, "It just needs a title."

"The Suicide Pact?" Lainey said.

Tyson looked as horrified as I felt. "God, no. That sounds like a cult where we promise *to* kill ourselves," he said.

"How about the Summer Pact?" I suggested.

"Yes. That's good," Tyson said, writing the words at the top of the page. He then dated it and drew three lines at the bottom. He signed on the first line, Lainey on the second, and I signed the third.

With our contract now executed, Lainey suggested a walk on the beach. We could build a fire, maybe go for a night swim. Tyson and I agreed, though I knew there was no way I'd be getting in dark, potentially shark-filled waters. We put on our shoes; grabbed a flashlight, a few towels, and some matches; then poured our remaining wine into a thermos before heading out the door.

The night was chilly. Too cold to swim, we decided. Instead, we built a fire in one of the designated pits on the beach. Spreading our blankets around it, we huddled together for warmth, sitting in silence as we passed the thermos of wine.

After a while, we began to reminisce about Summer, laughing one second and crying the next. At one point, when we really started to fall apart, Lainey lightened the mood, gesturing over to a nearby lifeguard stand, informing us that it was where she'd lost her virginity. We'd heard the story before but cracked up as she told it again, right down to the part where she projectile vomited all over the cop who had busted them.

As our laughter faded, Lainey sighed and said, "I can't believe Summer never got to have sex."

Tyson looked surprised. "She was still a virgin?"

"Yeah," I said, nodding. "She was saving herself."

"For marriage?" Tyson asked.

"Not for marriage necessarily. But for true love," I said, looking down, feeling the weight of all that she would miss in her life.

Lainey sighed and said, "She was so freaking *pure*."

Tyson nodded. "Yes. Good to the core. She would have made such an amazing doctor."

"And mother," I said.

We fell silent again, watching the fire die down, each of us lost in our own thoughts. As I shivered, Lainey suggested we head back to the house.

"Can I say a prayer first?" Tyson asked, looking at Lainey.

She didn't believe in God, but she nodded. We all held hands as Tyson closed his eyes and bowed his head. I did the same, listening to the sound of waves breaking on the shore.

"Heavenly Father," Tyson finally began, his voice soft but clear. "While we will never fully understand why Summer chose to leave us, we pray that her memory remains an eternal blessing and a reminder to walk gently through this fragile life . . . to love . . . to be loved . . . and to do our best to ease the pain, despair, and suffering of others. We ask for the strength to both follow this mission and keep the sacred promise we made to one another. Thank you for the blessings of our friendship." He paused, then whispered, "Amen."

"Amen," Lainey echoed.

"Amen," I said.

WHEN I GOT back from California, I knew I had to find a way to move on with my life. The promise we had made was about being there for one another and never letting tragedy strike again. But it was also about each of us finding our own path forward. I didn't have Tyson's brilliant mind or Lainey's charismatic personality. Nor did I have concrete career goals or any real passion. But I could still have a life of meaning.

For me, that meant marriage and motherhood. Maybe it had something to do with my mother and our complicated relationship, but I yearned for a family of my own. I wanted a husband and life partner with whom I could create a happy home and safe haven for my children. The idea of family was something Summer and I had talked about a lot. As ambitious as she was, she wanted marriage and motherhood as much as I did. She once told me that I would be her maid of honor and the godmother to her firstborn. I told her she would be mine, too. We joked that Lainey would feel relieved to be off the hook from those duties. It broke my heart that I could no longer do those things *with* Summer. But I knew she would still want me to do them.

So I got on with my life. I made a real effort at work, then got a job I liked more. I went on dates. I managed to have a little fun again. All the while, I could hear Summer encouraging me.

Then, one day out of the blue, Grady Allen called and invited me to dinner. One of my first thoughts was Summer. I distinctly remembered telling her about Grady, the cute older boy who lived down the street. He was my childhood crush—although that hardly made me unique. A lot of girls across town had been infatuated with Grady at one point or another.

I longed to share the news with Summer. Of course, I also wanted to confide my mortified suspicion that my mother had her hand in it, à la *Pride and Prejudice,* Mrs. Bennet style (a hunch that would later be confirmed). But I knew what Summer would have told me. She would have said something along the lines of, "Who cares how or why he called? Just go out with him!" I told myself that she would have been right, and that for once, my mother's meddling had paid dividends.

In any event, my first date with Grady was amazing. So were the second and third. As things progressed and we hit various relationship milestones, I continued to imagine my conversations with Summer. How thrilled she would have been for me after our first kiss; our first time having sex; and when Grady finally told me he loved me. I missed her every step of the way, and I missed her the most after Grady got down on one knee and asked me to be his wife.

The most until now, that is. As my heart is broken for the *second* time.

CHAPTER 1

HANNAH

IT STARTED WITH a small chip in my nail polish. Working in an interior design firm, I spent most of my days either moving furniture or hauling fabric, paint, and rug samples around town, so a chipped nail was hardly a rarity or anything I fussed over. But when a client called last-minute to cancel our four o'clock Friday meeting, I decided I might as well squeeze in a quick manicure before I went home to get ready for the double date Grady and I were going on with another couple.

On my way to the nail salon, I swung by Grady's house to pick up my favorite bottle of OPI polish—Mimosas for Mr. & Mrs.—which I'd left in his bathroom. Per my mother's wishes not to "cohabitate," I was waiting to officially move in with him until after the wedding. It was a waste of money, and a bit inconvenient, but there was something about the decision that felt romantic, too.

As I pulled into the driveway, I took a moment to admire the satisfying symmetry of the small but stately brick Georgian that

Grady had just bought with a chunk of his trust fund. He called it our "starter home," but I couldn't imagine we would ever outgrow it. I especially loved the huge old magnolia in the front yard. One high, sturdy branch was perfect for a swing.

I parked my car in the driveway, walked up the front path, and used my key to unlock the front door. As I stepped into the foyer, I heard the low thrum of music coming from upstairs. Grady was still at work—I'd just called him—so I assumed he'd left his Alexa on. Midway up the flight of stairs, I could make out Coldplay's "Yellow." Then, a couple of steps later, I heard the faint sound of moaning. *Female* moaning. I stopped in my tracks and held my breath, telling myself there was no way. There must be a benign explanation. Maybe Grady had left the television on this morning, along with his music. Maybe he had blown off work, too, and was indulging in a little Friday afternoon porn. It wasn't my favorite thought, but with Grady's sex drive, it wasn't outside the realm of possibility. That had to be it, I thought, deciding to abort my nail polish mission and save us both the needless embarrassment.

Yet the smallest kernel of paranoia lingered, propelling me down the hall and toward the bedroom door. It was only open a crack, but it was wide enough for me to peer inside and see a naked woman mounted on my naked fiancé, expertly riding him. They looked like a couple in a movie. . . . The scene was that airbrushed and golden, right down to the way the late afternoon sun streamed through the window and her long blond hair flowed down her tanned hourglass back. There was even a soundtrack, Chris Martin serenading them. *And it was all yellow.*

I stared in horror, my mind working overtime, wondering if she was a high-end call girl performing some sort of hazing cere-mony—a bachelor-party ritual. But as the two fluidly changed posi-tions, I had a hunch it wasn't their first time. And then, in another gut punch, I recognized her. Grady was having sex with Berlin Beverly, a young Instagram influencer whom I happened to follow, as did about seventy-five thousand other people.

Berlin's page was curated pastel perfection filled with artfully arranged images of balloon bouquets and fine china tablescapes and expansive floral arrangements. Mostly, though, Berlin's feed was full of Berlin, sashaying all over Atlanta—that is, when she wasn't posing and preening aboard luxury yachts and private jets. To say she was smug is an understatement, but she had always seemed harmless, her clichéd captions punctuated with hearts, butterflies, and clinking champagne flutes.

Several excruciating seconds ticked by as I watched them, wondering how this could be happening. Of course, I knew how in the literal sense. I knew that Grady had lied about being at work. I knew he must have parked his Porsche in the garage rather than in his usual spot in the driveway. I knew that Berlin lived two streets over, close enough to walk, which she must have done, as there was no sign of her Portofino blue Range Rover. I knew they had climbed the stairs, removed their clothes, and gotten in the upholstered bed that I'd bought with my designer discount.

How, though, was this *actually* happening?

I waited for the rage to kick in, knowing that I was supposed to follow the script of a woman scorned. Pull an Elin Nordegren and smash something. Curse at them. At the very least, interrupt their imminent orgasms. But I couldn't make myself move, feeling paralyzed with an irrational feeling of shame. It was almost as if *I* was the one doing something wrong, and I might, at any second, get busted by *them*. Instead, I made my escape, slowly backing away, then running downstairs and out the front door.

·   ·   ·

I MUST HAVE been on autopilot because I don't remember driving home or parking my car in the garage or taking the elevator up to my apartment. Somehow, though, I now find myself in my foyer, collapsed on the floor. As the shock starts to wear off, I break into a cold sweat. I feel nauseous and dizzy. Like I might vomit or faint.

I sit up, put my head between my knees, and take deep breaths, in through my nose and out through my mouth. At some point, I manage to lift my head and find my phone in my tote bag. I check my messages, a small part of me expecting to find a full confession from Grady. Instead, there is only a one-line text from him, letting me know that he'll pick me up at seven.

I close my eyes, wondering if Berlin is still in his bed. I picture the satisfied way he always looks after sex. His faint smirk.

I text back that I don't feel well and need to cancel. It's the truth. I have never lied to Grady. I stupidly add that I'm sorry.

What's wrong?

I feel nauseous.

Uh-oh. Could you be pregnant?

I'm tempted to write back: No. Could Berlin be pregnant? But I'm not ready to confront him. I'm too disoriented.

No. Probably just a bug. Give my regards to the Campbells.

He gives my text a thumbs-up and says he'll call me later, feel better. He then sends a lone red heart. I stare at it, questioning every heart he's ever sent me.

I'm not much of a drinker but decide I need something strong. I get to my feet, walk the few steps over to my kitchen, and survey my paltry selection of liquor. I opt for Tito's, pouring it into a juice glass, skipping ice and mixers. Vodka neat and room temperature. Is that a thing? It is now. I take a large swallow, then quickly drain the rest and head down the hall to my bedroom. I take off my shoes and pants, then crawl under the covers, curling into a tight ball.

Just as the vodka starts to kick in, my phone rings. It's my mother. I want to answer it. I want to pour my heart out to her and have her tell me that everything is going to be okay. But after thirty-two years, I know better than to answer. I know that she is incapable of making me feel better after a stumble or fall, especially one this serious. She just can't do it. She'll find a way to make me feel worse. She had worked so hard to infiltrate Grady's mother's Bible study group, then the inner sanctum of her tennis team, to arrange that first date, years ago. And now all her effort was for nothing. I know that will be her take, and I can't bear the thought of disappointing her. I can't bear the thought of *anything*.

I tell myself to pull it together. My fiancé cheated on me, but it's not the first time in human history that such a thing has happened. There are many people in the world struggling to *survive*—and in any event, suffering far more than I am right now.

But perspective is a hard thing to come by when your heart is broken, and I feel myself completely unraveling, believing this is proof that I'm destined to be alone, maybe even unworthy of having a happy family. Suddenly, all I want to do is call Summer. Hear her voice. Cry into the phone. She would know what to say. She would know how to ease my pain, if only a little.

And that's when I realize what I need to do. It's not a solution, but it *is* a path forward. A baby step. A promise kept.

CHAPTER 2

LAINEY

I AM SITTING IN Delta's Sky Club lounge at LaGuardia, nursing a vodka martini as I wait to board a flight to L.A. I have an audition tomorrow, so I really should be hydrating, but it's only one drink. My cellphone rings. I expect it to be my agent, Casey, whom I just hung up with. But it's my best friend, Hannah—which probably means she's sitting in Atlanta traffic. I honestly don't know how she stands all that time in her car. I'd go crazy.

I answer with my usual "hey," waiting for a mundane wedding update. Ever since Hannah got engaged last fall, our conversations have become a bit one-dimensional. As her maid of honor, I understand that comes with the territory—and it really *is* an honor. I also recognize that over the years, my drama has dominated the airwaves. But I can't lie; I'll be happy when the whole thing is over and we can get back to our regularly scheduled programming.

"Hi. Did I catch you at a bad time?" she asks, her typical starter. Her voice is faint, like she just woke up from a nap.

"No. I'm at the airport. Waiting for my flight to L.A.," I say.

"Oh, right. Your audition."

"Yeah. What's up?"

There is silence on the end of the line, and I wonder if we've lost our connection.

"Han? You there?"

"Yes," she whispers.

"I can barely hear you," I say, pressing my phone against my ear. "Where are you?"

"I'm home."

"Are you okay?"

"Not really, actually," she says, her voice shaking.

"Oh, crap. Your mother again?"

Hannah's narcissistic mother has been dormant for a couple of weeks—which means she's overdue for one of her manipulative stunts. You'd think Mrs. Davis was the one getting married. She definitely thinks it's *her* day.

"No," Hannah says. "Unfortunately, it's a bit worse than my mother."

My stomach drops, remembering the voicemail she left me ten years ago, after Summer committed suicide. And then my mother's call to tell me about the "tiny tumor" her doctor had found. Six months later, she was gone, too.

"Tell me what's going on," I say, bracing myself.

"Grady cheated on me," she says through sobs.

My jaw drops. It's the last thing I expected to hear. "When? Are you sure?"

"Today. And yes, I'm sure."

"Shit, Hannah. With who?" I ask, praying that it's not one of her "friends," though I wouldn't put it past a couple of them.

"Berlin Beverly," she tells me.

The name sounds familiar—one of the cast of characters Hannah sometimes mentions—but I can't place her.

"Should I know who that is?"

"She's an influencer. Here in Atlanta. I've sent you some stuff from her 'Like to Know It' page."

"Oh, *shit*. The blonde in the goofy *Little House on the Prairie* dresses?" I ask, as I pull her up on Instagram and confirm that I have the right suspect.

"Yeah. She's beautiful, isn't she?"

"Yuck. No," I say, scanning her feed with disgust. "She's fake as fuck. A plastic Barbie doll . . . although that's an insult to Barbie."

"She's twenty-*four*," Hannah says.

"And? So? Who the fuck cares how old she is?" I ask. "She's a dumb whore."

It's not the way I usually talk. I never slut-shame anyone, and not only because of my own lifestyle choices.

"Do you think he's in love with her?" Hannah asks.

"Oh, please, Hannah. He's not in *love* with her."

"What if he is?"

"Well, it doesn't really matter, does it?"

"It matters to me," she says.

I cast about for the right words, wishing Summer were still with us. She would know what to say. She *always* knew what to say.

"Are you sure about this? Maybe it's just a rumor—"

"It's not a rumor, Lainey. I *saw* them."

"Okay. But what did you see, exactly?" I say, imagining a lingering hug in a parking lot. Something shady but explainable.

"I saw them in bed. Having sex," she says, then starts to cry again.

My jaw drops for the second time. "Oh my *God*, Hannah! You

should have started with that! What happened? *You busted them?* How did they react?"

"They didn't. I just left."

"But they know you saw them, right?"

"No."

"*Wow*," I say, wondering how she could have such superhuman restraint. I would have castrated him on the spot. In fact, all I want to do is change my flight from L.A. to Atlanta and go do it myself. With a pair of kids' craft scissors.

"I know, Lainey. I know I'm pathetic," she says, sobbing again. "I didn't know what to do."

"It's okay, honey. It'll be okay. I promise," I say, feeling desperate for her. "Just take a deep breath."

She keeps crying, saying she doesn't know what to do.

"Okay," I say, gathering my thoughts. "For starters, you need to tell him you *know*. That you saw him."

"And then what?"

"And then you dump his ass."

"Oh, my God, Lainey," she says. "I can't believe this. I have to start over. I'm thirty-*two*."

"Thirty-two is *young*—"

"Not when it comes to having babies—"

"You'll have a baby, Hannah. I know you will."

"But I put everything into that relationship. It's all I have."

"It's not all you have. You have me. And Tyson," I say as adamantly as I can.

"My mother is going to lose her mind," she says. "My life is seriously over, Lainey."

My heart skips a beat, wondering how she could think such a thing, let alone say it aloud. "Don't say that. Don't you *dare* say that,"

I say, thinking of our pact. A promise to come together if any of us ever hits rock bottom. I'm pretty sure this qualifies.

"Have you told Tyson?" I ask.

"No. I can't bother him with this. He has a big trial next week—"

"Oh, *please*, Hannah. This is way more important. And anyway— you promised. We *all* promised—" I say, suddenly knowing what I have to do. "I'm changing my flight and coming to Atlanta. Tonight."

"But your audition."

"I don't care. It's a stupid, minor role," I lie.

"You still need to go—"

"*Hannah*. Stop it right now," I say as firmly as I can. "I'm coming down there. And that's final."

"Okay," she whimpers. "Thank you, Lainey."

THE SECOND WE hang up, I head straight to the ticket counter, pro- filing the three agents, wondering who would be most helpful to my cause. There is an older lady who looks like she bakes home- made cookies for her grandchildren; a girl about my age who is more likely to have seen my show (always useful in customer service matters); and a forty-something man I could flirt with.

I wind up with the older woman. According to the pin on her shirt pocket, her name is Lydia, and I use it twice as I tell her my predicament and how worried I am about my friend.

"That poor girl," Lydia says, going on a mini-tirade against men as she click-clacks on her computer, searching for flights to Atlanta. When she finally looks back up at me, she says, "Okay. So the good news is—I got you on the next flight to Atlanta—which you can just make."

"And the bad news?"

"Your bag definitely *won't* make it."

"That's okay," I say, handing her my credit card.

She runs it, explaining that my bag will be rerouted and then delivered to me. She jots down a number I can call if I have any problems, then hands it to me along with my new boarding pass.

"Thank you again," I say. "You're an angel."

"You're so welcome, dear," she says. "And best of luck to your friend. She's very lucky to have you."

A FEW MINUTES later, I've boarded my flight and am settling into my middle seat in the back of the plane. I text Hannah that I'm on my way, then call Tyson, knowing he won't pick up. Tyson hates talking on the phone. Most of our communication consists of exchanging funny memes or TikToks, with an occasional link to a human-interest story. Conjoined twins separated. A dog reunited with his owner after a hurricane. A toddler calling 911 to save his mother.

Sure enough, Tyson shunts me to voicemail. It's my pet peeve—the least he could do is let it ring through and *pretend* to have missed the call. I call him right back and he shunts me a second time.

Pick up, pls! I type. It's important.

Moving ellipses appear, followed by the words Can't talk now. What's up?

I type back: It's about Hannah.

My phone immediately rings.

"Is she okay?" he asks, sounding panicked.

"Yes. She's fine," I say, then lower my voice. "But Grady cheated on her. She caught him in bed with another woman."

I know that my seatmates have no choice but to eavesdrop, and out of the corner of my eye, I catch the lady in the window seat do a double take.

"Dang," Tyson says under his breath. "I knew that guy was trouble."

"Yeah. You did," I say.

"When did this happen?"

"Today. I'm actually on a flight to Atlanta as we speak—"

"*Really?*"

"Yes. Really," I say. "Why do you sound so shocked? We made a pact."

"Fuck," Tyson says. "That's where we are?"

"Yes. This is rock bottom for Hannah. Grady's her whole world."

"She has us."

"I know," I say. "That's why I'm going."

AS THE PLANE takes off, I lean my head back, close my eyes, and remind myself that I'm right about marriage and monogamy. Don't get me wrong—I'm not a man-hater. In fact, I *love* men. I love the art of flirtation, the cat and mouse games, and the thrill of being pursued. I love those early days, weeks, and sometimes even months of a romantic entanglement. It's the relationship and commitment and trust part that I can't get on board with.

Hannah's heartbreak underscores what I already knew. You can love *being* with a man, but you can't count on one. If you try, you will get burned.

I learned that lesson at the age of twelve when my mother sat me down and told me the truth about my father. For years, I believed that he was in the CIA, living overseas and handling top-secret assignments for the U.S. government. His job was the reason he didn't live with us and why we only saw him a few times a year. It was also the reason I wasn't allowed to show pictures of him to my friends. Every few months, he would visit, bearing gifts and promises that he would retire one day and the three of us would be together full-time.

It had all been a lie, my mother confessed that day. My father actually worked at the JCPenney corporate office in Plano *fucking* Texas. Not only that, but he had another family who didn't know we existed. A wife and two other daughters. Ashley and Olivia.

"How old are they?" I asked, reeling, expecting her to say that they were babies. That my father had cheated on her, then left her for the other woman.

Instead, she told me they were ten and thirteen.

"*Thirteen!*" I said, doing the obvious math. "So he was married when you met him?"

"Yes."

"Did you know he was married?" I asked, replaying their airport Starbucks meet-cute story.

She looked down and nodded.

"Then why did you like him?" I asked, aghast.

"It was love at first sight," she said. "And sometimes the heart wants what the heart wants."

My stomach turned at her flimsy explanation. I could only imagine the consequences of me doing something wrong, like shoplifting, then saying, *Sorry, Mom. But sometimes the heart wants what the heart wants.*

"Do you still love him?" I asked.

"Yes," she said. "We're very much in love."

"Then why isn't he with you? Why doesn't he get a divorce and live with us?"

My mother sighed and said, "It's complicated, Lainey-bug. Sometimes I get angry, but I have to accept the responsibility for my decisions, too."

I stared at her, processing that *I* was part of that responsibility. Having me. Raising me by herself. Hell, I was a *product* of their wrongdoing. I told her I needed to be alone, then went to my room.

That night, as I lay in bed, I connected all the dots. The real reason that I didn't have my dad's phone number or address and that he'd never met any of my friends or gone to any of my school plays or dance recitals. I then realized that he *was* doing those regular, fatherly things with Ashley and Olivia, and I felt my first wave of jealousy. It was so ironic. I'd always longed for a sister. Now I had two, and I was miserable.

Over the weeks, months, and years that followed, my resentment and anger grew. Whenever my father came to visit, I refused to see him, spending the night with a friend.

From that point on, when anyone asked about my father, I simply said he was "out of the picture." It was what I told Hannah, Tyson, and Summer on the night we met, and they all had the good sense not to ask any follow-up questions.

For the entirety of our first year, he was never mentioned again. Then one night early in our second year, Hannah came to talk to Summer and me, distraught over something her mother had done or said to her. I don't remember the specifics, only that Summer and I were both appalled.

"Y'all are so lucky to have such nice mothers," Hannah said. "I can't imagine that—"

Summer gave her a sympathetic nod, then said, "You have to remember, though, Han, no family is perfect."

"Yours is," I said, thinking of all the care packages her mother sent and how supportive both her parents were about her running, flying in from Chicago for most of her races. She was very close to her brother, too, a senior at Princeton who was also a star runner. In fact, she seemed to worship him.

"I love my family," Summer said. "But my parents *constantly* compare me to my brother. It's like nothing I do is ever good enough."

I stared at her in disbelief. How could anyone outshine Summer? She was a star. She was the *sun*. It was like hearing that Gisele Bündchen had a prettier sister. Frankly, it also explained a lot about Summer's perfectionism and the pressure she put on herself.

"Nothing is ever really what it seems," Summer added, a worried look on her face.

In that moment, I blurted out the truth about my father.

Hannah looked stunned and clearly had no idea what to say. But Summer immediately hugged me, then asked a series of calm questions, most of them about my sisters and what I knew about them. I confessed that I occasionally stalked their Facebook pages. Although their profiles were set to private, I knew that Ashley attended Texas Christian University and that Olivia was still in high school, playing tennis on the junior circuit. "I think she's at one of those sports academies," I added.

"Do you think you'll ever reach out to them?" Summer asked.

"I doubt it. Let sleeping dogs lie, right?"

"I don't know about that," Summer said. "I can understand that point of view, but there's a huge potential upside."

"And what would that be?" I asked.

"Having a relationship with your sisters," Summer said.

"I doubt that would happen. It's not like I'd be happy news."

"Maybe not at first, but they can't be upset with *you*."

"I wouldn't be so sure about that," I said.

Summer frowned, clearly deep in thought, then said, "Maybe you should talk to Tyson about this. He always gives great advice."

"Yeah, maybe," I say.

A few nights later, I brought him into the circle of trust. He was predictably furious at my father. Tyson had no patience for liars or cheaters. In his own life, he played by all the rules, once remarking that as a Black man, he had "zero room for error" and needed to be "beyond reproach." In *all* situations. It didn't come across as a complaint—more of an observation or fact, something he said his parents had ingrained in him from a very young age. Beyond the universal rules that everyone had to follow, there was a matrix of additional guidelines for him. In stores, for example, he was taught to make direct eye contact with the clerks; to never put his hands in his pockets; and to always get a receipt, no matter how small the purchase.

"You can't let your father keep getting away with this, Lainey," he said. "You need to out that son of a bitch."

"It's not my secret to tell."

It was a line I'd heard before, and I felt like it applied.

"The hell it's not," Tyson said. "You're his *daughter*. They're your *sisters*. The secret is very *much* about you—and very much yours to tell."

"I agree." Summer nodded, then turned back to me with the most earnest look. "Lainey, you have a right to know your sisters."

"Maybe one day," I said. "But for now, I have you guys. My friends are my family."

IT WAS THE truth. It was especially true since I'd lost my mother back in 2020. After she died, I had discovered a trove of letters from my father, along with a journal detailing their relationship. I questioned whether I should read them—it felt like such an invasion of privacy. But ultimately, I decided that if my mother hadn't wanted me to see them, she would have disposed of them.

So I opened a bottle of wine, sat down, and read every word of every page. I was shocked by how much my father had strung her along with false promises. He swore up and down that she was the love of his life, all while making excuses and moving the goalpost. Her diary confirmed that she believed him—that is, until her final entry.

It was written eight days before she died. In it, she pondered whether a secretive love could ever be *true* love.

"I don't know the answer," she wrote. "But if he truly loved me, wouldn't now be the time to show me? Maybe he's thinking that it makes no sense to ruin her life when mine is nearly over. I am trying to understand that. I'm trying not to let bitterness overtake my heart. I'm trying to focus all my thoughts and energy on Lainey. *She* is the love of my life."

Reading it made me nauseous. It made me *hate* my father even more than I already did. It was proof of everything I'd been telling myself about love.

And here I was, about to touch down in Atlanta to help my best friend, being reminded of this lesson all over again. Maybe love wasn't a *complete* farce, but in the end, it was never worth the pain.

CHAPTER 3

TYSON

'M AT WORK when I get an urgent text and phone call from Lainey, telling me that Hannah caught her fiancé cheating. It's a lot to process, especially given that I'm knee deep in trial prep, but I know I have to prioritize it. The three of us have significant history—tragic shit we went through together—and it's just not something I can blow off.

As devastated as I am for Hannah, though, I'm thrilled that her dick fiancé has finally been exposed. I've never liked or trusted the guy—not from the moment I met him, the weekend we all went to Charlotte to watch UVA play in the Belk Bowl. I remember arriving at the tailgate, spotting Lainey first. Unlike the rest of the girls, who were all dressed up, Lainey had on ripped jeans, an orange hoodie, and a pair of blue and orange midrise Air Jordans. At that point, she had yet to be cast in her Hulu limited series, but she'd landed a few small speaking roles in various films and television shows.

I gave her a hug and said, "Signed any autographs?"

"If you want my autograph, just tell me, Tyson," she said with a smirk.

A second later, we saw Hannah walking across the parking lot, hand in hand with Grady.

"Dear God," I said. "He's a clone of the last one."

Lainey laughed. "She *does* have a type."

"Yep. Tall, blond, and full of shit."

"C'mon, Tyson. How can you tell he's full of shit already?"

"By the way he's walking," I said. "The frat boy strut."

"*You* were in a fraternity."

I told her Black fraternities were a totally different universe, and she knew it.

"Just give him a chance. He seems like a nice guy," she said, having already met him during one of her visits to Atlanta.

I raised my eyebrows. "You know how I feel about that word."

"Oh, *right*. I forgot. It's *bad* to be nice."

I sighed and said, "It's not bad to be nice, but perfectly *nice* people looked the other way during the Holocaust."

"Jeez, Tyson! That's a bit extreme."

I shrugged. It may have been an extreme example, but it also happened to be true—and only one of many in the great span of fucked-up human history. At the end of the day, *nice* didn't count for shit.

"Well, he makes Hannah happy," Lainey said. "So please try and be—"

"Nice?" I quipped as Hannah approached us.

"Hey, y'all!" Hannah squealed, giving us both big hugs.

She then stepped back, beaming as she said, "Tyson, this is Grady! Grady, Tyson!"

I said hello, making eye contact, telling myself to give him the benefit of the doubt, just as he gave me an exaggerated upward-nod, chin lingering in the air for an unnatural beat.

"What's good, bro?" he said in a voice that I had to believe was several octaves lower than what was normal for him. If that weren't bad enough, he followed the question up with an awkward dap. It wasn't uncommon for guys like Grady to make such attempts, and on some level, I appreciated the effort. But I would have vastly preferred a neutral handshake to this awkward charade of solidarity.

"Nice to meet you," I lied, mostly for Hannah's sake.

"You too, man," Grady said, his chin still a tad high for my taste.

After some small talk about Virginia football and the Vegas line on the game, I tried to show interest in him. "So Hannah says you went to Ole Miss?"

"Yessir! Hotty Toddy!"

I forced a smile. "How'd you all do this year?"

"Not so good," he said. "Five and seven."

"That's rough," I said.

"Hey. It happens," he said with an affable shrug.

Maybe he wasn't so bad after all, I told myself. But over the course of the day, as Grady sucked down beer after beer, it became harder to maintain this position. He was everything I couldn't stand to be around. His stories were too long; he laughed too loudly; and he was the expert on everything. No matter the topic, he'd jump right in without the slightest hesitation.

At dinner that night, things went downhill even further when Serena Williams's recent U.S. Open match against Naomi Osaka came up. I braced myself as Grady launched into a tirade about her "poor sportsmanship."

I looked at Hannah, knowing she was a huge Serena fan. "I don't blame her for being upset," she said. "She was accused of cheating!"

"She *was* cheating. She was getting hand signals from her coach," Grady said.

"I don't believe that. She said she wasn't," Hannah replied. "Even the commentators were saying that Serena makes her own decisions on the court."

"Well, who the hell's gonna admit to cheating?" Grady said.

The comment was a huge red flag.

"Besides," Grady continued, "you can't throw a hissy fit just because things don't go your way."

"Why not? Men do it all the time," Lainey chimed in.

"And they get penalized when they do," Grady said. He looked at me. "Tyson, man, where do you come out on this?" he asked, clearly mistaking my silence for being on his side.

"Serena's the GOAT," I said.

"Okay. But do you think the ump was being sexist?" Grady pressed me.

Sexist and *racist*, I thought. At the very least, there was unconscious bias at play. But I'd made it a long-standing policy to only debate worthy adversaries, so I simply shrugged and said, "Hard to tell."

"Well, I still say she's a poor sport," Grady said. "And tacky."

"Tacky?" Lainey fired back.

"Yeah. Remember the ridiculous spandex suit she sported at the French Open?"

"What was so ridiculous about it?" Lainey asked. Shaming a woman for her clothing was a big no for her.

"She'd just given birth," Hannah said. "She wore it to combat blood clots."

"Still. You shouldn't be allowed to wear shit like that in tennis. It's a matter of decorum," Grady said, then doubled down on his racially coded language. "Tennis is a genteel sport. Nobody should behave that way. Black, white, or purple."

I stared at him, marveling at both his cluelessness and his brazenness. Here he sat, critiquing a Black female—two things he's not and never will be—with two women and a Black man. We were all more qualified to speak to Serena's experience, yet he was so convinced that he had all the answers.

I finally broke.

"You're right, Grady," I said. "She *can't* act that way. She's held to a different standard and has to be completely beyond reproach. She's gotta be twice as good and half as reactive knowing that she's going to get double the scrutiny. And on that day, she wasn't. When that ump accused her of cheating, she reacted like a normal, frustrated human being who'd just been accused of doing something she hadn't done. She lost her cool. So yeah. You're right. *She* can't act that way."

Grady nodded, then drained his pint of beer, obtusely triumphant. Meanwhile, Lainey squeezed my leg under the table, as if to tell me to calm down, he wasn't worth it. I wasn't going to change his mind, nor was I going to change Hannah's mind about him. I bit my tongue for the rest of the night, and during the few times I'd seen him since.

One thing life had taught me was how to keep my mouth shut. I was good at that.

But now, as I hang up the phone with Lainey, I realize that I'm off the hook: I can finally tell Hannah what I think of her asshole fiancé. *Ex*-fiancé.

Bottom line, I know Lainey is right. I know I have to fly down there and be with Hannah. We made a promise, and I don't break promises.

.   .   .

A FEW MINUTES later, I'm standing in Martin Strout's office door-way. Martin is the head of our firm's white-collar defense practice group and a D.C. legend. There's no one who understands the False Claims or Foreign Corrupt Practices Act better than he does. I've watched up close and in awe as he navigates complex issues of fraud, money laundering, and trade sanctions violations, defending heavy hitters in pharmaceuticals, financial services, retail, and energy.

He also happens to be a world-class asshole who believes that things must be done the way he did them back in the eighties. In other words, we all must be sitting together in a conference room, day and night, sometimes just watching him *think*. Even during the height of the pandemic, he expected us all to come in, and he made it clear that masking up annoyed him.

"Can I help you, Mr. Bishop?" he asks now, looking up at me with a scowl.

"Hi, Martin," I say. "Do you have a minute?"

"I have thirty seconds."

I nod, take a deep breath, and tell him that I need to go out of town this weekend.

"Come again?" Martin says, whipping off his wire-rim glasses with one hand. He flings them onto his desk, continuing to stare at me. It's one of his go-to intimidation tactics that I've witnessed in many depositions and trials.

I repeat my statement verbatim.

"We're going to trial next week, Mr. Bishop."

"I'm aware. And I apologize for the unfortunate timing. But this is an emergency."

"Has there been a death in your immediate family?" he asks, making it clear that attending the funeral of, say, a grandparent or cousin would not be an acceptable excuse.

"Nobody has died," I say.

"Are you on your own deathbed?" he asks.

"I am not."

"Then no," he says. "You can't go."

I shift my weight from one foot to the other but maintain eye contact. "Well, Martin, I wasn't asking for permission."

He stares back at me, his red face turning redder than it usually is.

"Well, Mr. Bishop, let me put it to you this way: If you're not in the office this weekend, then you're off this case."

I nod and tell him I understand.

"Good. So you decide which matter is of greater importance to you."

He gives me a smug look, confident that he's just laid down a trump card.

"Will do," I say with a curt nod. "Thank you, Martin."

"What are you thanking me for?" he grumbles.

"For framing the issue so clearly," I say, then turn on my heel, determined to have the last word.

"SO, WHAT ARE you going to do?" Nicole, my girlfriend of nearly a year, asks after I give her the update. We are sitting at the bar in a little bistro in Georgetown, waiting for a table to open.

"I'm going to Atlanta."

"*Seriously?*" she says, making a sharp ninety-degree turn on her stool.

I nod and take a sip of my beer.

"But you're up for *partner*—"

"Not anymore," I say with a laugh.

"Tyson. It's not funny. Martin doesn't play," Nicole says, looking aghast. A fellow lawyer at another big firm in town, she would know all about Martin even if she weren't dating me. "He might even fire you."

"I can't get fired," I say. "I already wrote my letter of resignation."

"*What?*" she says. "You quit your *job?*"

"Not yet," I say. "But the email is drafted and ready to go."

"You're going to throw everything away? Over *this?* You don't even like Hannah's fiancé!"

Her "this" instantly grates on me, as I say, "It's not about *me,* Nic. It's about Hannah. She feels like her life is imploding."

"O-*kay.* But I still can't believe she's asking you to do this."

"She didn't *ask* me to do anything. She doesn't even know I'm coming."

Nicole shakes her head but says nothing. She doesn't have to. I know how she feels about Hannah and Lainey and close male-female friendships in general. She doesn't believe they can work over the long haul. In her mind, if both parties are straight, someone always wants to sleep with the other. The classic *When Harry Met Sally* premise.

"I really want you to be okay with this, Nic," I say, doing my best to avoid an argument.

"And why is that?" she asks, crossing her arms.

It's clearly a test, and I answer carefully. "Because your feelings matter to me."

"Well, let me ask you this," she says, unfazed. "If I told you I'm *not* okay with it, would you go anyway?"

I stare back at her, thinking this is the problem with dating a fellow lawyer, especially one as smart as Nicole. I always have the feeling she's about to outmaneuver me. She often does.

"It might not change my ultimate decision," I say. "But the way you *feel* matters to me."

"Okay, Tyson," she says, taking a deep breath. "Aside from the fact that this is a disastrous career move, it just feels so . . . *excessive.*"

"How so?" I ask.

"Why do you have to fly down there? Why can't you just talk to her on the phone?"

"Is that what you would do for a close friend?"

"An extremely vulnerable *male* friend? Yes. Absolutely. A thousand percent yes."

I roll my eyes. "C'mon, Nic. Do you really think Hannah's on the prowl right now?"

"I have no idea. What I *do* know is that flying down to Atlanta in the middle of a huge trial in order to comfort a *female* friend is just too much. It's beyond the pale. And yes, it makes me uncomfortable. You asked me how I feel—and that's how I feel."

"Why does it make you uncomfortable? Do you not trust me?"

"It's not about trust. It's about respect."

"Please explain to me how my going to help a friend is disrespectful to you?"

"You don't see how flying down to Atlanta on a rescue mission—"

"That's so condescending."

"Condescending to whom? You or Hannah?"

"To both of us."

"Oh. *Us.* I see."

I don't take the bait, and after several seconds of silence, Nicole says, "What about Lainey?"

"What about her?"

"Why can't she go to Atlanta?"

"She *is* going. She's on her way there now."

"So why do you have to go, too?"

I take a sip of beer, debating how much of the truth to share.

Nicole knows about Summer, generally, but not about our promise to be there for one another in the worst of times.

"Because she's my friend," I say. "And she needs me."

"Well then," she says with a passive-aggressive shrug. "You gotta do what you gotta do."

"Yes," I say. "I do."

She nods, then says, "Once you get back? You might want to go talk to someone about the underlying issues here."

"Underlying issues?" I ask against my better judgment.

"Why those girls have such a strong hold on you."

"Nobody has a hold on me," I say. "Nobody."

"The framed photo in your *bedroom* says otherwise," she says, referring to the only photo I have of the four of us.

"It's just a photo," I say, bristling.

"A photo you keep next to your *bed*."

"Who cares *where* it is? You want me to move it to another room, I will."

She stares at me for several seconds, and I can tell she's debating whether to say something. She finally does. "Look, Tyson. Do what you will, but if you fly down on this rescue mission, we are done."

"Are you for real right now?"

"Yes, Tyson. I'm very much for real," she says. "If you go, it's over."

An uncomfortable staring contest ensues, a tough feat on side-by-side barstools. I wait a beat, expecting her to back down, at least a little. She does the opposite, grabbing her purse and throwing the strap over her shoulder. "Okay. I'm out. Let me pay for my drink."

"It's okay. I got it," I say, wondering why she'd start paying for things *now*. To be clear, I've never minded paying for Nicole, but at times, it does feel contradictory to her feminist position. Especially given that our salaries are the same.

"You're too kind," she says, getting to her feet. "But we already knew that, didn't we?"

LATER THAT NIGHT, after I eat takeout from the bar and pack my bag for Atlanta, I crawl into bed, exhausted. I think about Hannah, of course, and my thoughts quickly move to our pact and Summer. It's been a long time since I've gone there, and the memories hit me like an avalanche.

Throughout college, people asked me what was up with my three best friends. I know what they were getting at, and it annoyed me the way so many assumed I had to be hooking up with one of them. Most people suspected Lainey, as she was gorgeous and well built and turned heads everywhere she went. She was also a huge flirt. Some suspected Hannah, though—the cute blond, blue-eyed girl next door.

Summer was the least conventionally attractive of the three, but I liked her strawberry-blond hair, warm freckles, and intense green eyes. And I loved her strong legs and sleek, effortless stride. Sometimes I couldn't believe how fast Summer was.

As in awe as I was of her talent, though, I was even more impressed by her discipline and work ethic. I'd never seen anyone grind as hard as Summer. In addition to all the required team practices and lifts, she put in extra mileage every week, extra time in the weight room, and frequently did two-a-days. Some of our best conversations came during those cross-training sessions when I'd offer to keep her company. Whether doing the elliptical or aqua-jogging, her little "add-on" workouts were among my most grueling—and I have to admit that I preferred just riding my bike alongside her as she did her slower long runs. Nothing was more peaceful than those quiet moments on the wooded trails.

One night during the spring of our fourth year, Summer and I went on a long bike ride together. Her ankle had been bothering her, and she was giving herself a couple days off from running. As we biked, she confided the extent of her pain, expressing worry about her ability to compete in the postseason.

"Even if that happens, you gotta remember that you've already accomplished so much," I told her. "You're an All-American."

"But I've never won a championship," she said.

I could hear the stress in her voice, and I knew there was nothing I could say to reassure her. I tried anyway. "You can only do your best," I said. "I'll be proud of you no matter what."

"Thanks, Tyson," she said, sounding unconvinced.

"Seriously," I said. "I've never been so proud of anyone in my life." She smiled, then pedaled faster.

Later that night, Summer came to my apartment to watch her Cubs play in their season opener. I had picked up a six-pack of beer for myself, and she brought the snacks—popcorn and Reese's Pieces—making an exception to her no junk food rule. As we hunkered down in my double-wide La-Z-Boy recliner—our usual spot for watching games—something felt different. She even looked different. Her hair was in soft waves around her face when she usually wore it up in a ponytail or two side braids. She was wearing tiny pink running shorts, and her legs looked better than ever. I couldn't believe it—but I suddenly felt attracted to Summer.

Over the next several innings and beers, I imagined kissing her. Of course I didn't do it, knowing it was a terrible idea. Then, right after the seventh inning stretch, she very casually slung her left leg over my right one. It was the sort of touchy-feely thing Lainey sometimes did, but it wasn't Summer's style, and it made my body tingle. I tried to focus on the game—think about baseball, as it were—but that didn't work, and I could feel myself getting excited. Wearing mesh basketball shorts, I panicked, then did my best to hide the evidence with a bottle of Amstel Light.

A long minute passed, and then she suddenly turned in the chair, directly facing me, and said my name as a question.

"What's up?" I said, my heart pounding as I held her gaze.

She swallowed, then took a deep breath. "I'm really going to miss you next year."

"Me too," I said, my heart beating faster. "But if you end up going to Harvard, we'll be pretty close."

"Yeah. A two-hour and forty-seven-minute train ride," she said with a sheepish smile.

"Is that right?" I asked, getting more butterflies.

"Yes," she said. "I checked."

I smiled at her, and her cheeks turned as pink as her shorts.

"You should have applied to Yale," I said, going out a little further on the limb we were on.

"I know. I wish I had. If I don't get into Harvard, will you still visit me in the Midwest?"

"Of course I will."

"Good. Because I'm gonna want to see you," she said, her voice now a whisper.

"Oh, you'll see me," I whispered back.

Kissing her suddenly felt inevitable.

If not now, then eventually.

And if eventually, why not now?

I looked into her eyes, wishing I could read her mind. My gut told me she was feeling the same way I was, but I still felt vulnerable. A lot could go wrong.

In the back of my mind, I could hear my father warning me about the history of miscegenation and the potentially disastrous outcomes for Black men, even today. With Summer, my best friend, that risk felt virtually nonexistent. But regardless, kissing her would still change things. Forever. There would be no taking it back. Was I willing to roll the dice?

I decided I was—or maybe I just stopped thinking.

Overcome with attraction, I placed my open palm on her smooth thigh.

"You've got great legs," I said.

It was the first compliment I'd ever given her on her appearance, and my heart pounded in my ears.

"Thank you," she said with a shy smile.

"You're welcome," I said, holding her gaze.

"What are you thinking?" she finally asked me.

I hesitated, staring into her wide green eyes. "I'm thinking . . . that I want to kiss you," I breathed.

"Oh," she said, moving closer, her face only a few inches away from mine.

"Can I?" I asked, inhaling her sweet vanilla scent.

She gave me the slightest nod, looking as nervous as I felt. Then I leaned in, closed my eyes, and brushed my lips against hers. It was barely even a kiss, but it counted. In the background, I could hear that the Cubs had wrapped up their victory, three to one.

"Cubs win," she whispered.

"Yes," I said, finally opening my eyes. "They sure did."

"I should probably go," she said. "It's way past my bedtime."

"I know," I said, aware of how seriously Summer took her sleep.

She stood up to go. "So. We obviously aren't mentioning this to Lainey and Hannah, right?" she asked.

"I don't think we should. No."

"Good. Because I think they'd make a huge thing of it—"

"Totally. And it's really not a big deal," I said, testing her, and maybe myself, too.

"Not at *all*," she quickly answered. "I'm just glad we got that out of our systems."

"Right," I said, feeling a mix of relief and disappointment. "Me too."

OF COURSE, IT wasn't out of our systems, and over the next few weeks, we found every excuse to be alone. We made out a lot, but I always put on the brakes. In the back of my mind, I was worried about ruining our friendship for what would probably be a fling. No matter how compatible Summer and I were, or how attracted I was to her, a long-term romantic relationship was impractical. I had three years of law school ahead of me, and she had four years of medical school plus her residency.

As we navigated that weird terrain, taking one step forward then two back, Summer and I found ourselves in an argument. It wasn't our first, but it was one of the dumbest. In short, Hannah and I had gone to the mall, last minute. Neither of us had asked Summer if she wanted to come, both of us assuming she was too busy.

"Thanks for the invite," she said when I called her later. I could hear in her voice that she was upset.

"Oh. Sorry about that. We figured you'd be training or studying—"

"I actually would have gone with," she said, dangling her preposition in her cute Chicagoan way. "I still need shoes for graduation. . . . And you guys know I don't have a car."

I told her she was welcome to take my car anytime.

"That's not the point."

"What *is* the point?" I asked gently, really wanting to know.

"The point is—you and Hannah have always been this way."

"What way?"

"Exclusive."

I was shocked. We were a foursome, but we also hung out in every combination of twos and threes. I probably did the least with Lainey alone—but it was a toss-up between Hannah and Summer. More important, none of us ever kept score like that.

"You're always going off with her," Summer continued, citing a few examples, including a day trip we'd once taken to Washington, D.C., to check out a few museums.

"You had practice that day."

"Well, I didn't have practice *today*," she said. "I'm injured. *Remember?*"

I suddenly realized that this wasn't about the mall or Hannah. It was about the pressure of her sport and the nagging worry of her injury. "I'm really sorry we didn't call you—"

She cut me off. "Has anything ever happened between you two?"

For the first time, I regretted that Summer and I had crossed a line. "Are you *serious* right now?" I asked. I was angry, but my feelings were also hurt.

"It was just a question," she said. "You don't have to get so offended."

"It *is* offensive," I said.

"And yet you still haven't answered the question," she said.

"And I'm not going to," I said, hanging up the phone.

THE FOLLOWING NIGHT, I went to a party. On my way home, I stopped by Summer's room on the Lawn, knowing that she had stayed in to study for an exam. We hadn't talked since our argument, and I was still a bit chafed, but I wanted to see her.

When I got to her room, I knocked lightly. She came to the door in a white sports bra and navy track sweats. Her hair was in a messy bun, and her eyes looked wide and frantic.

"Hi," I said. "How's the studying going?"

"Awful," she said, crossing her arms.

"Okay. Well, I don't want to bother you . . . I just wanted to see you . . . and say hi."

She nodded, her expression too neutral to read, then said, "Do you want to come in for a minute?"

"I'd love to," I said.

As she uncrossed her arms, then stepped aside, I walked into the room, then turned to face her. "Are you still mad at me?" I asked.

"I was never mad. I just asked you a simple question," she said, pushing the door closed with her foot. "You're the one who got mad at me."

"Fair enough." I nodded, then took a deep breath. "Well, the answer to your question is no. Nothing ever happened between Hannah and me. Or Lainey and me."

She gave me a small smile, her shoulders relaxing, then said, "Good. I'm glad to hear that."

"And I'm glad that you're glad to hear that."

She smiled bigger, then asked if I had fun at the party.

"Yes," I said. "But I missed you."

"I missed you, too," she said. "And I'm *really* going to miss you next year."

"Same," I said, my heart fluttering. "I hope you get into Harvard. Then we'll be closer."

She took a deep breath, then exhaled, glancing nervously over at her desk strewn with index cards and Post-it notes. "Speaking of Harvard, I really better get back to it."

"Okay, but try to get some sleep," I said. "Even a couple of hours would do you good."

She shook her head. "I don't have time to sleep. I have so much left to do. But you're welcome to crash here if you want. . . ."

The offer was so tempting. I was tired and had a long walk back to my place, but mostly, I just wasn't ready to leave her. I hesitated, wavering, then said, "I probably shouldn't. Someone might see me leaving in the morning—"

"True," she quickly said, nodding.

I looked into her eyes, then leaned down and kissed her on the forehead. "Good luck, Summer."

"Thank you, Tyson."

She gave me a tight-lipped smile, then returned to her desk, where she sat, studying her index cards. I watched her for a few seconds, then quietly slipped out the door.

That was the last time I ever saw Summer.

CHAPTER 4

HANNAH

Tyson once likened Lainey to the next-door neighbor on a sitcom. The friend who pops over, providing a dose of comedic relief in every episode. I think of this description now as she sails into my apartment and says, "So I've been thinking about ways to kill Grady, and I think poisoning is the way to go."

She then bursts into the refrain of "Goodbye Earl."

I manage a smile, then tell her that Grady probably isn't worth a prison sentence.

"*That's* debatable," she says, dropping her tote bag on the floor and wrapping her long arms around me. Lainey's hugs are the best, and I lean into her, inhaling her no-nonsense perfume, which smells more like aftershave. "What a piece of shit."

"It hurts so bad, Lainey," I say, fighting back tears as I cling to her.

"Don't worry," she says, finally releasing me. "We will make him pay for this." Her brown eyes are piercing.

I nod, less concerned with revenge than with my broken heart, but at least she's distracting me. "How are we going to do that?" I ask.

"I have some ideas. But first—what do you have to drink?"

"Just vodka and some cheap chardonnay," I say, knowing her standards are higher than mine. They didn't used to be—she was a Boone's Farm girl in college—but a lot has changed in Lainey's life since then. She's still as down to earth as ever, but her tastes have become more expensive.

"Cheap chardonnay fits the mood, I think." She smiles.

We make our way to the kitchen, and I open my fridge, pulling out a screw-top bottle, then pouring two glasses.

"Go ahead and top mine off," she says with another smile.

I nod and fill both glasses to the top. We each take one, then head over to my sofa.

Lainey kicks off her boho-chic boots that seem so out of season but I'm sure are cool in New York and L.A. She curls her legs up under her while I put my feet on my coffee table.

"So I've been doing some digging," she says, taking a gulp of her wine. "And this Munich chick is absolutely *pathetic*."

For a second, I'm confused. Then I smile and say, "You mean Berlin."

"Munich, Berlin, Frankfurt, *whatever*. It's a stupid name. And don't get me started on her pathetic Instagram," she says, then immediately launches into a rant. "She photoshops the fuck out of everything. Does she think people can't see what she's doing?"

I know Lainey is trying to comfort me, but she seems to be forgetting that I just saw the woman in real life. Unretouched, naked, and flawless.

"And seriously—what's with those floral dresses? Good *God*. Those bows and puffy sleeves? She's a walking antebellum costume."

"I think she's going for wholesome," I say.

"Wholesome? She doesn't get to monetize a prim and proper Southern belle image, then fuck someone's fiancé. She needs to be held accountable. *Outed.*"

"Outed how?" I ask, picturing something crazy that only happens in urban myths—like a billboard on Peachtree Street or an ad in *The Atlanta Journal-Constitution.*

"Funny you should say that," she says, looking proud of herself. "So on my flight, I made a list of all her brand partnerships.... I also found a mutual friend of ours in the PR world. I reached out and told her I needed a tastemaker in Atlanta to help with a project. Guess who she suggested?"

"*Lainey!* No! Stop! Berlin's family is as connected as Grady's—"

"And? So?"

"So I don't have the stomach for this kind of conflict."

"Well, I *do.*" She blinks her long jet-black eyelashes. They look like extensions, but they're natural—like everything else about her.

I sigh, part of me wanting to unleash Lainey's wrath on both of them. As powerful as Berlin and Grady might be in Atlanta, Lainey has more cachet and a much bigger platform.

"I just don't want you to do something crazy," I say.

"It's not crazy to hold someone accountable. She knows Grady has a fiancée, right?"

I nod. The social circles we move in aren't that big—everyone knows everything. "I just don't get it," I say. "Why would he *propose?* And then do this?"

"Because he's a man. He wants to have his cake and eat it, too."

I get a nauseatingly graphic image and groan. "Do you think she's the only one? Or do you think there have been others?" I ask, as the possibility of sexually transmitted diseases crosses my mind for the first time.

"Who knows? Who cares? One is too many."

"I know, but I'd feel a lot better if this was the only time. Like a fluke . . ."

"A *fluke?*"

"You know what I mean—"

"No, I don't. And you need to stop it right now."

"Stop what?"

"Searching for ways to somehow excuse this—"

"I'm not doing that—"

"Swear to me. Swear you'll *never* take him back."

"I swear," I say.

It's mostly true, but a very, *very* narrow path to forgiveness *has* crossed my mind—one that would also involve a ton of groveling and therapy.

"So how do you want to confront him?" Lainey asks.

"Can't I just call him?"

She shakes her head. "No. It has to be face-to-face. And you need to look hot when you do it," she says, giving me the once-over. "No sweats."

"You want me to get dressed *up?*"

"Yes. And put on makeup. And do your hair."

"Jeez, Lainey. That's a really tall order."

"No, it's not. You can pull it together. And the good news is— your skin is glowing and you're in the best shape of your life—"

"Yep. The silver lining to getting cheated on while you're engaged."

"There are a lot of other silver linings here."

"Such as?"

"Such as—you found out *now*. *Before* you married him. It's a blessing in disguise. You dodged a bullet."

"Then why does it feel like I took a bullet to the heart?"

Lainey nods, giving me a look of pure sympathy. "I know it hurts. There is nothing worse than betrayal. *Nothing*. But this is who he is. This is his character. He's a dick."

"He can be difficult," I say. "But I didn't think he was a cheater—"

"It all goes hand in hand. The rules don't apply to him."

I sigh and nod, thinking of all the white lies I've heard him tell and all the lines and corners I've seen him try to cut, often getting away with it.

She looks at me, frowning, then says, "Were you really in love with him?"

I give her a confused look. Is she asking whether I was *actually* in love with Grady or whether I was *very* in love with him? Either way, it seems like a strange question. "Aren't most people in love with their fiancés?"

"I'd say seventy–thirty. . . . Maybe eighty–twenty at best."

I wait for her to laugh, but she stares at me, stone-faced. It's such an absurdly cynical Lainey statement that I just roll my eyes.

"I'm serious, Han. Marriage seems like a game of musical chairs. It's all fun and games until the music stops, then everyone's in a mad, frantic scramble to squeeze their butt cheeks onto a seat. *Any* seat."

"Grady wasn't just *any* seat, Lainey. I loved him." I hesitate, then say, "I still do."

She gives me a horrified look. "How could you *still* love him?"

"Because love isn't something you can just turn off like a switch."

"Okay. Well. Tell me what you love about him," she demands.

"Lots of things."

"Name them. Seriously. I want to know."

I take a deep breath and picture Grady at his best. "He's charming and funny, and he makes everything feel like an adventure. Just going to the grocery store . . . He made life interesting. And let's face it . . . I'm a little boring."

"You're *not* boring. You're just not an attention whore," she says.

I smile. "Okay. He can be a bit of an attention seeker. But we balanced each other out. Everyone loves Grady."

"Fine. But what I hear you saying is that you love how much *other* people love him." Lainey hesitates, giving me a knowing look. "And I bet I can guess who's at the top of that list."

"Who?" I ask.

"Oh, c'mon, Hannah. Don't play dumb at a time like this."

I sigh. "Okay. But just because my mother thought he was a great catch doesn't mean he *wasn't* a great catch."

"Yes. But again, listen to your word choice. 'Great catch'?" She makes air quotes. "What does that even mean? That he checks a lot of boxes? He's not even smart—"

"Maybe not book-smart. But he's very street-smart."

"He ain't *that* street-smart," Lainey says. "He got busted in bed with another woman."

"True," I say.

"Look, the bottom line is he may be seen as a 'catch' and he may check a lot of boxes and you might even think you love him—"

"I *do* love him—"

"Fine. But do you know what?" she says, staring into my eyes.

"What?"

"I never believed he was your *person.*"

"I thought you didn't even believe in that soul-mate stuff—"

"I don't. But you *do,*" she says. "And I never got that 'I can't live without him' vibe from you."

"You didn't?" I ask hopefully.

"No. I didn't. And for what it's worth, Tyson couldn't *stand* him."

"Seriously?"

"C'mon. You had to know that. Remember what an ass Grady was about Serena Williams? Honestly, Hannah, that whole thing was low-key racist and sexist—"

"I know it was," I say with a sigh, thinking that *low-key* was probably generous.

I always made excuses for Grady, rationalizing that he never said anything *overtly* racist or sexist. That his attitudes were more the results of an ingrained, unconscious bias. But deep down, I knew that was a distinction without a difference, and I was wrong to look the other way for so long.

"I know this is brutal, Hannah. And if you say you love him, I believe you do. But in the words of Tina Turner: What's love got to do with it?"

"At this point, I guess nothing," I say.

"Exactly. You can't marry a cheater. You just can't. It has to be over."

"I know," I say, nodding.

Part of me feels relieved that the situation is so clear-cut. There is no gray area to navigate, and there is peace in that. But another part of me knows that I've built the vision for my entire future around Grady. Without him, I don't know where I'm going or even who I am. The thought of figuring all that out is nothing short of terrifying, and it doesn't help to know that my new reality is going to shatter my mother's very conditional approval of me.

Lainey and I sit in silence for a few seconds before she suddenly jumps off the sofa. "Come on," she says, grabbing my hand and pulling me to my feet.

"Where are we going?"

"To your closet," she says, walking down the hallway toward my bedroom. "To pick out your revenge outfit."

I laugh and reluctantly trail behind her. In some ways, Lainey is the female version of Grady. Never a dull moment. The difference is that she would never in a million years stab me in the back.

A few seconds later, we are standing before my closet, my clothes neatly arranged by color. She points to a navy and white striped cardigan with nautical buttons. "You still have this thing?"

"What's wrong with it?"

"It's ancient. You've had it since college."

"So what? It's a perfectly good sweater. Just a few pills," I say, reaching out and picking several off.

"It's out of style."

"How can a simple cardigan be out of style?"

"The same way *anything* can be out of style. It's all about the cut and proportion and stuff like that. Didn't you see *The Devil Wears Prada*?"

I smile because I've always identified with Anne Hathaway's character.

"When did you wear it last?" Lainey says.

"I can't remember."

"Well, if you can't remember, it's time to say buh-*bye*," she says, yanking it off the hanger. "Out with the old. In with the new."

She tosses it on the floor, declaring it the start of our "donate pile."

She continues over the next several minutes, ruthlessly discarding three pairs of skinny jeans, two innocuous button-down blouses, and an emerald-green top. I fight back on the top, declaring it sentimental.

"Because of Grady?"

I shrug, knowing full well that I wore it on our second date.

She shakes her head, then rips it off the hanger and tosses it on the floor.

She works her way through the rainbow, ending with a white Brandon Maxwell minidress I recently ordered from Net-a-Porter. A splurge for me.

"Oh, wow. I *love* this," Lainey says, running her hands over the heavy silk. "It's gorgeous."

"Thanks. But it's going back," I say, grateful that I'm still in the thirty-day window for returns. "It was supposed to be my rehearsal dinner dress."

"And now it's your revenge dress." She gives me a diabolical smile.

"Meaning?"

"Meaning you're wearing this when you dump Grady."

"You want me to wear a dress over to his *house?*"

"No. I want you to wear it *out*. To dinner."

I stare at her. "You want me to break up with him at a restaurant?"

"Yes. A *nice* restaurant."

"Lainey, no! This isn't a television show."

"I know that," she says. "It's your *life*. That's why it's so important to do this in a strong way. You don't want to have any regrets."

"But I can't do it in public, Lainey. I'll fall apart."

"No, you won't. I'll be there with you."

"How would that even work?"

"You tell Grady that I came to town to see you. Last-minute visit. Maid of honor type stuff. And that I want to take you both to dinner. We get to the restaurant and order the most expensive bottle of wine on the menu, apps galore, pricey entrées. . . . Then, once everything is brought to the table, you dump his ass. Then we throw some wine in his face and stick him with the bill."

"We are *not* throwing wine!"

Lainey laughs. "I was kidding about that—but we will definitely stick him with the bill."

I give her a tiny smile, knowing how cheap Grady is. "That *does* sound pretty satisfying," I say. "But can I at least return the dress? I have no need for an expensive white dress."

"Yes, you do." She smiles. "You're going to need it for our trip."

"What trip?"

"The *fabulous* trip that we're going to take to get you over this whole ordeal," she says. "The trip where you'll have sex on a moonlit beach with a tall, dark, handsome stranger and regain your mojo. *How Hannah Got Her Groove Back!*"

I laugh, as Lainey stares at me, stone-faced. "You think I'm kidding?" she asks.

"Oh, I know you're *not,*" I say. "But sex with a stranger isn't going to fix this."

"It might not *fix* it. . . . But it'll be a damn good start," she says, then smiles. "And it's way more fun than musical chairs."

THAT NIGHT AS we get settled into bed, I try to distract myself from my heartbreak by asking Lainey about her life.

"There's not much to tell," she says, punching her pillow and turning on her side to face me. She is wearing one of my T-shirts as a nightgown, since her bag didn't make the flight and has yet to be delivered.

"Stop it. You have the most exciting life of anyone I know."

"People always think that. But it's like anything else. It's just work."

"Any new A-list interactions?"

"Um, let's see. . . . Does Debra Messing count?"

"Definitely. I love her."

"Same. She's a badass."

"Did you work with her?"

"No, she was at a party. At Donny Deutsch's townhouse. Oh—

and I also met Matthew McConaughey at Soho House. He was with his wife, Camila. They were so cute together."

"You do realize that regular people don't just forget to tell their friends they met Matthew McConaughey?"

"I thought I told you."

"No, ma'am, you did not."

She shrugs and says, "At the end of the day, they're just people."

"What about your *love* life?" I say. "Are you still seeing your neighbor?"

"*Seeing* is a stretch. But yeah, we're still hooking up," she says with a laugh. "Though he is kind of old."

"How old?"

"In his fifties. Oh! Get this. He told me this crazy story about getting his ex pregnant with twins who were then adopted by another guy. They're, like, twenty now."

"So he doesn't see them?"

She shakes her head.

I nod and say, "When's the last time you *really* liked someone?"

"I *really* like Neighbor Guy."

"No, you don't. You'd call him by his real name if you did," I say.

"Well, then I really like *Marcus*," she says with a shrug.

Lainey's use of nicknames started as a joke—a takeoff on the "Ugly Naked Guy" *Friends* episode. But she took it to another level, largely skipping names altogether. There had been Pilates Guy, Chess Guy, Unicycle Guy, Mafia Guy, Hockey Guy. Occasionally, she had to assign Roman numerals—as in: Firefighter Guy I and II.

In the past, I always felt a little sorry for her, believing that no matter how much fun she was having, she had to be a little lonely. Now she seems like the lucky one. No strings. No worries.

"Tell me more about Matthew McConaughey," I say, forcing a smile.

"He has the best bod," she says. "Arms. Chest. Ass. Holy. Shit."

I smile again, this time for real.

"If he weren't married . . ." Her voice trails off.

"You've never been with a married man?"

"No. Never. After watching my mother live her life as the other woman? No chance."

I nod, feeling a wave of guilt that I've only been thinking of myself, and that I haven't once thought of the parallels to Lainey's mother's affair. "Have you had any contact with your father?"

"Nope. Not since he didn't show up for my mom's funeral," she says.

I nod, feeling another stab of guilt that I wasn't there, either. But it was May 2020—the height of the pandemic. Only four guests were allowed in the chapel—Lainey and her mother's three closest friends. I watched the livestream of the service and did everything else I could think of, checking in with calls and texts, sending her flowers and cards and food. I still wish I could have done more, though. After all, that was *Lainey's* rock bottom.

"What about your sisters?" I ask. "Have you given any more thought to reaching out to them?"

She shakes her head, but I sense hesitation.

"Are you sure about that?" I ask gently.

She sighs and says, "I recently looked them up. Just to see."

"And?"

"And they're both still in Texas." She rolls her eyes. "Ever notice the way people from Texas never seem to leave Texas? They act like it's the damn Garden of Eden."

I can tell she's downplaying something, so I press her a bit. "What are they doing right now?"

"They're both private on Facebook and Insta—but I can see a bit. Ashley's definitely married, and Olivia's still playing tennis."

"Professionally?"

"Yeah. I think so. I didn't delve too deeply."

"Maybe you should. Wouldn't it be nice to have family in your life?" I say softly, thinking how unfair it is that Lainey's mother was an only child on top of everything else.

"It's crossed my mind. But it would just cause problems. I mean—there's no way they'd be happy to hear from me."

"Maybe not at first. But then they'd have *you*."

She laughs. "The ultimate prize, right?"

"*I* think you are," I say.

"Thanks, Han."

She gives me a smile, but I can tell she's sad now, too.

THE FOLLOWING MORNING, I open my eyes and see Lainey's long brown hair spilling over her pillow. For one second, I'm only happy to see her. Then it all comes rushing back to me—the reason she's here—and the pain is even more acute than it was yesterday.

It was that way when Summer died, too. As horrific as that first day was, my heartbreak only grew as our new reality set in. Obviously, there's no comparison between the two situations; they aren't in the same universe. But losing Grady in this abrupt way really does feel like a death. He was there one second and gone the next.

My phone vibrates. It's him. I freeze, panic, then make myself answer. Somewhere, deep in my soul, I hope that he'll confess. It would be his only way to salvation.

"Hi," I say, barely getting the word out.

"Morning, babe!" he says, his voice chipper and loud. "How're you feeling?"

"Better," I say as Lainey rolls over and looks at me.

I flash her my phone screen, showing her Grady's name.

"Put it on speaker," she whispers.

I do as I'm told, laying the phone on the bed between us.

"So what are you up to today?" he asks.

"Lainey's here," I say.

"Oh, cool. I didn't know she was coming. Is she filming something?"

"No. She just flew down to see me."

Lainey points down at her left ring finger, reminding me of her plan.

"She wants to take us to dinner," I say. "To celebrate our engagement."

Lainey gives me an encouraging smile and a thumbs-up.

"That's so nice of her! I'm in! Do you have a rez?"

"Not yet."

"Should I make one?"

"Sure," I say.

"Okay. I'll try Le Bilboquet. It's short notice, but I'll text the manager. I bet they can slide us in."

"Sounds good," I say, biting my lip so hard that it hurts, thinking that he's certainly mastered the art of *sliding in.*

THE HOURS TICK by. It feels like I'm treading water and on the brink of drowning. Lainey forces me to eat, but I can only manage a few bites of buttered toast. At some point, I notice that Lainey has taken down all the framed photos of Grady. It's a relief not to see his face, but I hope she hasn't gotten rid of them. I'm not ready to throw pictures away. I don't know that I ever will be.

Around three o'clock, Delta finally delivers Lainey's bag, and she goes to take a shower. As I curl up on my sofa, I hear a knock at my door. My heart starts to race, as I wonder if it could be Grady. Or my mother, whom I've been avoiding like the plague.

I nervously walk to the door and stare out the peephole. I can see a man's chest and shoulders but can tell it's not Grady.

"Who is it?" I ask, always a little paranoid.

"It's me," I hear a familiar voice say.

I quickly open the door and throw my arms around Tyson.

"Oh my God. You came!" I say, my eyes welling up. I've never been so grateful to see him.

He hugs me back and says, "Yep. Of course I did."

I finally let go of him, wiping away tears and telling him to come in.

He smiles, then walks into my foyer. "How are you holding up?" His voice is calm and soothing.

"Better now that you're here," I say.

"Good." He nods, putting his leather duffel bag on the floor.

"Did Lainey know you were coming?" I ask.

"No," he says, glancing around. "Where is your girl, anyway?"

"She's in the shower," I say. "And let me just warn you, she's in rare form."

"I figured. Why I came. I knew you'd need a little adult supervision."

"Wait till you hear her 'revenge plan.'"

"Oh, Lord. Do I even want to know?"

I lead him over to the sofa, explaining as I go. "Grady thinks she's here to celebrate our engagement. He's making a dinner reservation," I say, both of us sitting down. "She wants to ambush him."

Tyson shakes his head.

"It's a bad idea, isn't it?"

"Not necessarily. I guess it depends on how you feel about it?"

"Well, I like the idea of having her there with me. Even better if you're there, too. I really don't think I can do it alone."

He nods.

"But she wants me to get all dolled up. It seems a bit—I don't know—"

"Needlessly cinematic?"

"Yes. Exactly," I say.

"What does your gut say?"

I sigh, thinking. "My gut tells me to let Lainey do her thing. Burn him," I say, a little shocked by my answer. I'm even more shocked that the last two words give me a small rush.

"Well, then," Tyson says. "Let's do it."

I nod, hoping I can go through with it.

"I'm so sorry this is happening to you, Hannah."

I feel a *but* coming on just as he says it.

"But I never liked that guy."

"Why didn't you tell me?"

"Because that always backfires. And ultimately you are the only one who can decide what's right for you. I'm just glad you saw his true colors. The circumstances suck, but better late than never."

"Yeah," I say. "That's probably true."

"It *is* true. You're a really good person, Hannah. You deserve so much better."

I feel myself getting teary again just as Lainey rounds the corner in a short red robe. Her wet hair is wrapped in a towel, turban-style. She stops in her tracks when she sees Tyson.

"What the hell?" she says, grinning. "Why didn't you tell me you were coming?"

"I know how much you love surprises," he says. "Speaking of surprises, I heard about your ambush plan."

"It's good, isn't it?"

"I don't hate it . . . and it *is* probably easier to extricate Hannah from a restaurant than his house."

"Exactly," Lainey says. "And I also want to stick him with the big, fat bill."

"That's so petty," Tyson says.

"Yep." Lainey grins proudly.

"What happened to 'when they go low'?" Tyson says.

"When they go low, I go *lower.*" Lainey laughs.

"Okay. But remember, I don't want to make a scene," I say.

"No scene," Lainey says. "Soft voices. All smiles."

"So what are we going to do, exactly?" Tyson asks Lainey. "We sit down, toast the happy couple. And then—BAM. Hannah drops the bomb that she knows he cheated?"

"Something like that," Lainey replies. "You can refine the script. Maybe infuse it with some sort of cross-examination technique leading up to a *gotcha* moment."

Tyson nods, then looks at me. "What if—and I'm just spitballing here—you break off the engagement without telling him *why?*"

"So I wouldn't tell him what I saw?"

"Correct. You'd just tell him that it's over, and that you have your reasons."

"What's the point of that?" I ask.

"It's always an advantage to hold your cards close," Tyson says. "Knowledge is power."

I mull this over as Lainey shakes her head. "I don't like that plan. She has to bust him. It'll be *so* satisfying."

"In the moment, sure. She'd have instant gratification," Tyson says. "But long term, the wondering what happened will *wreck* him."

"He'll want a reason," I say.

"Tough. Tell him you had a change of heart. . . . That you just aren't 'feeling it' anymore," Tyson says. "Be vague."

"He won't buy that."

"He won't have a choice if that's all you give him."

"But won't he know that I know?"

"He might *suspect* it, yes. But he won't know for *sure*. And he can't very well ask you if it's because he cheated, now, can he?"

"Oh. Wow. True," I say.

"And the sense of rejection will feel exponentially greater if you don't provide a concrete reason."

"Okay. So when would I do this? In the middle of dinner? With y'all at the table? Or would I ask for a moment alone?"

"That's up to you," Tyson says.

"I think it's better to have an exact plan," Lainey says. "Or else you might not go through with it."

"Oh, she'll go through with it," Tyson says. "She *has* to."

He gives me a stern but compassionate look just as my phone buzzes and a text comes in from Grady, telling me that we have a reservation for seven o'clock at Le Bilboquet.

OK, I text back. But do you think you could change it to four people? Tyson just arrived.

Tyson? he says.

He's annoyed. He's always been jealous of my friendship with Tyson. It has stressed me out in the past, but now I relish it.

Yes, I type back. Such a wonderful surprise, isn't it?

I DON'T THINK I've ever been as nervous as I am getting out of our Uber at the valet stand in front of the restaurant. It doesn't help that I feel way overdressed. When we check in with the hostess ten minutes ahead of our reservation, I tell myself that it's better than looking as wan and sad as I feel.

She asks if we'd like to be seated before the last member of our party arrives.

"Yes. Absolutely," Lainey replies.

On the way to our table, I see two people I know, including one of Grady's co-workers. I smile and say hello but obviously don't stop to chat, reminding myself that whatever happens tonight, we cannot make a scene. When we get to our table, Lainey whispers instructions. *Grady goes in the corner. You sit across from him. We'll flank you.*

I nod, taking my assigned seat, my back to the main dining area, as one of the waitstaff arrives at our table, asking if we prefer still or sparkling water.

"Tap water is fine," I quickly say, feeling queasy and sweaty.

"And two bottles of Perrier, please," Lainey says.

The second my glass is filled, I down it, then whisper that I might throw up.

"No, you won't," Lainey says, shaking her head. "Just breathe and smile."

"She doesn't have to *smile*," Tyson says.

"It'll help relax her. It's a thing. It signals to the brain that everything is okay," Lainey says.

"Everything *isn't* okay," I say, feeling myself start to panic.

"Do you want to leave?" Tyson asks me. "We can still bail—"

"We can't *bail*," Lainey says, her eyes darting over to the entrance. "We're on a mission."

"It's her decision," Tyson says.

"Too late," Lainey says, glancing over at the door. "He's here."

"Oh, *shit*," I say under my breath, my mind going blank. "I forget what I'm supposed to say!"

"Say whatever you want," Tyson says, his voice low and reassuring. "If you want to tell him to fuck off the second you see him, do that. Otherwise, just follow our lead."

I nod and look at Lainey, watching her flip a switch and begin performing. She gets to her feet, turns on her biggest smile, and waves across the room at Grady.

A second later, he is standing beside me. I want to die.

"The groom has arrived!" Lainey says, kissing one of his cheeks, then the other. "Congratulations once again."

"Thank you so much!" Grady says as I feel the warm weight of his hand on my shoulder. "Hi, sweetheart."

I say hello without looking up, my heart in my throat.

He gives my shoulder a little rub, then reaches across me to bump fists with Tyson. "Hey, man! Good to see you! It's been a minute!"

"Yeah, it has," Tyson says with a tight smile as Grady circles the table and takes his seat. He looks as handsome as ever in a navy sport coat and a light blue button-down.

I force myself to make eye contact with him.

He smiles, then says, "You look gorgeous. Love the dress."

"Thank you."

"And I love your hair like that," he says.

"Thanks," I say again. "Lainey curled it."

"Well, she did a great job," he says, grinning at me like we're the only two people at the table.

I search his face for any sign of guilt or regret or remorse. But there isn't a trace. He is as confident and relaxed as ever.

"So. How was your day?" Grady asks, glancing around the table. "Did y'all do any wedding planning?"

I look at Lainey, unable to answer. She clears her throat and says, "We made a few decisions, yes."

Grady smiles and nods. "Such as?"

"That's top secret!" Lainey says with a wink as our server arrives to give us her welcome spiel, then ask if we'd like a cocktail.

"Tyson?" Lainey says, giving him a knowing look. "Didn't you want to order some wine?"

"Yeah. Sure. What does everyone like? Red? White?" Tyson asks, scanning the wine list.

"I prefer red," Grady says. "But white's fine, too. I trust you, man!"

"Trust is *very* important!" Lainey says, nodding effusively.

I give her a look to tone it down.

"How about this one?" Tyson points to a cabernet.

"Unless you have something even better? Something more special?" Lainey chimes in, looking up at our server. "We're celebrating—and really want to *splurge*!"

She tells Lainey she'll check with the sommelier.

"Perfect. And please also bring us your best champagne! We'll open both right away!" Lainey says, making a ridiculous double-fisted drinking gesture.

"I'll also take a Jack and Coke," Grady says.

"Oh, c'mon, Grady, you can do better than Jack *Daniel's*!" Lainey says. "We're celebrating here! My treat!"

Grady smiles, nods, then looks up at our waitress. "Make that a double of your best bourbon. *Neat*."

"Attaboy," Lainey says, leaning over to give his arm a playful punch.

As our waitress departs, Grady turns to Lainey and says, "So how's showbiz?"

"Great! Never been better! Having the time of my life."

"That's awesome. I'm sure Hannah's told you—we binged your series. It's so good—and you're hilarious."

"That's very kind," she says. "Thank you."

"So I gotta ask. What's Emma like in real life?" he says, referring to Riley Evans, the hottest girl on the show.

"Riley's a sweet girl, but very self-absorbed." Lainey glances at me with a glint in her eye. "Her Instagram is one big brag fest. Like— 'look at me and all my designer shit.'"

Grady laughs and says, "Yeah. I know the type."

"I'm sure you do," Lainey says.

I give her a horrified look, but there is no stopping her.

"Who's that influencer you follow here in Atlanta?" she asks me. "I think her name is Munich?"

"*Munich?*" Grady laughs as my heart stops. "What kind of name is Munich?"

"I think she's talking about Berlin Beverly," I say as nonchalantly as I can.

For one second, he looks stunned. But he quickly recovers. "So. What looks good to everyone?" he asks, glancing down at the menu.

"Everything looks amazing!" Lainey says. "I'm thinking about the lobster. Is it good here?" She turns to Grady, wide-eyed and innocent.

"I'm sure it's great," he says. "But I'm allergic to shellfish."

"Oh, my," Lainey says. "What would happen if you ate it? Would you *die?*"

"I could, yes." Grady nods somberly.

"What if *I* ordered the lobster?" she says. "Would *that* pose a threat to you?"

"Nah," he says. "As long as I don't eat it. . . ."

I tune their conversation out and feel relieved when our drinks arrive. I numbly watch as Tyson does the wine tasting and Lainey samples the champagne, both nodding their approval. After our glasses are poured, the server asks if we have any questions about the menu.

"No, I think we're ready!" Lainey says.

We give her our order, then Lainey asks for "all the sides," announcing that she wants the meal to be lavish and festive. She then lifts her champagne glass.

"How about a toast? Tyson—will you do the honors?"

"I think *you* should do it, Lainey," he says.

"Okay! My pleasure." She smiles, then pauses dramatically. "Here's to my best friend, Hannah. I don't know a kinder, more loyal, more amazing woman in the entire world. Grady—you're a lucky man. Don't screw this up or I'll have to kill you! With lobster—"

"Okay! Hear, hear!" Tyson says, cutting her off and raising his glass.

Grady does the same, making eye contact with everyone before sipping his bourbon. I take a hurried taste of champagne, then decide I can't take it another second.

"Lainey. Tyson," I mumble. "Could y'all excuse us for a moment?"

"Sure thing," Tyson says, immediately leaping up from his chair. "Let's go check out the bar, Lainey."

Lainey stands, picking up her glass. She gives me a final nod of encouragement, then turns to follow Tyson.

"What's up? Are you okay?" Grady asks as I meet his gaze. He's smiling, but I can tell he's at least a *little* worried.

"Not really," I say, shaking my head.

"What's wrong? Did I say something?"

"No. I just need to talk to you."

"About?"

I take a deep breath, then cut right to the chase. "I can't marry you."

Grady stares back at me with a bewildered expression. He chuckles uneasily and says, "Ha! Good one!"

"I'm not joking," I say.

He glances at my ring, as if checking to see if it's still there. I look down at it, too, then take it off and move it to my right hand.

"Okay, Hannah. Knock it off. This isn't funny—"

"I know it's not *funny*," I say. "It's very, *very* sad. I thought you were *the one*. But I was wrong."

"Hannah. Stop. What are you *talking* about? What's going on here?" he says with a tremor in his voice.

"I think you know," I say, fighting back tears. I tell myself I can't cry. It's *game over* if I let even one tear drop.

"I have no *clue*," Grady says in a frantic whisper. He leans across the table, close enough for me to see the stubble of his blond beard. "What is this about?"

When I don't answer, he looks past me, toward the bar. "Do your friends have something to do with this?"

I shake my head.

His eyes narrow as he shifts in his seat. "Are you sure about that?"

"Positive."

"You're sure nothing happened with you and Tyson?"

I stare at him, incredulous. *Pissed*. How dare he try to flip the script on me.

"No, Grady. Nothing happened with Tyson," I say, determined to stay calm. "That's ridiculous, and you know it."

He makes a scoffing sound, then says, "So I'm supposed to believe that it's purely coincidental that we're having this conversation right after he gets to town?"

I reach for my water glass, then choose my champagne flute instead, downing it.

"Well?" he demands.

I put my glass back down on the table and say, "They know nothing about this."

"I don't believe you," he says. "I think Tyson has a *lot* to do with this."

I bite my tongue, reminding myself that it no longer matters what Grady thinks or believes. I know the truth. I have the knowledge and the power.

"That guy has *always* had a thing for you." Grady doubles down, his fists landing on the table.

I blink, then clear my throat. "Are you projecting, Grady?"

"No, I'm not *projecting*!"

"Are you sure? Because they say the biggest cheaters always accuse their partners of infidelity."

"That's a stupid theory," he scoffs.

"So you've been faithful to me?" I say, daring him to lie to my face.

"Yes!" he says. "One thousand percent!"

I take a deep breath. "Okay, Grady," I say. "You have two choices. You can either confess to me what *you've* done or lose me forever—"

"Hannah! I have *never* cheated on you," he says, looking so wounded, so *deeply* offended that for a nanosecond, I stupidly doubt what I saw with my own eyes.

"Okay, Grady. If you say so."

He gives me a look of relief, unclenching his jaw and dropping his shoulders. I pick up my clutch and slowly get to my feet.

"Where're you going?" he asks, looking frantic.

"You made your choice," I say, staring down at him.

"What *choice*?"

"The choice to lie to my face."

"Hannah! I'm *not* lying. I would never, ever—"

"Stop talking, Grady. I'm leaving."

"What do you mean you're *leaving*?" he asks, looking more panicked than I've ever seen him.

"I mean—I'm leaving this restaurant. I'm leaving this relationship. I'm leaving *you.*"

"Hannah! Wait. Please, *please* don't do this," he says, his hands in prayer formation. "*Please*, Hannah. I love you."

I stare into his eyes, and for one fleeting second, I feel sorry for him. Then I remember the way he looked in bed with Berlin.

"Sorry, Grady. We're done," I say, shaking my head. "Have a nice life."

CHAPTER 5

TYSON

KEEP ONE EYE on Hannah while I sit at the bar. Lainey's back is to our table, so she keeps glancing over her shoulder. I tell her to knock it off before Grady sees her, so she demands a play-by-play. I tell her they're just talking.

Then, suddenly, Hannah gets up from the table and starts to walk toward us.

"Okay. She's coming," I say.

"Oh, shit. That was fast. How does she look?"

I tell her Hannah looks pretty calm—and her chin is up—but as she gets closer, I start to worry that she's almost *too* composed. Maybe she hasn't done the deed?

"What about Grady? What's he doing?"

"Nothing. He's just sitting there. Looking at his phone. Maybe she's going to the restroom?"

"Ugh. If she chickens out—I swear to God—I will go over there and do it myself. And wine *will* be thrown!"

"No doubt," I say, just as Hannah makes eye contact with me. She gives me a slight nod before making a sharp turn at the hostess stand, heading straight out the restaurant door.

"She just walked out," I say, getting pumped. "She must have done it!"

"Wow!" Lainey says, spinning around on her stool.

"Go get her," I say to Lainey. "Call us an Uber. I'll be right there."

Lainey gives me a confused look. "Wait. Are you going to tell him off?"

"No. I just need to settle up—"

"Tyson! You can't *pay*!"

"Can I at least get my beer?" I say, raising the glass in my hand.

"No! Transfer it to the table."

"It's one beer, Lainey. I'll look like a jerk if I walk out. Just go get Hannah—" I say. "I'm right behind you."

As Lainey runs after Hannah, I make eye contact with the bartender. When he comes over to me, I explain the situation as tactfully as I can, discreetly gesturing toward our table.

"Call me if he gives you any trouble with the check. He might. The guy's an asshole," I say, handing him a twenty, along with my business card.

The bartender nods, smiles, and says, "Got it. Thanks, man."

"No problem," I say.

On my way out the door, I make a point not to look back at Grady.

"SHE DID IT! SHE TOTALLY DID IT!" Lainey shouts as I join them in the back of our getaway car. Hannah is in the middle, and I give her a hug as Lainey giddily debriefs me.

"I'm really proud of you," I tell Hannah.

"I just followed the plan," she says with a shrug.

"Still. That must have been really tough."

She nods, looking shell-shocked as Lainey continues to whoop it up, replaying all the highlights. Hannah feeds off Lainey's energy, even laughing at moments, but by the time we get back to her apartment, I can tell her adrenaline is wearing off—and that she is about to fall apart.

"Why don't you change into something comfortable, and Lainey and I will order a pizza?" I suggest, settling onto the sofa.

"Unless you want to go out?" Lainey says, wildly misreading the room.

Hannah shakes her head and says no, she wants to stay in, and pizza sounds great. She then turns and walks to her bedroom.

The second she's gone, Lainey picks up Hannah's phone, enters her passcode, and starts looking through her texts.

"Uh, what are you doing?" I ask.

"Nothing."

She keeps scrolling, then takes a photo of Hannah's screen with her own phone.

"Lainey! Get out of there."

"I'm just getting Grady's number."

"Why?"

"I have some follow-up bidness," she says.

"Have you ever heard the expression 'Quit while you're ahead'?"

"Have you ever heard the expression 'Nevertheless, she persisted'?" she fires back at me. "I know what I'm doing here. Just order our pizza."

When Hannah returns to the living room, she's in pajamas. Her eye makeup is gone, her face red and blotchy. It's clear she's been crying.

"Do you want to talk about it?" I gently ask her.

She shakes her head. "No. Can we just talk about something else? Will you distract me?"

I nod, give her a smile, and say, "Okay. So, funny story. You're not the only one who broke up this weekend."

Hannah looks back at me, wide-eyed. "You and Nicole broke up?"

"Yep."

"When?" she asks.

"Last night."

She gives me a worried look. "Why have you waited to tell us?"

"Because we had bigger fish to fry," I say.

"Gosh, Tyson. I'm so sorry," Hannah says.

"Who did it?" Lainey asks.

I tell them it was mutual—that we have different priorities—hoping that they won't press me on the details.

Of course Lainey does, and I finally just admit what happened. "She didn't approve of my decision to quit my job."

"Oh my God!" Hannah says. "You quit your job *and* broke up with Nicole? What on earth is going on?"

I shrug and say, "It was time to make a change."

Hannah stares at me, wringing her hands. "Did either thing have to do with you coming here?"

"Not really," I say. "I mean, the trip may have been a *catalyst*, but both things needed to happen—"

"Shit. I knew it," Hannah says, shaking her head. "I feel awful."

"Well, *I* feel liberated."

"Congratulations on your newfound freedom!" Lainey says. "This is great news! Now you can come on our trip!"

"And what trip might that be?" I ask.

"The trip Hannah and I are taking. In lieu of her honeymoon."

I glance at Hannah, and she shrugs, giving me a look that says, *Just humor her*.

"Oh yeah?" I say. "Where are you guys headed?"

"We haven't decided. Maybe Bora-Bora or the Maldives," Lainey says.

"Terrific," I deadpan.

Her eyes light up. "Yay! So you're in?"

"Nah. I don't like the beach," I say.

"That's a ridiculous statement. You don't like *any* beach? In the world?"

"I don't like *your* kind of beach—"

"What's my kind of beach?"

"Beach resorts that are totally insulated from the country they're in."

"How do you know I like that kind of beach?"

"Well, I'm pretty sure you're not going to Bora-Bora to learn about the indigenous Maohi people."

Lainey laughs. "How the hell do you know their name?"

"I know stuff."

Lainey rolls her eyes. "Okay. So where would *you* want to go?"

"I'd have to think about it," I say, as it occurs to me that it's easier for me to say where I *don't* want to go than where I *do*. Come to think of it—the same is true when it comes to my job. And my relationship. Maybe Hannah's not the only one who needs a reset.

"What about you, Hannah?" Lainey asks. "Where do *you* want to go?"

"Oh, I'd go anywhere with y'all," she says, clearly just playing along.

"What if we each picked a place?" Lainey says.

"Like an *Eat, Pray, Love* type thing?" Hannah asks.

"More of an *Eat, Shop, Party* type thing," Lainey says.

Hannah smiles and shakes her head.

"Seriously. Remember how we were supposed to take that European vacation after we graduated?" Lainey asks.

Hannah and I nod. Of course we remember. We had planned a three-week trip with Summer, each of us picking one spot. I'd chosen Madrid; Lainey picked Amsterdam; Hannah picked Paris; and Summer picked Capri.

"Would you still choose Paris?" Lainey asks, looking at Hannah.

"I don't know. Maybe. I've *still* never been. Grady had no interest."

"No interest in *Paris*? Seriously?" Lainey says. "That's reason enough to break up with him. What the hell?"

"He doesn't like museums or churches," Hannah says.

"Of course he doesn't," I mumble under my breath. "What an idiot."

"We should go there," Lainey says, looking at Hannah.

"I don't know—the most romantic city in the world might be a little painful right now." She gives us a wan smile. "Then again, what was it that Audrey Hepburn said? Paris is always a good idea?"

"Always!" Lainey says. "I think Paris should be a front-runner here."

Hannah gives her a tight smile as Lainey turns to me and says, "And what did you have, Tyson? Was it Portugal or Spain?"

"Spain. Madrid," I say, remembering how excited I was at the prospect of seeing the great works of Goya and Velázquez and walking the Camino de Santiago.

"What about *that*, then?"

"Nah. I don't fuck with colonizers these days."

"Huh?" Lainey says.

I break it down for her as succinctly as I can. "I'm not interested in romanticizing Europe anymore. I know too much."

"Okay. So once again: where *would* you go? If you hate the beach and you're not down with Europe?" Lainey asks, as if that doesn't leave huge chunks of six other continents.

"I didn't say Europe—I said *colonizers*. There are plenty of European countries who never rolled up on anyone—" I start rattling them off: Bosnia, Croatia, Estonia, Cyprus, Finland, Belarus, Montenegro, Iceland.

"Okay. What about one of those?" Lainey says.

"What about Burundi?" I say, just to mess with her.

"Oh. That sounds nice!" Lainey says. "Is Burundi tropical?"

"Yes," I say. "It's in Africa. Beside Rwanda and Tanzania."

"Love that!" she says. "Do they have luxury safaris?"

"Nope," I say. "No safaris in Burundi."

"Beaches?"

"Nope. It's landlocked."

"So what *do* they have?"

"Well, let's see," I say. "They have high rates of corruption and crime and the lowest per capita GDP in the world. But I'm sure we would all feel very grateful for our current lives if we went there."

"You're *impossible*," Lainey says, then looks at Hannah. "Tell him to cooperate."

"Y'all," Hannah says. "This isn't a real thing, is it? Because there's no way I can travel right now—"

"Why not?" Lainey says.

"Because we're slammed at work. We have three huge installations coming up—and a photoshoot with *Southern Living*."

"Jada wouldn't let you get away for a bit? Given the circumstances?" Lainey asks, referring to Hannah's boss.

"She might," I say. "For a couple days. But certainly not for multiple *weeks*."

"You could always just quit," Lainey says with a breezy shrug. "Like Tyson."

"I can't just *quit*, Lainey," Hannah says. "I need the money. I'm not a famous actor."

"I'm not a *famous* actor, either," Lainey says. "I'm a *working* actor. And I'm sure you have more savings than I do. You're so good with money."

"Not lately, unfortunately," Hannah says. "I've spent way too much on that stupid house—" She inhales sharply, then lets out a long sigh.

"I thought Grady bought the house with his trust fund?"

"He did. But I've been paying for the furniture—"

"That's such *bullshit*," Lainey says. "He needs to pay you back for all of that. . . . And you need to sell your ring. That sucker would fund the whole trip."

"You think I should sell it?" Hannah asks, as I notice that it's no longer on her finger. She must have taken it off when she went back to her bedroom. It's a good sign.

"Of course you should sell it," Lainey says. "Why would you ever want to keep it?"

"Well, don't you think he's going to ask for it back?"

"Probably will. But tough shit," Lainey says.

"I agree," I say. "That ring is legally yours, Hannah."

"Are you sure about that?" she asks.

"I'd have to look up Georgia law to confirm," I say. "But most states say that an engagement ring is a gift. He could try to argue that it was a *conditional* gift—dependent upon marriage—but I bet Georgia has a 'dirty hands doctrine.'"

"I'd say he has dirty hands!" Lainey laughs.

"Which means if he did something to break the contract, the ring is yours," I say.

"Okay. But is keeping it the right thing to do?" Hannah asks.

"C'mon, Hannah. Don't play the martyr here," Lainey says.

I nod emphatically. For once, Lainey and I are a unified front. "She's right," I say. "About the ring *and* the trip."

Lainey and Hannah both look at me, surprised.

"I think it'd be great for you to get away for a couple weeks. Clear your head."

Hannah bites her lip and nods. "Maybe. I guess I could talk to Jada . . . see what she says."

Lainey is now off to the races, establishing the ground rules. Everyone will pick a destination, and no vetoes allowed, whether it's a beach *or* Burundi.

"Fine," I say. "No vetoes. I'm cool with that."

Lainey nods, then says, "We'll leave next week."

"Next *week*?" Hannah says.

"Yes," Lainey says. "No time like the present . . . YOLO, *bitches*."

LATER THAT NIGHT, after the girls have gone to bed and I've fallen asleep on the couch, I'm awakened by a tap on my shoulder. I open my eyes and find Hannah standing over me.

Startled, I ask if she's okay.

"Yes. I just wanted to talk," she whispers, sitting cross-legged on the floor next to the sofa so we're eye level. "I have an idea."

"What's that?" I ask.

"I think I'm going to pick Texas," she says, swallowing. "For my destination."

"Why in the world would you do that?"

"Lainey's sisters live there. I just did some digging. One lives in Dallas—the other one is in a small town called Dripping Springs."

"And? So?"

"I think Lainey needs to meet them. Her mother's gone. She has no family left. It's a gaping hole in her life—and I really think she needs to try to fill it...."

"Maybe you're right," I say. "And maybe it would help with her drinking."

"Exactly," Hannah says. "I've tried to talk to her about that—"

"So have I—"

"But she refuses."

"I know."

"Maybe if she got this big family secret out in the open—she could ... I don't know ... *rest* a bit," Hannah says.

I nod. It isn't the first time that Hannah and I have discussed Lainey's drinking—which seems to have gotten worse since the pandemic and her mother's death. But it's the first time it's occurred to me that it could have something to do with a vacuum in her life. I think of my own parents and shudder just imagining what it will be like when they're gone.

"That's really nice of you, Hannah. But you're the one in the middle of a crisis. Not Lainey. You should pick somewhere *you* want to go."

"Maybe so. But if you think about it, Lainey's crisis was her mother passing. And we couldn't be there for her."

"We did what we could," I say, thinking of how often I called Lainey during that time.

"I know, but we can do more *now*."

I nod, feeling a surge of admiration for Hannah's big heart.

"I guess it's worth a try," I say.

"Definitely." Hannah smiles. "And it will be an adventure."

"It's *always* an adventure with Lainey," I say. "But I really don't think she'll agree to this."

"Well, she's going to have to," Hannah says with a worried smile. "No vetoes. Remember?"

"Diabolical," I say, reaching out from under my blanket to give her a fist bump. "Downright cold-blooded."

CHAPTER 6

LAINEY

THE FOLLOWING MORNING, I awaken to the sound of Hannah crying. I reach across the bed and drape my arm around her.

"It's going to be okay," I whisper.

"No, it's not," she sobs. "Grady called my mother. Before I could talk to her. He's already turned her against me."

"How can that be?" I ask. "Did he tell her what he did?"

"Of course not," she says. "He's blaming everything on me. *I'm* the bad guy. *He's* the victim. So my mother is livid. With *me.*"

"Oh my God, Hannah. That's awful. I'm so sorry. . . . And could Grady *be* any sleazier?"

"He's the worst!"

As Hannah continues to vent, reading aloud Grady's latest text rant, I discreetly check my own phone. I am delighted to discover that I have not one but *two* responses to the messages I sent last night to Grady and Munich. Even better, it appears that they have failed to compare notes. *Rookies.*

As Hannah gets out of bed, I nonchalantly ask if I can borrow her car to run a quick errand.

"Sure. What do you need? I might have it here."

"I feel like I'm getting a UTI," I improvise. "I just want to get some cranberry juice and knock it out. Do you need anything?"

"I don't think so," she says. "But I can go with you—"

"That's okay," I quickly say. "You stay here with Tyson. I'll be back in a jiffy."

ABOUT TWENTY MINUTES later, I'm sitting in a maroon vinyl booth in the corner of Goldbergs, a strip-mall diner not far from Hannah's place. I have my back to the wall and my eyes on the door, mobster-style, as I nurse a cup of black coffee.

Across from me is a very disheveled Grady, sucking down a Coke as he waits for his order of biscuits and gravy—a telltale sign of a hangover.

"So how are you holding up?" I ask, feigning sympathy that is in keeping with the text I sent him last night.

"Terrible," he says.

"I know," I say, shaking my head and practically making a tsking sound. "The whole thing is shocking."

"So she didn't tell you what she was going to do?"

"No. It was totally out of the blue," I say, putting my acting chops to the test. "Tyson and I were *floored*. You two have always seemed so happy."

"I thought we *were*," he says. "But Hannah seems to think I cheated on her."

"I know," I say with a sigh.

"Why in the world does she think that?"

He is clearly trying to figure out what she knows. It's a solid strategy, but this isn't my first rodeo. "I have no clue," I say. "I guess it's a hunch?"

Grady nods, looking relieved. "Damn. I'm really worried about her. It's not like her to be so paranoid."

"Hmm," I say, sipping my coffee, keeping the concerned look on my face.

As he rambles on, I spot Munich walking through the door in a ridiculous frilly getup. Her blond hair is freshly curled, and even from a distance, I can tell she's wearing way too much makeup.

"Will you excuse me for one second, Grady?" I say as nonchalantly as I can.

"No problem," he replies, immediately pulling out his phone.

I slide out of the booth and trot over to the door, smiling. Munich beams back at me, exposing a row of oversize snow-white veneers. They are all the same rectangular length, giving her a horsey smile.

"Hello!" I say. "Thank you for coming!"

"Oh, it's my pleasure and honor. I'm such a big fan!" she gushes, pressing her left hand to the right side of her chest, where her heart isn't.

"Thank you," I say. "Would you like to come sit down? I have a table in the back."

"I'd love to," she says.

As I lead her back to the corner booth, I tell her I've heard great things about her "influencing" from our mutual friend, Liz.

"Oh, I'm so excited to help in any way I can," she says, clearly oblivious to my connection with Hannah.

A second later, we reach the booth, where Grady is scarfing down his biscuits. He looks up midbite, sees us together, and knows in an instant that he's been played. *Again.* His face falls, his lips covered with crumbs.

"Grady! *Heeey*," Munich says, looking surprised. "What are you doing here?"

"Oh my God! No way!" I say, slapping my thigh. "You two know each other? What a small world!"

I look at Grady, who has yet to utter a word, and say, "Don't be shy. Scoot over and make room for Munich!"

"Oh. My name is Berlin," she says, as Grady slides the whole way over to the wall with a look of sheer panic.

"My bad!" I say.

"It's *totally* okay," she says as we sit across from each other. "I can see how that could happen! They're both cities in Germany, after all!"

I smile and nod, relishing every second of her idiocy. "So, now that we're all here together, should we get down to business?" I say, resting both my forearms on the table, leaning into my killer instinct.

"Sure!" Munich says, pulling a day planner out of her white Birkin bag. "Should I be taking notes?"

"Up to you!" I say. "I'll let Grady kick things off. Would you like to start by telling *Berlin* how you and I know each other?" I ask him. "Or should I?"

He stares back at me, mouth agape.

"Okay, then! I will!" I say, shifting my gaze to Munich. "So. Crazily enough, I went to college with Grady's fiancée, Hannah. Oops. *Ex*-fiancée!"

Munich's smile instantly evaporates. She freezes, a deer in headlights.

"*Ex?*" she says, her face turning red.

"Oh. I'm sorry. You didn't hear the sad news?"

"No . . . I didn't know," she stammers. "I'm so sorry."

"That's funny. Because you didn't look very sorry on Friday afternoon," I say, dropping the mic.

"Friday afternoon?" she says.

"Think back, hon," I say. "Try real, *real* hard to recall what you were doing at around four or five o'clock, day before yesterday?"

"I don't remember," she whispers.

"Hmm. Well, might I refresh your recollection?" I say, using one of Tyson's favorite legal phrases. "You were with *him* on Friday afternoon, weren't you?" I point at Grady without looking his way.

Munich stares at me, furiously blinking back tears.

"Yes. We were together," Grady cuts in. "But nothing happened. Berlin just came over to help me with something."

"Oh. I see," I say, nodding. "What was she *helping* you with?"

"She was consulting on a gift. For Hannah. Berlin is very good at that stuff."

"Hmm," I say, holding his gaze a beat before pulling out my phone and staring down at it. "Well, from the looks of this little video, she seems to be pretty good at some other things, too."

"Video?" Munich says. "What video?"

"The video of you in Grady's bed. Would you like to see it? The videography is ah-maz-ing," I say with a chef's kiss.

"Fuck," Grady says under his breath as Munich sobs that she didn't "mean to do it."

"You didn't *mean* to do it? How does that work, exactly? Were you air-dropped into his bedroom? Right onto his dick?"

"I'm sorry," Munich sobs, mascara pooling under her eyes and streaming down her face. "I'm so sorry."

"So you knew he had a fiancée?" I ask her, not letting up.

"I did, but he said things weren't going well," she sobs.

"I didn't say that—" Grady says, turning on his co-defendant.

"Yes, you did, Grady!" she says.

"Well, the good news is—he's all yours now! Hannah doesn't want him anymore."

They both stare at me.

"So now that that's settled, let's get down to some more business, shall we?" I roll up my sleeves for effect.

Grady nods, savvy enough to understand that the jig is up, while Munich continues to cry. I ignore her, staring into Grady's cowardly eyes.

"So. Here's what I'm thinking," I say, rubbing my palms together. "Grady, I want you to go home, look around, and calculate the value of everything Hannah has either purchased or contributed to. Obviously, the big stuff, like furniture and rugs. But the little stuff, too. I don't care if it's a pot or a pan or a stick of deodorant. Add it *allll* up. Got it?"

"Got it," he says through clenched teeth.

"Great! Feel free to add an idiot tax to that. And a commission for Hannah's interior design services. Twenty percent. Maybe thirty?"

He nods as I shift my gaze to Munich.

"As for you," I say, my voice dripping with disdain, "I want you *off* Instagram. And all social media."

She stares at me, horror-stricken. It's clearly a punishment worse than death.

"I don't want Hannah—or anyone in Hannah's orbit—to have to see your sorry face. Are we clear?"

She nods, then wipes her nose with her napkin.

"What about the video?" Grady asks.

"What about it?" I say, putting my phone back into my purse.

"Who else has it?"

"Oh. Don't worry about that," I say. "You two act right, and it will be deleted."

"*Act* right?" he asks with a flash of anger in his eyes. "Are you *threatening* us? Because that sure sounds like a threat—"

"Of course not. I'd never threaten *anyone*," I say with a smile. "I'm simply giving you a small incentive to do the right thing."

"How long do I have to stay off of social media?" Munich asks.

"Hmm. How about forever? Does forever work?"

"But social media is my livelihood—"

I resist the urge to tell her she should have thought about that before she fucked my best friend's fiancé. Instead, I say, "That's for you to decide. A week? A month? It's entirely up to you. Use your judgment. Your *fantastic* judgment."

She nods and whispers okay, her tears still flowing.

I slide out of the booth, then pause at the head of the table. "All righty, then," I say, looking straight at Grady. "I gotta run. Do you mind paying for my coffee?"

"No problem."

"Why, thank you, Grady," I say. "You're such a gentleman!"

WHEN I ARRIVE back at Hannah's place, I find her and Tyson sitting together on the sofa.

"What's the latest?" I ask, settling into the chair across from them.

"I was just telling him about my mother," Hannah says, giving me a suspicious look. "What about you? Did you get that cranberry juice?"

I smile and say, "Would you believe that my symptoms cleared up?"

"Okay, Lainey," Hannah says, crossing her arms across her chest. "What did you do?"

I shrug, then say, "Nothing, really. I just had a brief meeting."

"A brief meeting with whom?" she asks.

"A brief meeting with Grady." I pause. "And Munich."

Hannah's eyes grow huge. Then she shakes her head and smiles. "You're too much."

"Thank you," I say.

"So spill it. What happened?" she asks, looking some combination of appalled and impressed and grateful.

"Well. The three of us met at Goldbergs . . . and had a nice little chat." I pause. "I may have also mentioned that we have an incriminating video—"

"Lainey!" Hannah groans. "You told them that I took a *video?*"

"Not at all. I just sort of implied that one was *obtained,*" I say. "Needless to say, you'll be getting your money back for all that furniture."

"Lainey! You *blackmailed* them?" Hannah says. "You could get in so much trouble!"

"I'm sure she didn't put anything in writing," Tyson says, raising his brow, studying my face.

"Of course not," I say.

"Good," Tyson says, then turns back to Hannah. "How about we just put Grady and Berlin on the back burner for now? We need to deal with your mother. I know you're exhausted, but you really need to go over there and set the record straight."

"I don't know if I'm up to that," Hannah says, looking utterly defeated.

"Yes, you are," I say. "And I'm going with you."

THE HOUSE HANNAH grew up in is a large white colonial with black shutters that has always reminded me of the *Father of the Bride* house, which is funny because Hannah's dad is a dead ringer for Steve Martin. Like Mr. Banks, the character he plays in the movie, Mr. Davis dotes on his daughter. *Adores* her. But unlike Mr. Banks, Hannah's father is painfully passive, unwilling to intervene when his wife treats their daughter like shit.

As Hannah parks her car under the vine-covered porte cochere, she lets out a long sigh.

"It's going to be okay," I say. "We got this."

"I don't know, Lainey. She's so impossible," Hannah says. "Every time I think I've 'got this,' she gaslights me . . . and finds a way to spin things around."

"Yes, but it's two against one today," I say. "Now, c'mon. Let's roll."

A few seconds later, we walk through the side door, directly into the kitchen, where Mrs. Davis is sitting at the counter, reading a magazine. As she hops off her stool, I notice that she has on kitten heels with bows. I can't think of a shoe style I dislike more.

"Hannah! You should have called first! The place is a mess!" she says, tidying an already neat pile of mail. Clearly, she is rattled, but she quickly recovers. "Lainey—it's so nice to see you, dear! What a wonderful surprise!"

"It's great to see you, too, Mrs. Davis," I say. "And your home looks beautiful. As always."

"Thank you, but I would have straightened up more if I'd known . . ." She gives Hannah a pointed look as Mr. Davis rounds the corner in a pink polo, khaki shorts, and loafers with tassels.

"Why, hello there, kiddo!" he says, giving me a big hug. "Great to see you in person! Congrats on all your amazing success!"

"Aw. Thanks, Mr. Davis," I say. "I appreciate that."

"Would you like some coffee? Have you eaten?" Hannah's mother asks me, completely ignoring her heartbroken daughter.

"Oh, I'm good, thank you." I pause, then say, "I just had coffee with Grady, actually."

She swallows, then takes a deep breath through her nose. "Oh?"

I nod, then say, "Maybe we should all sit down?"

"Well . . . of course. Let's do that," she says, leading us over to a sunroom off the kitchen. Hannah and I sit next to each other on a love seat while her parents opt for chairs across from us.

"So," Mrs. Davis says, staring at me. "How is Grady holding up?"

"Not so good, Mrs. Davis," I say. "Not so good."

"Yes. He sounded awful when I spoke to him, too. He just cannot understand why Hannah would make such terrible accusations—" She shoots her daughter a look.

"Hmm," I say, nodding. "Well, you may want to check back in with him. I think his story may have changed since you and he spoke."

"Oh? And why would that be?" Mrs. Davis asks.

"Because he knows that I know the truth about what he did. That's why."

Hannah's father stares at me, slack-jawed, clearly trying—and failing—to keep up.

"Did he tell you what he did to Hannah, Mrs. Davis?" I ask.

"No. But he told me that Hannah has a *male* visitor in town this weekend," she says, making a sour face.

"What?" Hannah says. "Is that what Grady told you? That I had a 'male visitor'?"

"Well? Is he wrong? Isn't Tyson a male?"

"C'mon, Mom! You know he's my *friend*. Lainey and Tyson are my *best* friends."

"Nobody's worried about Lainey," Mrs. Davis says.

"Nobody should be worried about *either* of them!" Hannah says, getting more upset by the second. "We're all just friends, Mom, and you know it. Grady knows it, too! This is absurd!"

"Well, you have to admit that the optics aren't great."

"Optics? What are you *talking* about?"

"Your *male* friend just happens to be in town—and at dinner with you—when you break off your engagement, completely out of the blue? You have to admit that doesn't look good, Hannah."

"Mom! I came over here to tell you that Grady *cheated* on me! My two best friends came to town *because* he cheated on me. You have the order wrong! You have *everything* wrong!" Hannah says, bursting into tears.

I wait for Mrs. Davis to have an "aha" moment. Realize that Grady manipulated her and she jumped to the wrong conclusion. At the very least, find it within her heart to comfort her clearly distraught daughter.

Instead, she gives Hannah a steely look, then says, "Grady denies any wrongdoing. He seems to think *you're* the one manipulating the truth."

"*Mom!*" Hannah says with the most anguished expression. "How can you believe him over *me?*" She lets out a loud sob.

Mrs. Davis stiffens, then blinks. "Hannah, please. Calm down. Pull yourself together."

"I can't, Mom. Not if you're on his side—"

"I'm not on his *side,*" she says. "I'm only trying to understand. That's all. I just have some questions. . . ."

I reach over and rest my hand on Hannah's leg as she wipes her face with her sleeve and takes a gulp of air.

"Okay, Mom. What's your question?" she asks.

Mrs. Davis pauses, then says, "Where is your friend staying while he's in town?"

I know what she's getting at, and the question is unbelievable—even for her.

"What do you mean?" Hannah asks.

"Did *Tyson* get a hotel room?" Mrs. Davis asks. "Or is he staying with you?"

"*Mom!* Are you *seriously* asking me that? I can't even believe you—"

I cut in, enraged. "I can answer that for you, Mrs. Davis," I say, my voice low and measured. "Tyson slept on Hannah's couch. I slept in her bed with her. As Hannah explained, this weekend wasn't planned in advance. It was a last-minute emergency visit after *Grady* cheated on *Hannah.* He's blatantly twisting the facts—*lying*—and it's very surprising that you'd believe him over Hannah."

Mrs. Davis nods, bites her lip, and says, "Be that as it may, the optics—"

"With all due respect, Mrs. Davis," I say, though she deserves *zero* respect, "if you truly cared about your daughter, I'm not sure you'd be focused on *optics* right now. But if you insist—what about the *optics* of Grady being in bed with another woman? The bed that Hannah just bought for their new house, which was supposed to be their marital home?"

Mr. Davis makes a groaning sound—his first contribution to the entire conversation, but I don't take my eyes off Hannah's mother. A staring contest ensues—one that I win.

"So," she says in an ice-cold voice, turning to Hannah. "You're not willing to forgive him?"

"*Ruth,*" Mr. Davis says under his breath. "Some things aren't forgivable."

"Our pastor would beg to differ," she snaps back at her husband. "Forgive our debtors. That's what it means to be Christian."

It is all I can do not to tell her what she can do with her faux Christianity.

"I know, Mom. You're right. God does want us to forgive," Hannah says, looking numb and drained. "And I will do my best to forgive Grady. One day maybe I can. But that doesn't mean I should *marry* him."

"And it doesn't mean you *shouldn't*—" she says.

"Seriously, Mom? You'd want me to marry a man who would do this to me?"

"He hasn't taken his vows yet."

"Right. And neither has Hannah," I say. "She's not his wife. She's under no 'for better or worse' obligation."

"I believe in forgiveness," Mrs. Davis says, her face pinched and her voice prim.

"Really? You'd have forgiven Dad if he had done this to you?" Hannah asks.

"Well, I wouldn't have just thrown in the towel. I would at *least* go for counseling—"

"Mom, Grady had *sex* with another woman—"

"Hannah Davis!" she says in an appalled tone, as if saying the word *sex* is worse than Grady actually *having* it.

"Sorry, Mom. But that's what happened. And I know none of us is perfect. But I'm not a liar. And I'm not a cheater. And I'm not going to marry one. Period."

I feel a burst of pride in my best friend. She is finally standing up for herself.

"Very well," Mrs. Davis says, now pouting. "How do you plan to notify our guests? The 'save the dates' already went out—"

"So you'd like me to send out 'release the date' announcements?" Hannah asks.

"Well, I think people need to be informed—"

"I'm pretty sure word will get around," Hannah says. "Bad news travels fast in this town."

"And what should *I* tell people? When they ask? Which they will."

Hannah shrugs. "Tell them the truth. Tell them that Grady cheated on me, and I broke up with him. Or tell them that it's none of their business. Frankly, I really don't care what you tell them!"

"But if they ask how Hannah's doing," I interject, "please tell them she's doing fine, under the circumstances. She's sad, but she's keeping her head up. And she's leaving town to travel with her two best friends."

"*Travel?*" Mrs. Davis says, looking at Hannah again.

"Yes, Mom," Hannah says. "Lainey, Tyson, and I are taking a trip."

"*Tyson's* going?"

"Yes, Mom," she says again. "The three of us are going together."

Mrs. Davis purses her lips and shakes her head. I stare at her, enraged. I may not be able to save Hannah in this moment, but I *can* punish her mother. My mind races for the perfect burn.

"Best friends for now!" I finally say. "But maybe Grady is on to something. Hannah and Tyson really *would* make a cute couple. And you really can't do better than a Yale-educated attorney, now, can you?"

Mrs. Davis gives me a horrified look as I jump up from my seat. "Anyhoo! We'd really love to stay and chat more. But we have travel plans to make! Right, Han?"

"Right, Lainey," she says, getting to her feet. "We certainly do."

CHAPTER 7

HANNAH

J UST AS LAINEY and I return from my parents' house, a new message comes in from Grady. He is singing a different tune now, and I read his text aloud to Lainey and Tyson:

Hannah, I'm so sorry for my terrible mistake. I was at a work lunch at Chops and had too much to drink. Berlin happened to be there. She offered to give me a ride home. It was innocent. She dropped me off and went home, then realized that I left my sunglasses in her car. She was going for a walk so came by to give them to me. When I answered the door, she barged in, wanting to see the paint color you'd chosen for the dining room. She admires your decorating. We ended up having another drink and one thing led to another. It meant nothing. It will never happen again. I'm so sorry, Hannah. Please, PLEASE give me one more chance. I will never let you down again. We are so good together. I love you.

I finish reading, then look up.

"Tell me that bullshit changes nothing," Lainey says.

"It changes nothing," I say.

"Can you say it with a bit more conviction, please?" she says, looking worried.

I repeat the statement with a little more chutzpah.

"Okay. Good. Now write him back."

"What do you want me to say?"

"Tell him to fuck off. Tell him he's the worst person ever. Tell him to never contact you again or that video—"

"No!" Tyson says. "Don't mention the video in writing."

"What *should* I say?" I ask him.

"Say nothing. Silence is powerful. He's not worth your breath," Tyson says.

Lainey sighs, then nods in reluctant agreement. "Okay. Fine. Don't reply. And block him."

"That's not a bad idea," Tyson says.

"You think? I mean—I'm not going to get sucked back in or take him back. Don't worry about that.... But won't there be logistics we have to cover? Like, I have stuff at his house."

"He can email you. And you can get to the logistics later. For now, he shouldn't have access to you," Tyson says. "More important, how did it go with your mother?"

"You don't want to know," I mumble.

"Oh, yes, he does!" Lainey says. "It involves him."

"*Me?*" Tyson says.

I give Lainey a look not to go there, but she can't be stopped. "Apparently, Grady told Mrs. Davis that you're banging Hannah."

"What?" Tyson says, looking horrified. "Seriously?" He shifts his gaze to me.

"Well, she didn't say *banging*—but yes," I say.

"Wow," Tyson says, shaking his head. "Does she actually believe that?"

"Who knows?" I say with a sigh.

"Oh, well. I guess it's not that surprising," Tyson says. "Your mom has never liked me."

"She doesn't even *know* you," I say. "She doesn't really know Lainey, either. She just pretends she does now that Lainey's famous."

"I'm not famous," Lainey says.

"Yes, you are. And she likes being associated with you," I say, as it occurs to me that in a weird way, the same was true for Summer. My mother couldn't have been any less interested in Summer before she died, but in the aftermath of the tragedy, she had the gall to put up a Facebook tribute.

"What's her beef with me, anyway?" Tyson asks. "Or is it just . . . the obvious?" He looks down at the back of his hand.

I know what he's getting at, and he's not entirely wrong. But I dodge his question, feeling ashamed.

"Honestly, her main issue has always been the Greek stuff," I say. "She blamed y'all for my not joining a sorority."

"She's not over that yet?" Lainey asks.

"She'll *never* be over that," I say, remembering how she didn't speak to me for a month after I told her I wasn't going to rush. That I was happy in a smaller friend group.

"But everyone will think you just didn't get a bid," she said to me at one point.

God forbid.

Another more recent memory pops into my head. Right after Grady and I got engaged, she took me out to lunch, just the two of us. One of her first questions was about the wedding party. Who was I selecting? I told her I had already asked Lainey to be my maid of honor—and was planning to ask my three closest high school friends to be bridesmaids. Of course, I got a sharp pang thinking about Summer, knowing that she would have been my maid of honor.

My mother got a wistful look on her face, and for one second, I foolishly believed that she sensed how I was feeling. I felt certain that she was going to say something comforting about Summer.

Instead, she pursed her lips and shook her head. "Only four bridesmaids?"

"Yes, Mom. Only four."

She sighed, taking a sip of her Arnold Palmer. "It's such a shame you don't have more friends from college."

I stared at her, gutted. "Yes, Mom," I managed to say. "It's a real shame Summer died."

I didn't expect an apology—my mother is incapable of saying she's sorry—but I thought she'd at least change the subject. Instead, she kept right on talking about her own wedding and bridesmaids, all of whom were her sorority sisters. I was so close to telling her off, but I didn't want to ruin our lunch. No matter how often she proved me wrong, I couldn't help hoping that someday she'd show me the warmth I craved from her. So I let it go. The way I always did.

As I tune back into Lainey and Tyson, I hear Lainey say, "So back to our trip . . . Where are we going? Who wants to go first?"

"I will," Tyson says.

Lainey rubs her hands together and says, "Well? Don't leave us in suspense!"

He smiles and says, "So Burundi will have to wait for now. I choose Capri."

Lainey's face lights up. "Even though it's a beach? And, you know, *Mussolini?*" she says, clearly forgetting that it had been Summer's pick. I gently remind her, and she nods, looking chagrined.

We sit in somber silence for a few seconds before I say, "I love that, Tyson. It's the *perfect* choice."

"Yes. It is," Lainey says. "It's a great idea."

Tyson exhales, then says, "So who's going next?"

"I will," I say. I have a pit in my stomach, knowing that Lainey is going to kill me. I look at her and take a deep breath. "Okay. So I know this is an odd choice, but just hear me out—"

"Oh, Christ," Lainey says. "Are you taking us somewhere cold and remote?"

I smile nervously and say, "No. It's neither cold nor remote. In fact, it's quite hot there. And there are easy direct flights."

She brightens a bit. "Is it near water?"

"Well . . . there are some springs. . . ."

"*Springs?* Oh! Like a geyser? Is it New Zealand?"

I brace myself, then spit it out. "No. It's Dripping Springs. Texas."

She stares at me and says, "Is this a joke?"

"No, but we're also going to Dallas. Which has a lot of very nice hotels."

"What the actual fuck," she says. "Veto!"

"No vetoes," Tyson says. "Your rule."

"Well, I'm *not* going to freaking Texas."

"Lainey, I know you've always wondered about your sisters," I say. "And that this secret has weighed on you. We just thought it would be cathartic to finally—"

"*We?*" Lainey glares at Tyson. "*You* were in on this?"

"It was *my* idea," I say.

"Well, it's a shitty idea," Lainey says.

"But what if you meet them and love them?" I ask her. "Isn't it worth a shot? Just think, you'd have family—"

"They won't love me," Lainey says, shaking her head.

"Listen. You aren't responsible for your father's decisions any more than they are," I say. "Maybe you can give them a chance and see if they can rise to the occasion. It's a big hole in your life, Lainey."

"I don't have any holes in my life. I'm fine," she says. "I'm great."

I glance at Tyson, my expression pleading.

"We know you're great, Lainey," he says. "But I think Hannah's right about this—and I know you've toyed with the idea over the years."

"Not really," Lainey says. "Not that much."

I nod, then press on. "It must be hard, though—especially since losing your mother. But just imagine if you meet your sisters and end up being close to them."

She rolls her eyes, but I can tell she's giving the idea some consideration.

"Ugh," she finally says. "This is the lamest pick of all time. Seriously. You have the whole globe to choose from, and you pick *Texas*?"

"We don't have to stay there long," I say. "Just long enough to tell them the truth—"

"Because the truth will somehow set me free?" Lainey rolls her eyes.

"Something like that, yes," Tyson says. "Even if you don't end up having an ongoing relationship with your sisters, I bet you'll feel a tremendous sense of relief to let go of this secret. And you deserve that. For yourself."

Lainey lets out a long sigh, then says, "Fine. Whatever. I'll do it. But it's not going to go well. Mark my words."

"It might not," I say, knowing that part of what she's doing is protecting her pride, putting on her armor of indifference. "But if it doesn't, you'll be no worse off than you are now."

She gives me a reluctant nod.

I smile and remind her that we'll be there with her every step of the way.

Then, before she can change her mind, Tyson tells Lainey that it's her turn. He smiles, adding, "What tropical beach are you gonna make me go melt on?"

"Well, *smart-ass*," she says, her face brightening a bit. "I'm actually not going to pick a beach at all." She pauses, keeping us in suspense. "As it turns out, you two aren't the only martyrs around here," she says.

Tyson smiles and says, "How are we martyrs?"

"Because you picked for Summer. And Hannah picked for me. So I choose Paris. For Hannah."

"Oh, *Lainey*," I say, feeling so touched.

"If you don't think Paris will make you too sad?" she asks.

I smile, welling up. "I'd *love* to go to Paris."

"Good," Lainey says, smiling back at me. "Fuck Grady. And romance. Your first trip to Paris is going to be with two people who love you unconditionally."

"Thank you," I say. "It's a wonderful idea."

LATER THAT NIGHT, I drive Tyson and Lainey to the airport, dropping them off in front of Delta departures. I get out of the car, and we embrace in a group hug. I start to cry, but Lainey reminds me that this isn't goodbye. We'll be seeing one another in Texas in less than a week. It was her idea to get that leg over with first, and Tyson and I agreed.

In the meantime, we all had work to do. Lainey was responsible for choosing our hotel in Dallas and confirming her sisters' addresses; Tyson had a letter of resignation to send in and a big conversation to have with his parents; and I had a wedding to unravel and a boss to disappoint.

THE FOLLOWING MORNING, twenty thousand dollars appears in my checking account directly from Grady's. It feels like a fair assessment of what I've contributed to his home, but it's a surreal and very upsetting feeling to know that our entire relationship has been reduced to a bank transfer. Not to mention one motivated by a tacit threat from my best friend.

What hurts even more, though, is how my mother continues to treat me. Since our face-to-face conversation, she's only communicated with me via a few brisk, businesslike emails, including one filled with bullet points of all the wedding vendors with whom we've signed contracts. She gives me a line-item list of all of our nonrefundable deposits.

I write back that I'm so sorry.

"It is what it is," she replies. "I just wanted you to know."

Against Lainey's advice to tell her to "fuck right off," I send my mother a long note of apology, saying, "I know how disappointed you are. We both are. I wish this weren't happening, and I'm so sorry for how much money you and Dad have spent. I will pay you back once I sell my engagement ring. I love you."

Her response is deafening silence. Although I should be accustomed to my mother's silent treatments, this one hurts more than usual.

Honestly, I don't know what I'd do if I weren't getting the hell out of Dodge. Maybe I'm running away from my problems—I guess that's *exactly* what I'm doing—but it's better than wallowing in misery. Meanwhile, my mind keeps returning to Summer and the hopelessness she must have felt in her final hours. I know that her pain has a lot to do with why Tyson and Lainey are now rescuing me, and although I am grateful, I also feel guilty that we couldn't support Summer in the same way. I decide I owe it to her to focus on my gratitude and make this time with my friends count. Tyson is right, it's what she would have wanted for us—and the thought keeps me afloat as I temporarily shut down my life in Atlanta.

The following day, I attack my to-do list. It's a helpful distraction. I pay my bills, clean out my refrigerator, and cancel appointments. From there, I start packing for our trip. So far, we've only bought one-way tickets to Dallas, but we've agreed that we won't return home between the three legs of our journey, so I do my best to keep things simple, packing a few versatile pieces. It's a far cry from the elegant wardrobe I'd envisioned for my honeymoon, but I tell myself the contents of my suitcase are the least of my worries.

Once all my logistics are tackled, I know it's time to face the hard part: telling people. I consider sending a mass email, but I hate the idea that it could get screenshotted or forwarded. It's not that I think my life is so consequential, or that anyone would want to intentionally hurt me, but lesser scandals have become fodder for gossip, and adding a famous actress and an Instagram influencer into the mix would only cause more temptation.

Ultimately, I decide that the only people I owe a conversation are my boss and my bridesmaids.

I start with Jada. As one of the most renowned interior designers in the Southeast, she can be a bit of a diva, but she's also been very good to me for nearly seven years—longer than I've been with Grady. I've been good to her, too, and I'm by far her most reliable employee. So when I walk into her office and tell her I need to take a few weeks off, effective immediately, she is more than a little taken aback.

"Hannah, there's no way. The Petersons' installation and photo shoot is next *week,*" she says, as if I could possibly forget about the clients who send me dozens of emails a day.

"I know. And I'm sorry. But I really have to get out of town for a while. . . ." My voice trails off.

She gives me a quizzical look, then says, "Are you okay? Is this health-related?"

"Grady cheated on me," I blurt out. "The wedding is off."

"Oh, Hannah," she says, her face falling. "I'm so sorry."

"Thank you," I say, bursting into tears. "You know I'd never want to leave you in the lurch—"

"I know. I get it," she says, pulling two tissues out of the fabric-covered box on her desk and handing me one. She dabs her own eyes with the other. "We'll be fine here. Don't worry about work at all."

"Thank you," I say again. "I really, *really* appreciate this. You have no idea."

She stares at me for a few seconds, then says, "Unfortunately, I do." She smiles, but her eyes look pained. "I was left at the altar."

"At the *actual* altar?"

"Pretty much. I was the consummate jilted bride."

"*Jada.* I had no idea."

"Well, it's not something I make a point of bringing up." She forces a smile.

I hesitate, then say, "He just . . . never showed up?"

"Correct," she says. "I was in the bridal room in the church base-ment. The organ was playing, and the guests were all seated." She takes a deep breath. "Then, just as my father came to walk me down the aisle, one of the groomsmen appeared and asked if he could 'have a word.' I knew right away that it was bad. . . . Like—car acci-dent bad. Or cold feet bad. I wasn't sure which would be worse." She laughs, as if it's a joke, but on some level, I can tell she means it. "Anyway. It wasn't a car accident."

"Was it ... someone else?"

"No. As it turned out, he was gay. *Is* gay. He's been happily married to a wonderful man for ten years."

The soft look on her face surprises me. She's clearly forgiven him. "Are you still friends?" I ask.

"I wouldn't say *friends*, but we speak every blue moon. He's been very sweet about my career. Always congratulates me when I win an award. That sort of thing. It took some time, but I came to feel a lot of compassion for him. He's from a very traditional Southern family, and the pain of hiding—and trying to be something he wasn't—must have been excruciating. But I still felt betrayed and lied to. And of course, on that day, I didn't know any of this. I was just a humiliated, heartbroken bride."

"God," I say, shaking my head. "I can't imagine how horrible that must have been."

She takes a deep breath that is more like a shudder. "It really was. But you know what?" She pauses and smiles. "I got through it. And you will, too."

Her words comfort me. Until I remember that Jada is in her midforties and still single. I always assumed this was her choice—that she was just one of those women with different priorities. Like Lainey. Now I wonder if it has more to do with trust issues. I almost ask the question, but stop myself, afraid of what her answer might be.

When I get home from work, I call my bridesmaids, one at a time. I stick to the basics: Grady cheated on me; the wedding is off; and I'm headed out of town for the next few weeks with my college friends. We'll talk more when I get back.

They are all shocked, upset, and very much on my side, but I also sense something else. I can tell they are questioning my judgment and whether, in the words of my oldest friend, Abby, I should be "throwing it all away."

I tell her that I wasn't the one who threw anything away—Grady was—and she quickly backtracks. She says she knows I'm right; she's just so sad. Her husband and Grady are close friends, and she had always pictured our kids growing up together.

"I did, too," I say, my heart aching. "All I want is a family."

"You'll find someone else," she says.

"I hope so," I say, blinking back tears as I suddenly picture Berlin in Grady's bed.

"You will," she says. "You're so beautiful."

"Thank you, Abby," I say. I know she's doing her best, but she's ill-equipped to make me feel better. "I think I just need to get out of here for a while."

CHAPTER 8

TYSON

WHEN I GET back to D.C. on Sunday night, I head straight into the office. After finishing a few tasks for partners I don't hate, I clean out my desk, boxing up all my personal belongings. Around two in the morning, I send the last email from my computer—a letter of resignation to the managing partner of the firm. I apologize for my abrupt departure, citing personal reasons.

The next morning, I call my father and ask if he can meet me for dinner. I tell him I have something important to discuss—and that I'd rather do it just the two of us. He knows what this means, of course. That it's a topic I'm not ready to share with my mother.

At his suggestion, we meet at his private club. I arrive early, which to him is on time, and we are promptly seated by one of the more obsequious staff members. My father takes the fawning in stride— deflecting it graciously—but it all feels so over the top, and I can't help wondering why he enjoys such a stuffy, snobbish scene. The food is top-notch, but to me, no rib eye is worth the foolery that comes with it.

I wait until he is on his second scotch to break the news: I quit my job; I broke up with Nicole; and I'm taking a few weeks to travel with Hannah and Lainey. Before I can think better of it, I debrief him on their respective situations.

"So let me get this straight," my dad says, stroking his beard and pausing for what feels like forever.

I brace myself, knowing that the longer the silence, the worse it's going to be. "Now that you're unemployed and single, your plan is to waste money and time, road-tripping with two lost souls?"

I stare back at him, debating whether to stick to the big picture or dive into semantics. For some reason, I can't resist the latter.

"I wouldn't characterize it as *road-tripping*," I say.

"It's a goddamn boondoggle," my dad scoffs. "And your friends sound like they belong on *The Montel Williams Show*."

"That show was canceled fifteen years ago, Dad."

"You know what I mean."

"I don't, actually." I shake my head. "Lainey and Hannah aren't airing their dirty laundry on television."

"But their problems are so—"

"*Real*, Dad. They both have legitimate problems."

"They'll both be just fine," he says. "Trust me."

I sigh, knowing what he's getting at—that Hannah and Lainey enjoy certain privileges that don't belong to us.

"Moreover," he continues, "I'm not concerned about the well-being of your friends. I'm concerned about *you*. And I just don't understand why you'd want to get mixed up in all of that drama while turning your back on an esteemed and lucrative job—"

"A job I detest, Dad."

"A job you have because your mother and I put you through law school and college and fourteen years of private school before that."

"So you're including Montessori preschool in the guilt trip here?" I smile, doing my best to diffuse the tension.

It backfires.

"I'm glad you're amused," he says, stroking his beard again.

"I'm sorry, Dad."

He raises his hands, palms out. "You know what? Let's forget *your* education. Let's talk about *ours* for a second. Let's talk about your mother and me. Let's talk about your grandparents—three out of four of whom went to college—"

"I'm aware, Dad—"

"Do you have any idea how rare that is—"

"Yes, I do," I say. "And I'm proud of them."

"You don't need to be *proud*. You need to be grateful."

"I'm proud *and* grateful," I say. "I'm just not sure what any of that has to do with my life right now—"

"You're not sure what your grandparents' blood, sweat, and tears have to do with your ability to nonchalantly walk away from your law firm?"

"I'm not doing *anything* nonchalantly," I say. "I'm just asking why their education means I have to be miserable in my job—"

"Why do you think they call it a *job*, Tyson?"

"You and Mom love your work."

"Mom does. I'll give you that. But trust and believe, I'd rather be doing a lot of other things."

"So why don't you do them?"

"Look, son. Your mother and I sacrificed for you. We invested in you. And you're throwing away that investment—"

"I'm not throwing anything away. It's time for me to make a change. And it happens to coincide with my friends needing me. Hannah's in a dark place right now—"

"And I feel for her—"

"No, you don't," I say. "And that's fine. There's no need to sit here and pretend you care about either of them."

"Fair enough. But I *do* care about you—"

"I'm fine, Dad. Especially now that I resigned," I say. It's the truth. In fact, I feel like a weight has been lifted from my shoulders.

Several seconds pass before my father clears his throat, then says, "So is this why you and Nicole broke up? Because I know she wouldn't put up with you traveling with two females—"

"Nicole and I weren't right for each other."

"You're dodging the question."

"Okay, fine. Yes. She's not thrilled with my female friendships. But more important, Nicole and I want different things." I pause, then say, "She wants *your* life."

"Meaning?"

"Meaning things like this club," I say, glancing around the room.

"Oh. You don't enjoy this club?" he snaps back.

"It's nice," I say. "It's very nice. . . . I just might want another kind of life."

"Oh? And what kind of life is that?"

"I don't know, Dad. That's what I need to figure out."

He sighs so loudly that it sounds like a groan. "So you're taking this trip to *find* yourself?"

"That feels dismissive."

"I'm not dismissing you. I'm just asking you."

"Okay. Yes. I'm going on this trip, in part, to take a step back and figure out what I want my life to look like. So, yeah, I guess you could characterize that as 'finding myself.'"

He stares at me, then shakes his head.

"Why is that so wrong?"

"It's wrong because you don't come from generational wealth and the mindless sense of security that comes with that. You don't have the luxury of that kind of fallback plan."

"Dad, I understand what you're saying. But I *do* have a fallback plan. I have my degree—*two* degrees—and I have plenty of money saved and invested. And isn't that the point? Didn't you and Mom and your parents work hard so that I don't have to feel trapped? So that I can be in the position where I *can* go find myself if that's what I need to do? Aren't you the man who taught me that 'necessitous men are not free'?"

"That's true to a point, son. But quitting your job on a lark—" He pauses, shaking his head. "That sort of entitlement feels disrespectful. To your mother and me. To your grandparents. To *their* parents."

"It's not a *lark*, Dad. It's something that I've been thinking about for a long time."

I almost mention Summer—and our pact—but can't bring myself to share that much. It's too risky. If he dismisses my feelings about her in any way, the conversation could really take a bad turn. I can't let that happen.

"Look, Dad, I'm sorry you don't agree with my decision, but my friends aside, this is something I need to do. For my own mental health."

My dad stares at me, then slowly nods. It's hard to argue with mental health, even for his generation.

"Just remember where you came from, Tyson."

"I will, Dad."

"And remember there's a difference between your history and your legacy. Your history is what happened. Your legacy is what you set in motion."

I nod again.

"You are *my* legacy," he continues. "And I'm proud of you. I also want you to be happy. But your decisions—the ones you make today and tomorrow and the next day—will ultimately impact *your* legacy. What do you want that to be?"

I nod, feeling the weight of his words. "I'll keep that in mind, Dad. I promise."

"Good. Thank you."

I pause, then give him a half smile. "Now," I say. "Can I just ask for one small favor?"

My father shakes his head. "Nope," he says with a chuckle.

"You don't even know what I'm gonna ask!"

"Oh, yessir, I do," he says. "And the answer is no. You're telling your mother all on your own."

"Dang. Can you at least give her a heads-up?"

"Sorry, son," he says. "I've got enough problems."

THE NIGHT BEFORE I fly to Dallas, I find my mother in her office. With a working fireplace, an extensive library, and a West Wing–style desk I used to play under when I was a kid, it's my favorite room in their five-story Kalorama townhome.

"Hi, Mom," I say, standing in the doorway, inhaling the musty scent of old books.

"Well, well," she says, putting down her pen, then taking off her reading glasses. "Another country heard from."

I smile at one of her favorite expressions and ask if she has time to talk.

She nods and says, "You know my door is always open."

This is true—both literally and figuratively. No matter how busy my mom has been over the years, she's never made me feel like I'm interrupting her. I take a seat in the armchair facing her desk.

"So I think you may know why I'm here," I say, crossing my legs, then uncrossing them.

"I may have an inkling."

I hesitate, wondering who her source is—my father or Nicole—and what exactly they told her.

She holds my gaze for several long seconds, her expression inscrutable. "So you're really doing this?"

The question feels a little bit like *Are you still beating your wife?* so I clear my throat and ask for clarification. "Doing what, exactly?"

"Quitting your job, breaking up with Nicole, and traveling with two females?"

I fight the urge to look down. "Yes. I need to figure some stuff out," I say. "This feels like the best way."

"Hmm," she says, nodding.

"I just need some time away. With old friends," I say, deciding not to delve into Hannah's and Lainey's issues. I know that angle will fall as flat with her as it did with my father.

"Everyone has stuff to figure out, Tyson. We can't just run away from our problems."

"I'm not running away. I'm just taking a little time for myself."

"Okay. Well, you're grown," she says with a sigh. "It's your life."

"I know, but I don't want you to be upset with me—"

"I'm not upset. But I *am* worried. And a bit disappointed."

"Please don't worry, Mom," I say, although her disappointment is what hits me the hardest. I can't stand letting my mother down. For some reason, it feels even worse than letting my father down.

"I'm your mother. Worrying is part of the job, Tyson," she says.

"I know. And I'm really sorry. But it's all going to be fine."

She gives me a look, then says, "It won't be fine with Nicole. You realize that, right? She's not going to sit around and wait for you."

"It's already over with Nicole, Mom. It was over the minute I went down to Atlanta."

"Well, it will be even *more* over if you go on this trip. *Death-knell* over."

"I know," I say, nodding, although a small part of me thinks that if we were really meant to be, we could overcome just about anything.

She stares at me a long time, then says, "Can I ask you a question?"

I nod, bracing myself, somehow knowing it will be a challenging question without an easy answer.

Sure enough, she says, "Does this trip have anything to do with Summer?"

I look at her, shocked. It's been years since we've discussed Summer.

My throat tightens as I slowly nod. "In some ways, yes," I say.

She holds my gaze, looking deep in thought.

"You can't change the past, Tyson," she says.

"True. But I can learn from it."

She gives me a curious look, then says, "Meaning what?"

"Meaning I need to do this," I say, treading carefully.

"And you need to do it with Lainey and Hannah?" she says. "You have so many other friends who might be able to support you more."

I nod, knowing what she's getting at—that I have *Black* friends who are more settled and arguably better equipped than Hannah and Lainey to understand me.

"I know, Mom," I say. "But I made a promise to *them*. And to myself."

She nods, then says, "Well, I'm proud of you for being a man of your word. You're a good friend."

"Thank you, Mom."

"Maybe not the best *boy*friend," she says with a smile. "But a good friend."

"I'm sorry things didn't work out with Nicole. I know how much you like her."

"I do," she says. "But maybe not for the reasons you think . . . I just know how much she loves you."

"She told you that?" I ask, surprised.

"Not exactly. But she understands that you have some unresolved emotions," she says, confirming that the two of them have recently talked. "And she really wants what's best for you. That's love."

"Dang," I say under my breath.

"And for the record," my mother says. "I want that for you, too."

CHAPTER 9

LAINEY

I
T'S ONLY BEEN a few days since I left Atlanta, but it feels like much longer, perhaps because I've been on a bit of a bender since I last saw my friends. I didn't plan on that happening, but after digging around on the internet and finding all sorts of nuggets on my sisters, including Ashley's sappy wedding announcement, I got a little triggered. Drinking helped calm me down.

Last night with Marcus, aka Neighbor Guy, was a particular doozy. We started out at Socialista, a Cuban-inspired cocktail lounge in SoHo; then moved on to the Wiggle Room, a nightclub in the East Village; then Musica, which I only remembered after seeing the photos on my phone. This morning, I woke up in his bed, my clothes nowhere to be found. I must have undressed in my apartment, but I have no idea how I got down the hall without them.

Somehow, though, I managed to make my flight to Dallas. As I sit on the plane now, I order a Bloody Mary—a little hair of the dog—which takes the edge off not only my hangover but also my anxiety about what's to come.

I still can't believe Hannah convinced me to go to Texas. I know she has a pure heart and the best intentions, but I can't help having second thoughts about the mission. I tell myself that I'm not locked into anything other than a couple nights at a luxury hotel. I'll be able to sort the rest out after we check in and if need be, to talk my friends out of this half-baked plan.

MY FLIGHT LANDS slightly after Tyson's and Hannah's, and when I get to baggage claim, they are waiting for me, Starbucks in hand.

"Dallas in June!" I say as they hug me. "Everyone's dream destination!"

Hannah smiles, looking sheepish, while Tyson says, "C'mon, now. Positive attitude."

"Yep. Just call me Pollyanna!" I say, eyeing the carousel as luggage starts to drop from the chute.

"So do we have a plan?" Tyson asks, looking at me, then Hannah.

"Well . . . I confirmed the addresses," I say, feeling squeamish.

Hannah nods, then says, "I was thinking maybe we do a little scouting first—"

"Oh, like a stakeout," I say, rubbing my hands together. "Fun, fun!"

"Not exactly a stakeout," Hannah says, missing my sarcasm. "More like getting the lay of the land. At least here in Dallas. Dripping Springs is a bit of a haul—"

"We could always put a letter in their mailboxes," Tyson says.

I nod, thinking. As my heart fills with dread, I feel myself shifting into a reckless mode. "Nah. I say we go right up to the front door."

"And do a cold call?" Tyson asks, looking wary.

"Yep. We're in Texas now, baby," I say, twirling an invisible lasso. "Go big or go home."

. . .

NESTLED IN A grove of trees strung with tiny white lights, the Mansion on Turtle Creek looks more like a private residence than a hotel. As we pull into the driveway in our rental car, I nod approvingly. We get out of the car, a bellman taking our bags, then walk into the lobby.

"It's gorgeous," Hannah says. "Nice job, Lainey."

I smile, then stride over to the front desk, checking us in and collecting our AmEx amenities, including free breakfast and a spa credit.

"Lainey, you should get a massage!" Hannah says on our way to the elevator.

"I'm gonna need it," I say under my breath.

A moment later, we are rolling into our suite. As Hannah gushes over the décor, I announce that it's five o'clock somewhere, diving into the minibar and selecting a local IPA.

"Anyone else?" I ask, cracking it open and taking a long sip.

"I'm good for now," Hannah says.

"Tyson?" I ask.

"Nope," he says. "I'm driving."

"How about a little pool time first?" I say.

Tyson glances at Hannah, then looks back at me. "We could do that, but why not just do what we came here to do?"

I sigh, then sit down on the bed, taking another long swallow of beer.

"Guys. I'm really nervous," I finally confess. "Ashley is not going to be happy when I show up and interrupt her perfect life."

"Nothing's ever perfect," Hannah says.

I give her a look, remembering that's what Summer said when I first told her about my father. Boy, did that turn out to be true.

"I know. But I just can't think of a world in which she's going to be happy to know about me. Her parents just celebrated their thirty-fifth wedding anniversary." I open my mouth, insert my index finger, and make a gagging sound.

"You never know until you try," Tyson says. "And really, what's the worst that can happen?"

"I guess so," I say, though deep down, I know what the worst thing is. I know I could be rejected.

"How about we drive that way, check things out, and see what your gut says? If you're still not feeling it, we can bag it and come back to the pool," Tyson says.

"Fine," I say, giving my friends a reluctant nod. "Let me just finish this beer."

LESS THAN AN hour later, we are turning down a residential road in some random suburb of Dallas. The neighborhood is nice but modest. Tyson is driving and Hannah is navigating, reading off the numbers on mailboxes, looking for Ashley's house. I'm in the backseat, feeling sick to my stomach.

"That's it," Hannah says, pointing to a two-story stucco home with a yellow front door.

Tyson nods, then slowly pulls over to the curb before putting the car in park.

"Who the hell paints their front door *bright yellow*?" I say, feeling a wave of negativity coming on.

"I like it. It's cheerful," Hannah says.

"It's hideous," I say under my breath.

"Well, that probably shouldn't be your opener." Tyson looks over his shoulder at me and smiles.

I smile back at him. "You don't think that works? . . . 'Hi there. Your door is fugly, and I'm your father's love child?'"

Hannah lets out a nervous laugh as I eye the house, feeling more nauseous by the second.

"You don't have to do this," Hannah says. "It's your call."

"What do you mean 'you'?" I ask. "I think you meant 'we,' right?"

"Of course. Yes," she says. "*We* don't have to do anything."

"She might not even be home," Tyson says.

I sigh, then suddenly make my decision. I'm tired of carrying around this heavy baggage. It's time to blow some shit up—or at least rip off the Band-Aid.

"Let's do it," I say.

"Are you sure?" Tyson says.

"I'm sure," I say.

He turns off the ignition, but nobody makes a move. Within seconds, the inside of the car is an oven, and I'm sweating my ass off. I take a deep breath, then open my door.

"You know what?" Tyson says. "I think you two should go alone. I'll hang back."

"Why wouldn't you come with us?" I demand.

"It's a terrible idea for me to be randomly knocking on some white lady's door in the state with the highest number of firearms in the country. That doesn't really work out for people who look like me."

"That's a good point," Hannah says, nodding earnestly.

"Nice try," I say to Tyson. "You're coming with us."

"All right," he says with a shrug. "But this is how we end up getting shot."

"Tyson! That's not funny!" Hannah says.

"It wasn't a joke," he says, biting his lip.

I nod, feeling sheepish because I hadn't thought of that angle—how freely I can walk up to a front door in suburbia without fear of violence.

"You're right," I say. "But Hannah's definitely coming with me."

"I'll come, too," Tyson says. "But you two should lead the way."

"Fine," I say, getting out of the car and slamming the door.

I march right up to the front porch with Hannah and Tyson trailing behind me.

"Here goes nothing," I say, pushing the doorbell.

We listen to the classic ding-dong chime followed by the sound of footsteps.

A second later, the door opens, and we are standing face-to-face with a middle-aged woman in a pink velour tracksuit. Her bleached hair is cut in short architectural layers. I hate it.

"Good afternoon," I say. "We were looking for Ashley Sheffield—*Richards*," I correct myself to her married name. "But I think we may have the wrong house?"

"Oh, my *gawd*. You're that actress! On that show!"

It's a curveball that I didn't see coming, but I do my best to appear unfazed. "Hello. Yes. I'm Lainey."

"This is incredible! Ashley didn't tell me she knows you!"

"So she *does* live here?" I ask.

"Yes! I'm sorry. I'm visiting this weekend. Ash is at the hair salon! She should be back any minute."

"Great," I say. "We'll just wait in the car—"

"Absolutely not!" the lady says. "Come in! I insist! Was Ashley expecting you?"

"No. We were just . . . passing through town."

The woman nods, beaming, then looks at Tyson and Hannah. "Are y'all actors, too?"

"No, ma'am," Tyson says in his polite courtroom voice. "We're just friends of Lainey's. I'm Tyson, and this is Hannah."

"And I'm Sharon! Ashley's mom! Please come in! All of you!"

My heart stops. She's changed her hair color and cut from the one photo of her I saw on Facebook years ago, but how did I not instantly recognize my mother's nemesis? My father's *wife*.

We are already stepping into the foyer as my brain absorbs this information. I know I should abort the mission, but for some reason, I keep going, operating on a weird, dread-filled autopilot.

As we pass the point of no return, Hannah grabs my hand and squeezes it while Tyson calmly asks if we should take off our shoes.

"Up to y'all!" Sharon says. "They aren't a 'shoes off in the house' family. But do whatever makes you comfortable! I love going barefoot!"

As she points to her toes, the nails painted a sparkly teal, I feel another wave of nausea.

The three of us opt to keep our shoes on, walking down a short hall and into the family room, scattered with toys, including a vintage Fisher-Price barn I recognize from my own childhood. It occurs to me that it probably originally belonged to Ashley and her sister, and I feel something break inside me.

"The triplets just went down for their nap, thank goodness. They're quite the handful," Sharon says with a laugh, bending over to pick up a stuffed animal and a board book, tossing both into a wicker basket. "Now, c'mon, have a seat!" she says, pointing to a denim-blue, slipcovered sectional. "Can I get you some iced tea?"

We all decline the offer, taking seats on the long side of the sofa, our backs to the wall. I am in the middle, Tyson and Hannah flanking me.

"So how do you know Ash?" Sharon asks me. "Did y'all go to TCU?"

I shake my head, fumbling for an answer, as my father suddenly materializes at the sliding glass back door. Oddly, he doesn't appear to have aged at all. It's like seeing a ghost, and he's staring back at me the same way.

"Hon, look who it is!" Sharon says.

When he doesn't immediately respond, she continues. "It's Yvette Gregory!" she says, using my character's name. "Live and in the flesh!"

Sharon laughs, then says, "I'm sorry! I guess I should say Lainey Lawson! But Yvette feels *so* real!"

I force a smile and thank her.

"It's true. You're the best part of that show. Right, hon?" she asks, looking over at my father.

"Yes," he replies, making fleeting eye contact with me. "You're a terrific actress."

An awkward few seconds tick by before we hear a garage door rumbling.

"Yay! Ash is home!" Sharon says. She bolts up from the sofa and runs out of the room.

I stare at my father, feeling a swell of anger as I wait for him to speak.

"I've been trying to reach you. How have you been?" he asks in a low, shaky voice.

"Peachy fucking keen," I say, my heart pounding in my ears.

A second later, Sharon bursts back into the room. Ashley trails behind her, looking confused.

"Hey, y'all," Ashley says tentatively while scanning our faces.

"Hi, Ashley. I'm Lainey."

Ashley smiles, blinks, and says, "I'm sorry. I have baby brain since the triplets were born. Have we met?"

"We have *not*," I say. "But this meeting is long overdue—"

"Lainey—" Tyson cuts in with a low voice. "Maybe you want to speak to Ashley in private?"

"No, thank you, Tyson," I curtly reply. "I think everyone should stay for this."

Ashley and Sharon exchange an intrigued look before sitting down on the short wing of the sectional.

"So, *Dad*," I say, feeling my nervousness turn to anger. "Would you like to tell your wife and daughter why I'm here? Or should I?"

Ashley looks at me, then him, then back at me. "*Dad?*" she asks, her voice rising.

"Yes. *Dad*," I repeat.

She looks back at her father, then says, "Why did she call you that?"

He clears his throat, takes off his glasses, and wipes his eyes.

After several seconds of silence, I look at Ashley and say, "Perhaps I can help him explain. *Your* father had an affair with *my* mother. Resulting in me."

"Dad? Is that true?" Ashley asks, her voice shaking as her face turns white.

I glance at Sharon, feeling a stab of guilt. I know that none of this is her fault—or Ashley's, for that matter. I also know that I'm being needlessly cruel. I can't stop myself, though, years of grief and anger pouring out of me.

"Well, I wouldn't count on *him* for the truth," I say. "My mother sure couldn't. He told her that she was the love of his life. And yet here we are—" I gesture grandly around the room.

"That's enough, Lainey," Tyson says under his breath.

I feel an ounce of remorse as Sharon runs out of the room, but the pound of hatred for my father outweighs it. Especially when he has the gall to get up and follow her without a word to either of his daughters.

Ashley's eyes are steely as she stares at me. "Why did you come here? What do you want from us?"

"I don't *want* anything—" I say. "My friends convinced me to come meet my *sister.*"

"You're not my sister," she says, her voice ice cold.

"I'm afraid I am," I say with a laugh.

"Ashley. We're sorry. . . . We didn't know your parents would be here," Tyson chimes in.

"Yet she still chose to make this announcement in front of my *mother?*" Ashley spits back at him.

"Welp," I say, clasping my hands together for effect. "I figured I might as well get everything out in the open."

"You came here to hurt us," Ashley says, staring at me with pure disdain.

"That's not true," Hannah pipes up, surprising me. "It wasn't her intent to hurt you. She's been very hurt by your father's actions, too."

"What about her *mother?*" Ashley spits back at Hannah. "She's the homewrecker here."

"Ha. That's *rich,*" I say, glancing around the room. "Your home looks far from wrecked."

"You're a spiteful person—which I assume you got from your mother. Tell her I said congrats. Mission accomplished."

"My mother passed away four years ago."

"Am I supposed to say I'm sorry?"

"I don't care *what* you say."

"C'mon, y'all," Hannah says. "All else aside, you're *sisters.*"

"Like she already said, we aren't sisters," I say, getting up from the sofa and giving Ashley a disdainful shrug. "We just happen to share the same asshole father."

"Get the hell out of my house," Ashley says.

"With pleasure," I say with a smile, then calmly walk out the door.

"WELL, THAT WENT swimmingly," I grumble on the way back to the car.

My heart is racing, and my hands are shaking, but I also feel vindicated. I knew all along this was going to backfire, and I was right. Absolutely nothing good came from it, except for finally bringing my father to justice—and even that wasn't worth the way I feel now.

Hannah gives me a furtive glance. "I'm so sorry, Lainey."

I can't tell if she's apologizing for how shitty the whole scene was—or for her role in suggesting it in the first place. Either way, I just shake my head and say, "Whatever."

I wait for Tyson to chime in with an apology of his own—or at least an acknowledgment that I was right; this was a terrible idea. Instead, he strides ahead of us, gets in the car, and slams his door shut. He's clearly pissed—and I have a feeling that it's *not* at Ashley, or even my father.

"What's his problem?" I say under my breath.

"He's just upset for you," Hannah says.

"Well, he sure has a funny way of showing it," I say, climbing into the sweltering backseat and slamming my door harder than he slammed his.

"I'm so sorry, Lainey," Hannah repeats as she fastens her seatbelt. "That was awful."

"A total fucking shitshow," Tyson scoffs as he turns on the ignition.

"Yep. Just like I told you it would be," I say.

"You made sure of that," Tyson snaps at me.

I stare at the back of his head, fuming. "What's that supposed to mean?"

He looks over his shoulder, glaring at me. "It means, you couldn't have been any less tactful."

"I thought you were all for telling the truth," I say in a snide voice.

"The truth is one thing," Tyson says. "But you threw a grenade in there—"

"Are you for real right now?" I shout back at him. "What did you think was going to happen? I told you that this was a bad idea!"

"You're right, Lainey," Hannah says in her most placating tone. "You are a hundred percent right, and I take *full* responsibility for this—"

I cut her off, still shouting. "And if you think I'm going to go meet the other *bitch* in the family, you can forget it! Ain't gonna happen!"

"Why didn't you just try to talk to Ashley alone? One on one?" Tyson asks as he pulls away from the curb. "Why would you say all that stuff right in front of her mother?"

"I'm sorry I don't have a whole lot of sympathy for that woman and her *triplet* grandchildren!"

"What do the grandchildren have to do with this?" Tyson asks. "You're not even making any sense!"

"Oh, I'd say they have *plenty* to do with this!"

I know I'm being irrational, and that he's right—it's not relevant how many children Ashley has or that she birthed three of them at once. But somehow, they feel like one more slap in the face. Because of *course* she has a big happy family. And of course her children have doting grandparents who babysit while their mother goes to the salon.

As for my father, he is exactly who and what I've known him to be for years. The truth has been underscored: his so-called love story with my mother wasn't complicated or star-crossed. It was all a lie. And *my* mother—not *Ashley's* mother—was the true victim. The one who paid the ultimate price.

NO ONE SPEAKS for the rest of the car ride back to the hotel. When we walk into the lobby, Hannah suggests that we go put our swim-suits on and head out to the pool. Tyson nods, but as they walk toward the elevator, I veer off.

"Lainey!" Hannah calls after me.

"What?" I say, glancing back at her.

"Where are you going?" she asks with a worried look—her de-fault expression.

"To find the bar."

"For lunch?"

"Nope," I say. "For a martini."

Hannah glances in Tyson's direction, as if torn.

"Go with Tyson," I say, deciding for her. "I want to be alone right now."

THE MANSION BAR is cool and dark with a clubby, masculine décor and leather-clad banquettes. Fittingly, the bartender is a classic guy's guy, and there are also three men at the bar. Two are older—in their forties, maybe fifties—dressed in well-tailored suits and expensive shoes. The third is younger than I am, wearing Wrangler's, cowboy boots, and a plaid shirt. He has nice brown eyes and looks easier to talk to, so I pick him. I'm not in the mood for a challenge.

I hop on the barstool next to his. "Hi," I say. "Is this seat free?"

"*Hi,*" he says. "And yes! It's free!"

"Thank you," I say, giving him a seductive smile.

He smiles back at me. I glance down at his left hand, wrapped around his pint glass. No ring.

"I'm Lainey," I say, loud enough for the other two men to hear. Might as well kill three birds with one stone in case this one doesn't pan out. *Four* including the bartender, who is now standing in earshot of us.

"Gus," he says, eagerly extending his hand.

I shake it, saying, "That's a cute name."

"Thanks," he says. "It's gotten trendy, but growing up, I was the only Gus in my grade."

"Your parents were ahead of the curve, I see."

"Yeah. I suppose they were!" he says, grinning, as the bartender asks what he can get me.

"An extra-cold, extra-dirty vodka martini," I say, giving him a flirty smile.

"Vodka preference?" he asks, all business. For now.

"You choose. I trust you."

He nods, then turns to make my drink while Gus asks me whether I'm here for business or pleasure.

"Neither," I say. "I'm here because my friends made me come down to Texas to meet my sister. Who didn't know I existed until about an hour ago."

"Wait. Your sister didn't know you existed?" he asks. "How's that?"

I sigh and say, "My dad was married when he met my mom. They had an affair. I was an accident that he never told his 'real' family about."

"Hmm. Well, you look pretty real to me," Gus says, grinning at me.

"Yeah. A little *too* real for my sister."

"Uh-oh. The meeting didn't go well?"

"That's an understatement. It was a bloodbath. Hence, the martini."

"Wow. That sucks."

"Yeah. But whatever." I shrug. "What about you? What brings you to Dallas?"

"Work," he says. "But I'm not staying at this hotel."

"Are you meeting someone here?"

"No. I just wanted to check this place out. I love nice hotels. The lobbies and bars, that is. I wouldn't know about the rooms." He smiles. "Can't afford 'em!"

I smile back at him, though he's boring me so far. "What kind of work are you here for?" I ask.

"Litigation. A trial."

"Oh. You're a lawyer?" I ask.

He shakes his head. "No. I'm a *witness*."

"Was it Mrs. Peacock? With a candlestick? In the conservatory?" I deadpan.

He laughs and says, "No one was murdered, thank goodness. It's a *civil* litigation."

"So what happened? Were you a witness to a slip and fall? Banana peel in a grocery store?"

"No. I'm actually an *expert* witness," he says, looking proud.

"Nice!" I say as the bartender returns with my martini, placing it on the bar in front of me. I thank him and take a sip.

"Would you like to start a tab?" the bartender asks.

"Definitely," I say.

I take a second sip. I already feel better.

"So. What kind of an expert are you?" I ask, turning back to Gus.

"I'm a cynologist," he says, sitting up straighter on his stool.

"A *who?*"

"It's like a canine specialist."

"Like a dog trainer?"

"More like a dog behaviorist, though I have trained some dogs in my day."

"So are you, like, just obsessed with dogs?"

"I love them. And I respect them. Both my parents are legally blind. We always had Seeing Eye dogs."

"Wow," I say. "That's really interesting."

He nods and says, "Yes. Dogs are fascinating."

"What's the most interesting fact you can tell me about them?"

"How long do you have?" He smiles.

"All day. And night," I say with a wink. I know I'm being cheesy, but I can tell he likes it.

"Okay. Interesting facts," he says, his face lighting up even more. "Let's see. . . . So dogs can tell when we're sad. They can read all sorts of human emotions. Anxiety and worry and depression. They internalize those feelings and feel worries themselves. . . . What else? . . . Prolonged eye contact with a dog releases oxytocin."

"For the person or dog?"

"Both."

I nod. "What else you got?"

"Um . . . Dogs have associative learning capabilities. There are two main types. Classical or Pavlovian conditioning, and operant or Skinnerian conditioning."

"I know Pavlov! The bell!"

"Yeah. That's a basic example. But the point is—they can learn associations between contiguous events. . . . Like, when you put a certain pair of tennis shoes on, they know they're going to be walked. Some dogs can discern the sound of your automobile—"

"Your *automobile,* huh?" I say teasingly.

He laughs and says, "Sorry. They know the sound of your *car*. They can hear it up to a mile away."

"Impressive," I say. "So what's this trial about?"

"It's a dog bite situation—"

"And you're defending the dog?"

"Kind of. Yeah. I'm testifying for the dog owner."

"Who did the dog bite?"

"A neighbor."

"A child?"

"No. An adult. Who happens to be six-foot-six and was trespassing—"

"To do something nefarious?"

"Well, no. But the dog didn't know that."

"So you're basically testifying that it wasn't the dog's fault?"

"I'm not opining on fault or liability. I'm simply explaining that the dog was likely traumatized by something very specific based in her past—maybe another tall adult male—and that the circumstances aren't likely to present themselves again. Basically, I don't think the pup should be put down—"

"You think he will be?"

"*She*. And hopefully not. But likely yes."

"Wow. That's sad."

"Very."

"Where are you from?"

"Tulsa."

"They couldn't find someone in Texas?" I smile.

He laughs and says, "I'm a good value," he says. "Just starting out."

"How old are you, anyway?"

"How old do you think I am?"

"Hmmm," I say, looking for laugh lines. There are none. "Twenty-four?"

"Twenty-*eight*, thank you very much. And you?"

I've never cared about my age, and unlike Hannah, I had no problem when I turned thirty, but I still play it coy. "Older than you."

He smiles. "What about you? What do you do?"

"Oh. I'm between jobs."

"In what industry?"

"Entertainment."

"Are you an actress? You're very pretty."

"Thank you for the compliment. You're pretty cute yourself."

He smiles, looking flustered, both of us aware that he's in over his head.

I cut to the chase and ask what he's doing for the rest of the day.

"Not much," he says.

"Do you want to hang?" I ask. "We could go to a dog park."

He smiles. "I *do* have a life apart from dogs."

"As in . . . a girlfriend?"

He shakes his head.

"No girlfriend? That's surprising."

"What can I say? I'm *between* them." He smiles.

It's his first real attempt at flirting, and although it's a bit clumsy, he pulls it off. Or perhaps he pulls it off *because* it's clumsy.

"Touché," I say, putting my hand right on his knee.

BY THE TIME Tyson and Hannah find me in the bar, I'm on my third martini and getting very cozy with Gus.

"Oh, hey," I say, giving them a nonchalant wave. Hannah is wearing a white eyelet cover-up and platform sandals. Tyson has on navy swim trunks and a gray T-shirt. They both look like they'd rather be anywhere but this bar.

"Hi," Hannah says, glancing at Gus, then looking back at me.

"This is Gus. From Tulsa. He's here for a dog trial." I hiccup, then laugh. "He's defending the dog."

"The dog's *owner*," Gus clarifies.

"Cool," Hannah says, nodding.

Tyson stands behind her, looking pissed.

"Ask him something about dogs," I say to Hannah. "Anything."

She thinks for a second, then says, "Is it true that a dog's IQ is the same as a toddler's?"

"It is! Dogs' mental abilities are comparable to those of a two-and-a-half-year-old human child," Gus says, nerding out. "Of course, the intelligence of individual dogs differs, just as it does with humans—"

"How many of those have you had?" Tyson cuts in, pointing to my martini glass.

"What are you, my father?" I ask in a snide voice. "Oh, shoot. No. He's the one with triplet grandchildren, isn't he?"

"No, Lainey. I'm *not* your father," Tyson says. "I'm your friend. Who thinks you need to lay off the vodka."

"Thanks for your advice, *friend*. But I'm good."

Tyson stares me down. "Okay. Do your thing, Lainey. Have fun."

"Oh, I *will*," I say. "Don't you worry."

Tyson stalks off as Hannah says, "Lainey, please come out to the pool with us. Gus—you should come, too."

"Nah. We're good here," I say.

Hannah stares at me for a few more seconds, in full angst mode. "Okay. Just please be careful," she says.

"Will do," I say.

As Hannah turns to follow Tyson, I look at Gus. He gives me a
yikes expression.

"Don't worry about them," I say. "What do you say we get out of
here?"

"And go to the pool?" he asks.

I shake my head and tell him I have something better in mind.

A FEW MINUTES later, after I pay for our drinks, I am leading Gus
through the lobby, over to the elevator, and up to our room. As we
walk in, Gus glances around.

"Wow," he says. "This is so nice."

"Yeah," I say as he stares down at a pair of Tyson's sneakers on the
floor outside the bathroom.

He looks back up at me, concerned. "You're sharing a room with
your friends?"

I nod.

"So they could come back any second—"

"That's what these things are for," I say, latching the security lock,
then walking over to the bed. I sit down and immediately start unbuttoning my blouse, then take it off. He follows me like a puppy,
watching as I remove my bra, then my jeans.

I'm down to my thong when Gus finally sits down and starts
kissing me. He's a bit awkward, but he has nice lips. We make out for
a few minutes, then I start unbuttoning his shirt. A few charged
seconds later, we are both completely naked. I pull him on top
of me.

He is rock hard, but still hesitates. "I don't have any . . . uh . . .
protection."

"That's okay. I'm on the pill. And I've been recently tested. All
good. You?" I ask—which is always the full extent of my inquiry.

"Oh. Yes. All good here, too," he says with a nervous laugh.

"Awesome," I say, kissing him again, ready to get the show on the road.

He pulls away, then says, "And you're . . . not too drunk to consent?"

"No, Gus," I say, thinking that if he keeps it up, I'll be too *bored* to consent. "I'm all set."

CHAPTER 10

TYSON

"Y OU THINK WE should go check on Lainey?" Hannah asks as we sit poolside on chaise lounges. Mine is under the shade of an umbrella, while hers is angled toward the sun.

"Nah. She's a big girl," I say, sipping my margarita. I'm not one to drink during the day, but after the morning we've had, the tequila hits just right. "She's got a higher tolerance than both of us combined."

"I'm not talking about her tolerance," Hannah says.

"You mean Dog Guy?" I say—which is how Lainey will undoubtedly refer to him from now on, though Dog *Boy* might be more accurate. "Lainey could eat him alive."

"Yeah. But I mean . . . I'm just worried about her mental state *generally.*"

"She'll figure it out," I say. "She always does."

"Maybe so. But I think she's really struggling."

"I know," I say. "But I find it hard to muster much sympathy for her. That shit at her sister's house was *so* unnecessary. She went in there *looking* for a fight."

"I think that was a defense mechanism. She was scared—"

"Oh, *please*," I say. "Lainey's never scared."

"Maybe not *scared* scared. But she was definitely afraid of rejection. She wanted to hurt them before they could hurt her."

I swipe my thumb along the salted rim of my plastic cup, then lick it off. "Well, she pulled that off in spades."

"I just wanted to help her," Hannah says. "But coming down here was clearly a bad idea."

"Yeah. With hindsight. But how were we to know Lainey would be that combative? She's one of those people who is so hard to help. Her own worst enemy."

Hannah sighs, then lowers the shoulder straps on her bathing suit top before reclining. I put my sunglasses on, picturing Summer's perpetual runner's tan lines—which, with her pale skin, were more often burn lines. She was constantly applying sunscreen to her nose and cheeks, determined to keep her freckles at bay. I close my eyes, feeling a wave of haunting regret that I never told her how much I loved her freckles. Her face. So many things about her.

"Are you okay?" I hear Hannah say.

I open my eyes and realize that I'm frowning.

"Yeah," I say, relaxing the muscles in my face, taking a deep breath.

"What were you thinking?"

I take another deep breath, then tell her the truth. "I was just thinking about Summer."

Hannah nods and says, "What about her?"

"How much she hated her freckles."

"I know," Hannah says. "I *loved* them."

"Same."

"She didn't know how pretty she was."

"She really didn't," I say.

"Looking back, I can see that she was insecure. About a lot of things," Hannah says. "I never saw it at the time. She was such a star."

"I know," I say, thinking of the argument Summer and I had a couple days before she died. I'd been so annoyed with her, but now I see how vulnerable and fragile she actually was.

"Sometimes I still can't believe she's gone," Hannah says.

I take off my sunglasses, look at her, and nod.

"Do you ever forget? For, like, one second? And think you can just pick up the phone and call her?" she asks.

"That used to happen to me all the time. But not so much anymore. I hated when her parents cut her phone off," I say, remembering how I used to call and listen to her outgoing message. Then, suddenly, one day there was a recording saying her number was no longer in service.

"Oh my God. Yes!" she says. "That 'no longer in service' message was the *worst*."

We sit in silence for a moment, before Hannah looks at me and says, "She really was our sun, wasn't she? I mean, we were a foursome, but in a lot of ways, she was our center."

"Yeah," I say, getting a bit uneasy with the direction of the conversation. "She was our leader. From the very beginning. But who knows how that might have changed over the years. . . ." My voice trails off.

"Why would that have changed?"

"Oh, I don't know. Just that 'sliding doors' concept. Lots of things could have changed our dynamic. We might have had a fight or a breakup—" I stop suddenly, realizing what I've just said.

"A *breakup*?" Hannah asks.

"Well, not a breakup per se, but a rift or a fallout—" I stammer, trying to cover for myself.

Hannah gives me a suspicious look.

I put my shades back on and close my eyes, but I can feel Hannah staring at me.

"Tyson?" she says after a few seconds.

"Yeah?" I say, bracing myself. Somehow, I know what's coming even before she asks the question.

Sure enough, she says, "Did you ever have feelings for Summer?"

My heart skips a beat and my jaw clenches. "What do you mean?" I ask.

"You know what I mean, Tyson. *Romantic* feelings."

"Why would you ask that?" I say, my eyes still closed.

"I'm just curious," she says. "I always suspected that she had feelings for *you,* but did you have feelings for *her*?"

I inhale deeply, my chest rising. I start to lie, but I can't do it anymore. For all these years, telling the truth felt like a betrayal to Summer. Now, suddenly, it feels like a betrayal *not* to tell the truth. To both Summer *and* Hannah.

I glance over at Hannah. She is staring at me intently. *Knowingly.* I take a deep breath as she sits up in her chair, turning to face me.

I remove my sunglasses, turn my head, and look her right in the eye.

"Yes," I finally say, knowing that I'll never be able to put the genie back in the bottle.

"Oh my God," Hannah says. "Did she know how you felt?"

"Yes. She did," I say, feeling light-headed.

"So y'all . . . *talked* about it?"

I take a few measured breaths, then sit up and face her all the way, my feet planted on the sundeck. "We more than *talked* about it, Hannah."

She stares at me, looking shocked. "You were . . . *together*?"

"Sort of," I say. I take a deep breath and start rambling. "It started in April. Before graduation. I kissed her—and we hung out a few times after that. I was in her room the night before she died. . . . Nothing happened. She was just studying. But I saw her for a few minutes—"

"Oh my God, Tyson," she whispers. "I had no idea."

I bite my lip and nod, feeling a wave of familiar guilt that I was the last person to talk to Summer in any meaningful way. I'd been in the best position to prevent what happened. I could have stayed in her room. And I didn't.

"How have you kept this secret for so long?" she says.

I shake my head and say, "I didn't see how telling you would have helped the situation."

"Wait. Does *anyone* know? Did you tell Summer's parents?"

I shake my head. "No. You were the only one I considered telling. I almost did. So many times."

"What stopped you?" Hannah asks.

I sigh and say, "I don't know. I could never get the words out. And part of me felt it would be disloyal to Summer. . . . It was her secret, too."

Hannah nods, her eyes wide. "Well, I'm glad you finally told me. And I hope you feel a weight lifted. I can't believe you've lived with that all alone for all these years."

I nod, realizing that I do feel lighter. But I can't help wondering if Hannah now blames me, on some level, for what happened. Something on her face seems slightly off.

"I want to talk about this more," she says, her voice sounding funny, too.

"We don't have to, actually," I say. "There's not much more to say."

"Still. I'd like to," she says. "But for now, we should probably go check on Lainey."

"Probably," I say, grateful for a subject change.

We gather up our things and head back inside. The cold, dark bar is a shock to the system and a bit depressing after being out in the bright sunlight. We look around, but there is no sign of Lainey or Dog Boy.

"Oh, snap," I say under my breath. "This isn't a good sign."

"I'm sure she just went upstairs to sleep it off."

I raise my eyebrows. "Sleep it *off*—or sleep *with*—"

"Tyson. Stop."

"Well, don't act like that's not a distinct possibility."

"No way. They just met. It's the middle of the day."

I shake my head at her "middle of the day" comment, guessing that Hannah is a sex-at-bedtime kind of girl—and only after her teeth are brushed and flossed.

"Besides, he's not her type," Hannah says. "He seems a little nerdy for her."

"Oh, please. Lainey doesn't have a type. Anything goes," I say.

We ride the elevator in silence, and a few seconds later, we're in front of our door. I put my key card up to the sensor. It turns green, but as I push the door open, I discover that Lainey has the security guard latched.

"Oh, hell no," I say, giving the door a hard pound. "Now we're locked out of our own room?"

"Calm down," Hannah says in a low voice.

"She's so rude. I told you she's fucking him—"

"You don't know that, Tyson. I always put the security latch on when I'm in the room alone."

I pound on the door again.

"Chill out!" we hear Lainey shout. "I'm coming."

A second later, the door swings open. Lainey looks sheepish and disheveled in an oversize T-shirt and quite possibly nothing else.

I blow past her but stop when I see Dog Boy sitting there on the edge of the bed, shirtless and shoeless.

"Jesus," I say under my breath.

"What?" she snaps back. "We were just talking."

"Yeah, right," I say, staring the guy down as he quickly finishes dressing.

"I was just leaving—"

"Whatever, man," I say, waving him off.

As much as I know that Lainey was the ringleader, I'm angry with him, too. What kind of a guy takes a drunk woman he just met up to her hotel room?

"Leave him alone, Tyson," Lainey says. "Don't be a bully."

"No. This is my fault," Dog Boy says. "I should go."

"I think that's an excellent idea," I say, following him to the door. "And I would tell you to stop taking advantage of drunk women in bars, but in this case, I think maybe you were the one who got taken advantage of."

He gives me a sheepish look, then mumbles an apology before shuffling off down the hall.

"You're such an asshole," Lainey says the second I shut the door.

I ignore her as Hannah steps in to play mediator. "He's not an asshole," she says as I head into the bathroom. "He just cares about you."

"He might care about me, but he's self-righteous as fuck. I'm sick of his morality policing," I hear Lainey say.

Her rant continues as I relieve myself, then wash my hands. I can't make out most of what she's going on about, but I hear something about "Saint Tyson coming to the rescue for his slutty, fucked-up friend."

"Nobody called you a slut, but you *are* selfish as fuck," I say when I get out of the bathroom.

Her face crumples. I instantly regret my words, but not enough to take them back or apologize, especially because they are true. She *is* being selfish.

She tries to flip it on us, saying, "I told you this would be a dumpster fire!"

"Well, yeah. *You* set the fire," I say.

I wait for her to clap back at me. Instead, she bursts into tears. I look at her, shocked. Lainey never cries. *Almost* never. As I get a vivid flashback to Summer's funeral, I lower my voice and say, "Okay, Lainey. You're right. Coming here was a bad idea. I'm sorry. Hannah and I are both sorry."

"*Very* sorry," Hannah says, standing frozen in the middle of the room. "This is my fault. It was my idea—and it was a horrible one."

"I just want to go home," Lainey says.

She climbs onto the bed, pulling her T-shirt over her knees. "I'm going to book a flight back to New York," she whimpers.

"No," I say, my voice calm but firm. "You're not going home, Lainey."

"Yes, I am. You guys should go on the rest of the trip alone," she says. "It will be better without me, and we all know it."

"No," I say again. "We're sticking together. We *all* need this trip."

Silence fills the room as Lainey and Hannah both stare at me.

"It's what Summer would have wanted, and it's what we're doing," I continue, my voice as strong and steady as I can make it. "I know she's up there, watching us. . . . Rooting for us to get our shit together."

"I don't believe that," Lainey says, shaking her head. "I don't believe she's *anywhere.*"

"Well, I *do*," I say. "In fact, I'm absolutely certain of it. So if you don't want to stay for Hannah or me or yourself, I need you to stay for her."

She stares at me for a long few seconds, then slowly nods. "Okay," she says. "I'll stay. On one condition."

I nod and say, "What's that?"

"No judging me for the rest of this trip. I'm a grown woman."

"Okay," I say, resisting the urge to tell her that she really needs to start acting like one. "I won't judge you—but will you please try to take better care of yourself?"

"I'll try," she says, sniffing.

"That's not very convincing," I say.

Before she can respond, we hear Hannah say she's going downstairs for a minute but will be right back.

When the door opens, then closes, Lainey rolls her eyes. "Classic Hannah," she says.

I nod and smile. "Yeah. She really finds any conflict unbearable, doesn't she?"

Lainey nods, then immediately looks worried. "Wait. You don't think she's going downstairs to call Grady, do you?"

"No," I say. "She wouldn't dare."

"God, I hope not."

"See?" I say.

"See *what?*"

"The protective way you feel about Hannah is the way *we* feel about *you.*"

She nods, granting me the point.

"So what do we do from here?" I pause, then say, "I'm guessing you don't want to check out those dripping springs?"

"No way, Tyson," she says. "No *fucking* way."

I raise my hands in surrender. "Okay. I was just confirming."

"Confirmed," she says. "Now get me the hell out of Texas."

CHAPTER 11

HANNAH

W E ARE TWELVE hours into the Texas leg of the trip, and so far, things haven't been smooth sailing. To say the least. Our meeting with Ashley was a disaster; Tyson dropped a bomb that he and Summer were romantically involved; and Lainey just had sex with a random guy she met in the hotel bar.

As I listen to Tyson and Lainey argue, I feel a sense of overwhelming guilt. Mostly I feel guilt that it was my idea to come here in the first place, but I also feel guilt toward Tyson. I know it's not my fault, but I feel like I should have somehow intuited that he was dealing with another layer of grief about Summer.

Deciding I need a minute alone, I excuse myself, go downstairs, and wander into a courtyard where a bustling waitstaff is setting up for an event. Based on the lavish centerpieces of white roses and pale pink peonies, and candles, I have a strong hunch that it's a wedding.

As I sit down on a small bench, a wave of loss crashes over me, along with a barrage of questions. *What would have happened if I hadn't caught Grady in the act? Would it have happened again? Had it happened before? Was she the first? Does he have feelings for her?*

I tell myself that none of it matters. What's done is done.

I learned that lesson in futility when we lost Summer. For years, I've struggled to understand why she took her life. Even if the cheating rumor were true, why had she felt the need to make such a drastic decision? I have replayed our final conversation hundreds of times, wishing I could go back. I know exactly what I would tell her.

So what if you do poorly on one stupid test? The world will keep turning. You will still go to medical school and become a doctor. You will still get married and have children. You will still have a beautiful life.

Would it have made any difference? The what-ifs were excruciating, and now, knowing she and Tyson had something going on, I have even more questions. At the top of the list is why hadn't she confided in me?

I told Summer *everything,* including troubling things about my mother—things that I'd held back from my high school friends, too worried that something might get back to my mother via one of their mothers. I thought she had told me everything, too. The fact that she hadn't both confuses me and hurts my feelings. Maybe she didn't trust me the way I trusted her. I try to talk myself out of those doubts.

I tell myself there are other reasons she might have kept that secret from me. Maybe she feared my reaction. I like to think I would have been supportive and happy for her, but maybe I would have worried that my friendship with one or both of them would become less important. Maybe I would have made *their* relationship about *me.* Maybe that's what I'm doing now. The mere thought of that makes me feel petty, small, and ashamed.

I think back to Lainey and the scene I just witnessed upstairs in our hotel room. I wonder what she would say about this news. It's so hard to know. Lainey and I are such different people. As much as I love her, it's sometimes a real struggle to understand her.

I flash back to the time I was most confused by Lainey. It was the immediate aftermath of Summer's death, when her parents came to Charlottesville. They reached out to me upon their arrival, asking if Tyson, Lainey, and I could meet with them to talk. They were looking for any small clue or insight we might have.

The following day, thirty minutes before we were due to meet them at their hotel, Lainey came back to the apartment that she and I shared. It was three in the afternoon, and she was already wasted.

What the fuck is wrong with you? I remember Tyson yelling at her as she insisted in a slurred voice that she'd only had one drink.

Needless to say, we went without her.

When we arrived at the hotel, I told myself that I had to be strong. As we sat down, Tyson gave our condolences. I nodded, noticing a bleach mark on Mrs. MacFarland's navy sweatshirt. I recognized immediately that it was one of Summer's sweatshirts—the same one she was wearing the night before her final exam, when we last talked.

Her mother caught me looking at it and said, "It was in her hamper. It still smells like her."

She extended her arm, offering me the sleeve. I lowered my head and inhaled the familiar scent of my best friend. Tears filled my eyes. I did my best to fight them off, but I couldn't. As they rolled down my cheeks, Tyson had to do all the talking for us. I still remember the lost look on his face after he'd answered all of their questions and it was time to go. There was a group of Summer's track teammates standing in a cluster in the lobby, clearly waiting to speak with her parents next.

"We loved your daughter so much," he said as we got up from the table. "Lainey did, too. She's sorry she couldn't be here with us."

The following morning, Lainey left for Myrtle Beach. Going

there the week between exams and graduation was tradition at UVA, and it was what the four of us had planned to do before Summer died.

I didn't judge Lainey for still going—particularly because we couldn't get our money back on our rental—but Tyson was outraged. I did my best to calm him down, pointing out that staying in Charlottesville was too painful.

"She could come with *us*," he said, as we were planning to stay at his parents' place in D.C. for a few days.

"I know," I say. "Everyone handles grief in their own way."

"Handling grief? Is that what we're calling drunk sex at the beach?" Tyson asked.

"You don't know she's going to do that."

"Oh, yes I do," he said. "And so do you."

Looking back, I don't know how I got through that week. I couldn't have done it without Tyson, that's for sure. While his mother fed us the most delicious homemade meals, he and I sat in a dark room, watching movies for hours on end. Everything made me cry—comedies and dramas alike—but *Stand by Me* hit me the hardest. Tyson and I had both seen it before—it was one of our favorites—but the death of River Phoenix's character broke my heart in a whole new way now. In the last scene, Richard Dreyfuss, playing a grown-up Gordie Lachance, reflected back on his childhood friendships. I burst into tears as I watched him type on his computer screen: *I never had any friends later on like the ones I had when I was 12. Jesus, does anyone?*

As the credits rolled and that haunting Ben E. King song began to play, I looked over and saw that Tyson was bawling as hard as I was. In that moment, I realized how much we take friendship for granted when we're young, unable to grasp its significance until later in life. For Tyson and me—and Lainey, wherever she was tonight—that "later" had come. Our perspective would never be the same. That's the thing about innocence. . . . Once it's gone, it's gone forever.

By the time we got back to Charlottesville for graduation, Tyson had let go of his anger toward Lainey. Or maybe he was just too exhausted or numb to show it. It took enough energy just to walk up the Lawn and collect our diplomas. After the ceremony, we hugged one another goodbye and left the campus for the last time. None of us has ever been back.

In some ways, Lainey's life has changed so much since then. In other ways, though, she is still the same old Lainey. A bull in a china shop. Breaking things. Breaking *herself*. As I think about the way she just looked upstairs, cradling her knees on a hotel bed after having drunken sex with a stranger, I no longer buy her "I am woman, hear me roar" routine. I don't know why it has taken me so long to see her bravado for the façade that it is.

I feel a sudden rush of worry that borders on fear—fear that something really bad might happen if we don't find a way to help her. I take my phone out of my purse and pull up Instagram, desperate to do some kind of damage control. I type as fast as I can:

Hi Olivia, I'm Lainey's best friend, and I was with her today at your sister's house. I just wanted to apologize for how we handled things and for the hurt we have caused your family. We didn't know your parents were going to be there. Lainey is a wonderful person, and I hope one day you have the chance to get to know her. Please extend my apologies to the rest of your family. Sincerely, Hannah

My first thought after I hit send is that Lainey is going to kill me and maybe rightly so. My intentions are pure—just as they were with Ashley—but they had still backfired in that case. Badly. Why would I think that this effort will turn out differently? I try to remember how to unsend direct messages on Instagram. I know there's a way. Before I can figure it out, a response comes in.

Hi Hannah, I think you must have the wrong Olivia??

I stare at the screen, confused, returning to her profile, reading her bio. Could there be *two* people named Olivia Sheffield who went to the University of Texas and have a reference to tennis in their Instagram bio? It seems highly unlikely.

Does your sister have triplets? I text back, thinking surely that narrows it down to one person.

Her reply is immediate: Yes. But are you sure this matter concerns me? My sister and I lead very separate lives.

I read the message twice, parsing every word, trying to decipher the meaning. One thing seems certain: Olivia doesn't know about our visit today.

Having a voice-to-voice conversation is pretty much the last thing I want to do, but I text back: Yes, I think I should probably explain. I then type my phone number, asking her to please give me a call if she can.

My phone vibrates within seconds.

"This is Hannah," I say, my heart racing and my palms sweating, suddenly terrified that I might be making a bad situation even worse.

"Hi, Hannah. It's Olivia," she says in a low, raspy voice. Oddly, there is no trace of a Texas accent.

I take a deep breath and say, "So this is sort of a long story, but I'm just going to come out with it." I pause, then force myself to say the rest. "Your father had an affair with my best friend's mother. We went over to Ashley's house today to tell her about it. It was a bad scene, and I just wanted to tell you how sorry I am."

There is silence on the end of the line, and I wonder if she's hung up on me.

Then she clears her throat and says, "I'm confused. When, exactly, did my father have this affair?" Her voice is strangely calm.

"Um. Well ... Lainey's thirty-two now," I say. "So I guess it started, like, thirty-three, maybe thirty-four years ago?"

"*Ohh*. So are you saying that ... Lainey is my *sister*?"

"I'm sorry, yes," I say, realizing I left out the most important part.

"Wow," she whispers. "*Wow*."

"I know this must be so hard to hear."

"Yeah," she says under her breath. "I can't . . . I'm just a little shocked right now."

"I know. I'm *really* sorry. About the affair and all."

"It's okay. That's not your fault, obviously," she says.

I stare into the distance, shocked by her ability to show any grace in this moment.

She asks me a few questions about our meeting with Ashley, and I tell her everything, right down to getting thrown out of the house.

"Yikes," Olivia says.

"Yes. We should have left as soon as we realized your mother was there."

"Yeah. I feel bad for her. . . . But I'm not surprised that Ashley handled it so poorly. She's not one to rise to the occasion."

I pause, then say, "So y'all aren't close?"

"No. Not at all."

"I'm sorry," I say. "Family dynamics can be so complicated."

"Yeah. And politics don't make it any easier," she says.

"True," I murmur noncommittally.

My political views have always been moderate—falling under the "why can't we all just get along" umbrella—but in the past several years, I've discovered that middle of the road is no longer safe terrain. Both extremes will eventually come for you. The good news is that having a deeply self-absorbed mother has taught me a lot of survival skills. I know how to appease just about anyone on any topic, including politics.

"I'm not really speaking to anyone in my family right now," Olivia continues. "In part because of politics."

Trying to show empathy, I blurt out that I don't get along with my mother. "She's a bit of a narcissist," I say.

"Are the two of you estranged?"

"No. But at the moment, *she's* not talking to *me*."

"Ah. The good ol' silent treatment. Been there, done that."

"With your mother?"

"No. With Ashley. But my mother enables her."

"That's what my father does," I say, thinking about the years of manipulation I've witnessed. "Everything is always about my mother. It's like he doesn't exist apart from her."

"Yes. Exactly. Ashley has to be the center of attention. She was always jealous if I was happy, but when I got upset about something, that was an issue, too. If I was tired, she was flat-out exhausted. If I was sick, she was certain she had inoperable cancer. And God forbid my feelings be hurt about anything she said or did. Because that made *her* feel bad."

"Oh, *wow*. You're describing my mother to a T," I say.

"Yep. It's all straight out of the narcissist's playbook."

"Why are they like that?" I say.

"I don't know. I've read all the books. I follow all those accounts on Instagram. And I still don't fully get it. Their mentality is so sick."

I tell her that I follow similar accounts—and sometimes they just randomly show up in my algorithm.

"Do you follow Lee Hammock?" Olivia asks.

"Yes! Mental *Healness*! He's a hoot," I say.

"Yeah, he cracks me up," she says, then does a perfect imitation of him.

I laugh as she continues, saying, "But no matter how much you study their behavior and analyze the patterns and employ the 'gray rock method,' you just have to accept that they're never going to change. They simply can't."

"I know." I sigh.

"Which is why boundaries are so important."

"Yes," I say, suddenly feeling a bit blown away that we are having such a deep conversation right out of the gate.

"So," Olivia says, her tone brightening. "Please tell me Lainey isn't self-absorbed, too?"

"Oh my goodness, not at all! She has a *huge* heart." I hesitate, then say, "It's probably a little TMI, but my fiancé cheated on me, and Lainey was the first person I called. She came running to be with me, booking a last-minute flight to Atlanta."

"God. That sounds traumatic," Olivia says. "I'm really sorry."

"Thank you. It *was* traumatic," I say, taking a deep breath. "Thank God I have Lainey. She's such a special person and dear friend. I couldn't have gotten through the past week without her. Truly."

"Oh, wow. This *just* happened?"

"Yes," I say. "It's part of the reason why we're here. Lainey and I and another college friend. We realized that it wasn't just me who needed to get away. Lainey had family stuff to confront—and our friend Tyson is also at a crossroads in his career and relationship. So the three of us decided to take some time to travel together."

"That's amazing," Olivia says. "You're lucky to have such strong friendships."

"Yeah," I say. "Hopefully the rest of our trip goes a bit smoother."

For the next few seconds, we sit in a silence that should be awkward but feels strangely comfortable.

"So. How far is Dripping Springs from Dallas?" I finally ask her.

She laughs and says, "You really did your homework, didn't you?"

"We did a little stalking, yes," I say, feeling sheepish. "Sorry about that."

"That's okay," she says. "I get it, under the circumstances."

"Gosh. I wish we had gone to see you first," I say.

"Yeah. I wish you had, too," she says. "But if it makes you feel better, I'm actually out of the country right now. So I'm glad you didn't drive all that way."

"Are you in a tennis tournament?" I ask.

She laughs and says, "*Excellent* research. But no. I'm training with a new coach for a few months in Italy."

"You're in *Italy*?" I bolt up off the bench, then begin to pace excitedly around the courtyard.

"Yeah."

"You'll never guess where Tyson, Lainey, and I are going from here."

"No fucking way," she says, reminding me of Lainey with her casual F-bomb.

"*Yes* way!" I say, grinning into the phone. "We're going to Capri. Where are you?"

"Northern Italy. In a little town called Bordighera. It's on the coast near the French border."

"Is that close to Capri?"

"Not that close. But nothing is that far apart in Italy, either. Maybe we could meet up?"

The wheels in my head start turning, but I catch myself and slow down. "I wish we could. But today was really bad. I don't think Lainey would go for that. Not at this point, anyway."

"Oh. Okay," Olivia says. "So I take it she doesn't know you're calling me?"

"Correct," I say.

"Would she be upset with you?"

"Yes. Probably. She really hates your father," I say, realizing that there are nuances I haven't explained, including that Lainey's mother has passed away.

"Well, it's hard to blame her for that," Olivia says.

"How do *you* feel about him?" I ask.

"I love him. I love *both* my parents. But they're problematic. I had to take a break from my whole family."

"I get that."

"Maybe you could tell Lainey that? It might make her feel better."

"Maybe. I just need to think things through a bit," I say, my mind racing. "Could I do that and reach out again?"

"Of course," she says. "Anytime."

"Thank you," I say, feeling a rush of unexpected affection for this woman on the phone. Lainey's *sister*.

WHEN I GET back to our room, Lainey is passed out on the bed, snoring with her mouth wide open, while Tyson sits a few feet away from her, reading a book. I ask him if we can talk, then lead him out to the hallway.

"You'll never believe what just happened," I say, then quickly tell him the whole story, right down to Olivia being in Italy. "Maybe Lainey would want to see her?"

He grimaces, then says, "Hannah, no. I don't think this is a good idea."

"But she's *so* nice," I say. "She's nothing like Ashley. I really think Lainey would like her."

"Maybe down the road. *Way* down. But for now, I really think we need to respect her feelings," Tyson says. "If we tell her that her other sister is in Italy, she'll lose her mind and go back to New York."

I start to protest, but Tyson cuts me off. "Look, Han. I know your heart is in the right place, but trust me, we need to put a pin in this sister stuff."

I sigh and nod. "You're probably right," I say, thinking of how my fairy-tale notions of love and family have contributed to my *own* problems, and wondering when I'll ever learn.

CHAPTER 12

LAINEY

TWENTY-FOUR HOURS LATER, we are boarding our flight to
Rome. Our seats, booked late last night, are in the very back of
the plane. But at least we got three together. As we approach our
row, I call dibs on the window seat, feeling certain Hannah will give
it to me despite my assigned middle seat.

Sure enough, she shrugs, declaring the middle seat "cozy." She's
normally accommodating, but this is over the top even for her. Everyone hates the middle seat, especially on an international flight. I
figure she must be feeling really guilty about the scene at my sister's
house.

As we settle into our seats, she kicks off her sneakers and puts on
a pair of fuzzy socks. "I can't believe we pulled this off," she says with
a contented sigh. "A trip to Italy! It feels like a dream."

"I know," Tyson says, almost smiling.

"I don't think I've ever been this excited," Hannah says.

"Well, that's a telling statement," I say. "I wish Grady could hear
you say that."

"Facts," Tyson says with a nod.

"C'mon, y'all. If you're talking about getting engaged, that was sort of a given after all those years," she says. "Almost more of a relief than anything else. This is so . . . *spontaneous.*"

I nod. The word *spontaneous* makes me think of Gus, who's been texting me nonstop. I look at my phone now, seeing a new message, telling me that he signed up for Hulu just so he could watch my show.

I start to write him back, but I get distracted watching Hannah pull up Instagram on her phone, then type a DM. She angles her screen away from me, which only piques my interest. She must sense that I'm trying to read over her shoulder because she quickly swipes out of the app.

"Who were you just messaging?" I ask.

"No one," she says.

"Yeah, right. I know a sneaky maneuver when I see one," I say with a laugh.

"It was just a friend," she says.

"As long as it's not Grady," I say.

"It's not. He's still blocked."

"And he hasn't tried to email you?"

"No. But he did Venmo me five dollars—"

"What the hell? Why?" she asks.

"So he could send me a message and confirm that I got it. Can't do that with email."

"What a cheapskate," Tyson says.

"Yeah," I say. "Send him a dollar back and tell him if he has something further to say via Venmo, it'll cost him a grand."

Hannah smiles as I ask what his message said. She pulls it up, reading in a monotone: "Hi, Hannah. I hope you're doing well, wherever you are. I miss you and hope you'll give me a call sometime soon. I just want to hear your voice." She stops suddenly and says, "Blah blah blah."

"Shut the fuck up, man," Tyson says, giving Hannah's phone a dismissive wave. "Nobody wants to hear your shit."

"Literally *nobody*. It's driving him *crazy* that he doesn't know where you are. But at least he knows *who* you're *with*," I say, giving Tyson a knowing look.

"You really think Tyson bothers him?" Hannah asks me.

"Yes. It's one thing to skip town with your girlfriends, it's another to jet-set with this hottie. . . ." My voice trails off, as I demonstratively look Tyson up and down.

"Thank you?" Tyson says.

"You're welcome," I say. "And on that note, I think it's time for a strategic Instagram story."

"But he can't see my story," Hannah says. "He's blocked."

"He can still see *my* story," I say, pulling my phone out of my bag.

"Rest your hand on Tyson's leg and look here," I say to Hannah. I know it's a bit childish, but I can't help myself.

"Lainey!" she says. "I'm not gonna put my *hand* on his leg!"

"Okay, fine. But at least look at him and smile. Tyson, pretend you just said something funny."

They both sigh and cave. I take a few pictures, then swipe through them, looking for the best one of Hannah.

"This one's perfect," I say. "You look happy."

She gives me a tight smile. "I'm trying to be."

"You'll get there," I say. "And in the meantime, everyone will see *this*."

I start to upload the photo to my story, then decide it needs a caption. I brainstorm for a few seconds, then type: And we're off! Here's to new beginnings!

Now reading over *my* shoulder, Hannah laughs and says, "You're too much."

"I almost wrote something worse," I tell her.

"Oh, Lord. What was that?"

"Here's to the Mile High Club." I laugh.

"Lainey!" Hannah gasps. "You wouldn't!"

"Wouldn't write that caption, or wouldn't join that club?" I ask.

"The caption," Hannah says. "Both!"

"I'm sure she's already a platinum member of the club," Tyson says with a smirk.

"Platinum?" I say, making a *pfft* sound. "Try *diamond*."

CHAPTER 13

TYSON

PLANES, TRAINS, AUTOMOBILES, and ferries.

It's a long journey to Capri, and it crosses my mind that people need to stop saying they "love to travel" when the actual traveling part sucks. Especially when it involves jet lag and Lainey.

I'm mostly kidding about Lainey, though she does have a way of making things more complicated than they need to be. When we arrive in the Naples train station, she suggests that we take a long, expensive Uber ride in the direction *away* from our ferry to a pizzeria that she once read about in a novel. We are literally surrounded by pizza, yet she wants to eat a slice that a fictional character declared orgasmic.

I put my foot down and tell her that ain't happening—I just want to get to Capri and relax. She lets the dream die, but is now in a souvenir shop by the ferry landing, trying on straw hats. She models each one for the young male clerk while Hannah and I watch her from outside the store.

I feel myself start to get agitated. "If we miss our ferry, I'm going to be so pissed," I say to Hannah.

She nods, glances at her watch, and says, "I know. But we should be fine. Give her a few more minutes."

A second later, she emerges, beaming in her new hat, then leads the charge to the ferry.

"See?" she says, giving me a smug look. "I told you we had plenty of time!"

WHEN WE FINALLY pull into Marina Grande, Capri's main seaport, I'm exhausted. It doesn't help that deboarding the boat is a complete cluster, everyone clamoring to collect their baggage from a holding pen crammed with suitcases. The concept of a queue is clearly nonexistent in this country, and the lack of order stresses me out. I remind myself that we are on vacation—not in a law firm. I have no obligations or schedule. I can just go with the flow.

As I grab my bag, step off the boat, and merge into the crowd on the pier, I realize that the feeling is equal parts liberating and disorienting. Although I relish the freedom of being my own man on my own timetable, I'm not quite sure what to do without all the usual goals that have guided my life. Some of that pressure has always come from my parents, but a lot of it has been internal, the way I'm wired. For as long as I can remember, I've had the deep desire to achieve and climb the next rung of the ladder of success. Get into college, then law school, then a top law firm, then make partner. It was one of the reasons I could relate so much to Summer. She was the same way. I remind myself why we are here—and that I need to take this opportunity to do some soul-searching.

I look beyond the crowd on the pier and take in my first glimpse of Capri. It's just like a postcard, the scene somehow glamorous and quaint at once. A mix of large yachts and small, rustic fishing boats are anchored in the sapphire-blue waters. A pebble beach stretches along one side of the paved street while cliffs hugged by colorful pastel buildings rise dramatically on the other. Lush vegetation dots the landscape in every direction, and the balmy air smells of citrus and salt. If only Summer could be with us. She was right about this place.

"Holy smokes!" Lainey says in a voice so loud that an entire family of five turns to look at her. "It's freaking gorgeous!"

"Gosh. It really is," Hannah says, glancing around with wide eyes.

When we get to the end of the pier, Lainey looks at me and says, "Where to next?"

We turn onto the street and stand on the shoulder as I study a map to get my bearings, remembering the email I received from our hotel concierge. "Depends on whether you want to take a taxi or the funicular," I say.

"The *fun*-icular sounds more fun," Lainey says.

"Let's do it." I smile, then lead the way down to the station.

The ride is an efficient five-minute climb through lemon groves. The views are amazing, and when we exit the station at the top, the panoramic vista is even more dramatic. Lainey pulls out her phone and starts taking pictures like crazy. She takes a few selfies, too, changing her pose every few seconds, smiling into the camera.

I watch her, marveling that she can be so unself-conscious.

"Hannah! Come here and get next to me!" she clamors.

Hannah shakes her head. "No way. We've been traveling for twenty-four hours!"

"But we have to memorialize our arrival!"

I watch for as long as I can bear it, then finally turn, heading toward the heart of the square. Refusing to look back, I feel like a parent strategically walking away from a stubborn child, knowing Lainey will eventually follow, if only to avoid being abandoned.

Sure enough, she scrambles after me, her roller bag making a racket on the cobblestones, while Hannah keeps pace at her side.

"Wait up, jerk!" Lainey happily yells.

I wait for them to catch up, then quietly remind her she might not want to be the loud American.

"And *you* might not want to be the American who can't stop to smell the roses."

"How about the tired-as-fuck, jet-lagged American who just wants to check into his hotel and take a shower? Can I be him?" I ask her, as I do my best to orient us in the busy square.

"Look. They have a Tod's!" Lainey says, pointing to a storefront. "Let's get matching loafers!"

"Maybe later. But for now, look for Via Emanuele," I say, scanning the street signs affixed to buildings.

"Everything looks so upscale," Hannah says, sounding surprised.

I nod, a little surprised at how cosmopolitan the scene is given that the town is situated on such a tiny island. The crowds are dense—which is a bit of a bummer—but I love the energy, and I make sudden eye contact with a gorgeous woman. She smiles at me, and I smile back.

It's a harmless exchange, but Lainey catches it and says, "And *I'm* the flirt? *Sheesh.* Could you be any more obvious?"

"What?" Hannah says.

"Tyson just tried to pick up some hot chick."

"*Please,*" I say, thinking that I can't recall the last time I randomly picked up a girl at a bar, let alone walking down the street. "And for the record, I'm focused on my *friends* right now—not looking for action."

I give Lainey a pointed look that she clearly misses, seemingly forgetting all about Dog Boy. Instead, she turns to Hannah and says, "Do we believe him?"

"I do," Hannah says.

Lainey stops walking, then says, "Care to place a bet on that? Fifty bucks?"

Hannah takes the bet as I roll my eyes and keep us moving toward our hotel.

"How about a wager on *your* action?" I say to Lainey over my shoulder.

"No line on that," she says, grinning. "That's a lock."

CHAPTER 14

HANNAH

B Y THE TIME we check into our hotel, an enchanting oasis tucked between the sea and a lush garden of pink bougainvillea and pomegranate trees, I've already fallen in love with Capri. I have been to some beautiful places in my life, but I've never felt this transported. The scenery is otherworldly, and I keep getting the feeling that we are stepping back in time. I know the island has ancient roots, dating back to Greeks and Phoenicians in the eighth century B.C. But for me, Capri evokes the golden age of Hollywood. With every twist and turn we take, I envision Audrey Hepburn biking in a pair of pedal pushers; or a bikini-clad Brigitte Bardot frolicking by a cliffside pool; or Grace Kelly lounging aboard a yacht, donning oversize sunglasses and a headscarf.

The vibe is both romantic and nostalgic—two things that should make me miss Grady. Yet I don't for some reason. Perhaps it's because his trashy antics with Berlin feel like the antithesis of that refined bygone era. His cheating aside, I'm ever so slowly starting to believe that maybe Grady really hadn't been the right person for me.

"Have you ever seen anything so beautiful?" I ask Tyson and Lainey.

We are sitting on our hotel's rooftop terrace, looking out over the island's iconic rock formations, which rise dramatically from the cobalt sea.

"So dreamy," Lainey says, sipping her Aperol spritz. She'd ordered us a round of the Italian aperitif from the bar for our official welcome-to-Capri toast. "Gosh, this is delicious."

Tyson takes a small sip of his. He has discarded his straw, along with the mint leaf and orange slice garnish.

"Do you like it?" Lainey asks him.

"It's okay, but I'm not really a *spritz* guy."

"Too manly for a colorful cocktail?" Lainey says.

He smiles and says, "It's just a little too sweet for me. Sort of like you."

Lainey laughs, gazing back out over the ocean. "At least we can all appreciate this view!"

"Yes, we can," Tyson says. "Tell me if there is another spectacle on earth which can compare with this."

"*Whoa!*" Lainey says. "Did you just come up with that?"

"No. I read it on the hotel website. It's a quote by Alexandre Dumas."

"Who?" Lainey asks.

"French novelist. He wrote *The Count of Monte Cristo*."

Lainey shakes her head. "Never heard of it."

"How about *The Three Musketeers*?"

"The candy bar?" Lainey grins.

As their banter continues, I covertly check my messages. Since yesterday afternoon, Olivia and I have been texting back and forth.

On the surface, and given the circumstances of our meeting, I know our communication is a bit odd. I also know Lainey would kill me if she knew we were talking at all, let alone so often. But I rationalize that other than a brief sidebar about Lainey's acting career, most of our conversation has had nothing to do with her.

Instead, we chat about random things, like travel and music and tennis. I tentatively ask about her career, hoping she doesn't think I'm a complete weirdo. She doesn't seem to, though, freely sharing details about the pro circuit. She tells me that the Williams sisters are as amazing as people as they are as athletes—warm and funny and kind. I wish I could tell Grady *that*.

Bottom line, our rapport feels so easy and natural—and is a complete departure from my insular world back home. Our interaction actually reminds me of those early days in college with Lainey, Tyson, and Summer.

I smile down at my phone now, reading Olivia's latest text, which is a response to a selfie I sent her when we got off the funicular.

Beautiful shot, she replies.

"Okay. That's it. Who the fuck are you texting?"

I look up and see Lainey staring right at me. I panic, flipping my phone over, which I'm sure looks even more suspicious.

"My mom," I say.

"I thought she was giving you the silent treatment?"

"She is," I say. "I just wanted to let her know we got here safe and sound."

"You're so full of shit!" she says with a laugh. "You better not be texting Grady!"

"I swear I'm not."

"Then let me see your phone," she says, grabbing for it.

I hold it out of her reach, then tuck it under my thigh, laughing.

"Do you swear that you're not texting Grady?"

"I swear," I say, raising my right hand, my thumb holding down my pinky.

"Wow. The Girl Scout salute," Lainey says with a laugh, then looks at Tyson. "She's gotta be telling the truth!"

I smile.

"Okay, if it's not Grady, who is it?"

I take a deep breath, then a long drink through my straw, buying myself a few extra seconds.

"Olivia," I finally say.

"Olivia *who?*" she says.

"Your sister Olivia," I say.

"Tell me you're kidding," Lainey says.

"Please just hear me out," I say.

She slams her glass down on the table. "No! I don't want to hear anything about her! Haven't I made that clear?"

"Pretty clear," Tyson says, giving me a look.

"But she's nothing like Ashley. They don't even speak—"

"I don't care *what* she's like or *who* she speaks to!" Lainey says. "I don't want anything to do with her. Or my father. Or anyone he's related to by blood or by marriage. Why don't you get that, Hannah? Didn't you do enough damage in Dallas? You thought another round of rejection would be fun for me?"

"But that's the thing. . . . She's not rejecting you."

"I don't care!"

"I'm sorry," I say, my heart racing.

She stares at me a beat, then says, "I'm not like you, Hannah. I'm not obsessed with this fairy-tale notion of marriage and family. You see where that got you with Grady?"

I know she's not trying to be mean, but her words are a gut punch.

"And your own mother. *Jesus.* The shit you put up with simply because you're related to her. . . . It's unfathomable to me."

"C'mon, Lainey," Tyson says in a low voice. "You have the right to be upset, but don't be mean. She said she was sorry."

I nervously nod.

"Okay, but I'm serious," Lainey says. "This is the last straw. I just want to have a fun trip, and if you guys aren't capable of that, tell me now. Please."

"I *am* capable of that," I say. "I promise."

I look down, feeling ashamed. She's right. Who am I to say that she should try to have a relationship with her sister? What do I even *know* about relationships? My mother isn't speaking to me, and as much as I love my father, I'm not close to him, either.

"I'm sorry," I say again.

"It's okay," Lainey says with a sigh, her voice and expression returning to normal. Her outbursts remind me of summer thunderstorms; they are intense but usually pass as quickly as they come. "I'm sorry if I overreacted."

"You didn't overreact," I say, shaking my head. "I understand."

"*Well* . . . maybe she overreacted a *little*," Tyson says. He holds his thumb and index finger a centimeter apart.

It lightens the mood somewhat, and I give him a grateful look.

"Shut it, Tyson," Lainey says.

He holds up his hands, palms out, with a slight smirk on his face. "Sorry. I'll be quiet."

"Good," Lainey says, rolling her eyes.

She then switches gears, announcing that she's going to discuss dinner options with our concierge, Alessandro—a handsome man with whom she's already been flirting.

She gets up, grabs her Aperol spritz from the table, and marches back inside.

I look at Tyson with a rueful expression.

"I warned you," he says with a shrug.

"I know. You were right."

"What are you and Olivia even texting about?" he asks.

"Lots of stuff," I say. "I really like her. I feel like I've made a new friend."

Tyson gives me a skeptical look. "Okay," he says. "Just be careful. I'd really like to avoid another blowup on this trip."

CHAPTER 15

LAINEY

AFTER THE FIASCO in Dallas, I seriously can't believe Hannah would reach out to Olivia. Especially when I made it crystal clear how I felt. At the same time, I feel a little guilty for blowing up at her, especially at such a fragile point in her own life. I excuse myself, explaining that I'm going to go work on our dinner reservation with our concierge.

I find Alessandro at his desk.

"Good evening, Miss Lawson," he says.

"Good evening, Alessandro," I say, sitting in the chair across from him. "Please call me Lainey!"

"As you wish, Lainey," he says, giving me a nod that reminds me of a royal bow. "How might I assist you this evening?"

"My friends and I were wondering if you could recommend a restaurant for dinner. Something casual—and nearby. We're starving."

"Of course." Alessandro nods. "Capri is all rather casual and easy—"

"Yes, but *this* casual?" I say, gesturing down at my cropped white jeans, cotton top, and flip-flops.

"Yes. Sei bellisima," he says, his brown eyes twinkling.

I can tell it's a compliment, but I still say, "I'm sorry. I don't know much Italian."

"You look beautiful," he says.

"Ohh. *Grazie,*" I say. "You're bellisima, too."

He laughs a deep, rich laugh. "La ringrazio."

I smile back at him as he folds his hands across the leather blotter on his desk, then says, "So tell me. What sort of cuisine are you and your friends looking for this evening?"

"Hmm. I think we want to go out on a bit of a limb tonight and try . . . Italian."

He laughs again and says, "Excellent choice. Just give me a moment and I'll make some calls for you."

"La ringrazio," I say with a wink. "I'll be back in a jiffy."

I get up from the desk and head to the bar, grabbing one more drink. By the time I return to the lobby, Tyson and Hannah are waiting for me. Alessandro informs us that he has booked us a table at Da Giorgio, a nearby local favorite, then gives us easy walking directions.

I thank him, then ask what I should order.

"Everything is fabulous," he says. "You can't go wrong."

"But I want to know *your* favorite," I say.

"In that case," he says, "I always get the spaghetti alle vongole."

"Okay!" I say. "Well, then that's what I'm having!"

As we exit the lobby, Tyson calls me shameless. "That's what I'm having," he mimics in a high, flirty voice. "Do you even know what *vongoles* are?"

"No," I say. "But they sure sound good in that accent!"

"Pretty sure *we're* the ones with the accent right now," Tyson says.

"Yeah, but when he's speaking *English*, he has an *Italian* accent," I say.

"She's got a point," Hannah says.

I give Tyson a smug smile, then take Hannah's hand in mine, intertwining our fingers. It's my way of telling her that I've fully forgiven her, and she gives me a grateful smile.

"This feels so European, doesn't it?" I ask, swinging our arms.

"What's that?" she says.

"Holding hands with friends . . . It's nice."

"Europeans aren't as homophobic as Americans," Tyson says. "It's not uncommon for straight men in Italy to kiss hello, hold hands, or even fix each other's hair."

"And order spritzes!" I say.

"Touché," Tyson says.

A FEW MINUTES later, we arrive at Da Giorgio, which is connected to a hotel of the same name. Passing under a stucco archway, we check in with a hostess who directs us down a narrow corridor toward a large, bright dining room. The vibe is casual and homey—devoid of glamour but in a nice way. Even better, an entire wall of windows offers incredible harbor views.

The cuisine turns out to be as amazing as Alessandro promised, and as the sky gradually darkens, turning a deep indigo, I feel a growing contentment and affection for my friends. I know some of that has to do with my deepening buzz, but it's not only that.

"I love you guys," I say as we finish our wine.

"We love you more," Hannah says.

"Well, maybe not *more*." Tyson smiles.

"Hey, I'll take whatever I can get from *you*," I tell him.

"You always do," he quips.

I laugh, then look over at Hannah. "I'm just glad we're here to-gether. And that you got out of that relationship. It's the silver lin-ing to busting Grady the way you did. Without firsthand proof, you might have married that guy."

Hannah sighs and nods.

"Even without the cheating, you would have been settling," Tyson says.

"Totally," I say, waiting for Hannah's reaction.

When she doesn't respond, I ask her directly. "Can you see that now?"

"I guess. Now that I've taken a step back. But I still miss him. Or at least who I *thought* he was and what I thought we had." Hannah pauses, then continues, "And I'm not going to lie—I'm very worried that I'll never find someone."

"Yes, you will," I say. "You *totally* will."

"I hope so. I really want a family."

"You'll have that. And at thirty-two, you still have plenty of time. But if you're really worried, you could just freeze a few of your eggs."

"Yeah," she says. "I just wish I could look into a crystal ball and know that I won't end up alone."

"Well, I'd hope you know that by now," Tyson says, lowering his voice.

She looks at him, nodding earnestly. "I do. And it's made all the difference. I can't even tell you—" Her voice breaks. "I just wish Summer could have known that she was *this* loved."

"You don't think she knew that?" I ask. "I think she did."

"Maybe she did," Hannah says. "Let's just admit it. She was every-one's favorite."

"Wait. *What?*" I say, pretending to be shocked and dismayed. "I thought *I* was the favorite."

Tyson laughs, then says, "Nope. But you're the most . . . *special*."

"What was it about Summer, anyway?" I say.

"A lot of things," Tyson says. "She was good at everything she did."

"Yeah. I know that. But we didn't love her for her fast times on the track or her stupidly high GPA."

"Well, *obviously*," Tyson says. "We admired her for those things, but we didn't *love* her for that."

"Exactly. So what was it that we loved about her?" I press.

I'm asking the question specifically about Summer, but in a sense, I'm asking it about myself. And Hannah. And Tyson. What makes a friendship? What makes us choose to love the people we love?

"Well, she was fiercely loyal, for one," Hannah says. "We all had little arguments along the way, but she never once said a single negative thing about either of you. Or anyone, really."

"Um. I hate to break it to you, sister," I say, grinning at Hannah. "But she trash-talked you on the regular. Didn't she, Tyson?"

Tyson laughs and plays along. "Yep. All the time."

We sit in silence for a few seconds, our smiles gradually fading, before Tyson says, "For me, it was her passion. How fully she lived and deeply she loved."

Hannah stares at him, blinking. "Yes," she says. "That's so true."

"It was almost as if she felt things *too* deeply." I pause, then say, "Remember Hurricane Sandy?"

"Oh my gosh, yes," Hannah says, as we all fall silent, remembering how obsessed Summer got with the coverage, even starting a fundraiser on campus.

"And how about when Whitney Houston died?" Tyson muses. "I mean, I *loved* Whitney. She was in my top five. Maybe three. But—" He shakes his head.

"I know," Hannah says. "It was as if she *knew* her."

"She must have watched *The Bodyguard* three times that month," I say.

"I can't even listen to that song," Hannah says.

Tyson nods, humming, *I will always love you.* He stops, shakes his head, and says, "Damn."

"What about you, Lainey?" Hannah asks me. "What did you love most about Summer?"

I think for a second. "This might sound selfish," I say, cutting my eyes to Tyson. "But I loved that she always saw the best in me. Even when I messed up. She never judged me."

"She really admired you," Hannah says.

"She did?" I ask.

I'm so used to everyone else thinking of me as the wild, out-of-control fuckup that I don't quite believe it.

Hannah nods, adamant.

"Yes. She once told me she would kill to have your way with people," Hannah says. "The way you can talk to anyone. It's like Grady—but unlike Grady, you make everyone feel good about themselves."

"I hope I made *her* feel that way."

"You did," she says, nodding.

"I really hope so. I wish I had gone to more of her races."

"You went to plenty."

"Not as many as you guys did—"

"That's okay. You did other things with her. Think of all the times you took her shopping," Hannah says.

I smile. "That's true. That was our thing. She had her own style."

"What style was that?" Tyson says with a laugh. "She lived in sweats and athletic wear."

"Not when she went out—"

"She went out?" Tyson laughs.

"Well, rarely. But when she did . . . Remember her little overalls?" I say.

"You hated those overalls!" Hannah says.

"No, I didn't," I say. "I teased her, but I thought they were so cute on her."

"And her pigtails," Hannah says.

I smile. "Yes. But the pigtails did *not* work with the overalls."

"Or with her flannel shirts," Tyson says as we all laugh.

"She was such a Midwestern girl," I say.

"Through and through," Tyson says, nodding.

"You think she would have settled down there?" Hannah asks us.

"Probably so," Tyson says. "God, she would have been a hell of a doctor."

"And such a good mother," Hannah says. She takes a deep breath, then looks at Tyson. "I'm really glad you picked Capri. It makes me feel closer to her."

"Me too," he says, looking out the window. "I really feel her here."

I follow his gaze, wishing I felt the same way. It must be a huge comfort to believe in some sort of an afterlife. For me, though, death is a blackout. The end of the line. It was the end for Summer; it was the end for my mother; and one day, it will be the end for each of the three of us, too. It's a grim thought if you dwell on it too much, so I decide not to. Instead, I order one last glass of wine.

CHAPTER 16

TYSON

WAKE UP ON my rollaway cot, shocked to discover that it's after nine o'clock. I never sleep this late. For my father, beating the sun is a point of pride—only the weak and lazy sleep in—and his mentality has rubbed off on me. I get up, feeling sheepish, finding Lainey and Hannah out on the balcony, drinking coffee in matching white hotel robes.

"Good morning, Mr. Sleepyhead!" Lainey says as I sit down with them at the small round table.

"Morning, ladies," I say, getting a hit of dopamine as I stare out at an expanse of bright blue sea and sky.

"Want some coffee?" Hannah asks, gesturing toward an Italian press.

I nod and pour myself a cup as Lainey asks if we should order room service or go downstairs to eat.

"I don't like room service," I say.

"How can you not like room service?" Lainey asks.

"It's the awkward dynamic—a waiter coming into the room where you're sleeping, often when you're still in pajamas." I yawn, waking up.

"You're so weird," Lainey says, then points down to the rock formations below. "What are they called again?" she asks me for at least the third time.

"The Fa-rag-li-oni," I say as slowly as I can. "How are you able to memorize so many lines in your scripts when you seem to have zero retention in real life?"

"Because dialogue is intuitive. It flows. And also—my scripts are in English."

"Would it help to know that *faraglioni* is Italian for *rock stacks*?"

"Nope," she says, shaking her head. "Doesn't help."

"How about that it comes from the Greek word *pharos*, which translates to *lighthouse*? Which they were once used as."

"Nope. Doesn't help, either." Lainey shakes her head.

"How were they used as lighthouses?" Hannah asks, looking intrigued.

I nod. "Back when it was all one giant rock, people climbed up there and built a fire pit at the top so they could signal the land to passing boats."

"Wait. How did they become three separate rocks?" Lainey says.

"There are actually four. There's a smaller one you can't really see from this vantage point. . . . But to answer your question: erosion. Thousands of years of pounding wind and water. And to further tax your memory," I say with a smile, "each rock has its *own* individual name."

"Uh-oh," Lainey says.

"That one's Stella," I say, pointing to the rock on our left, closest to the shoreline.

"Well, that's darling," Lainey says. "And easy to remember!"

I point to the one farthest from land. "That one's Faraglione di Fuori—"

"Fuori? As in fury?" Lainey asks.

"No. It's taken from *foris,* the Latin word for 'door,' which can also refer to anything beyond a threshold—like outside," I say, amazed by how often I use my high school Latin.

"And the middle one?" Lainey asks, pointing to the most distinctive rock of the three, with its small open archway at the bottom.

"Take a guess," I say.

She smirks and says, "Lisa? Angela? Pamela? Renée?"

I laugh at her old-school hip-hop reference. "Nope. *Di Mezzo.*"

"*Mezzo* means 'middle,' right?"

"Yep. You know—like *mezzanine* . . . or *mezzo-soprano,*" I say. "Legend has it that if you kiss your sweetheart under the arch of the di Mezzo, you stay with them forever."

"Oh, wow," Hannah says with a wistful look.

I assume she's thinking about Grady until she glances at me and says, "Summer would have loved that."

"Why?" Lainey asks. "Because she was so superstitious?"

"Well, yeah. That too," Hannah says. "But I meant the romantic part."

I look down, feeling uneasy, just as I did last night at dinner. It's hard for me to get used to Hannah knowing what happened between Summer and me. Maybe it's in my head, but I still have the feeling that she's not entirely comfortable with it—or more likely, that she's upset I kept such a big secret for so long.

I tune back in to hear Lainey and Hannah discussing Summer's obsession with rom-coms. Lainey mentions *Sixteen Candles* and *Mystic Pizza,* then starts quoting from *Notting Hill.* "'I'm just a girl, standing in front of a boy—'"

"'Asking him to love her,'" Hannah finishes with a sigh.

"She ate that stuff up," Lainey says.

"Every bite," Hannah says.

"And how about her love of Taylor Swift?" Lainey says.

"You have to give her credit, though," Hannah says. "She was a Swiftie before it was cool to be a Swiftie."

"You mean before Travis Kelce put her on the map?" I quip, trying to get a rise out of them. They don't take the bait.

"Gosh," Hannah says. "How much would she have loved the Eras tour?"

"I know." Lainey sighs. "I thought about Summer the *entire* show. Especially when Taylor sang her old stuff."

Same, I think, getting a sharp pang in my chest. I'd gotten tickets for Nicole for her birthday, but I'd be lying if I said my mind wasn't on Summer at the concert.

The girls finally fall silent; then Lainey asks if anyone is in the mood to go shopping.

I make a face and tell her it's too nice a day to spend inside stores. "How about a hike down to the sea?"

"Why do we have to hike? Didn't you hear Alessandro say that we can take the hotel car down—"

"Christ, Lainey. This isn't Machu Picchu. It's more of a *walk* than a hike. And it's *downhill.*"

"Okay, fine. *Fine,*" Lainey says, rolling her eyes. "I'll do the stupid hike."

"Attagirl," I say, giving her a light punch on the shoulder.

AFTER A QUICK breakfast, we walk over to the nearby Augustus Gardens. Hannah goes crazy for the flowers, naming them all, from the more familiar geraniums, begonias, and dahlias to a shrublike yellow flower called "broom" that I've never heard of. I agree they're pretty, but I'm more interested in the history, including a marble monument to Vladimir Lenin, of all people. According to the plaque, it was commissioned in the nineteen-sixties by the Soviet Embassy.

The best part about the gardens, though, has to be the sweeping views in all directions. On one side, you can see the Faraglioni. On the other side, you look down over Marina Piccola and the incredible Via Krupp, a dramatic switchback road zigzagging down the cliff, connecting the gardens to the beach.

As we walk, I play tour guide, telling them that the road was commissioned by German industrialist Friedrich Alfred Krupp so that he could get from his own mansion in town down to his marine biology research vessel.

Lainey looks bored until I add a footnote. "Old man Krupp also used the path to get to his secret grotto, where he had sex orgies with local youths."

"Oh my God!" she says. "Like Jeffrey Epstein!"

"Yep," I say. "There's always one of those guys."

"That's terrible. Those poor children." Hannah shakes her head. "Did he go to prison?"

I pull up Wikipedia on my phone. "No criminal charges, but he was eventually booted off the island—and out of Italy, for that matter. Later, they changed the name of Krupp Gardens to Augustus Gardens."

"They should have changed the name of his stupid path, too," Lainey says, frowning. "Are you sure you want to take that route? Isn't there a straighter shot down?"

"Nice try," I say, knowing she's just trying to get out of the trek. "But if it helps, I read that the walk is very Instagrammable."

She smiles and says, "In that case, I'm in."

. . .

TRUE TO FORM, Lainey takes photos the whole way down the foot-
path. Mostly, she takes pictures of the scenery or selfies with Hannah, but occasionally she insists on a group shot of all three of us,
which is a tedious process. First, she recruits a stranger, never bothering to gauge whether said stranger is in a hurry or in the middle
of a conversation or has their hands full. Second, instead of just giving her Good Samaritan creative license, she issues detailed instructions about her preferred composition. *Vertical, please. Just a tad
higher! Did you get the sky? Make sure you don't cut off our feet!* Third,
and my least favorite part, is that once the favor is granted, she holds
the stranger hostage while checking their work, deciding whether
to release them or ask for "one more shot." I keep waiting for someone to lose patience with her, almost *hoping* that they will. But not
only does everyone indulge her every request, they seem downright
enchanted by her.

Needless to say, her shenanigans slow us down quite a bit. By the
time we get to the bottom, we are all starving, having long since
burned off our breakfast. I suggest we get lunch before we hit the
beach.

"Can we go to La Fontelina?" Lainey asks.

"Is that the beach club you showed me on TikTok?" Hannah asks.

"Yes," Lainey says. "With an attached restaurant. Okay with you,
Tyson?"

"Sure," I say, consulting a map, then leading us down a path lined
with wildflowers and sea grass.

About three hundred meters later, we arrive at what is clearly a
very popular spot. The open-air restaurant has a line of people waiting to get in.

"Darn," Hannah says. "We should have gotten a reservation."

"Hmm. Let me call Alessandro. I bet he can hook us up," Lainey says without missing a beat.

We haven't even been in Italy for a full twenty-four hours, and she is already working her connections.

A few seconds later, Lainey looks over and gives us a big smile and a thumbs-up.

"All set," she says as she rejoins us. "Alessandro's best friend is Chef Mario!"

She beams at us, like we're supposed to know who that is, and a moment later, we are being seated at a prime table under a rustic straw-covered pergola, overlooking a small rocky beach. Instead of sand, there are slabs of limestone scattered with blue-and-white lounge chairs and matching parasols. The jet-set crowd is chic but laid-back.

Hannah and Lainey are seated across from me, and they keep up a running commentary on attractive men in our vicinity. They seem to be especially taken with a guy behind me who Hannah says is giving her Jude Law in *The Talented Mr. Ripley* vibes.

Lainey slaps the table and says, "Oh my God! Yes!"

I glance over my shoulder, then turn back to face them. "The foppish dude with the sideburns?"

Hannah nods as Lainey tells me to stop being so obvious.

I shrug and look out into the distance, my thoughts making their way back to Summer. I picture her now, warming up before a race. The determination and concentration on her face as she went through her routine, a combination of light jogging and dynamic stretching. Then, at the starting line, she always did one explosive jump, high into the air. I never asked why, but I assumed it was to wake up her nervous system—give it a jolt before the gun.

I tune back in to hear Hannah pointing to the cliffs. "That's the spot where the Sirens bewitched Odysseus," she says.

"The *who*?" Lainey says.

"The Sirens," Hannah says. "In *The Odyssey.*"

"Oh. Never read it," Lainey says, looking proud.

"Didn't *everyone* have to read *The Odyssey*?" Hannah asks.

"I did," I say. "Twice. In high school and college."

"Well, I didn't go to a fancy prep school," Lainey says. "So don't leave me in suspense—who are the Sirens?"

Hannah explains that they were mythological winged monster women, part bird, part human. "They'd hypnotize sailors with their angelic voices, luring them off course before drowning them," she finishes.

"How *ruuude*," Lainey says with a laugh. It's one of her catchphrases from college, which she got from some sitcom.

"Wait!" Hannah suddenly says. "Do you remember what book Summer was reading the night we all met?"

Lainey shakes her head. "No clue."

I look over at Hannah, thinking. I remember a lot about that night. I remember I was watching the Yankees–Orioles game. I remember thinking that all three girls were attractive and seemed cool. I remember being impressed with Summer as we discussed her running. But I do *not* remember what Summer was reading—if I ever knew in the first place.

"*The Odyssey*!" Hannah finally says.

"Oh, wow. That's wild," Lainey says. "Do you think that had anything to do with her wanting to come to Capri?"

"Tyson would know better," Hannah says, giving me a loaded look that Lainey doesn't miss.

"Wait. Why would *Tyson* know better?" she asks Hannah.

Hannah shrugs, still looking at me.

"I feel like I'm missing something," Lainey says.

"You're not missing anything," I say, giving Hannah a warning look that Lainey *also* picks up on.

"Guys. What's going on here? I have the right to know!"

"And why's that?" I ask. "Why do you have the *right* to know?"

Lainey stares at me, incredulous. "Because it's obvious that you told Hannah something you aren't telling me!"

As Hannah not so subtly raises her eyebrows, Lainey ratchets up her inquisition. "Tyson! Tell me right this second! Did you and Summer hook up or something?"

"Jesus, Lainey," I say under my breath.

"What?"

"That expression. 'Hooking up.' I hate it. You sound like a teenager."

Lainey is undeterred and unabashed. "Fine, then. Did you and Summer ever *kiss?*"

I stare back at her, then say, "And what if we did?"

"Wow. Wow. *Wow,*" Lainey says, shifting her gaze to Hannah. "How long have *you* known about this?"

"Only a couple of days. He told me in Dallas."

"This is crazy!" Lainey says.

"Why is it so crazy?" I ask, getting more annoyed and defensive by the second.

"Because. I always suspected that *she* had a crush on *you,* but I didn't think she was your type."

"I don't have a type," I say, bristling.

"Yes, you do."

"No, I don't."

"Give me a break, Tyson. Your last three girlfriends are the same exact type—"

"First of all," I say, now annoyed for multiple reasons, "three people is not a statistically significant sample size. Second of all, how are they the same type? Are they all lawyers? Are they tall?" I ask, thinking specifically of Laurie, my girlfriend preceding Nicole, who was a very petite yoga instructor.

"No. But they're all drop-dead gorgeous Black girls—"

"So by that logic, Dog Guy must be the same type as Surfer Guy?" I ask, cutting her off.

"Okay." Lainey nods, looking a little sheepish. "I get your point."

"Besides," Hannah says, "it's not really about how someone *looks*. Tyson and Summer had a lot in common. . . . They both loved baseball . . . and books."

I glance away, remembering how Summer and I used to pass novels back and forth. We loved all the same stuff and shared several favorite authors: John Green, Khaled Hosseini, Ann Patchett, and Curtis Sittenfeld. Summer had actually introduced me to Sittenfeld's work, and I still had her copy of *Prep*. I'd thought about giving it back to her parents, but I couldn't bear to part with it, as it had all of her little notes in the margins. Summer annotated books even when she was reading for fun, underlining passages, highlighting the names of new characters, and circling words she didn't know. We had talked about teaching high school English once—how satisfying we thought the job would be. Looking back, I think we both discarded the idea for the same reason; at the time, it didn't seem ambitious enough. I can see now that we were both thinking about life the wrong way, and for the first time, I wonder if Summer had truly been passionate about medicine.

"So were you guys in *love?*" Lainey asks me now.

I look back at her, my stomach twisting in knots, so many emotions hitting me at once. I feel the usual grief, of course, but also remorse and guilt that I hadn't better understood the pressure she was feeling. I'm also angry that Lainey feels entitled to these answers. What happened between Summer and me is none of her business. I almost lash out at her but manage to hold back.

"Lainey. Please," I say instead. "I really don't want to do this—" My voice cracks, surprising both of us.

She stares at me, looking worried and appropriately sheepish. She might not understand all the emotional layers I'm feeling, but at least she seems to realize there is subtext to my resistance. "I'm sorry," she says. "I didn't mean to upset you—"

"It's fine," I say. "Can we just move on?"

"Of course," she says, nodding. "We can do that."

"Thank you," I say.

After several long seconds, Lainey finds my hand under the table. She wraps her fingers around mine, then squeezes. The warmth and subtlety of her gesture catches me off guard, but what surprises me even more is that I don't pull away.

CHAPTER 17

HANNAH

As we make our way down to the harbor, I feel at peace in the company of my two best friends, surrounded by such incredible natural beauty. Frankly, it also helps that more than five thousand miles and an entire ocean separate me from Grady and my mother, and I'm in a place with zero memories shared with either of them. It occurs to me, not for the first time since our flight took off yesterday, that Grady had never expressed any real desire to travel beyond his mainstays of St. Bart's, Aspen, and Nantucket—the favored destinations among my old circles. Now that I'm no longer tied to him, I will inevitably get to see more of the world. It's a silver lining.

In a recent text, Olivia asked how we chose Italy. It led to a conversation about travel—and a lot of the places she's been—and I found myself perusing her Instagram. She isn't a prolific poster, but I've gleaned quite a bit about her. I know she has a bleeding heart, especially when it comes to animals. I know she loves sports, and her teams are the Astros, the Cowboys, and, of course, the Texas

Longhorns. She's obsessed with music of seemingly all genres and loves going to concerts. She seems to spend as much time as she can outdoors—biking and hiking and even fishing.

One thing I *can't* discern from her social media is her relationship status, past or present. My guess is that she is one of those people who scrubs her page after a breakup, and I decide that I will do the same as soon as I can stomach looking at Grady's face long enough to delete old posts. Incredibly, I feel like I'm getting there.

WE ARE NOW having lunch at a restaurant down by the water. As Tyson looks out over the sea, I notice a wistful expression on his face. I wonder if he's thinking about Summer. I glance away, hit by a wave of intense sadness. It suddenly doesn't feel right to avoid the pain. For *any* of us. I look back at Tyson and decide to push him to tell Lainey what I already know about their relationship. It feels like the right moment—or at least it feels like the *wrong* moment *not* to tell her.

Unfortunately, the conversation doesn't go well, and Tyson gets upset. Once again, my instincts have proven wrong.

My stomach in knots, I head to the restroom, hoping the tension will dissipate by the time I return to the table.

On my way back, I stall, lingering by the bar and checking my phone. There are several new texts from Olivia, including a funny anecdote about her coach. Smiling, I start to type a reply, then feel someone hovering nearby.

I look up and find myself face-to-face with the Jude Law doppelgänger. With wavy blond hair, glacier-blue eyes, and golden skin, he's even more striking up close.

"Hello," he says, smiling at me.

Flustered, I smile back, glad that I touched up my makeup in the bathroom. "Hello."

"How was your lunch?" he asks. I can't place his accent but hear a lilt that sounds Australian, South African, or maybe Irish.

"Delicious," I say. "Yours?"

"Excellent," he says.

We grin at each other for a few more seconds, until I do a quick glance over at Tyson and Lainey.

He follows my gaze, then says, "I'm sorry. Do you need to get back to your friend? Boyfriend? Husband?"

"No," I say, shaking my head. "Both of my *friends* are fine."

"In that case," he says, taking a step closer to me, "I'm Archie."

"Oh, my goodness! I had a cat named Archie when I was little!" I blurt out before I can stop myself.

"You better keep that info under wraps," he says. "Someone could steal your identity with that sort of 'childhood pet' intel."

"That's true," I say, giggling. "That *is* a common security question."

He grins and says, "Wait. By any chance, is your name Biscuit?"

"No. It's Hannah," I say, laughing. "Biscuit was your childhood pet?"

"No," he says. "You just look like a Biscuit."

I laugh harder. "Why, thank you for such a kind compliment!"

Archie smiles, then asks if I'm from the States.

I nod and say, "Yes. Atlanta, Georgia."

"Where Donald Trump got arrested?"

"Ugh. Sadly, yes," I say, embarrassed that my home state is known for an election shitstorm. "What about you?"

"Have a guess."

"Ireland?"

"Close. They're our Celtic neighbors."

"Oh! Scotland?"

He nods.

"Whereabouts in Scotland?" I ask.

"Aberdeen," he says. "It's north of St. Andrews and east of Balmoral. On the coast."

"How close to Balmoral?" I ask, wondering if he's ever seen the royal family traipsing around the castle.

"Not far. About an hour. And no, I never saw the queen, God rest her soul. Or the king. Long may he reign."

I laugh. "How'd you know I was going to ask that?"

"Because you're American," he says, smiling. "Americans love the royals."

"So? *Have* you seen any of them?"

"I once saw Princess Anne whilst tractor shopping."

"*You* were tractor shopping? Or *she* was?"

"She was! Pure dead brilliant lady."

"She does seem really cool," I say, thinking of how she rode horseback, in full military regalia, to both her mother's funeral and her brother's coronation. "So are you here with friends?"

He nods. "Yes. I'm here with my good mate Ian, but he's absolutely stocious at the moment—"

"Stocious?"

"Minced. Pished. Sloshed." He grins, gesturing toward his beer. "Currently sleeping it off back at our hotel."

"Ahh," I say, smiling. "That's unfortunate."

"And why's that?" he asks.

"Because my friend Lainey might want to meet him," I say with a slight head tilt and strategic smile. My flirting skills are rusty, but not nonexistent.

He smiles back at me, then asks what we're doing this evening.

"No plans yet," I say. "You?"

"We're going to Lanterna Verde. A piano bar up in Anacapri. You and your friends should come."

"Maybe we will."

"Okay. Well, I'll let you get back to them," he says.

I nod. "Yes. I better do that."

"In case you can't make it tonight, here's my number," he says, handing me a business card. "I'd love to see you again."

I take it and smile, feeling a rush. "Me too," I say.

"GO, HANNAH!" LAINEY says when I get back to the table. "Give us the scoop!"

"There's really no scoop," I say with a shrug.

"What's his story?"

"His name is Archie. And he's Scottish."

"Well, that's *adorable*. Does he own a kilt?"

"Darn it," I say, snapping my fingers. "I forgot to ask. Maybe we'll find out tonight."

"What's happening tonight?" she asks, while Tyson stares off in the distance.

"He suggested we meet up. He's here with a friend."

"I didn't see a friend," Lainey says. "Wasn't he eating alone?"

"The friend is hungover," I say. "Back at their hotel."

"Oh, so he's fun!" Lainey says, rubbing her palms together.

"Or maybe he's just an alcoholic," Tyson mutters.

Lainey ignores him and announces that she's proud of me.

"For what?" I ask.

"For getting back on your horse!"

"Well, I'm not sure about any *horse*." I smile. "But it did feel good to flirt a bit."

"So. What else did he tell you about his friend? Is he hot, too?" Lainey asks.

"Shoot." I snap my fingers. "Didn't ask that, either."

"My prediction?" Lainey says.

"What's that?" I ask, already amused.

She puts both thumbs down, shakes her head, and says, "A guy that fine always has a sloppy sidekick."

I laugh, picturing Zach Galifianakis in the *Hangover* movies. "But they're usually funny."

"Good point," Lainey says. "And besides, I can work with just about anything."

AFTER LUNCH, THE sky turns cloudy, and nobody is in the mood for the beach. Lainey insists on a taxi back to the hotel, and this time, Tyson doesn't balk. He is quiet on the ride home, and the second we walk in the room, he changes into workout clothes.

"Where are you going?" I ask him.

"For a run," he says.

"Where?" I ask, thinking that Capri's hilly terrain and narrow roadways aren't well suited for running.

"Gym treadmill," he says, putting his AirPods in his ears, then looking down at his phone.

"Okay. Have a good workout," I say.

He nods and says thanks, walking out the door.

I look at Lainey, then grimace. "I think he's upset with me."

"Why would he be upset with you?"

"For forcing his hand. About Summer," I say, as we both sit on the bed.

"As you should have. He should have told us his secret a long time ago. And you *both* should have told me in Dallas."

I look away, thinking of *another* secret I've been keeping from her.

Lainey sighs and says, "I feel so sad for him. It's hard enough to lose a friend. . . ."

"I know." I clear my throat. "And I can't help but wonder if that's why he broke up with Nicole. Maybe he compares everyone to Summer. Maybe he feels that nobody can measure up—not only to Summer but to the unfulfilled potential of their relationship."

"That's really sad," Lainey says.

I nod.

"What do you think would have happened with them?" she asks.

"I don't know. But they could be married with kids by now. . . ."

"Wow," she says. "Can you imagine?"

"Then again," I say, thinking about the conversation Tyson and I had at the pool in Dallas. "It could have been a disaster. They could have broken up on bad terms. We might have had to pick sides."

"As if you'd *ever* pick a side," Lainey says with a friendly eye roll. "Ms. Switzerland."

I smile and shrug.

"Maybe you should talk to Tyson," Lainey says. "About all of this."

"And say what?"

"I don't know. Something about not comparing other women to Summer? Or at least giving them more of a chance?"

I nod, then lean my head back on my pillow, thinking.

LAINEY'S IN THE shower when Tyson finally gets back to the room. I give him a hug. His clothes are damp with sweat, but I don't care.

"I'm sorry," I say.

"For what?" he says without hugging me back.

"For what you lost. With Summer. I feel like I didn't say enough when you told me in Dallas," I say, releasing him as I look up into his eyes.

He stiffens. "You were fine," he says. "I'm sure it was surprising."

"Still, I wish I had said more. . . . And I'm sorry for earlier, too. I should have let you tell Lainey on your own terms."

"It's okay. It's better that it's out," he says, glancing past me. "Where is your girl, anyway?"

"She's in the shower," I say, then ask if we can talk for a second.

"Sure," he says, nodding.

After we walk out onto the balcony and sit down, I cut right to the chase. "Do you think that what happened between you and Summer is holding you back?"

He freezes for several seconds, then says, "What do you mean?"

"I mean—with other women? With Nicole?"

"Oh, shit," he says. "You're *really* going in now."

"I have to," I say. "I care about you."

He lets out a long sigh, then says, "Maybe. A little. I still feel so guilty."

"Guilty for what?"

"That I didn't protect her."

"You had no way of protecting her," I say, thinking about the phone call I didn't make sooner. "There's no way anyone could have known what was coming."

He nods. "I know that. Rationally. But it's still hard. . . . I was right there in her room. . . . I almost stayed over. *Fuck*. If I had just stayed with her."

"You can't think like that," I say.

"It's impossible not to—"

"I know—"

"And a small part of me wonders if Summer felt . . . I don't know . . . that I didn't have her back."

"That's crazy talk," I say. "You *always* had her back. You were her number one supporter."

"Yeah. In some ways . . . And I know I was a good friend. . . . But I feel like I would have disappointed her."

"How?"

"It's hard to explain. . . . The road we were on was just . . . complicated. . . . I was attracted to her—and of course I loved her—but deep down, I think she wanted more from me than I might have been able to give her. It's almost like I feel guilty for something that never even happened."

I nod, trying to process what he's telling me. "Wait. Are you talking about a breakup?"

"Yes," he says.

"Oh," I say, things shifting around in my mind. "So you think you may have broken her heart?"

"Yes. I worry that I would have," he says again. "And I can't bear the thought of it."

"Oh, Tyson," I say.

He hesitates, then tells me about an argument they had a couple of days before she died. Summer had been upset that Tyson and I had gone to the mall without asking her to join us. She'd even gone so far as to ask Tyson if he'd ever kissed me.

I look at him, shocked. It doesn't sound like Summer at all.

"You told her no, right?"

"Of course I did. But the whole thing just confused me. It made me feel like we shouldn't have crossed that line. I regretted kissing her. At the same time, I wanted to kiss her again. . . . Either way, I was scared that I was going to mess up not only my relationship with her but the friendship of all four of us."

"That didn't happen, though," I say.

"I know that," he says, nodding. "But, Hannah, don't you see?"

"See what?"

"What *did* happen was way worse."

"Meaning you'll never know what could have been?" I ask him.

Tyson gives me an incredulous look, then shakes his head. "Meaning she *died*, Hannah. I mean, who the fuck cares what would have happened between the two of us? Even if we'd had an ugly breakup—and it blew up our friendship—she'd still *be* here. I was worried about the wrong things."

I lower my eyes and nod.

CHAPTER 18

LAINEY

THAT EVENING, HANNAH and I are in the bathroom, primping for dinner, when my agent texts. She says she's about to call, and I need to pick up—it's important.

The phone rings one second later. I answer it on speakerphone, so I can finish contouring my cheeks with a bronzing stick.

"Are you sitting down?" she asks me.

Hannah and I exchange a look in the mirror.

I freeze, then yell at her. "That's a terrible question, Casey! This better be good news."

"It *is*. It's *fantastic* news."

I breathe a sigh of relief and resume my contouring. "You're lucky," I say. "What's going on?"

"You remember the big audition you just blew off?"

It's clearly a rhetorical question considering the amount of shit she gave me for the decision.

"Vaguely," I say as Hannah winces.

"Well, it turns out that your little hard-to-get maneuver worked. Because . . ." Casey pauses, keeping me in suspense. "They. Want. *You.*"

"They want me for what? Sales Associate Number 2?"

"No, Lainey. They want you for the lead! They want you to play the Pigeon Girl."

Hannah gasps, then covers her mouth with both hands.

"Is that so?" I say, waiting for the catch.

"Yes. I just got off the phone with Brad."

"*Pitt?*" Hannah whisper-shouts.

I shake my head.

"Lainey?" Casey says. "Did you hear me? You're Brad's first choice!"

Hannah grabs my forearm, gripping it tightly in excitement.

"Ow," I say, pulling away from her.

"Lainey? Are you there?"

"Hmm. Yes. I'm here," I say. "So who else passed on it?"

"Nobody. They asked you first."

"Wow. That's incredible," I deadpan, then whistle. "They wanted me over *Margot Robbie?*"

"Margot Robbie is way too pretty for this role."

"Why, thank you." I smile.

"You know what I mean, Lainey. This character is not a blond bombshell. She's a quirky brunette. You read the script, didn't you?"

"Yeah," I say, though it was more of a quick skim than a read. I had been planning to do a deep dive on my flight to L.A. But then Hannah called.

"So if you actually *read* it, you should realize that Margot Robbie isn't right for this role—"

"What about Issa Rae? Rose Byrne? Kristen Bell? Anna Kendrick?

America Ferrara?" I rattle off. All comedic actors. All bigger names than I am.

"They're too old to play this role. At thirty-two, you're on the cusp of being too old yourself."

"Again. Thank you." I laugh.

"Hey. No point in sugarcoating it."

"What about Emma Stone? We're around the same age."

"Jeez, Lainey. I don't know. Maybe Emma *was* their first choice. Maybe she had a scheduling conflict. Maybe the script didn't speak to her. Maybe she was too expensive for their budget. This is a small indie film. But it's an amazing opportunity for *you*. Why are you trying to give this role away?"

"I'm not trying to give anything away. I'm just managing expectations," I say. "And besides, I don't like being lied to."

"Well, then you're in the wrong business, my friend." Casey chuckles.

I sigh, conceding the point, then ask if they've made me an official offer.

"No. They wanted to check on your availability first."

"And? What's the timing?"

"Well, that's the only small catch. They would need you soon."

"How soon?"

"Next week."

"Next *week*?"

"Yes, but only for two scenes. It's, like, a four-day shoot. Five max. The rest of the filming is scheduled for August and September."

"Well, then it's a moot point. Next week doesn't work for me," I say.

Hannah looks at me, aghast, then whispers, "Yes! It does!"

"Why doesn't it work for you?" Casey demands.

"Because I'm on a trip with my friends. I already told you that," I say, as Tyson pops his head into the doorway.

He's clearly been eavesdropping on our entire conversation; he looks as appalled as Hannah.

"I'm sure your friends will understand once you explain."

As Tyson and Hannah start nodding, I close my eyes and turn my back on them, feeling my stubborn streak kicking in. "I'm sorry, Casey. Next week is out of the question," I say, determined not to let work—*any* work—interfere with our time together.

Casey groans and calls me impossible.

I apologize again but hold firm.

After a long pause, Casey says, "Okay, Lainey. If that's your decision, that's your decision. But as your agent, I have a duty to tell you that I think you're making a huge mistake. And as your *friend*, I can tell you that you're a complete idiot—"

"It won't be the first time," I say. "Or the last."

Casey lets out a loud, weary sigh, then says, "When do you return from your trip? I can see if they can push it back a bit."

"Not for another couple of weeks. We're in Capri now—as you know—and then we're headed to Paris. We don't even have a return flight booked."

She sighs. "Okay. But could you at least ask your friends how they'd feel about a few days in Buenos Aires instead of Paris? They could come with you."

"Hell, yes!" Tyson says right out. "I'd love to go to Argentina!"

Casey hears him and says, "See?"

Tyson grabs the phone from me and says, "The answer is yes, Casey."

She laughs. "Thank God! Someone there has some sense!"

"Yes. *Someone* does," Tyson says, smiling. "I'll give the phone back to Lainey now, but please know that her entourage will be sure she gets to Argentina."

THE SECOND I hang up with Casey, Hannah and Tyson both pile onto me, hugging me as hard as they can. Hannah's enthusiasm is on brand, but Tyson's reaction is surprisingly effusive.

"Are you sure about this?" I say, looking at Hannah. "I feel bad about Paris."

"Are you kidding me?" she replies. "Paris can wait."

"But you've already been waiting so long," I say.

"Exactly. So what's a little longer? Besides, we're going to Buenos Aires!" Hannah says.

"Vamos, Argentina!" Tyson belts out, pumping his fist in the air.

I smile, then say, "Maybe we can still go to Paris *after* Argentina?"

"Maybe," Hannah says. "But I think I'd be pushing my luck with Jada if we did that."

I nod, as Tyson and Hannah both stare at me, grinning.

"Holy hell, Lainey," Tyson says. "This is incredible."

"I know! You're going to be a *movie* star!" Hannah says.

"Yeah, right," I say, waving them both off. "You heard her. It's a small indie film."

"Still. It's a *movie*," Hannah says.

"Yeah. You got the lead role in a goddamn *movie*." Tyson smiles and shakes his head like he can't believe it.

He proceeds to walk out of the bathroom, and a second later, I hear him on the phone, calling down to Alessandro. He shares my news and asks for a bottle of champagne to be sent to the room. He then asks if we can possibly change our reservation to something less casual. More celebratory.

After a long pause, Tyson says, "Yes. That's perfect. I appreciate you, man."

I walk into the bedroom, look at him, and say, "Who are you and what did you do with Tyson?"

He shrugs, giving me an "aw shucks" look. "I can't help it," he says. "I'm so proud."

"Of little ol' me?"

"Yes, *you.*" He grins.

I smile back at him, a feeling of warmth filling my chest. He's always been supportive of my acting, but this time feels different—probably because it is. I can act blasé all I want to, but the three of us know that this is a way bigger deal than being part of a large ensemble cast on a Hulu show.

Hannah and I finish doing our makeup, then join Tyson on the balcony.

"So what did Alessandro say, anyway?" I ask.

"He said to congratulate you. He didn't know you were an actor."

"That's sweet," I say. "But I meant what did he say about *dinner?*"

"Oh. That. He got us into L'Olivo. In Anacapri. It has two Michelin stars."

"We don't need anything *that* fancy," I say.

"Yeah, we do," Tyson says. "This is big-time. Now, c'mon. Give us the full scoop."

"I really don't know much yet," I say, trying to remember what Casey told me back when I thought I was a long shot for the part and that going to L.A. was probably a waste of my time. "It's a romantic comedy. Called *The Pigeon Girl.*"

Tyson's eyes light up. "Oh, very cool. I love pigeons."

"And you made fun of Gus for loving dogs?" I say with a smirk.

"First of all, I didn't make *fun* of him. I just told him to get the hell out of my room. Second of all, pigeons are actually *smarter* than dogs."

"Yeah, right!" I laugh.

"True statement," Tyson says, nodding. "I saw a documentary on them. They're smart as shit. They pass the mirror test of self-recognition. They can differentiate letters of the alphabet, as well as human faces. One just sold for almost two million dollars in a bidding war."

"Why would *anyone* spend that kind of money on a bird?" I ask.

"Pigeon racing. It's a thing."

"That's nuts," I say, as the reality of my news starts to sink in. I sit up a little straighter, feeling a wave of pride.

"And what does the Pigeon Girl do, exactly?" Tyson asks.

"The typical romantic comedy thing," I say. "She falls in love, gets her heart broken, pieces her life back together. You know the drill."

"Yes. But I mean—what does she do with *pigeons?*" Tyson asks. "Why is she called that? Does she train them? Raise them? Collect them?"

"I didn't read the whole thing yet. But she has, like, one as a pet—and I think she has it deliver a message to this guy she likes—"

"See? That's what I'm trying to tell you! They're smart as shit!" Tyson says.

"Is it a happy ending?" Hannah asks.

Tyson immediately puts his hands over his ears, closes his eyes, and says, "Hey. No spoilers."

"It's a romantic comedy, Tyson," I say. "There's your big clue that the ending is happy."

"Whatever. I like to be surprised."

"Since when?" I ask.

"Since *now*," he says.

"Who else is in it?" Hannah asks.

"I'm not sure. Casey mentioned Adam Driver a few weeks back, but I don't know if they got him. . . . Oh! And Andrew McCarthy is my father."

"Oh my gosh!" Hannah says. "Summer would be so happy! She loved *Pretty in Pink*!"

"And *St. Elmo's Fire*." I glance nervously at Tyson. If he's fazed by Hannah's mention of Summer, he hides it.

"Who's the director?" he asks.

"Ed Burns . . . Oh, and I lied," I say, smiling at Hannah. "My agent actually *was* talking about Brad Pitt."

"Oh, my goodness! I knew it!" Hannah squeals.

"Wow," Tyson says, shaking his head as he stares at me with such sweet sincerity and pride. "This is incredible, Lainey. Congratulations."

"Thank you," I say, hit by a wave of déjà vu. The moment feels so familiar, yet I know it hasn't happened before. I chalk it up to a dream.

A few minutes later, the champagne arrives. Tyson opens the bottle, then pours our glasses. As he raises his and says, "To our movie star," I realize where I've seen the expression on his face.

It was the way he used to look at Summer during her races. I can so clearly picture him now, leaning over the chain-link fence encircling the track, yelling her name, and cheering for her. At cross-country meets, we could get closer to her, finding her at the finish line. Sometimes she'd be gripping her knees, catching her breath, her chest heaving, her cheeks bright red. Other times, she would be collapsed on the ground, flat on her back, covered with sweat and grass and dirt—and sometimes, when she got spiked, blood.

Regardless of her performance, Tyson always looked at Summer with pure respect and intense admiration.

"Thank you," I say now, holding his gaze, then smiling at Hannah just before we all take our first sip of champagne.

As Tyson looks out over the horizon, I admire his profile. At some point I think you stop noticing the way your friends look. You just see them as who they are. But in this moment, he looks so handsome.

I feel a wave of affection for him—along with a deep appreciation for his friendship. I'm just so glad he's in my life. That he and Hannah *both* are.

He suddenly turns and looks at me. "What?"

I shake my head and smile. "Nothing."

"Then why are you giving me that look?" he asks, almost seeming self-conscious.

I lower my gaze and run with it. "Your jacket," I say.

"What about it?"

"It's wrinkled."

"It's linen," he says, smoothing one lapel, then the other. "Linen can be a little wrinkled."

"Hmm. Well, it's a *lot* wrinkled. You might want to iron it or something."

"You might want to mind your business," he says.

"You might want to get a life."

He stares at me a beat, shrugs, then says, "Why the fuck you ain't eat it cold?"

I burst out laughing as Hannah looks at both of us, confused. "Eat *what* cold?" she asks.

"A ham sandwich," I say, still laughing as Tyson beams back at me.

"Huh?" Hannah says.

I try to explain the viral video Tyson shared with me a few years back. It was an argument between two little boys in which one burns his sandwich and the other asks him why he didn't just eat it cold.

"I still don't get it," Hannah says.

"It's like the 'Charlie bit me' video," I say. "You have to see it to get why it's funny."

"Oh," she says, nodding.

"Trust me," I say, smiling at Tyson and enjoying our inside joke. "It's hilarious."

CHAPTER 19

TYSON

'M SO PROUD of Lainey. I always have been—more than she probably realizes. As much as she half-asses a lot of things in her life,
she really *is* talented. I have her entire series recorded, and when
I'm doing laundry or other housework, I play back the episodes.
Her scenes always shine, and she never fails to make me laugh out
loud.

But I sometimes wondered if I was a bit biased. Or simply enjoying the novelty of seeing a friend on the screen. Now I know that's
not the case. If anything, it means she's even *better* than I thought
she was, and I'm so damn happy for her big break. Part of me also
hopes that this will be the catalyst she needs to start taking her life
a little more seriously.

After a champagne toast on our balcony, we head out to dinner.
For the second time in one day, Alessandro has scored us
reservations—this time at a fancy restaurant inside the Capri Palace
Jumeirah. Afterward, we are meeting Hannah's new friend at a
nearby piano bar.

The girls are both wearing black dresses. Hannah's is knee-length and, according to Lainey, "very Audrey Hepburn." Lainey's is short, tight, and, I must admit, hot.

As we enter the hotel lobby, Alessandro rushes up to Lainey to congratulate her. He is a perfect gentleman, calling us a taxi and even coming outside to open the car door for us. But as Lainey climbs into the backseat, I catch him staring at her legs. It's harmless—and I can't blame the guy for copping a discreet look— but I still feel protective of her. I also find myself hoping that she doesn't drink too much tonight and put herself in a bad position.

It's clear what's on her agenda, though. As we pull out of the hotel driveway, she immediately says to Hannah, "I hope Archie's friend is cute."

"If he disappoints, you are more than welcome to Archie."

"No chance! He's all yours—"

Hannah laughs. "Hardly," she says. "I don't even know if I'm interested."

"Stop it. He's gorgeous."

"I think you like him more than I do! You should take him."

"Say it one more time, and I will," Lainey says with a laugh.

I shake my head and smile at her. "Are you ever *not* shameless?"

"Are you ever not self-righteous?" she says, smiling back at me.

"Okay, you two," Hannah says. "We're celebrating tonight, remember?"

"I'm trying," I say, suppressing a smile. "But the Pigeon Girl isn't making it easy."

Lainey laughs, then says, "You know what? I think we should make a deal. We all get laid tonight."

"Lainey, hush," Hannah says under her breath. She glances up at the taxi driver, looking mortified.

"Oh, don't be such a prude," Lainey says.

"I'm not being a prude," she says. "That's just so . . . I don't know . . ."

"Predatory?" I finish for her.

"How is that *predatory*?" Lainey says. "We'd obviously be with consenting adults!"

"Still. How would you like to be on the receiving end of that kind of 'deal'?" I ask her.

She raises her eyebrows. "That would depend entirely on how good looking he is."

I shake my head, smile, and say it again: *Shameless.*

OUR DINNER IS as incredible as Alessandro promised. We go with the tasting menu plus wine pairings, and every dish looks like a work of art. *Too pretty to eat,* Hannah keeps saying, as Lainey snaps photographs of her plates. After dessert and a sweet Vin Santo, the bill comes. I grab it.

"What are you doing?" Lainey asks.

"I got this one," I say. "My treat."

Hannah thanks me as Lainey pats my arm and says, "I guess chivalry's not dead, after all."

"It's not chivalry. It's just my official congratulations to you," I say. "Don't get used to it."

Lainey laughs, then says, "Shall we head to this piano bar or what?"

"Can we go over a few safety guidelines first?" I say.

"Safety guidelines or morality policing?" Lainey asks.

"Just don't go wandering off, please. And keep your eye on your drinks."

"Oh, wow. You think Archie is going to try to roofie Hannah?" Lainey asks me with a smirk.

"Who knows?" I say. "I'm sure he's great. He's probably a good guy, but you just never know. Ted Bundy seemed great."

"Jeez! You're such a buzzkill!" Lainey says. "And I really don't think there's much crime on *islands*. The escaping part would be a challenge."

"Well, let's put aside the fact that we already covered Friedrich Krupp and Jeffrey Epstein—both committing sex crimes on islands. Have you ever heard of Mary Jo Kopechne?"

"Who?"

"Chappaquiddick? An island," I say. "Or how about Natalee Holloway on Aruba? Also an island."

Lainey shudders. "That story still haunts me. Thank God they finally got that asshole to confess."

"All right. Now that we've established that bad shit can happen to you while on a piece of land surrounded by water . . . can everyone please make sure they have their Life360 turned on?"

"I do," Hannah says, as Lainey nods.

"And let us know if you leave the bar," I say, staring at Lainey. "Okay?"

"Sure thing," Lainey says. "And if I get in any trouble, I'll send you a message via carrier pigeon."

"Okay, smart-ass," I say, trying not to smile. "Get yourself kidnapped. See if I care."

ACCORDING TO GOOGLE MAPS, the bar where we're meeting Archie and his friend is only nine hundred meters from the restaurant. But the streets are dark, and we're all a bit tipsy, so we grab a cab. The ride is so quick that we laugh at ourselves as I pay the fare and we all pile out at the San Michele Hotel.

We go inside, following the sound of music to Lanterna Verde.

The bar is carved out of white limestone and has a wall of windows overlooking the Gulf of Naples. With pulsing dance music, swirling colored lights, and a cheesy star-spangled ceiling, the vibe is more psychedelic nightclub than chill piano bar, but I have a nice buzz and roll with it.

On our way to the bar, Hannah spots Archie and his friend, sitting at a table by the windows, beers in hand. She and Lainey walk over to them.

Trailing behind, I watch Hannah tap Archie on the shoulder. He turns, beams up at her, then stands and kisses her on one cheek, followed by the other. By the time I catch up, introductions are under way.

"This is Ian," I hear Archie say as the girls greet him.

I smile to myself because Lainey nailed the description of the jovial sidekick right down to his beer belly and unruly beard.

Hannah follows suit, introducing Lainey and me.

We both say hello, and as Ian immediately starts working Lainey, Archie turns to me and smiles.

"How're you liking Capri?" he shouts over the music.

"So far, so good," I shout back.

Archie points out the window. "Stunning views around here, aren't there?"

"Yes," I say, looking down at the sparkling lights of the town and harbor. "Everywhere you turn."

Archie smiles, then says, "Hannah says you went to uni together?"

"Yeah. A long time ago," I say. "How about you and Ian?"

"Known each other since birth," Archie says. "Our *mums* went to uni together."

"That's real," I say.

Archie smiles, then holds up his empty pint glass. "I'm getting another. What can I get everyone?" he asks, looking around at all of us.

"I'll get this round," I say, thinking there's no way I'm going to let another guy buy our first drinks. "What do you girls want?" I ask Hannah and Lainey.

"A glass of prosecco, please," Hannah says.

"Dirty martini," Lainey says. "Extra cold, extra dirty."

I look at Ian and Archie. Ian says he's good, while Archie offers to come with me. We head toward the bar. It's crowded, but we manage to find a sliver of real estate. As Archie rests his elbow on the counter, I notice that his wrist is adorned with several braided leather bracelets with gold hardware. They look expensive, as do his clothes.

"So where are you from, Tyson?" Archie asks me.

"Washington, D.C.," I say.

He nods and asks if I work for the U.S. government.

"No. I'm just a regular lawyer," I say, remembering that I'm currently an *unemployed* lawyer. "What about you?"

"I work in agriculture," he says cryptically.

I nod, getting the distinct feeling that Archie isn't out there farming the land himself. "Any particular crop?" I ask, wondering if it's a stupid question.

It doesn't seem to be, as Archie says, "Oh, gee. A bit of everything. Spring barley, winter wheat, strawberries, raspberries, black currants, turnips, and swedes."

"What's a swede?" I ask.

"It's like a rutabaga."

"Gotcha," I say, although that doesn't really clear things up for me.

"Barley is our main crop, though."

"Is this a family business?" I ask, suddenly picturing Randolph and Mortimer Duke illegally trading on orange crop reports in the Eddie Murphy classic *Trading Places*.

Archie nods as it occurs to me that Hannah has only ever dated wealthy white guys. That might be part of her problem, I think. I remind myself there is nothing that precludes rich white men from being good guys—Archie could very well be one of them.

A second later, the bartender approaches us. I order the girls' drinks, then motion toward Archie.

"I'll take a pint of Birra Moretti," he says.

"Make that two," I say, sliding my credit card across the bar.

As we wait for our drinks and listen to the band, Archie and I continue to chat. At one point, I look over my shoulder, making eye contact with Lainey. I pause, expecting her to smile or wave or even flip me off, but she just stares back at me with an odd look on her face. I turn around as the bartender puts down our drinks and hands me the receipt to sign.

I sign my name while Archie grabs one of the pints along with Hannah's prosecco. "Thanks, mate," he says with a nod.

"No problem," I say as Lainey suddenly appears beside me.

"What's up?" I ask as she takes Archie's place at the bar. "Did you change your mind?"

"About what?" she asks.

"About your drink?" I say, gesturing toward her martini.

She shakes her head, plucks it off the bar, and takes a big gulp.

"So why'd you come over?" I give her a suspicious look, then say, "You're not about to order a shot, are you?"

"Oh my God, Tyson. I'm not getting a *shot*," she says, as if that isn't her very common M.O. upon arriving at a bar. "I just came over to thank you." She holds up her martini, then takes another sip.

"It's only a drink, Lainey."

"It's not *only* a drink. It was dinner, too. And the champagne before dinner—" she says.

"The champagne's going on our hotel bill," I say.

"You know what I mean," she says, staring solemnly into my eyes.

I wait for the punch line or the dig, but she just keeps looking at me, without a trace of a smile or any of her usual antics. "You're being really nice—and I appreciate it."

I nod, then say, "Well, I'm very happy for you. And proud of you."

"Thank you. That means a lot," she says.

Her expression is so serious that I start to feel off balance.

"Okay. What's going on? Did something happen with Ian?"

She shakes her head. "No. Nothing *happened*. What could have possibly happened? We just got here."

"I know, but you're acting kind of weird."

"I'm not acting weird. I just wanted to thank you." She pauses, then takes a deep breath. "I also wanted to say that I'm sorry. About our conversation. At lunch."

"You have nothing to be sorry for," I say, brushing her off.

"Yes, I do," she says. "I shouldn't have pressed you like that."

"It's okay, Lainey."

"No, it's *not* okay. It was insensitive." She takes a deep breath, then says, "And since lunch, I've been thinking about that terrible week. How upset you were with me after it happened—"

It, I think.

A singular, neuter, impersonal pronoun—and one of the simplest two-letter words in the English language. And yet, right now, out of Lainey's mouth, *it* covers so much. *It* sums up the worst hour, day, week, and month of my life, as well as the *end* of Summer's life. *It* sums up Lainey getting drunk and blowing off Summer's parents, then going to party in Myrtle Beach.

"Lainey, you've already apologized for that, too. It's ancient history."

"I know it's ancient history—but I can see now that my actions must have hurt you even more than I realized. We all lost our best friend . . . but you lost even more than that. And I'm just so sorry."

"Thank you," I say. "That means a lot. I promise we're all good."

She lowers her head, then nods. I put my arm around her shoulders.

"Now, c'mon," I say. "Let's go have a good time."

THE NIGHT TURNS out to be pretty fun. Archie and Ian are both cool, and the five of us mix it up with other random people, too. Funnily enough, the girl Lainey accused me of flirting with when we first arrived in town is here. Lainey points her out in a wildly obvious way.

"Who dat?" I say, squinting across the dance floor.

"You know exactly who *dat* is. You never forget a face," she says as the woman starts swiveling her hips on the dance floor. "Or an ass."

"Whatever, Lainey." I laugh just as the woman catches us staring at her.

Lainey motions for her to come over to us.

"What are you doing?" I say.

"I'm getting the show on the road. You obviously need help."

"Trust me. I do *not* need any help," I say as the woman approaches us.

The Lainey effect, I think. Everyone follows her orders. People taking photos for her, hotel concierges, pretty girls in bars. *Everyone.*

A second later, the woman is standing in front of me, smiling. "Didn't I see you in the Piazzetta the other day?"

"You did," I say.

"And he's been talking about you ever since!" Lainey says.

I roll my eyes and smile. "I'm Tyson," I say. "This is my trouble-making friend Lainey."

The woman laughs and says, "Ciao, Tyson. Ciao, Lainey. I'm Amore."

"Amore?" Lainey says, nudging me with her elbow. "As in *love*?"

Amore laughs and nods.

"Well, could that be any more perfect?" Lainey says, looking at me.

Amore laughs again as I point over at Ian. "Hey, Lainey. I think your boy is looking for you. You better get going."

She gives me an over-the-top wink before sashaying back to Ian.

"Your friend is funny," Amore says.

I shake my head and say, "You have no idea."

We both smile as I ask where she's from.

"I'm from Torino."

"Ah, Turin!" I say, nodding. "That's close to Milan, right?"

"Sì." Her eyes light up as she gives me an alluring smile. "Would you like to dance?"

"Sure," I say.

Before I know it, I'm twirling Amore around the dance floor to a Shakira song.

When it finally ends, and Amore makes her way back to her friends, Lainey finds me and says, "I thought you hated to dance?"

"I *do* hate it," I say.

"Could've fooled me. I wish I had a video of all that do-si-do stuff." She snaps, then holds up her phone. "Oh, wait! I *do* have a video."

"Lainey!" I say, grabbing for it. "Delete that right now!"

She pulls her phone out of my reach, then slides it back into her purse. "Nope! I may need it one day."

I shake my head, pretending to be more bothered than I am, as Lainey motions toward Hannah, who is getting cozy in the corner with Archie. "They seem to be hitting it off."

"Yep." I nod, feeling happy for Hannah.

"What about Amore?" Lainey asks me. "You gonna do her?"

I blink, determined not to give her the reaction she wants. "You gonna *do* Ian?"

She grins. "Maybe. He's cute. I like his beard."

"You should go for it," I say.

"Hey. What happened to 'you're going to wind up dead in the ocean'?" Lainey says.

"Well, I'd prefer that you come home with me—" I stop, realizing how that sounds.

She hears it, too, raising her eyebrows. "Oh, really?"

"Not like *that*!" I say, rolling my eyes. "What I *meant* is, I'd prefer that we all call it a night. But you're gonna do what you're gonna do."

"Yes. I am," she says, giving me a sultry look as she pulls her shoulders back and pushes her breasts out.

The maneuver isn't unprecedented; Lainey flirts like she breathes. But it's been a long time since she's tried it with me.

I shake my head.

"What?" she asks, her voice turning coy.

"Nothing." I smile, determined not to play her little games.

.   .   .

THE FIVE OF us are now in a taxi van, heading back down the mountain toward our hotel. Lainey is sitting between me and a very eager Ian, who is busy firing off jokes and desperately trying to get her attention. Archie and Hannah are behind us, in the third row, whispering and giggling and, by the sound of it, kissing. As we approach our hotel, I wonder if Hannah will be getting out of the car or going back to Archie's. I can't tell what Lainey's plan is, either, but at one point, she puts her hand on Ian's thigh.

When the cab pulls up to the front door, I get out of the car, waiting to see what the girls do. When neither makes a move, I pull a twenty-euro note out of my wallet, reach across Lainey, and offer it to Ian.

"No way, mate," he says, shaking his head. "You got more rounds."

"Yeah. We still owe you," Archie chimes in.

I thank them, then ask the girls if they have a room key.

"I have one," Hannah says.

"Okay, then. Stay together. I don't want to get out of bed to open the door."

"Yes, sir!" Lainey says, giving me a salute.

I shut the door and head into the hotel, feeling an irrational dash of disappointment that the night is over. I tell myself it's for the best. I've had a lot to drink and need to go to bed.

I pass Alessandro's desk, his lamp turned off for the evening, then reach the elevator. As I push the button, I hear the clack of footsteps on the marble floor behind me, along with Lainey's voice calling, "Wait up, dummy."

I suppress a smile, then turn around to look at her. "What happened?" I ask her. "Did you change your mind?"

"Change my mind about what?" she asks, as we step into the elevator.

"About Ian," I say, pushing the button for our floor.

"No, I didn't change my mind about *Ian*," she says as the doors close. "I changed my mind about something *else*."

"And what's that?" I ask, feeling a jolt of energy pass between us.

"You'll see," she says.

CHAPTER 20

HANNAH

W E LEAVE THE bar well after midnight, the five us getting in a cab together. Tyson tells the driver that we'll be making multiple stops, then gives him our hotel first. It feels like a foregone conclusion that I will be going back to Archie's hotel. The two of us pushed the envelope of good taste on the dance floor. PDA has never been my style—not even in college bars and frat houses, where such things were commonplace. But right now, in the far back of the taxi, as Archie kisses my neck and runs his hand over the bodice of my dress, it occurs to me that maybe it *is* my style. Maybe my mother just programmed me to be prudish, believing that owning your sexuality was shameful, something "nice girls" didn't do.

I get an involuntary flashback of Grady and Berlin in bed together. Although the images are still disturbing, they are no longer gut-wrenching, and for the first time, it crosses my mind that perhaps a physical connection was missing from our relationship. I always found Grady handsome, and I could tell he thought I was attractive as well, but there was never much passion between us, not even in the early days of our relationship. Looking back, I have the feeling he almost viewed me as a doll—*his* doll—something to be shown off in public but never ravaged. To be fair, I wasn't that into sex with him, either. Once we got going, I liked it fine, but it often felt obligatory.

As we pull up to our hotel, Tyson gets out of the cab while the rest of us stay put.

"Where to next?" Ian asks, glancing back at Archie, then looking over at Lainey. "One more drink in town?"

Lainey pauses, then says, "I'm beat, actually. Raincheck?"

"Sure. Cool," Ian says, sounding more than a little disappointed.

As Lainey gets out of the car, closing the door and scampering after Tyson, Archie suggests a nightcap at La Capannina.

"That sounds great," I say.

"You kids go ahead," Ian says, yawning and playing the good wingman. "I'm pretty knackered and going to head back to the hotel."

"You sure?" Archie says.

"Positive, mate," Ian says with a wink. "And no need to be quiet when you get back. I'm a very sound sleeper."

"SO LAINEY WASN'T into Ian?" Archie asks as we stroll into town. The streets are wet from a brief rainstorm, and a mist rises from the cobblestones.

"I think she's just anxious about her movie and getting rest. She wants to read the script tomorrow."

"I can't wait to check out her work," he says.

"And I can't wait to see her on set next week. Hopefully, they'll let us watch. I've never seen her in her professional milieu."

"So they're filming in Argentina?"

"Yeah. We were supposed to go to Paris next week, but we figured what the hell." I hesitate, then tell him about Grady and the whole genesis of our travels.

"Holy *crap!*" Archie says. "What a hurdie."

"I'm assuming that's not a compliment?" I ask with a laugh.

"Definitely not," Archie says. "I'm really sorry that happened to you, Hannah."

"Thank you. But I think it's for the best," I say, realizing that I just broke the cardinal rule of first dates, hangouts, or whatever this is. *Don't talk about your past relationships, especially your most recent ex.* I wonder if Archie now sees me as damaged goods, the way my mother does.

As we walk through the Piazzetta, I change the subject by pointing to a German shepherd lying down in the middle of the square and intently watching as a young street performer plays her violin.

"What a sweet dog!" I say. "He's listening!"

Archie pauses and smiles, then tosses a few euros into the open violin case. We resume our walk, turning onto a narrow street that feels more like an alleyway, quickly approaching the entrance of La Capannina. The stucco wall outside the restaurant is plastered with photos of celebrities who have dined here over the decades. I scan the wall, spotting Steven Tyler and Sylvester Stallone. Tucked into the corner beyond the pictures is an enchanting arched doorway— a literal hole in the wall that reminds me of illustrations in children's books of tree trunk homes inhabited by woodland creatures. I get a pang, thinking of Mole's house in *The Wind in the Willows*. It was my mother's favorite book when she was a child, and the only one I can remember her reading aloud to me. I tell myself not to start getting sentimental now.

Archie holds the door for me in a way that doesn't feel performative. So much of what Grady did was for show. He was far less likely to open my car door if we were alone. Of course, my mother ate it right up. Never mind if he cheated *behind* closed doors, so long as he held *other* doors open for me.

Archie checks in with the hostess before we make our way to the wine bar, settling into two cozy red velvet chairs in the corner. A friendly bartender immediately says hello, then tells us they offer more than four hundred labels.

"Just let me know if you have questions," she says, handing us a wine list.

As she turns aways, Archie asks what I'm in the mood for.

"I'm thinking red," I say, knowing that's a ridiculously basic answer when you're sitting in a wine bar in Capri. "Why don't you just pick for me?" I add with a smile.

As Archie nods and studies the list, I take the opportunity to check my phone. Olivia and I have been chatting on and off all evening, and there's a new text from her now.

> Okay. Just going to throw this out there. What if I came to Capri tomorrow? I have a free day, and my gut is telling me to come. Carpe Diem and all of that. . . . I'm obviously dying to meet Lainey, but if you really think that's a bad idea, I would still love to meet her best friend! ☺

I stare down at my phone, feeling a rush of excitement as I type, Please come! I want to meet you!

My heart racing, I return the phone to my clutch, tuning back in to hear Archie asking the bartender about a particular Amalfi wine. She reports that it has notes of ripe, dark fruit, smoked meat, and tobacco with a spicy finish.

Archie nods, then says, "I'm not sure about smoked meat and tobacco. Maybe something a bit lighter?"

A back-and-forth ensues until Archie finally makes a decision, going with two of the best-known appellations of Aglianico wines—one from Campania's Taurasi and the other from Basilicata's Aglianico del Vulture.

"We can compare and share," he says. "Our own mini-tasting."

I smile and say, "Perfect."

"Now, where were we?" he says, leaning closer to me.

"I can't remember," I say, doing my best to suppress a yawn.

I don't know whether it's my buzz wearing off or that I'm too busy thinking about Olivia's text, but my mood has shifted.

"You look so tired," Archie says. "Am I keeping you up past your bedtime?"

His question seems sweet, not passive-aggressive, but I still feel guilty—like I'm not being a fun date. I tell myself that's ridiculous. I'm allowed to be tired. I'm allowed to change my mind about what I want to happen tonight. And I'm allowed to respond in a way that might not please a man.

"I *am* pretty sleepy," I say.

"Should I cancel our order?" he asks me.

"Maybe we should just split a glass?"

Archie hesitates, then says, "Let's get both, but we don't have to finish them."

I nod and smile. Over the next thirty minutes, we share a pleasant conversation and two glasses of exceptional wine.

Afterward, Archie pays the bill and we stroll back to my hotel. When we arrive, he walks me the whole way into the lobby and over to the elevator, pressing the button. I can tell he's disappointed by the way the evening is turning out. A small part of me feels a letdown, too—it would have been nice to be swept away by passion, drunken or otherwise.

"What are you all doing tomorrow?" Archie asks me.

"I'm not sure," I say—which I guess isn't a total lie.

Archie nods, then says, "Ian and I may do the Blue Grotto if the weather is nice. You're welcome to join."

"Okay. And if not tomorrow, let's definitely get together before we leave," I say, thinking I'm not sure it's going to be a love connection, but I'm glad we met and would love to stay in touch.

As the elevator doors open, Archie smiles, then leans down and kisses my cheek. "Nighty night, Hannah," he says.

CHAPTER 21

LAINEY

S OMETHING IS HAPPENING between Tyson and me. It feels like a gravitational pull, though I'm having trouble figuring out if it's one-sided or mutual. Whatever the case, it grows stronger the more I drink and the later it gets. I want to be near him in a way that I've never felt before. It makes no sense. It makes even *less* sense that I find myself feeling territorial and a little jealous as Tyson dances with the gorgeous woman he first spotted in town yesterday. He actually turned his head and did a double take *both* times he saw her. I can't say I blame him. She looks like a runway model.

My jealousy takes me by complete surprise. I'm *never* jealous when it comes to guys—or really anything. It's an unfamiliar and uncomfortable emotion, and I do my best to make it go away.

Ian provides an excellent distraction. He's not nearly as handsome as Archie, but with cool tattoos and a beard, he has a certain grungy sex appeal. He's also a surprisingly good dancer.

As I feel myself approaching wasted territory, Tyson brings me a large glass of water and tells me to drink it.

"You said you wouldn't judge," I say, taking it from him and chugging it.

"I'm not judging. I just don't want to clean up puke tonight." He smiles.

"Fair enough," I say, kissing his cheek, then drinking the rest of the glass.

"Where's Amore?" I say.

"She left."

"Did you get her number?"

"As a matter of fact, I did."

"Look at you!" I say, punching his shoulder, then stumbling a bit.

"Easy there," he says, grabbing my elbow and steadying me.

A few minutes later, he brings me a second glass of water. This time he hands it off to Ian and says, "Make sure she drinks that, please."

"Will do," Ian says.

Tyson thanks him, then turns and walks back to the bar.

"Are you sure he doesn't fancy you?" Ian asks as he gives me the water.

"He one hundred percent doesn't *fancy* me," I say, charmed by the expression. "He's just a bit overprotective."

Ian raises his eyebrows and says, "And you've never been together?"

"Never," I say. "Not once."

"Hmm," he says, smirking at me. "He's a better man than me."

I look at Ian, thinking, *Well, duh. Tyson is better than everyone.*

BY THE TIME we leave, I've had a test run with Ian, making out with him in a dark corner of the bar. He's a good kisser, more than meeting my expectations. As the guys hail us a cab, I tell Hannah that I think we should both go back to their hotel with them.

She gives me an uncertain look.

"You don't like him?"

"I haven't decided," she says.

"Could've fooled me," I say with a laugh. "C'mon, Han. Tyson will give me shit if I try to go there without you."

Hannah nods and says okay.

But when we pull up to our hotel, I feel that damn pull again. As Tyson gets out of the taxi, I suddenly change my mind. All I want to do is follow him.

I say good night, quickly jumping out of the car.

WHEN I CATCH up with Tyson in the lobby, he seems nonplussed. I do my best to get a reaction from him on the elevator, but it doesn't work, and as we walk back into our room, Tyson informs me that he's going to take a shower.

I raise my eyebrows and smile. "A *cold* shower?"

"No, Lainey," he says slowly, like he's speaking to a child. "A *regular* one."

I kick off my wedges, watching as he pulls a pair of basketball shorts and an old UVA T-shirt out of his duffel, then heads toward the bathroom.

"Leave the door unlocked in case I need to get in there," I call after him.

He mumbles okay, and a second later, I hear the door shut and the shower turn on.

Feeling antsy, I connect my Spotify to the speaker in the room, looking for something to set the right mood. I go with Noah Kahan, then open the balcony doors, inhaling the scent of the sea.

Meanwhile, I try to gauge my buzz. I still feel it, but it's starting to fade, so I head over to the minibar, open an airplane-size bottle of vodka, and take a long swig. *Better,* I think, then figure I might as well finish it.

I take the last swallow, then reach around to unzip my dress. After stepping out of it, I take off my strapless bra and thong, debating what to put on. I select a short black nightgown that I think will get Tyson's attention but then decide I'd like a quick shower, too.

I walk over to the bathroom, open the door, and say, "You almost done in there?"

"Yeah," Tyson yells back. "Give me two minutes."

"Okay," I say, glancing at the glass shower door, now completely fogged by steam.

I stand there, leaning naked against the sink, waiting for him to come out and see me. I know he'll accuse me of being an exhibitionist—which I guess I kind of am.

Then, suddenly, I get a better idea. Am I bold enough to do it? Of course I am. I never back down from a dare, even if it's one I invent for myself. I take a deep breath, then open the shower door just wide enough to slip through. I step in and meet his gaze. Shock value at its finest. I wait for a reaction, but he just stands there calmly holding my gaze in what feels like an R-rated game of chicken.

"Was I really taking that long?" he asks, his eyes fixed on mine. He's clearly determined not to look down, and I admire his discipline.

"Kind of," I say with a smirk, watching the water run over his shoulders and chest.

"So do you want me to get out?" he asks, blinking, then pointing toward the only exit route from the shower—which I'm currently blocking.

Suddenly, I'm speechless. Inexplicably so. I swallow, then manage to shake my head.

"Is that a no?"

"Yes, it's a no," I say. "I don't want you to get out."

"Okay, then," he says, staring back at me. "What are you doing here, exactly?"

His expression is impossible to read. It could be anything from pissed to annoyed to bored to amused. He might even be turned on, but that feels like a long shot given that he's still not lowering his eyes.

I stand there, now not only speechless but flustered.

"No comment, huh?" he asks me with the slightest trace of a smile.

I shiver, then say, "I just wanted to join you. . . . I was cold."

He raises his eyebrows, nods, then moves toward the wall, making space for me under the showerhead.

"Well, then," he says. "Come on over."

When I still don't move, Tyson takes a step toward me. He reaches out and encircles my waist with both of his hands, then gently pulls me closer to him. It's an incredibly hot maneuver, but I still can't tell if he has a sexual thought in his head. Frustrating and intoxicating at once. His face and body now inches from mine, we stand under the hot water together.

As I take a deep breath, his hands slide slowly from my waist to my hips.

He pulls me even closer, then whispers in my ear. "There," he says. "Is this what you wanted?"

CHAPTER 22

TYSON

SHOULD HAVE KNOWN when Lainey gave me that look in the elevator that she was up to something. Baiting me. She talks a big game, but she also backs it up with action. Still, I never would have predicted that she would take it this far—stepping naked into the shower with me. It's over the top even for her, and she looks incredibly proud of herself.

I've seen Lainey naked before—but only a flash here and there. This time is different. *Much* different. I carefully consider my next move. I know what I *should* do. I know I should get out of there posthaste and go straight to bed. But I feel my own stubborn streak kicking in as I hold my ground, then point-blank ask her what she's doing.

For once, she doesn't have an answer—and something in her brown eyes looks different. Softer. Almost vulnerable.

"I just wanted to join you," she says, shivering. "I was cold."

I make room for her under the water and tell her to "come on over."

She doesn't move.

After a few seconds, I reach out and gently grab her waist, pulling her toward me and under the water. I'm surprised by how small she feels in my hands and how easily she folds into my arms. I'm even more surprised that she follows my lead with none of her usual gamesmanship. It's almost as if she's a different person. As I look into her eyes, a feeling of warmth washes over me.

"There," I say right into her ear. "Is this what you wanted?"

She shudders as I move my hands to her hips, pulling her closer. She puts her face on my chest and makes a soft *oh* sound. I take it as a yes, moving my hands to her ass.

"God*damnit,* Lainey," I whisper, kissing her neck and earlobe. "Your body—"

She looks up at me and smiles. She knows how good she looks, and her confidence drives me crazy. At the same time, I feel a sense of calm. Touching Lainey feels surprisingly comfortable and familiar. Maybe I shouldn't be surprised, though. After all, there has never been any pretense or bullshit with Lainey. She is *exactly* who she has always said she is. I'm dying to kiss her, but I make myself hold back, knowing that we will take things too far if I do. Lainey isn't one to put on the brakes, and my resolve is starting to slip, too.

I look into her eyes, the warm feeling expanding in my chest. I want to freeze this moment. Savor it. But we are at a crossroads, and I know that we have to move forward or stop altogether. It's an extremely close call, but I choose the latter.

I kiss Lainey's forehead, then step around her to get out of the shower. I towel myself off and quickly throw on my shorts and a T-shirt before walking back into the bedroom.

Holy shit, I think. *What just happened?*

A moment later, Lainey appears in the bedroom, wrapped in a

towel. I look over at her, then watch as she approaches me with a subdued expression.

"Why did you get out?" she asks me.

"You know why," I say. "The better question is—why did you get *in?*"

"Because I wanted to," she says, standing in front of me and looking right into my eyes. "I'm attracted to you."

I swallow and nod. "I'm attracted to you, too," I say.

"Then why did you stop?" she asks me, looking genuinely curious.

I pause, then say, "Because I need to process this. We can't fuck up our friendship on a drunken whim."

"I guess you're right," she says, nodding.

"Yeah," I say, thinking there are other reasons, too—reasons that I can't quite articulate, even to myself. I think they have something to do with Summer and the idea that I'd be crossing a line with the second of my three best friends. It doesn't feel right.

"But for what it's worth," Lainey says, "I don't think it's a whim...."

I bite my lip, then choose my words carefully. "Maybe not, but we need to be sure."

She nods, staring at me with her big eyes. "Can we at least cuddle?"

The warm feeling invades my body again, this time overtaking me completely.

I nod, then lead her over to the bed. We lie down, putting our heads on the same pillow, her towel still wrapped around her.

"Come closer," I say, my heart beating funny.

She slides the whole way over to me, resting her head on my shoulder.

"What's happening here?" she whispers.

"I don't know," I whisper back.

"Well, what do you *think* it is?"

"Shhh," I say.

She turns her face toward me and smiles. "Did you just shush me?"

"Yes." I gently palm her face and say, "Sometimes it's okay to be quiet, Lainey."

"Okay, *Tyson,*" she whispers, putting her head back on my shoulder.

Her retort is playful, but the way she says my name makes my heart race. It doesn't make any sense. It's just Lainey, after all, my friend who has uttered my name thousands of times before. But something has changed between us.

I'm not sure how long we stay like that, but at some point, I can tell she's drifted off. Then I fall asleep, too. When I awaken, I panic, remembering Hannah. I nudge Lainey, and we both sit up.

"What time is it?" she asks, rubbing her eyes.

"It's time to get up. Hannah could be back any minute. You should probably put some clothes on," I say, as her towel slips from her body.

Lainey pulls it up, then turns her back to me and quickly changes into a pair of pajamas. It's the most modest I've ever seen her. She sits back down on the bed, but several feet away from me. I turn on the BBC. They are covering the latest in Gaza, but I can't concentrate on the news right now.

"I think you should sleep here tonight," she says, looking over at me. "In the bed with me."

"I wish. This mattress is so comfortable."

"Is that the only reason?"

I smile, but before I can answer, Hannah opens the door and walks into the room. "Well, aren't y'all adorable!" she says. "Watching TV in bed like an old married couple."

Lainey gives me a knowing glance, then looks back at Hannah. "And guess what? Tyson said he wants to sleep here tonight. With me."

"I said no such thing." I shake my head.

"Well, I don't mind taking the cot," Hannah says. "We really should be rotating anyway."

"Well, if we're rotating," I say, "*Lainey* can take the cot."

"Why *me?*" she says, the whine back in her voice.

"Why *not* you?" I say, the sharpness back in mine.

"Okay, Tyson. Please stop pretending that you aren't dying to share a bed with me. We can all see through your act."

"Well, maybe you could give me some acting lessons," I say.

Hannah ignores us, heading into the bathroom. The second the door closes, I look at Lainey, smile, then whisper, "What the heck are you doing?"

"Nothing," she says with an innocent shrug. "I'm just trying to be regular."

I give her a look that says, *Nothing about this situation is regular.*

Then I get up from the bed.

"Where are you going?" she asks me.

"To my cot. So I can think," I say, walking over and putting in my AirPods before lying down on my back.

A second later, Hannah walks out of the bathroom, and Lainey starts grilling her. I stare up at the ceiling, listening to Jason Isbell on low volume.

"So what happened with Archie?" I hear Lainey ask her. "Give us the scoop! Did you have hot sex?"

"How'd you guess?" Hannah says, rolling her eyes.

"Wow! What a coincidence. Tyson and I just hooked up, too!" Lainey says. "In the shower!"

Hannah laughs and says, "I don't think he can hear you. He has his AirPods in."

"Yeah, right," Lainey says. "He's ear-hustling. Oldest trick in the book."

I smile, then open my eyes, looking over at her. "Trust me, Lainey. I'm trying *not* to hear you."

"Likely story," she replies before turning back to Hannah. "Now. C'mon. Tell me what happened!"

"Nothing," Hannah says. "We just had a glass of wine in town."

"Why didn't you go back to his hotel?" Lainey asks.

"I thought about it . . . but I was really tired. . . . What about you and Ian? Why didn't you go back with him?"

"Meh," Lainey says. "I just wasn't feeling it."

I can't help but smile to myself.

CHAPTER 23

HANNAH

WAKE UP THE next morning with a feeling of anticipation, but it takes me a second to remember why: *Olivia is coming.* As I roll over and find Lainey still sound asleep, my excitement quickly dissipates, replaced by acute nervousness.

In the bright light of day, without the cloud of alcohol, I realize what an untenable plan Olivia and I made last night. Lainey is going to kill me. Panicking, I reach for my phone, wondering if there is still time to cancel. But I quickly discover that it's nearly eleven o'clock and Olivia's travels are well under way. She sent a text at nine-thirty that says: Getting to Naples around noon and will try to make the 12:40 ferry.

A second text just came in, reading: Hello? Are you getting these? Still okay that I'm coming??

There is no mention of Lainey, but I know that's what she means by her last question.

I take a deep breath, then text her back: Sorry! I just woke up! I will be at the dock when you arrive!

I put my phone down, looking at Lainey again. I don't like keeping a secret from her—or Tyson, for that matter—especially on a trip like this one. But I remind myself that I'm not meeting Olivia for *Lainey;* I'm meeting her for *me.* It feels like an acceptable loophole.

If, later in the day, Olivia and I decide to tell Lainey that she's come to Capri, the ball will be in her court. If she wants to meet her sister, she can. If she chooses not to, that is also fine.

Our pact, along with this trip, is about the sanctity of our friendship, but it's also about following our guts. Tyson followed his gut by breaking up with Nicole and quitting his job, and Lainey always does *exactly* what she pleases in whatever moment she's in. It's my turn now. I need to be true to myself.

I ease my way out of bed, doing my best not to disturb the sheets and blankets wrapped around Lainey. The longer she stays asleep, the more time I have to figure out what to tell her I'm doing today. I could always use Archie as my alibi, but I don't want to overtly lie. A lie of omission feels bad enough. I have a couple of hours to figure it out.

I take a shower, then apply loads of sunscreen and a little bit of makeup. After debating what to wear, I go with a canary yellow cotton midi dress and white canvas sneakers. Just as I'm leaving the room, Lainey says my name.

I turn and smile. "Good morning!"

"Where are you off to?" she asks, her head still on the pillow.

"I was just going to get some coffee. Do you want anything?"

"That's okay," she says as she sits up and gives me a once-over. "Why are you dressed so cute? Are you seeing Archie today?"

"This isn't *that* cute," I say, dodging her question.

She nods, then says, "You look good."

I thank her.

"Where's Tyson?"

"I'm not sure. He was already gone when I woke up. Maybe he's working out."

"Working *out?*" she says. "You don't think he's hungover?"

"You know Tyson doesn't really get hungover," I say. "He always stops himself before he goes too far."

Lainey nods, and I slip out the door before she can ask me any more questions.

I MILK THE clock for as long as I can in the hotel restaurant, drinking coffee and eating a chocolate croissant. When I finally return to the room, I find Tyson and Lainey on the balcony. They are both on their laptops, looking engrossed. I brush my teeth, then grab a small crossbody bag, gathering my credit card, my phone, and a room key.

"All right, y'all!" I call out to them on my way to the door. "I'm headed out for a bit."

"Wait. Where are you going?" Lainey asks me.

"For a walk," I say, my heart racing as I make nervous eye contact.

Lainey nods, then says, "I'd come with you, but I'm going to start working on my script."

"And I'm helping her," Tyson says.

"We can meet up with you a little later," Lainey says. "Assuming you aren't with Archie."

"Sounds good!" I say, turning back around.

"Have fun!" Lainey says. "Don't do anything we wouldn't do!"

I SPOT OLIVIA the second she steps off the ferry. She is wearing chambray shorts, a white tank top, and tennis shoes, with a sweatshirt tied around her waist. Her dark hair is in a short ponytail, and her only luggage is a backpack slung over one shoulder. Her gait is strong and confident, and as she nears the top of the pier, I can tell how muscular her arms and shoulders are. She definitely looks like a professional athlete, and for a second, it almost makes me want to go lift some weights.

I watch her for a few more seconds, feeling worried again. Hopefully, this visit won't result in an argument with Lainey.

As Olivia steps off the pier, she looks right at me but doesn't react. Apparently, she hasn't been stalking my Instagram the way I've been studying hers.

"Hi, Olivia," I say.

"Oh, hey!" she says, smiling, switching her backpack from one shoulder to the other. It would appear by the size of her bag that she might not be planning to stay overnight—which means we'd only have a few hours before the last ferry departs for Naples. I tell myself to make the most of our time together.

"How was your trip?" I ask.

"It wasn't too bad. Easy flight."

"You *flew*?"

"Yeah. It's, like, an eight-hour drive to Naples. I actually took a train to Genova, then flew to Naples," she says.

"Oh my gosh! I had no idea you were going to that much trouble. . . ."

"It's no trouble," she says. "It was actually very efficient."

I smile. "Well, I'm glad you're here. Are you hungry? Should we have lunch?"

"I'm always hungry!"

We stand there, grinning at each other for a few seconds, before we start walking down the narrow road, single file. A couple of minutes later, as we reach a stretch of shops and cafés, we cross the street to check them out. We pass by the first few options but eventually find a restaurant that feels nice. Ducking inside, I ask a lady clearing tables if they're still serving lunch. She nods as Olivia asks her a follow-up question in Italian. The lady responds, gesturing toward the seating area.

"Do you want to eat inside or outside?" Olivia translates.

I glance around the dining area, then point to a small table in the corner right next to an open window—a compromise. "Maybe that one?"

"That works," she says, striding over to it. She drops her backpack on the floor before taking a seat.

"Your Italian is really good," I say, sitting across from her. "Have you picked that up in the last few weeks?"

She smiles and says no, telling me that she's been working on it for a few months.

I tell her I'm terrible at foreign languages—that I took eight years of French and never achieved any sort of fluency.

"The trick is—don't be embarrassed. Try whenever you can. There is no shame in trying," she says.

I nod, thinking her advice applies to many things in life. As we review the menu, I also glance at the wine list, debating whether to have a glass. It feels a bit early in the day, especially given how much I had to drink last night.

I look back up at Olivia. "Are you going to have a glass of wine?"

"I shouldn't. Training and all of that," she says. "But you should have one. . . . And maybe I'll have a sip of yours."

I smile back at her. I've had a good feeling about Olivia since that first time we spoke on the phone, but now I *really* like her. Weirdly, it also feels like I've known her a very long time. Maybe that's because she's related to Lainey, but I doubt it, given the very different feeling I had in Ashley's living room.

Our waiter is in no rush to take our order, which seems to be

normal here. I don't mind, though. In fact, I like the feeling that
nobody ever seems to be in a hurry or bothered. When he finally
makes his way to our table, Olivia orders the risotto alla pescatora,
and I go with the spaghetti alla posillipo, ordering in Italian. I also
choose a glass of red wine.

"Good job," Olivia says, giving me a thumbs-up.

Our eyes lock, and we both smile as butterflies invade my stomach.

"Are you okay?" she asks.

"Sorry. I'm just a little nervous. I'm not sure why. . . . I guess because I haven't told Lainey you're here."

Olivia bites her lip and nods. "I figured. . . . What does she think
you're doing right now?"

"I told her I was going for a walk . . . and possibly meeting up
with this guy we all met. . . ."

Olivia raises her eyebrows and smiles. "Oh?"

"Nothing like *that*. . . . I mean, he's very cute . . . but no."

She nods, then says, "Too soon?"

"I don't think it's *that*. The idea of a rebound is appealing," I say.
"It just wasn't there, I guess. That spark."

"How are you feeling generally? About the breakup?" Olivia asks.

"I'm doing surprisingly okay. I think it might be a different story
when I get back home," I say, my heart sinking at the thought. "But
for now, I'm holding my own."

"Have you heard from your ex?"

I shake my head and say, "No. And nothing from my mother, either."

"Good," she says. "But be careful of the stealth attack. They often
come when you least expect it."

I nod, then say, "Yeah. I dread going back to it all. I really wish I
could just move away for good."

"Why can't you?"

"I don't know. . . . Where would I go?"

"Um . . . literally *anywhere*—" She gives me a big, warm smile that reminds me of Lainey.

"True," I say. "But in a way, that makes the idea of moving even more overwhelming."

"I get that," she says. "And I know your roots are in Atlanta. But if the tree is dying—" She makes a quick slashing motion that gives me a sense of what she must be like on a tennis court. "Maybe it's time to cut it down."

I nod, my stomach fluttering again.

"So. Where can you see yourself living? New York City?"

I shake my head and say, "No. Not another big city."

She nods. "What about the West Coast?"

"Too far."

"Too far from *what*?"

I smile. "Good point."

"Have you spent any time in California?"

"A little. I went to a wedding in Napa once." I hesitate, then say, "And Tyson and I went to Lainey's hometown, Encinitas. We stayed at her mother's house at the beach."

Olivia nods, then quickly looks down, rearranging the napkin on her lap.

"I'm sorry," I say. "I shouldn't have mentioned Lainey's mother."

"That's okay," she says, looking back up at me. "It is what it is."

I nod and sigh. "Yeah. I guess so."

"Is her mom still in California?"

I feel my shoulders tense, as I shake my head. "No. She died a few years ago."

"Oh, shit. I didn't know," she says. "Poor Lainey."

"Yeah," I say. "They were very close. It was terrible. . . . But I probably shouldn't be talking to you about that. I feel like it's not my place to go there with Lainey's life—"

"I understand," she says.

"I mean, we can talk about your father—and *your* relationship with him—"

"Yes. I totally get the difference," she says, nodding. "And you're right."

I smile, feeling relieved.

Olivia sighs, looking deep in thought, then points to my wine. "May I?"

"Of course. Help yourself."

She picks up my glass, then takes a sip. "Hmm. That's really good," she says, putting the glass back down in front of me. "I may need to make an exception to my training rule."

I smile, then push the glass to the middle of the table. "We can share this one."

Olivia takes another sip before she says, "I've been thinking about my father a lot lately. I guess that's no surprise, is it?"

"Not at all." I shake my head, waiting for her to continue.

"It's so messed up. What he did. All those lies. My God . . . it's astonishing that someone could lie for that long about something so big—"

"I know. But maybe he just felt trapped," I say, instantly regretting my words. I quickly backpedal. "Not trapped by your mother and you and Ashley. But by the whole situation. Trapped by the lies."

"I knew what you meant," she says. "But I find myself wondering who he *truly* loved. I know it's possible to love two people—but what was in his heart? I'd love to ask him."

I nod as she continues. "A big part of me hopes it's my mother, of course, because I know she's so in love with him. But that's not the real reason—"

"What's the real reason?" I ask, threading the needle, doing my best to avoid mention of Lainey's mother.

"Because if he wasn't in love with my mother—that meant he stayed in a relationship that he didn't want to be in. And as bad as the lies are, there's nothing worse than living an inauthentic life."

I nod, riveted. She makes it all sound so simple—and maybe it *is*—but in this moment, her statement also feels profound.

"I don't think my dad is happy," she continues. "In his marriage or his job. I think he's settled his whole life. He should have been a musician. He used to be in a band—he played the guitar and has a really cool singing voice, a raspy baritone."

"Your voice is raspy, too," I say.

"Yeah," she says with a smile. "People say that. . . . But there's no way he's happy working at JCPenney for all these years. Especially after they filed for bankruptcy. So depressing."

I nod. "Does your mother have a career?"

She shakes her head. "No. She stayed home with us. She was a great mother in a lot of ways. Doting on us. Homemade cookies when we got back from school. Carted me to tennis tournaments all over the country. But she's also *so* narrow-minded in a way that he isn't."

I nod, then reach for the wineglass, waiting for her to continue as I take a sip.

"Everything really came to a head when I came out to my parents," she finally says.

I look back at her, surprised. For some reason, Olivia being gay has never crossed my mind. "When did you come out to them?" I ask.

"In college. When I got into a pretty serious relationship."

"What was her name?" I ask for some reason.

"Zara. She was my best friend for a long time. And then it was

more. And I just couldn't hide it anymore. I didn't want to hide it—
or her. So, I went home and broke the news."

"What did you say?" I picture my own mother, feeling impressed
by Olivia's bravery.

"I cut right to the chase." She clears her throat, then says, "'Mom,
Dad. I'm in love with Zara. She's my girlfriend. I'm a lesbo.'" She
smiles, but there is something troubling in her eyes.

"What did they say?"

"My dad said nothing."

"Nothing?"

"*Nothing*. Zilch. Total silence. Although to be fair, there wasn't
any oxygen left in the room after my mother's reaction."

I wince. "Oh, no. What did she do?"

"She cried buckets. She asked if it was 'just a phase.' When I told
her no—that this was the way I'd always been, the way I'd been
born—she insisted that that couldn't be true because—get this—I
played with Barbies as a kid." She shakes her head.

"Wow," I say.

"Yeah. Then she told me I needed to talk to my pastor. When I
reminded her that I didn't have a pastor, nor did I believe in God,
there were more tears."

"Gosh," I say, shaking my head. "That must have been so hard."

"It was. And what hurt the most was that my father just sat there
the whole time. A few days later, after I'd gone back to school, he
drove to Austin and took me to lunch. He told me he loved me no
matter what—and said Mom would come around. Eventually."

"And did she?"

"In her own way. But she still goes to some megachurch that
preaches hate from the pulpit. And my dad goes, too . . . even though
I know he's only doing it for her. Eventually, I just couldn't take it
any longer."

I nod, then say, "When did you know you were gay?"

"Oh. That's hard to say. Growing up, I had crushes on girls. And I was obsessed with this one babysitter when I was about ten." She smiles. "But I didn't see it as a queer thing at the time. I just thought she was the coolest ever."

I nod, thinking of the platonic girl crushes I've had over the years.

Olivia continues, "Then, in high school, I had a boyfriend. He was *so* cute. But—" She shakes her head. "Let's just say I'm definitely *not* bisexual."

I smile, thinking of Lainey's belief that sexual orientation falls on a continuum, ranging from exclusively opposite sex to exclusively same sex with every possible combination in between. She has always insisted that very few people are at one of the extremes. I reconsider her theory now, as Olivia and I both reach for the wineglass.

"Sorry," she says, pulling her hand back.

"No, go ahead."

She takes a sip, then hands me the glass. "You seem surprised."

"About what?"

"That I'm gay."

I start to deny it but force myself to be honest. "I'm a little surprised. I don't know why, though—"

Olivia nods, putting me at ease. "I get it. I present as straighter than some . . . but obviously those are just stereotypes."

I nod, then blurt out, "Just so you know—I fully support the LGBTQ community."

She nods, seeming to suppress a smile.

"Is that a dumb thing to say?"

"No, it's not at all *dumb*. It's nice." She hesitates, then says, "Do you have gay friends?"

Her question is gentle, but I still feel defensive. "I work with quite a few gay men," I say. "But I wouldn't say I'm close with any of them."

She smiles. "So I can be your first?"

"Yes, please," I say, smiling back at her. "I'd *love* for you to be my first."

CHAPTER 24

LAINEY

THOUGHT I HAD processed what happened between me and Tyson. Long after he and Hannah had fallen asleep, I was still replaying it all. But as I wake up this morning, sober and in the light of day, I'm in a state of disbelief.

As bold and flirtatious as I can be, Tyson and I have never crossed the line of friendship. Not once in all these years. I've always known better than to try anything with him, as everything he does is aboveboard—even when he's drinking. I try to pinpoint what made me go there last night, but I can't figure it out. All I know is that something felt different between us. The fact that he reciprocated at *all* confirms that it wasn't just in my drunken head.

Even more surprising than what actually happened, though, is the way I felt as Tyson held me in his arms. I'm not one to enjoy cuddling, but last night, I loved the feeling of closeness, and right now I almost miss it. And *him*. To be honest, it's all sort of blowing my mind.

As Hannah heads out the door, I casually ask her if she knows where he is. She says she doesn't. My guess is that when he returns to the room, he will act as if nothing happened. At most, he will address it, acknowledge that it was a drunken mistake, and recommend that we never speak of it again.

The second Hannah leaves the room, I check my phone, wondering if he's texted. He hasn't—and I feel a small stab of disappointment, wishing he had at least said good morning. I tell myself not to be silly. When have I ever waited for, wanted, or needed a guy to text the morning after sex, let alone the minor stuff that happened between us?

Then again, in some ways what happened between Tyson and me felt *more* intimate than sex. In any event, I text him:

Good morning!! If you're out and about, can you please bring me an extra-hot, extra-large, whole-milk cappuccino? If they don't do larges, please get me two. Everything here is served in a thimble! ☺

A few seconds later, Tyson gives my text a thumbs-up. Nothing more.

For a second, it annoys me that he didn't even say a simple good morning, and I wonder if his lack of a meaningful response indicates regret. I tell myself it doesn't matter. Either way, it won't happen again, and I need to stop overthinking and get ready to face my day.

I get up, wash my face, and brush my teeth, trying not to look over at the shower. I then return to the room, grab my laptop from my bag, and check my emails, seeing several from Casey, including a PDF of the latest revision of the script. Ready to work, I head out to the balcony to start reading. I'm about three pages in—and totally loving the dialogue—when Tyson returns.

"That coffee better be for me!" I call out, trying to act normal.

As he walks out onto the balcony, both of us avoid eye contact.

"It is for you. And look. It's bigger than a thimble," he says, putting it down in front of me, along with a white bag.

"What's that?"

"A muffin. You're welcome."

"Thank you," I say, as he sits down in the chair across from me and opens his laptop. He clears his throat and says, "Are you reading your script?"

I look up and nod, finally meeting his eyes.

"Can you send it to me?" he asks. "I want to read it."

My heart skips a beat as I nod, then forward him the PDF.

"For your eyes only," I say with a smile.

He nods, all business.

We read in silence, neither of us speaking or looking over at the other. At one point, he makes a *hmm* sound that seems approving. I catch him smiling twice, too. About thirty minutes later, Hannah returns. She putters around for a few minutes, then announces that she's going out again. I tell her not to do anything we wouldn't do, winking at Tyson.

The second she's gone, he says, "You're too much."

I shrug and smile.

"So I take it you didn't tell her?"

"Tell her what?" I give him a wide-eyed look.

"So you're going to do *that* routine, huh?"

I laugh. "Sorry. No."

"No, we aren't going to do that routine? Or no, you didn't tell her?"

"Both."

"Good."

"Good we're not going to do that routine? Or good I didn't tell her?" I smirk.

"Both," he says. "I know you're usually an open book—and I'm not going to tell you what you can discuss with Hannah—but I would prefer if we kept last night private. Between the two of us."

"Oh, I'm sure you would, Mr. Keep a Secret for Ten Years." I smile, but the second the words are out, I regret them. A reference to Summer just isn't appropriate right now. His stone-faced expression and tight jaw seem to confirm that I miscalculated.

"I'm sorry," I say.

He nods, then gazes out over the water.

After several seconds, he clears his throat, looks at me, and says, "I think we should talk about last night."

"Okay," I say, a nervous knot in my stomach.

"Do you remember everything?"

I nod. "I wasn't that drunk. Were you?"

"I wasn't drunk at all," he says, staring into my eyes. He clears his throat, then says, "How much of that was alcohol driven?"

Flustered by the question, I stammer that I'm not sure. "I probably wouldn't have gotten in the shower with you sober, if that's what you mean. But I don't regret it."

"Are you sure you don't?"

I take a deep breath. "No. I don't deal in regret. It's a waste of time.

"What about you? Do you regret it?" I hold my breath, knowing that I'll be crushed if his answer is yes.

He shakes his head. "No."

I feel a rush of relief.

"That's not to say we should ever do it again," he quickly adds.

My heart sinks but I quickly nod and say, "Totally agree. We should just forget it happened and move on."

He bites his lip, staring at me. "I should also point out that if the gender roles were reversed—"

I give him a quizzical look.

"I could never just get into the shower with a woman. *Uninvited*."

"Oh," I say, suddenly getting his point—and the inherent double standard I live by.

"That said . . ." He pauses, then gives me a small smile. "It was *very* hot."

I smile back at him, my cheeks on fire.

"You looked incredible."

"Thank you," I say, feeling light-headed.

"You're welcome."

I hold his gaze for as long as I can stand it, then look away before he does.

FOR A COUPLE of hours, Tyson and I immerse ourselves in *The Pigeon Girl*. We read the entire screenplay, start to finish, then run through a few scenes, discussing my character's arc and motivation as well as various themes in the film.

At one point, Tyson asks me what I think about the Pigeon Girl's ultimate epiphany that being alone doesn't mean she's *lonely*.

"That resonates with me," I say. "Most people assume that the key to happiness is through marriage and children. And so many seem to wind up miserable."

He gives me a noncommittal nod. "I hear you. I don't think there's anything lonelier than being in a bad relationship—or even the *wrong* one."

I nod and say I agree.

Tyson gives me a playful look. "Um. Don't you have to be *in* a relationship to know if you're in the *wrong* one?"

"Shut up." I smile. "Although you know what's weird?"

"What's that?"

"Sometimes I can't tell whether I'm *always* lonely or *never* lonely."

He nods like he can relate, looking as unguarded as I'm starting to feel. A hundred questions run through my mind—things I want to know about Tyson. I wish I had paid more attention to his love life over the years.

"What was the name of the girl you dated in law school?" I ask, trying to remember.

"Kendra," he says. "Why?"

I shrug and say, "No reason ... She was *gorgeous*."

"Yeah," he says. "She was cool, too."

"Why'd you break up?"

"I wasn't ready for a relationship. It was ... too soon."

I start to ask a question, then decide I better not.

"What are you thinking?" he asks.

I hesitate, then say in a gentle voice, "I was just wondering ... and you don't have to answer if it makes you uncomfortable ... but do you think you would have ended up with Summer?"

He stares at me, his expression impossible to read.

"I'm sorry. I don't know why I keep going there," I say, wondering if it comes from the belief that Summer should be the one sitting with him now, not me. Mostly, though, I think I just want to understand Tyson better.

"It's okay. I don't mind when you ask thoughtful questions," he says, then pauses. "But I don't have an answer. I really don't. I'd say it would have been a long shot—just given our age."

I nod, murmuring that that makes sense, as I find myself wondering what it would be like if Tyson and I were together. *Together together.* It's an absurd thought—untenable for so many reasons—and would pose an existential threat to our friendship. The chances of things working out with us would be nil, especially given that "working out" implies a permanent relationship, and I have no interest in that. With *anyone.*

I take a deep breath, then switch gears, suggesting we take a stroll around town.

"Sure. That sounds nice," he says.

I smile, then get up, heading inside to change my clothes.

"Wait a second," Tyson says with a laugh as he follows me over to the closet. "Is 'a little stroll in town,' a euphemism for 'shopping'?"

I smile and shrug, quickly selecting a white romper that I "borrowed" from my television character's wardrobe.

"Yep," Tyson says. "I've just been played."

I laugh. "Why do you say that?"

"Because you're about to put on that expensive onesie from your show."

I laugh, surprised that he was actually listening to the conversation I had with Hannah yesterday about the fact that I probably should have returned the outfit.

"It's not a *onesie,*" I say. "Babies wear onesies. Onesies snap at the crotch."

"Hey. Some girls wear tops that snap at the crotch. I've seen them."

"Oh, I'll bet you have," I deadpan. "And those are bodysuits, buddy boy. Not onesies."

"So what is *that* thing called?" he asks, pointing to it.

"This *thing* is a Valentino romper," I say, although the costume designer had actually referred to it as a *playsuit*—a name that only made me like it more.

"More like Romper *Room*," Tyson says.

I laugh and blow him a kiss before turning in to the bathroom to change.

CHAPTER 25

TYSON

AM SITTING ON the balcony with Lainey, reading her script and trying not to think about last night. Her body is incredible and our chemistry undeniable, but more than anything sexual, I keep returning to that vulnerable look on her face in the shower. In that moment, she really *did* seem like a different person.

I tell myself it was an illusion—the confluence of alcohol, attraction, and something in the Italian air—and that she's the same old Lainey. But as we read the script—which, incidentally, is surprisingly deep for a romantic comedy—I find myself wondering if maybe I have it backward. Maybe last night's glimpse of her—stripped bare of all her usual bravado and defense mechanisms—is closer to the *real* Lainey.

Watching her in her element reinforces this idea, especially as she reads a few scenes aloud. I'm struck by how difficult it must be to convince an audience that you're someone else—and how adept Lainey is at it. She really seems to lose herself in the character, and her serious approach to her work not only fills me with admiration but turns me on. At one point, I find myself getting hard, wanting to touch her.

Fortunately, Lainey suggests we take a stroll.

"Sure. That sounds nice," I say, thinking that if we don't get out of this room soon, I won't be able to resist kissing her.

WE START OUT on Via Camerelle, which Lainey calls the Wilshire Boulevard of Capri. As we wander in and out of all the high-end shops, like Gucci, Pucci, and Dolce & Gabbana, Lainey teaches me the concept of *atelier*. For the first time, I really stop to consider the craftsmanship that goes into couture clothing.

From there, we go to Carthusia, Capri's famed perfumery. While Lainey tries on scents, I delve into the history, reading all the placards adorning the walls. I give her the recap, explaining that in 1948, the Prior of the Carthusian Monastery of Saint Giacomo discovered the formula for the perfumery's original scent, which had been lying in the monastery's library since the fourteenth century.

"Love that!" She grins at me, then goes to buy two bottles—one for her and one for Hannah.

Our next stop is Amedeo Canfora, one of several sandal-making shops in town, and apparently the one favored by Jackie Kennedy and Grace Kelly. I look around at the displayed memorabilia, including a photograph of Jackie taken the night she came into the store. The caption, in Italian, reads "Wife of President Kennedy." Next to it is a log of her purchases and a tracing of her right foot, which includes her measurements: twenty-two centimeters for the width and twenty-three centimeters for the span of her arch.

Meanwhile, Lainey gets to work designing her sandals. After much agonizing, she chooses a flat base, a medium-brown leather T-strap, silver hardware, and little jingle bell charms. We watch as an older lady (who happens to be the daughter of the original owner) gets to work making Lainey's sandals.

Once they're made, Lainey tries them on. She loves them so much that she decides to wear them out of the store, putting her other shoes in the box.

"Now your turn!" she says.

"I'm not really a sandal guy."

"Oh, c'mon," she says. "When in Capri!"

"Fair enough," I say, pointing to a wall of premade shoes for men. "Just pick a pair for me."

"*You* pick. You have great style."

"Yeah, right," I say.

She insists that I do, and we end up agreeing on the same pair—a simple, classic brown leather slide called the "Tomas." I try them on and like them.

"We'll take these," Lainey tells the sales associate, handing over her AmEx.

"What are you doing?" I ask, reaching for my wallet.

Lainey looks at me, smiles, and says, "Really? You're going to look a gift horse in the mouth *again*?"

I smile and thank her.

ONCE BACK OUT on the street, Lainey asks if I've had enough shopping.

"Oh, I got a little left in me," I say, throwing her a bone.

Her face lights up, and she leads us to a narrow street called Via delle Botteghe.

"This area is supposed to be a little less pricey," Lainey says. "With more boutique international designers."

I nod, following her into a shop called Blu, then watch her systematically inspect garment after garment, feeling the material, checking the price, and occasionally asking for my opinion. The process is intriguing, and I like seeing what she likes. When she goes to try stuff on, I make myself comfortable in an armchair outside the dressing room, hoping she will show me the outfits. She does, of course, emerging first in a long, loose-fitting dress that looks hand painted and beaded.

"This one's by Dassios—a Greek designer," she says, twirling around. "Isn't it fun?"

"Yeah. It's cool," I say, thinking that it's not her usual style.

She smiles, then pops back into the dressing room. A few minutes later, she pokes her head out again and says, "Hey, Tyson. C'mere for one sec."

There is a glint in her eye, and I can tell she's up to something.

I take a deep breath and make my way over to her. "I'm here," I say through the velvet partition.

She pulls the curtain back, then turns around, exposing her naked back, a sliver of a white lace thong, and her perfect ass.

"Can you zip me up, please?" she asks, giving me a seductive glance over her shoulder.

I nod, then take my time, enjoying the view.

"There," I say, once she's zipped.

"Thank you," she says, turning to face me.

I look down at the bombshell black dress clinging to her curves. This one is pure Lainey.

"What do you think?" she asks.

"I think," I say, leaning close to whisper in her ear, "that you're going to get us in trouble."

CHAPTER 26

HANNAH

After lunch, Olivia and I take a leisurely walk, stumbling upon the base of the Scala Fenica—a.k.a. the Phoenician Steps. While eavesdropping on an English-speaking tour guide, we learn that the stone staircase was constructed by the ancient Greeks between the seventh and sixth centuries B.C.—and that it was the only pathway up to Anacapri until a road was built in the late nineteenth century. The guide goes on to explain that before that time, residents had to collect fresh drinking water from a spring in Marina Grande, then carry it up all 921 stairs.

"Shall we?" Olivia says, shielding her eyes from the sun and gesturing up the stairs.

"Climb a *thousand* steps?" I ask her—which is my way of saying, *no, we shan't.*

"Not a *thousand.* Only nine hundred and twenty-one!"

"Well, in that case, what are we waiting for?" I laugh. "Let's do it."

She smiles, turns, and starts climbing.

The first thirty or so steps are shallow, and I trail behind her, admiring her well-defined calf muscles. The stairs become steeper as we go, and within a couple of minutes, I feel like I'm doing the StairMaster on the highest level and my thighs and lungs start to burn.

Meanwhile, Olivia bounds effortlessly up the steps while still chatting. By the time we reach the top of the staircase, I'm drenched with sweat and panting.

As I slowly catch my breath, Olivia leads us to a spot of shade and pulls a water bottle out of the side pocket of her backpack, offering me the first drink. I take a few swallows, then hand it back to her.

"You're in unbelievable shape," I say.

"Thanks. You're pretty fit yourself." She smiles.

I smile back at her, feeling grateful that I recently added more cardio to my yoga-heavy exercise regimen, even though my effort was more about looking good in my wedding dress than about my health.

We walk toward the heart of Anacapri, stopping when we get to a piazza with a gorgeous old church called the Chapel San Michele. The architecture is beautiful, and we take a quick peek into the nave, admiring the exquisite ceramic floor. In the center is an angel with a flaming sword and what appears to be Adam and Eve in the Garden of Eden.

Olivia points to a serpent wrapped around the trunk of the Tree of the Knowledge of Good and Evil and says, "Yikes. I guess that's the devil."

"God, I hate snakes," I say.

"Yeah. This place kind of gives me the creeps," she says, backing her way toward the door.

I follow her outside, and we take a moment to study a map of Capri.

"What do you say we hike the Sentiero dei Fortini?"

"What's that?" I ask, more than a little worried about Olivia's notion of a "hike."

"It means the Path of the Forts. It's a trail along the coast," she says.

"How hard is it? . . . I mean—for someone who *isn't* a professional athlete?"

"It doesn't look difficult at all. And it's short," she says. "Looks like three miles from start to finish, but we can pick up the trail somewhere in the middle."

I nod, knowing that distances can be deceiving when you're talking about rough terrain. As I make a quick search on my phone, a boldface warning jumps out at me: *This is a rigorous hike with many twists, turns, and sheer drops to the sea.*

Once again, I tell myself I can do it—and that I'm a lot tougher than I thought.

"Sure," I say. "Sounds fun."

A FEW MINUTES later, we board a bus in downtown Anacapri, headed toward the coast. I check my phone, surprised but also relieved that I've yet to hear from Lainey or Tyson. After a short ride, we hop off, making our way down to one of four forts. We peruse the placards, learning that they were originally built to defend Anacapri from the Saracen pirates and were later occupied by the British and French. We take a few minutes to explore, then proceed along the wooded trail. Over the next hour, we pass the three other forts, while taking in gorgeous views of the coastline, cliffs, and various little coves.

It's all very pleasant until the trail suddenly narrows, quickly gaining elevation. The result is steep drop-offs and dizzying views to the water below. Even worse, there are no guardrails at this point. I try not to look down, my stomach twisting in knots.

"Hold on one second," I call out to Olivia, my voice as shaky as my knees.

She turns and says, "Uh-oh. Are you afraid of heights?"

I nod, taking a deep breath but otherwise feeling frozen.

"Hold on. Stay there," she says.

She retraces her steps and extends her arm, reaching for my hand. As Olivia's fingers wrap firmly around mine and she uses her body to shield me from the view, the gesture feels oddly chivalrous. *Can chivalry be platonic?* I wonder. I decide that it can—and in this instance it is.

Still, as she grips my hand more tightly, pausing every few seconds to ask if I'm okay, I feel flustered and confused. Not about Olivia's intentions—but about my *own* feelings. It's almost as if I have a crush on her. I tell myself that's impossible. I'm straight, and I've never been attracted to a woman. Any feeling I have about Olivia holding my hand surely stems from friendship, security, and the warmth of human touch—no different than how I felt when Lainey held my hand on the way to dinner the other night. But somehow, it *is* different, and it suddenly crosses my mind that maybe Lainey's belief in a sexuality continuum is right—and that maybe I'm not where I thought I was on that spectrum. It's a scary but exhilarating thought that feels amplified by my fear of heights.

A few seconds later, the sheer drop-off disappears and the trail widens. I breathe a sigh of relief, but still feel disappointed as Olivia finally relinquishes my hand. We stop to lean on a split-rail fence doubling as a guardrail and admire the most incredible view below.

The sun is a bright ball of fire, lowering toward the horizon, turning the sky and water a thousand shades of pink and orange. A handsome red-striped lighthouse looms over the rocky beach below.

"Damn. I don't think I've ever seen a sky this gorgeous," Olivia says in her raspy voice.

"Me either," I say. "It looks like a watercolor painting."

"A painting that changes every second."

We enjoy the view for a few more minutes before I start to worry about Lainey. Surely she and Tyson are wondering where I am. I pull my phone out, checking my texts. Olivia must know what I'm doing because she says, "Have you heard from her?"

I exhale, then say, "She just texted."

"What did she say?"

I read Lainey's text aloud: Hey! Hope you've had a nice afternoon! I assume you're with Archie?? How's it going? What's your dinner plan? Do you want to meet up with Tyson and me or are you guys doing your own thing? We are flexible and cool either way. Hope you're having fun!

Olivia bites her lip, staring at me.

"What should I tell her? Should we head back now?" I ask her.

"I guess we *should*," she says, looking a little reluctant. "But if we go now, we'll miss the sunset."

"Good point," I say.

I hesitate, then text Lainey back, avoiding any mention of Archie. Went for a hike. You would have hated it. ☺ About to watch the sunset—so y'all should go to dinner without me. Let me know where you'll be! XX

AS THE SUN slips lower in the sky, Olivia and I end up at a little beach bar called Malibù. A violinist is serenading the crowd. His sound is unique to me—more pop than classical—but Olivia seems to know all about the genre.

"You've heard of Lindsey Stirling, right?" she asks, as we sit shoulder to shoulder with a view of the water.

I shake my head. Olivia explains that Lindsey is a YouTuber who came to fame on *America's Got Talent*. "She plays the violin, fusing classical, rock, hip-hop, and dubstep."

"What's dubstep?" I ask, noting that Olivia is one of those cool girls who doesn't try to be cool—or make you feel dumb because you're not cool.

"It's a kind of electronic dance music that blends two-step rhythms and dub productions with other elements," Olivia says, her face getting more animated by the second. "It originated in South London as a garage band offshoot."

I nod, even though she might as well be speaking Italian.

"So is this guy any good?" I ask her.

"*I* think he's good, but art is subjective," she says. "What do *you* think?"

I listen intently for a few seconds, then shake my head. "I can't tell."

"You can't tell if you like it?" She smiles.

"Oh," I say, nodding. "If that's what you mean, then yes, it's catchy and . . . *happy*."

"Then we agree. He's good," Olivia says, her smile widening.

A second later, a waitress comes to take our order.

Olivia gestures for me to go first.

"Un limoncello, per favore," I say.

"Fanne due," she says, holding up two fingers. "E possiamo avere i calamari, per favore?"

"Assolutamente," the waitress says, turning back toward the bar.

"Wait," I say. "Did you just order a limoncello and calamari?"

"I did! Nice translation," she says, giving me a fist bump.

Her smile fades as she looks into my eyes.

"Are you worried about Lainey?" I ask.

Olivia shakes her head. "No. I'm not really thinking about Lainey right now."

My heart skips a beat. "What *are* you thinking about?" I ask her.

"I'm thinking that I like you," she says, angling her shoulders toward mine and holding my gaze.

"Oh," I say, feeling a small rush. "I like you, too."

"I like you, *and* I admire you," Olivia says.

"You *do*?" I say.

"Yes. Very much."

"Why do you admire *me*?" I ask. I'm not being self-deprecating—at least I'm not *trying* to be—but I really can't imagine why she'd say such a thing.

Olivia swallows, her eyes locking in on me. "Well, let's see. . . . I admire you for caring about Lainey so much that you flew down to Texas and walked into Ashley's living room with her. . . . I admire you for reaching out to me. I admire you for coming to Italy when you could be curled up in a ball in Atlanta, feeling sorry for yourself. . . . Or worse, going through with the wedding . . ."

"Wow," I say, feeling touched. "Thank you, Olivia. That's really nice of you."

"It's just the truth. You're a badass," she says, smiling.

I smile back at her, my whole body feeling warm.

"Can I ask you a question?" she says.

I nod, getting butterflies in my stomach.

She takes a deep breath, then slowly exhales, looking as nervous as I'm suddenly feeling.

"I was just wondering," she says. "Have you ever kissed a girl?"

I let out a nervous laugh, then say no.

With the smallest smile, she stares into my eyes, then says, "Have you ever *wanted* to kiss a girl?"

"You mean . . . before now?" I ask, my heart racing.

It is by far the boldest thing to ever come out of my mouth, and I watch as Olivia's smile spreads across her face.

"Yeah," she says, nodding. "Have you ever wanted to before now?"

"Not before now, no," I say, shaking my head.

"And how about now?" she whispers, leaning in so close that I can feel her breath on my face.

My eyes flutter shut. I know what's about to happen, but I'm still blown away as I feel Olivia's lips grazing mine. They are the softest, sweetest lips I've ever felt. For several seconds, I am frozen. Then I kiss her back, finally answering her question.

CHAPTER 27

LAINEY

WHEN I LEAVE the dress boutique, I find Tyson standing a few storefronts down, gazing in a window. I pause, watching him for a few seconds, soaking in the moment. It's been a magical afternoon, and I don't want our time alone together to end. Fortunately, I have yet to hear from Hannah, so when I catch up to Tyson, I ask if he wants to get a drink before we head back to the room.

"Sure," he says. "A cold beer sounds perfect."

The café on the Piazzetta is very crowded, so we keep walking, going over to one near the funicular. As we check in with the hostess, an outside table opens. She offers it to us, and we take it.

We settle in our chairs, bags at our feet, and look out over the Gulf of Naples. I let out a big sigh, feeling a wave of intense contentment.

"You good?" Tyson asks.

"Yes," I say, keeping my eyes on the horizon for another second before I look back at him. "I just love being here so much."

With you, I think.

"Me too," he says.

We sit in silence for a few minutes, reviewing the menu and enjoying a cool breeze off the bay. Tyson orders a beer, and I go for an Aperol spritz.

When our drinks arrive, Tyson clears his throat, raises his glass, and stares into my eyes.

"To whatever it is that's going on here," he says.

I nod, staring back at him, then raise my glass.

We both take a long sip.

"It's weird, isn't it?" I say.

He nods without hesitating. "It's *very* weird. And out of nowhere."

"Yes," I say, my heart racing. "Out of the blue."

"Yes," he says. "But it didn't start last night in the room. At least it didn't for me."

"When did it start for you?" I ask him.

"It happened at lunch. When I told you about Summer. Well. *After* I told you." He hesitates, then adds, "When you took my hand."

I feel a rush of emotion and relief. As much as I have always loved the thrill of seduction, I'm glad to hear that Tyson's feelings for me run deeper than seeing me naked in the shower.

We stare at each other for a long few seconds as I work up the courage to ask my next question.

"What do you think Summer would say about . . . *this*?" I ask.

He takes a deep breath, then sighs loudly, shaking his head. "I don't know. I think she would just want us to be happy. Whatever that looks like." He hesitates, then continues. "I think she'd tell us that you only live once. . . . That life is short—way *too* short. . . . And you never know what can happen."

I nod, concentrating as hard as I can, trying to stay in the moment, but my thoughts are racing in a million different directions.

He swallows, then says, "I think she'd also tell us to be careful. She'd tell us that our friendship is precious, and we need to protect it at any cost."

I nod. "Yes. She would."

He looks into my eyes. "I'm very attracted to you, Lainey. . . . But whatever is happening between us isn't about that. Even last night . . . in the shower . . . I was completely mesmerized, but not for the reasons you might think."

I stare back at him, my heart in my throat.

"It was that look on your face," he says.

"What look?"

"That soft look in your eyes. It's the same one you have right now."

"Oh," I say, my cheeks burning as I glance out over the water.

"Look at me," he says.

I meet his gaze again.

"Seriously, Lainey. Don't play games. Like that shower stunt," he says. "Don't do that shit to people. More important, stop doing that to yourself. . . . This isn't about judging you or slut-shaming you or any of that. I'm just telling you. . . . You can have whatever you want, Lainey. The world is your oyster. Just be certain. Be clear. With *yourself.*"

I stare into Tyson's eyes, too overwhelmed to speak. I nod instead, basking in his concern and the feeling of being understood. As his words sink in, I have a premonition that I will one day think back to this moment. That it is a turning point.

"What about you?" I finally manage to say. "Are you always sure about what you want . . . before you do things?"

"I try to be."

"And?" I say, my heart fluttering. "What *do* you want?"

He takes a deep breath and says, "I want peace . . . and honesty . . . and the freedom to be myself. Something I've never truly felt before. With anyone."

"So you didn't have that with Nicole?"

"No," Tyson says. "But part of that was my fault. I didn't really tell her the truth. . . ." His voice trails off.

I hesitate, then say, "The truth about Summer?"

"Yes. Summer. And other things, too."

"Are you tempted to go back and tell her those things?"

"It has crossed my mind. She's such a good person. I've wondered if things might have turned out differently if I'd been more open."

"Maybe you should try again," I force myself to say.

He shakes his head. "No. That's not what I want to try."

"Oh," I say, my heart pounding, surprised by how shy I feel. "What *do* you want to try?"

"I'm figuring that out," he says, his eyes locking in on mine. "But once I decide . . . you'll be the first to know."

I can't tell if it's from his words or from another cool breeze, but I shiver, getting goosebumps.

"In the meantime, we should probably reach out to Hannah," Tyson says.

"You're right." I nod.

I get my phone out of my bag and fire off a quick text to her. She responds right away, saying she went for a hike and is going to watch the sun set.

I read it aloud, then look back up at Tyson. "So I guess it's just the two of us," I say.

He smiles and nods, looking as happy as I feel. "I guess it is," he says. "Are you getting hungry?"

"Yes. Starving," I say, realizing that the only thing I've had to eat all day is the muffin that Tyson brought me for breakfast. "We forgot to eat lunch."

"We sure did. Wonder how that happened?" he deadpans.

I shrug and smile. "Should we eat now? Or head back to the hotel?"

"We can do whatever your little heart desires," he says, smiling back at me.

I laugh, my mind racing. As much as I want to go straight back to the room and make the most of our alone time, I show restraint like I never have before. "How about we order a little something to eat . . . and maybe one more drink?"

"Sounds great to me," Tyson says.

AS DUSK DESCENDS upon the bay and the sky darkens, Tyson and I eat and drink and talk, staying longer than we planned. The mood is so peaceful and our rhythm so natural. Then, suddenly, he looks past me, bewildered.

"That's weird," he mutters, squinting into the darkness.

"What's weird?" I ask, glancing over my shoulder.

"Isn't that Archie and Ian?" he asks, pointing. "Over there with those women?"

I turn all the way around in my chair, spotting our Scottish friends with a couple of girls.

I look back at Tyson. "I guess Hannah changed her mind," I say, feeling a wave of disappointment.

"Yeah. I guess she did." He nods, looking equally disappointed. "She must be back in the room."

"Hold on. I'm gonna find out," I say, getting to my feet and dropping my napkin on my plate.

I turn and stride over to their little group. Ian is holding court, a cigarette in his hand.

"Hello, gentlemen!" I call out in a loud voice.

Archie and Ian both look up at me and smile as the girls step back. I give Ian a hug, inhaling the scent of weed on his sweater.

"How's your day been?" Ian asks me.

"Great," I say. "Yours?"

"Awesome. We went to the Blue Grotto," Ian says.

"And did you enjoy the sunset?" I ask, looking at Archie.

"Ack. We missed it," he says, shaking his head.

"What do you mean you missed it?" I ask, confused. "Weren't you with Hannah?"

"Nope. She blew me off," he says with an affable shrug.

"So . . . wait . . . when did you leave her?" I ask, more confused by the second.

"Last night," he says. "When I walked her back to the hotel. Why?"

"Oh, it's not important," I say. "Look, I gotta go right now, but maybe we'll see you guys later."

"Hope so," Ian says, raising his eyebrows.

I nod, smile, then rush back over to our table.

When I get there, Tyson is staring down at his phone.

"Hannah's not with them," I say, sitting back down. "She hasn't been with them all day."

Tyson looks up at me and frowns. "Yeah. I just pulled up her Life360."

"And? Where is she?"

"It looks like she's at a hotel. . . . It's close. . . . Only about a hundred and fifty meters from here—" He looks up at me, an uneasy expression crossing his face.

"Tyson?"

"Yeah?"

"Do you know something you're not telling me?"

He sighs, chews his lower lip, then slowly nods.

"Well? What is it?"

He takes a deep breath, then says, "Olivia's in Italy."

I stare at him, floored. "You're kidding me, right?"

He winces. "I'm sorry I didn't tell you sooner—"

"Whatever, Tyson." I get to my feet so abruptly that I knock over my chair. "Let's go."

"Where are we going?" he asks.

"To wherever Hannah is," I say, crossing my arms, waiting for him to stand.

"Maybe we should just call her first," he says, glancing back down at his screen, clearly stalling.

"No. Don't call her. Just take me to her now," I say, fuming. "Right *fucking* now."

CHAPTER 28

TYSON

DON'T KNOW FOR sure that Hannah is with Olivia, but that's my best guess, and if I'm right, it's not gonna be pretty. Lainey is now *three* drinks in—which isn't helping matters. She's not a belligerent drinker, but she's definitely an emotional one, and as the two of us approach the entrance of a small, nondescript hotel, I can tell she's enraged.

I reach out and catch her arm right before she walks in.

"Lainey," I say. "You have every right to be upset. But can you please take a deep breath?"

"A deep breath? You think a deep breath is going to help right now?" she snaps back at me.

"I just want you to try to calm down a little. For your sake—"

"*Don't* tell me to calm down, Tyson," she says, pointing her finger in my face.

I quickly surrender, palms up and out. "Okay. I'm sorry."

She spins back around, storming into the hotel.

I trail behind her, cringing, praying that Hannah just chose to spend a quiet day alone. Instead, I turn the corner and spot her cozied up to a bar with a woman who could easily be Lainey's sister. They have the same dark hair and broad shoulders. I watch Lainey descend upon them.

"Why, hello there, Hannah! So lovely to see you!" she says in a loud voice. "How was that sunset with Archie?"

Fuck, I whisper under my breath, approaching in time to see Hannah's dumbstruck expression.

"And nice to meet you, Olivia," Lainey says. "What a coincidence that you're here on this same little island!"

Olivia smiles hesitantly, then offers Lainey her hand.

"Wow," Lainey scoffs, staring disdainfully at her extended arm.

"Lainey—" I say, touching her arm again.

She spins and looks into my eyes. "Don't you dare," she says in a fierce whisper.

I nod and keep my mouth shut.

"I asked you guys for one thing," she says, swiveling her head as she looks at me, then Hannah, then back at me. "*One* thing."

Hannah's face contorts in an unsuccessful effort not to cry as she tells Lainey how sorry she is.

"It's my fault," Olivia says. "Hannah told me this wasn't a good idea."

"No. It's *not* your fault," Lainey says, dismissing Olivia with a quick wave of her hand. "You owe me nothing. You're irrelevant."

Olivia's mouth opens, then closes, as Lainey continues her rant. "But my friends *did* owe me something." She turns and gives me a long death stare. "So much for that."

"Lainey, please," Hannah says, tears rolling down her cheeks. "Can I explain?"

"I don't want to hear it. From either of you. From *any* of you," Lainey says. "You three have fun. I'm out."

A second later, she is flying out of the bar and back toward the lobby. I start to follow her but stop myself, knowing it's futile—and could possibly be even more damaging. There is no way we can have a productive conversation until she calms down.

"Dammit," I say under my breath, turning back to face Hannah. "What a mess."

"I'm sorry I didn't tell you where I was today," she says. "I didn't want you to have to lie for me."

"Yeah," I say. "Except I already knew Olivia was in Italy—and I told Lainey I knew that. So now she assumes I was in cahoots with you."

"I'm *really* sorry," Olivia says. "You should both go talk to her. Tell her I'm leaving on the first ferry in the morning."

"No. We need to give her a minute alone." I hesitate, then say, "I'm Tyson, by the way."

She nods. "It's nice to meet you ... despite the circumstances."

"You too," I say, relieved that Hannah is right: she seems *nothing* like Ashley.

I grab the barstool on the other side of Hannah and order myself a bourbon, neat.

ABOUT THIRTY AWKWARD minutes of small talk later, I tell Hannah I'm going to head back to the room.

"Hopefully, Lainey's there," I add with a sigh.

"I'll go with you," Hannah says.

I nod, pulling my wallet out to pay our tab.

"Let me get the drinks," Olivia says.

I don't have the energy to push back, so I just thank her.

"I'm sorry again," Olivia says. "I really didn't mean to cause all this trouble."

"I know you didn't. I hope we can sort it out," I say, looking at Hannah, who hasn't budged from her stool. "Are you coming?"

"Yeah. Just give us one sec," she says, biting her lip and glancing nervously at Olivia. It seems odd—in fact, they've *both* been acting a bit odd—but I remind myself that it's been an emotional day for everyone.

I nod, then say I'll wait in the lobby. But the second I get there, I decide I should probably go back to the room alone. As angry as Lainey is with me, I might have a better chance of laying the groundwork for a reconciliation without Hannah.

I turn around and walk back, popping into the bar just in time to see Hannah and Olivia sharing a sweet hug. It's a heartwarming and hopeful sight. I walk toward them, then stop in my tracks, watching in disbelief as Hannah gives Lainey's sister a long kiss on the lips.

CHAPTER 29

HANNAH

"THANK YOU FOR coming today," I say to Olivia once Tyson leaves the bar and the two of us are alone again. "It's been really special."

Olivia nods. "Yes. It has been. I'm just sorry for how it ended—"

"I know," I say. "I hate that you met Lainey like this."

"Me too," she says.

"Ninety-nine percent of the time, she's really easygoing," I say, knowing how much Olivia hates the drama her other sister creates. "She's very different from your description of Ashley."

"I can tell," Olivia says. "She seems legitimately hurt, whereas Ashley just *plays* the victim."

I nod, then remember that Tyson is waiting for me. I tell her I'd better go.

"Yes. Go," she says, reaching for my hand as she gives me a tight smile.

"Okay," I say, stalling a few seconds more. "I'll reach out as soon as we talk to her. What time do you think you'll go to sleep?"

"Oh, don't worry about that. Call anytime. I want to know that everything's okay."

"I will," I say, finally getting to my feet as Olivia does the same. She's a good five inches taller than I am, so I tilt my head up to look in her eyes. "Bye for now."

"Yep. Bye for now," I whisper back, hit by a wave of affection and attraction. The attraction part still confuses me, but not as much as it did a few hours—and kisses—ago.

She gives me the cutest smile, then wraps her long arms around my waist, embracing me so tightly that it's hard to hug her back. I find a way, though, wondering if she'll give me one last kiss. I decide not to wait to find out, kissing her instead.

I FIND TYSON in the lobby.

"Sorry," I mumble.

"No worries," he says, gathering the shopping bags at his feet.

As we walk out onto the dark street, it takes me a few seconds to clear my senses of Olivia.

"Any word yet?" I ask.

"Nope," he says.

I glance at him, trying to gauge his mood. I know he's frustrated and worried, but I can't tell if he's also angry with me.

"Just so you know," I say, "I didn't actually *lie* to Lainey."

"Huh?" he says, giving me a sideways glance.

"I never *told* her I was with Archie. She just *assumed* . . ." My voice trails off.

"Look, Han," Tyson says, pausing midstride to look at me. "Your business is your business. You're entitled to have your own friendships and privacy. We're all adults here."

He takes a deep breath as I feel a *but* coming.

Sure enough, he says, "But I can understand why Lainey saw this as a breach of trust. Bottom line, it feels reckless."

I nod, ashamed.

"And honestly—I really don't know how you expected to pull this off on a speck of an island," he says, walking again.

"You're right. I'm sorry. I was going to tell y'all . . . and then the hours passed . . . and I chickened out. I should have just told Lainey the deal this morning—"

"What *is* the deal?" he asks, cutting me off and giving me a look.

"I don't mean deal like *that*," I say, not ready to get into anything other than concern for Lainey. "I just mean . . . I should have told you both that Olivia was coming to Capri. And that we've become friends. And that you were both welcome to join . . . or not."

"Yeah," Tyson says, quickening his pace. "That would have been a whole lot easier than this fiasco."

A FEW MINUTES later, we are back at our hotel. I brace myself the whole way up in the elevator, then down the hall to our room.

Tyson unlocks the door and pushes it open.

"Lainey?" he calls out.

There is no response, and it takes us all of three seconds to determine that she's not here. Further, it would appear that she hasn't been back since housekeeping cleaned the room, as the bedding and bathroom look undisturbed.

I point this out to Tyson, and he says, "Yeah. She definitely hasn't been back."

"Where do you think she went?"

He sighs. "I have no idea. But I bet it involves alcoholic beverages."

"Wait!" I say. "Did you check Life360?"

"I did. She turned it off," he says, then suggests that I call Archie. "We saw them on the square right before we came to find you. She might have linked up with them."

I nod and pull out my phone, wishing that I hadn't blown off Archie's earlier text messages—all *three* of them. I put that thought aside and call him. It goes straight to voicemail.

"Hi, Archie," I say, my voice sounding as strained as Tyson's expression. "Sorry for not replying earlier. Any chance you're with Lainey now? Long story, but Tyson and I are looking for her. Please give me a call if you've seen her."

I hang up, then watch Tyson furtively type with his thumbs.

"Are you texting her?" I ask him.

He nods.

"What are you saying?"

He finishes, then looks at me. "Exactly what you'd expect me to say.... 'Where are you? Please come back. Be careful. Don't drink too much.'"

I take a deep breath, then say, "Tyson. I'm *really* sorry—"

"Hey, Hannah?" He cuts me off.

"Yeah?"

"Stop saying you're sorry. What's done is done."

I nod, watching him pace back and forth. He suddenly stops, then grabs a jacket and his room key.

"I'm gonna go look for her," he says. "You stay here in case she comes back."

NIGHT TURNS INTO late night. As I call and text Lainey from the room, Tyson scours Capri's nightclubs and restaurants, checking with bartenders and bouncers.

Nobody has seen her, he reports back to me, again and again.

Archie finally returns my call just after one in the morning. There is loud music in the background, and for a second, I'm hopeful. Then he tells me that he hasn't seen Lainey since their conversation earlier this evening.

"Is everything okay?" he asks.

"Not really," I say. "We had an argument, and Tyson and I are worried about her."

"Oh, no," he says, sounding genuinely concerned.

"I'm sure she's okay," I say, trying to convince myself. "But keep your eye out for her. And if you happen to see her—"

"I'll call you straightaway," he says.

"Thank you, Archie," I say.

As I hang up, my stomach fills with dread.

CHAPTER 30

LAINEY

AM SHAKING WITH anger as I storm out of the bar and exit the
hotel. I glance over my shoulder to confirm that my friends
aren't following me. I guess they know better than to try when I'm
this upset, but their lack of effort is even more hurtful.

I really can't believe it. Hannah's lies and betrayal are astonishing, especially given how much I've had her back. But the fact that
Tyson was in on it, too, is even more devastating. I was feeling so
close to him, and I foolishly believed he was feeling the same way.

How could I have been so stupid? I never make this sort of error.
I know better. I think back to last night when I got out of the cab
and followed Tyson into the hotel. I should have stayed with Ian.

I tell myself it's not too late, quickly returning to the spot where
I last saw him. But when I get back to the Piazzetta, he and Archie
are nowhere to be found. The girls they were with are still lingering,
though, and I walk over to them.

"Hi. I was wondering if you might know where those Scottish
guys went?" I ask. "The ones you were talking to?"

"Don't know. They probably went back to their hotel," the shorter girl says in an accent that sounds Eastern European.

"Do you happen to have their number?" I ask. "Or know where they are staying?"

"No. Sorry," the short girl says.

"It's okay. Thank you, anyway."

I start to walk away, then stop myself, feeling desperate. I turn back to them. "Look. I won't get in your way if you're interested in them. I was just looking for something to do tonight—and my friends and I had fun hanging out with them last night."

"No worries," the short one says, finally loosening up. "I'm Petra."

I nod, attempting a smile. "I'm Lainey."

"And I'm Iris," the tall friend says.

I tell them it's nice to meet them both, then ask where they're from.

"Croatia," Petra says. "But we live here now. You?"

"New York City."

An awkward beat follows before Petra says, "We're going to a yacht party later. Down at Marina Grande. The boat is called *Andiamo*. You should come. We're just going to change first."

"Cool. That sounds fun," I say, nodding. "Maybe I'll do that."

I wave goodbye and continue on my way, walking another few minutes before I find an available taxi. I make eye contact with the driver as he leans against his car, smoking.

"You need a lift, miss?" he asks.

"Yes, please," I say.

He takes one last drag of his cigarette, then crushes it out before opening the back door for me. I climb in.

"Where to?" he asks me after sliding into the driver's seat.

I hesitate, then say, "Marina Grande, please. Where the yachts dock."

He nods and starts to drive.

As we wind our way downhill, I put my head back on the seat, close my eyes, and picture my next drink.

A FEW MINUTES later, we arrive at a dock close to where our ferry anchored. As I pay my fare and get out of the car, I can hear music coming from the water.

It doesn't take long to figure out that it's coming from the very yacht my new friends just told me about: *Andiamo*. I look up and see people dancing on the top deck. It's definitely a party. I walk toward the boat behind a chic couple. The woman is wearing a Missoni dress and five-inch wedges.

I watch as they both stop, remove their shoes, and lay them in a woven basket, boarding the boat via a wooden plank. I follow them; it won't be the first party I've crashed.

As I enter the main cabin, I pass about a dozen people lounging, talking, and drinking. I walk over to the makeshift bar, helping myself to a glass of champagne. I throw it back, then start to refill my glass.

"Would you like something stronger?" I hear a voice behind me say in an American accent.

I turn around to find a very attractive man with a Gatsby vibe. He's older—but not too old.

"What did you have in mind?" I ask him.

He smiles and says, "The bartender upstairs makes the best vodka gimlets."

"Well, then. Let's go," I say.

He smiles and says, "Yes. Andiamo!"

"Wait. Does *Andiamo* mean *let's go*?" I ask.

"It does," he says, giving me a wink. "Welcome aboard."

"Oh, shit," I say with a laugh. "Is this *your* yacht?"

"It is," he says, looking smug but friendly.

Feeling a bit sheepish, I say, "So I guess you're aware that I'm not an invited guest?"

He laughs. "It's fine. I'm just glad you could come."

"That's awfully kind of you," I say. "I'm Lainey."

"Hello, Lainey. I'm Jonathan," he says.

I try to shake his hand, but he takes mine and slowly raises it to his lips, kissing the back of it. It's pretentious as hell, especially for an American, but at the moment, I don't mind.

Jonathan leads me up a ladder to the top deck, where the party is in full swing. We head over to the bar as he cuts the line, saying hello to everyone before asking the bartender for two of his famous gimlets.

A moment of small talk later, Jonathan hands me one of the glasses. I take a long sip, then another.

"Oh, this is delicious," I say.

Within minutes, I start to feel euphoric, the alcohol surging into my bloodstream. I know I need to slow down and pace myself. But when I hear Tyson's voice in my head, admonishing me to be careful, I do the opposite. I drain my gimlet, then order another.

I lose track of my drinks after that. I lose track of *everything*. All I know is that I'm having fun. I'm the life of the party. I'm mixing and mingling and dancing, making the most of every delicious moment, knowing I can't last much longer. The only real question is whether I will pass out or *black* out. Either way, the crash is coming. The crash always comes.

CHAPTER 31

TYSON

As troubling as Lainey's disappearing act is, I manage to stay relatively calm until I finally decide to return to our hotel at four in the morning. At that point, knowing that even the late-night bars and nightclubs have closed, I can't keep my panic at bay.

Lainey has probably gone home with someone—or back to their hotel. The idea of her having drunken sex with a stranger makes me sick to my stomach, but the possibility that something more nefarious could be happening terrifies me. I tell myself very few people in the world are outright evil—and the chance of Lainey falling into the hands of one of them is minuscule.

Of course there is also the possibility of a run-of-the-mill accident—and the odds of having one of those only increases when someone is shit-faced. A horrifying image of Lainey floating face-down in a pool pops into my head. I shudder, then force it out of my mind as I run back to the hotel.

As I walk into the lobby, I see Hannah talking to Alessandro. He is not dressed in his usual suit and tie—and my first thought is he may have received some news about his favorite hotel guest.

"What's going on?" I ask, rushing over to them.

"I heard Lainey is missing," Alessandro says.

"How did you hear that?" I ask.

"My colleague working the night audit rang to tell me you spoke with her. She thought I would want to know." He hesitates, then says, "And she was right."

"That was kind of her," I say. "And of you to come in. Thank you."

He nods, then says, "I was just telling Hannah that I think we should go around to all the hotels. At this hour, that might be more efficient than ringing them. We can talk directly with the front desk and security. I also want to speak with some of the taxi drivers. They see and hear a lot. I've reached out and left some messages already."

"That sounds like a great plan. Thank you so much," I say, overcome with gratitude.

"Of course," Alessandro says. "My car's out front."

FOR THE NEXT couple of hours, Alessandro drives us all over the island. We take turns getting out of the car, going inside hotels, asking questions, showing Lainey's photo. No luck. Nobody has seen her.

Then, right as dawn starts to break, the sun slowly blooming on the horizon, Alessandro's phone rings.

He grabs it and answers, "Pronto."

"Buonogiorno, sono Gianni."

From there, I can't understand what they're saying, but I hear Lainey's name, and I don't need a translator to tell me that we finally have a lead.

Alessandro hangs up, his eyes bright. "That was my taxi driver friend Gianni," he says. "He saw the photo I sent of Lainey. Says he drove her last night."

"Drove her where?" I ask.

"Down to the marina. To the private dock."

"So she could have sailed off on a random yacht?" Hannah asks, looking panicked.

"I suppose that is possible," Alessandro says. "But it's unlikely that a yacht would leave the dock at night—unless it just took a quick cocktail cruise around the island. Even if it did set sail to go farther, she can't get out of the country without her passport. Does she have it with her?"

"No," Hannah says. "I checked. It's still in the safe."

I breathe a small sigh of relief, although the possibility that Lainey could be out on the open sea isn't particularly comforting. I tell myself to stay positive and keep my faith in Lainey's street smarts. Even when she's wasted, she has always managed to escape any real problems.

TEN MINUTES LATER, Alessandro has parked his car at the marina, and we are walking out onto a dock lined with yachts. We stop and talk to the first person we see—an older man reading a paper on a beautiful wooden sailboat.

He looks up and gives us a friendly wave. "Buongiorno."

"Ciao. Buongiorno," Alessandro says back, then starts speaking in rapid Italian.

The man nods, listening intently as Alessandro holds up his phone, showing him Lainey's picture.

"No. Non l'ho vista," he says—which I assume means that he has *not* seen her. He then says another few sentences, pointing down the dock.

"Grazie," Alessandro says.

"Prego. Buona fortuna."

The man returns to his newspaper as Alessandro looks back at us.

"He said to try the boat with the turquoise hull. They had a party last night."

We nod and follow Alessandro to the yacht in question. When we get there, he calls out, "Ciao! C'è nessuno?"

There is no response, only the sound of water slapping the side of the yacht and seagulls squawking overhead.

As Alessandro calls out again, I see Hannah looking down at a basket filled with shoes. I immediately recognize the pair of sandals that Lainey just bought.

"These are hers!" I say, bending down to grab them.

"No, they're not—"

"Yes, they are! She got them with me yesterday. She has to be here," I say, barreling up a wooden gangway, then boarding the boat.

"Hey! What the hell are you doing?" a man shouts in an American accent.

I look up to see him standing on the deck of the boat, wearing a silk robe. "This is private property!"

"We're looking for my friend. These are her shoes!" I yell back, waving Lainey's sandals at him.

"I don't know who your friend is, but *this* is private property, and you need to get off my goddamn yacht!"

"Look, sir. We're so sorry to bother you," Hannah calls up from the dock. "But we're really worried about our friend. Will you at least look at her photo and tell us if you remember seeing her?"

The man looks down at Hannah and sighs, clearly disarmed by the pretty white girl. "Fine. Show me the picture."

I pull up Lainey's photo on my phone and hold it up for him. The look on his face gives me chills. He's definitely seen her.

"Yeah. I saw her. She was a disaster. Out of her mind drunk. Thank God she left—"

"She was out of her mind drunk, and you just let her *leave*?" I say.

"That girl was not my responsibility. I didn't invite her onto my boat in the first place. She was trespassing. Like you are right now," he says, getting angrier. "Now I'm going to ask *you* to leave, one more time, before I call the police—"

I glare at him, trying to contain my fury, as another man approaches us. Wearing pressed khaki shorts and a white polo with a nautical logo, he appears to be a crew member.

"I'll handle this, sir," he says in a low voice with an Italian accent.

"Don't worry. I'm leaving," I snap back at them both.

As I walk back down the gangway, Alessandro starts speaking to the crew member in calm Italian. Their conversation couldn't be more different from the one I just had, and I listen hopefully and prayerfully.

After several seconds, Alessandro thanks him profusely, then turns to us and says, "We need to go. I think I know where she is. . . ."

CHAPTER 32

HANNAH

O N OUR FRANTIC jog back to the car, Alessandro gives us the update.

According to the deckhand, Lainey was so intoxicated that she fell down one of the ladders on the yacht and injured herself. While he and his colleague were administering first aid, Lainey vomited, and the owner threw her and her friends off his yacht.

"Her friends? What friends?" Tyson asks.

"Two Croatian girls. I think I know them—"

"How do you know them?" I ask.

"*Everyone* knows them—" He gives us a look that I quickly translate. "But they're very nice girls. I'm sure they took care of Lainey."

"Do you know where they live?" Tyson asks. "Or how to get ahold of them?"

"I could probably track them down," Alessandro says, as we all get back in his car. "But I think we should check the hospital first."

Tyson nods in numb agreement as I start to cry. He looks at me over his shoulder and tells me it's going to be okay.

"Do you really think so?" I ask, my heart pounding in my chest.

"Yes," Tyson says, staring into my eyes. "It has to be."

FORTUNATELY, THERE IS only one hospital on the island, and it's very close by. Unfortunately, it also happens to look more like a small, run-down health clinic than a proper hospital. There is trash in the parking lot; paint is peeling off the walls; and the small waiting room is loaded to the gills.

"This place doesn't look equipped to handle serious injuries," I whisper to Tyson. We are hovering behind Alessandro as he talks to the lady at the front desk.

"If she's here, she probably just needed stitches or something small," Tyson says. "Otherwise, I'm guessing she would have been airlifted to the mainland."

"Tyson!" I say, my heart in my throat.

"My point is—I'm sure she's getting the care she needs. Italy has good doctors."

I take a deep breath, but inside I'm freaking out. What if Lainey hit her head when she fell down the ladder? She could have suffered a traumatic brain injury, and they might not have realized the extent of her injuries until it was too late to get her to a better hospital.

Just as I start to really spiral, Alessandro turns to us and says, "She's here."

"How is she?" Tyson asks.

"I don't know. She just confirmed that Lainey is here. Someone is coming out to talk to us—"

"When?" I ask.

"Hopefully soon."

The next few minutes are torture as we sit and wait in complete silence. Meanwhile, my guilt compounds. I can't believe that I'm the cause of all of this.

Finally, a woman in a white coat emerges from the crowded corridor. She says Alessandro's name, glancing around the room.

"Sì. Qui," he says, getting to his feet.

She walks calmly over to us.

Tyson and I stand, too, watching and listening while she speaks to Alessandro in Italian. Although I can't follow what she's saying, she sounds very confident and competent. I tell myself that Tyson is right. This hospital might not be fancy, but that doesn't mean the doctors here aren't knowledgeable and caring. This woman has kind brown eyes, and she gives me a compassionate smile as she turns to go.

"What did she say?" I ask, my hands trembling.

Alessandro clears his throat, then says, "Lainey was in very bad shape when she got here."

"From the fall or the alcohol?" I ask.

"Let him finish—" Tyson says, putting his hand gently on my arm.

"Sorry," I say, nodding and taking a deep breath.

"Let's sit," Alessandro says.

We sit back down, and Alessandro continues, telling us that Lainey has alcohol poisoning. She was having a lot of trouble breathing when she was brought in. They gave her oxygen to protect her vital organs, IV fluids for dehydration, and thiamine and glucose to prevent brain damage.

"Oh my *God*! *Brain* damage?" I say.

"It's probably just precautionary," Tyson says. "You know— standard protocol with alcohol poisoning."

Alessandro nods. "They're running more tests now."

"Are they doing a CT scan?" Tyson asks.

"I don't know," Alessandro says. "She mentioned X-rays. It sounds like Lainey may have broken her arm when she fell."

"Are they going to let us see her?" Tyson asks, his expression stoic.

Alessandro shakes his head. "Not yet. The doctor said she'll let us know when we can go back."

I start bawling, and as Alessandro leans over and gives me a hug, I catch Tyson wiping away tears of his own.

OUR WAIT IS agonizing, the minutes slowly ticking by in the dingy waiting room.

At some point, I remember my promise to call Olivia and step out to the parking lot.

She answers on the first ring. "Please tell me you found her?"

"Yes. We're at the hospital, waiting to see her."

"Oh, no! What happened?"

I bring her up to speed on everything, then say, "Now we're just waiting. We hope to know more soon."

"Okay," she says with a sigh. "Will you please keep me posted?"

"Yes. I promise I will," I say. "What time is your ferry?"

"I haven't checked the schedule yet," she says. "But I'm not leaving until I know she's okay—"

"You really don't have to stay. I know you need to get back. Besides, there's nothing you can do at this point—"

"Hannah, I can't go yet. Not unless you want me to?"

I hesitate, thinking of Lainey—and Lainey only.

"I don't want you to," I say. "But I think maybe you should. Just in case she asks. . . . But I promise I'll keep you updated."

"Okay," Olivia says. "I understand."

LAINEY LOOKS EVEN worse than I had braced myself for. I can't tell if she's unconscious or asleep, but her face is pale and covered with cuts and bruises; her right arm is in a sling; and tubes and wires connect her to various machines.

I stand frozen in the doorway, fighting off a fresh wave of tears as I watch Tyson walk over to her bed, peering down at her. He is trying to be strong, but I can tell he's shaken, too. The language barrier isn't helping matters. Alessandro finally had to leave for work, and neither the hospital worker who ushered us from the waiting room nor the nurse speaks much English.

I tell myself that Lainey has to be stable—otherwise they wouldn't have let us see her. But it's impossible to know for sure, and I'm still worried about an undetected brain injury.

As I watch Tyson reach down and gently stroke Lainey's matted hair away from her forehead, I force myself to walk the whole way into the room and over to her bedside. As horrible as she looks, and no matter what happens from here, I'm grateful for this moment. It's something we never had with Summer.

Lainey's eyes suddenly flutter open. She looks up at us with a terrifyingly blank stare, like she has no idea who we are.

"Hi, Lainey," Tyson whispers. "It's me. Tyson."

Lainey blinks, still staring.

"Where am I?" she finally asks in a faint whisper.

"You're in the hospital," Tyson tells her.

Lainey's eyes turn watery, tears rolling down her cheeks and her lips trembling. It is a heartbreaking sight, but also hopeful. She knows who we are, and she understands what Tyson is telling her.

"I'm sorry," she says.

"Shh," Tyson says. "It's okay. It's all going to be okay."

She looks at me now, then tries to say something else, but Tyson stops her.

"Don't try to talk. We can talk later. Right now, you need to rest."

Lainey gives us the slightest nod before her eyes flutter shut.

"We love you, Lainey," Tyson says.

"We love you *so* much," I whisper.

She doesn't reply, but I tell myself she can hear us.

CHAPTER 33

LAINEY

ONE MINUTE I'M partying on a yacht; the next minute I'm waking up in a strange bed, staring at fluorescent lights. The room is freezing, and cool air is flowing into my nose.

I try to look around, but my eyelids are too heavy. So I listen instead. I can hear the low-pitched whir of a motor, a steady beeping sound, the rattling of wheels rolling along a hallway, and voices speaking Italian. Some are near, others are farther away, still others sound like they're coming from a television or radio.

The din is eerily familiar, taking me back to the end of my mother's life. I don't know what happened to me, but my body feels numb—like it's not my own. It crosses my mind that I could be paralyzed. Or dying.

WHEN I FINALLY open my eyes, I see Tyson's face. Then Hannah beside him. They are both peering down at me with expressions that scare me. I ask where I am, my voice coming out in a scratchy whisper. My throat is dry and sore. Tyson confirms that I'm in a hospital. I can't remember how I got here, but I'm guessing that it was my fault. I drank too much. I may have done drugs, too. I remember dancing with the Croatian girls that I met on the Piazzetta. I remember having sex. I remember falling. After that, my memory is a black hole.

Overcome with regret, I stare into Tyson's eyes and whisper that I'm sorry.

"It's okay," he says. "It's all going to be okay."

I try to reply, but Tyson stops me, telling me I need to rest.

I do as I'm told, closing my eyes.

I CAN'T TELL whether it's morning or night, but at some point, a doctor comes to talk to me. Standing at the foot of my bed with a clipboard in her hand, she informs me that I fractured three ribs and my humerus. I look down at my right arm, now in a full cast, as she explains that they were able to do a closed non-surgical reduction to set and realign the bone in the two places I broke it.

She goes on to say that I suffered acute alcohol poisoning. She tells me that if I hadn't been brought into the hospital when I was, I may have lost my life. My heart and liver were that distressed.

As I stare at her, trying to process everything she is telling me, she clears her throat, then says, "Lainey, you also had some bruising and bleeding that can be consistent with sexual assault. Were you assaulted?"

I shake my head.

"So the intercourse was consensual?" she asks.

I nod, choosing to believe that it was. I can't bear to consider the alternative.

She gives me a look like she isn't sure whether to believe me, then asks if I have any questions.

My mind races as I look down at my arm. "How long will I have this cast?" I ask.

"Ten to twelve weeks," she says.

I nod, fighting back tears, knowing that I will likely have to give up my movie role.

"How much longer will I be here?" I ask her.

"That depends on your bloodwork and other tests. We want to make sure you're stable before we discharge you. For now, you need to rest."

I nod as she gives me a small smile, hangs my chart on a hook, then walks out of the room.

A SHORT TIME later, Hannah and Tyson appear in my doorway with furtive expressions.

"Good morning," Hannah says. "We brought you a cappuccino. Extra hot."

"Thank you," I say. "I'm *dying* for some coffee."

She hands me the cup and I raise it to my lips, inhaling the delicious scent, then taking a long sip.

"That might be the best thing I've ever tasted," I say.

"Wait till you try these croissants." Tyson smiles, then asks how I'm feeling.

"A bit sore," I say.

"I bet," he says.

I don't know what to say, so I give them a rundown on my doctor's report, minus the sex part. They both nod, listening intently. When I'm finished, I brace myself for the inevitable questions about what, exactly, happened. At the very least, I expect them to mention our argument or explain how they found me.

But they don't go there with any of it. Not that morning or during any of their following visits that day. At first, I'm relieved, but as the hours pass, their silence is unnerving.

Maybe they know how ashamed I already am. Maybe they feel too much guilt of their own for lying to me about my sister. Maybe they are just waiting for me to broach the subject. I know I need to—and that I also need to call my agent—but I can't quite find the courage.

THAT EVENING, HANNAH and Tyson get permission to take me outside in a wheelchair. The sky is filled with stars. There has still been no mention of our fight or anything else that happened during those blacked-out hours. As we sit in silence, enjoying the night air, Alessandro walks up to us with a big pink teddy bear.

"You're just the woman I'm looking for," he says, handing me the bear.

I cradle it in my arms and tell him thank you.

Alessandro smiles, then pulls a Sharpie out of his breast pocket. "May I be the first to sign your cast?"

"Yes, please," I say, watching as he uncaps the pen and scrawls his signature across my forearm.

"You know, Lainey," Tyson says, "this guy led the search for you."

It's the most detail I've been given about those missing hours of my life, and I am filled with simultaneous shame and gratitude.

"Thank you," I say. "So much."

"Prego," he says with a small bow. "We're just happy that you're okay."

We chat for a while longer before Alessandro says he has to go. Once it's just the three of us again, my heart fills with increasing dread, and my stomach turns in somersaults. I can feel the conversation coming, and I know that even if they don't bring it up, I need to face the music. All of it.

"Well. I guess I better call my agent tomorrow," I say.

Tyson nods, then says, "Yeah. You probably should do that."

"I'm going to lose my role," I say, glancing down at Alessandro's signature on my cast.

I look back up in time to see Hannah's sympathetic expression.

"Yeah. I don't remember the Pigeon Girl having a cast on her arm," Tyson says. At first, I think he's attempting to lighten the mood, but he doesn't smile. Clearly nothing about this is a joking matter.

"And I'm guessing the Paris leg of our trip is out, too?" I ask.

"For now, yes," Hannah says.

After a painfully long stretch of silence, I give my friends a pleading look. "Guys. Please. Talk to me. Lecture me. Yell at me. Say *something*."

Tyson stares into my eyes and says, "We're not going to do that, Lainey. This has to come from you."

Hannah gives a somber nod in solidarity.

I take a deep breath, searching for the right words. *Any* words.

"I know I drink too much," I finally force myself to say. "At least I do when I'm upset."

Tyson nods, then says, "It's a relief to hear you say that. Because we're really worried about you."

"Worried how? Do you think I'm an alcoholic?"

"Do *you* think you are?" Tyson replies.

"I don't *think* so. . . . I mean, I don't drink alone or in the morning or at work.... And there are some days when I don't drink at all," I say, although those days are few and far between.

Tyson nods, studying my face.

"Do *you* think I am?" I ask him.

He sighs. "I don't know, but you definitely have a troubled relationship with alcohol. And I think it's all a very slippery slope."

Hannah nods, then says, "There are definitely some red flags. Once you start drinking, it seems hard for you to stop. And too often, you can't remember things."

"You should *never* be blacking out," Tyson says. "It's so dangerous."

"I know," I say, then confess that I sometimes use alcohol to numb myself.

Tyson bites his lip, staring at me intently. "Look. Maybe you just need to talk to a good therapist. Maybe if you sort out some of the underlying issues—the stuff you've been through with your father and losing your mother—you won't feel the need to drink when you're upset. There are so many better ways to cope."

I nod, then say, "I'm so sorry for putting you guys through all of this."

"I'm sorry, too," Hannah says. "I wasn't a good friend to you—"

"Yes, you were," Lainey says. "You *always* are."

Hannah shakes her head. "No, I wasn't. I wasn't forthright with you. But there are a few things I need to explain."

I stare at her, ready to listen.

"For one, Olivia was already in Italy when we got here. She's here for tennis. Training with a new coach. It was a complete coincidence," she says.

"Oh," I say, thinking that softens the blow of her deceit a bit.

"Also," she says, clearing her throat, "Tyson didn't know Olivia was coming to Capri. I wasn't forthright with *either* of you."

I look at Tyson. "You really didn't know she was with Hannah?"

He shakes his head and says, "I tried to tell you that—"

"Wow," I say, filled with mixed emotions. As much as I regret not giving him the benefit of the doubt, I'm also relieved that he didn't lie to me.

"There's one more thing. Something I haven't told either of you." Hannah takes a deep breath, wringing her hands. "So . . . I don't know how it happened . . . or what it is, exactly. . . . But somehow . . . Olivia and I seem to have . . . a connection—" She stops suddenly, looking more nervous than I've ever seen her.

"Um. Yeah. About that," Tyson says. "I think I saw something I wasn't supposed to see. In the bar."

I look at Tyson, then Hannah, completely lost. Then I remember how Hannah and Olivia were sitting together when we found them. They were so close.

"Holy *shit*. Are you and my *sister* . . . ?" My voice trails off, thinking there's no way. Hannah is as straight as they come.

She gives me a sheepish, starry-eyed smile. "I don't know," she says, her cheeks turning pink. "Maybe? I really like her."

"Well, *damn*," I say, blinking. "I didn't see *that* coming."

"I know. Believe me, I didn't, either. And I know you didn't want me talking to her, but we just clicked. . . . Then she asked to come see me here in Capri. And I said yes. I was afraid to tell you." The words come rushing out of her.

I stare back at her, speechless, as she continues. "I'm telling you because I want you to know why I didn't leave well enough alone when you asked me to. It's not an excuse—just an explanation. I made the wrong decision—and I take full responsibility for what happened." She sighs.

"I wish you hadn't lied to me. But it's not your fault that I almost killed myself. I can't put that on you—and you can't put that on yourself."

Hannah takes a deep breath, as if to brace herself. "Your sister is wonderful, Lainey," she says. "If you ever decide you want to know her, I am positive you will love her. But that's your call entirely."

"I trust you," I say, then look at Tyson. "I trust *both* of you."

"Good. Because we will always have your back," he says. "Even if we make some mistakes along the way."

I nod. I know I have a lot to work through, but I also know that anything is possible with these two at my side. They're all I need to get by. "I have both of your backs, too," I say, tearing up.

"We know you do," Hannah says. "You've helped me more than you could ever know. This trip has meant everything to me."

"Me too." Tyson nods.

My heart skips a beat as I think of the intimate moments we shared. I wonder if we will ever have more of them.

"God, Lainey." He swallows, a visible lump in his throat. "We almost lost you."

"But you didn't. I'm here." I force a smile. "A bit broken and battered, but I'm still here."

"We've all been through a lot. We're all a bit broken and battered," Hannah says. "But the important thing is that we kept our promise—"

Tyson nods. "Yes, we did."

"Summer would be so proud of us," Hannah says, staring up at the velvety sky.

"Yes, she would. All three of us," Tyson says.

I take his hand in mine, then gaze up at the stars. For the first time since Summer died, I can feel her with us. I can also feel tears running down my cheeks.

I try to wipe them away, but they come too fast, and I finally just let them fall.

"It's going to be okay," Tyson says.

"Better than okay," Hannah says.

I nod. Because I believe them.

ONE YEAR LATER

HANNAH

Tyson, lainey, and I finally made it to Paris. It was well worth the wait. The City of Lights is everything I hoped it would be and more. We are only a few days into our trip, but we've already experienced so much—from the Eiffel Tower and Notre-Dame to the Louvre and the Musée d'Orsay; to a riverboat cruise on the Seine and a stroll down the Champs-Élysées.

But so far, my favorite part of the trip has been our early morning runs around the city. It is something I never would have predicted back in January, when Summer's brother first reached out to us about the Chicago Marathon. His email explained that he and a few family members were organizing a tribute team to run in Summer's memory while raising money for the American Foundation for Suicide Prevention. Several of Summer's former high school and UVA teammates would be joining them, and he hoped that we would, too.

Tyson agreed on the spot, while I wrote back that although Lainey and I "can't run," we would be thrilled to help with their fundraising efforts—and of course be in Chicago that weekend to cheer everyone on.

"What do you mean you 'can't run'?" Tyson said a few minutes later on a three-way call.

"We literally can't," Lainey said.

"No, you literally *can*," Tyson replied. "If your legs work, you can run."

"Fine," Lainey said. "Technically, we *can* run. But we sure as hell can't run twenty-six point two miles."

"Nobody can run a marathon without training."

"I'm not even sure I could run the point two part," I said with a laugh.

"Then just do point *one*," Tyson said. "And build from there."

"But, Tyson . . . Ugh. Maybe a 5K—even a 10K. But a *marathon*? There's no way. It's too hard," Lainey said.

"C'mon, Lainey. You've done something way harder than a marathon," Tyson quietly reminded her.

He was obviously referring to her sobriety journey, which began shortly after we returned from Capri. At first, Lainey pushed back on the idea of rehab. But with much encouragement, she agreed to keep an open mind. From there, we did research—a *lot* of it. Lainey ultimately decided on Crossroads in Antigua, joking that it might be her only way to spend a month at the beach.

During her stay, she learned to put aside the stigma of certain labels and simply acknowledge that she had a problem. From there, she focused on the issues contributing to that problem. In other words, her drinking might only be a symptom, but it still needed to be addressed.

Since returning to New York, she had been taking things one day at a time, seeing a therapist, attending AA meetings, and following their mantra "to thine own self be true." Right before this trip, she texted us a smiling selfie with a purple medallion marking her ninth month of recovery.

In the end, Tyson convinced us to "put ourselves out there" and join #TeamSummer.

And here we were, running in Paris. Our pace was incredibly slow, but we still felt proud of our effort.

"Honestly? I don't know what is more shocking: that I'm *not* drinking in Paris or that I *am* running in Paris," Lainey says to me now as we finish a leisurely six-mile run along the Seine.

"I know," I say, as we begin our cooldown. "Who would have thunk it?"

"Not me," she says. "We've both come a long way."

I nod, thinking about my own journey over the past year.

After I returned home from Capri, my mother and I quickly fell back into our old patterns. In fact, she seemed to take strange, sick pleasure in breaking the news to me: Grady and Berlin were officially together, and he had slotted her right into my old life. My high school friends pledged their undying loyalty to me, swearing that they'd never accept Berlin in their circle, but there was still inevitable social overlap. Grady was friends with their husbands, fiancés, and boyfriends, and there was nothing to be done about that.

After three miserable months, I knew it was time to make a drastic change in my life and get the hell out of Atlanta.

Fortunately, Jada agreed with my decision and made phone calls to some of her interior design friends across the country. I was open to living pretty much anywhere, but in the end, I chose Austin, Texas, in no small part because of Olivia. After finishing her training in Italy, she had returned to Dripping Springs, and we had started to spend more time together, traveling back and forth between Texas and Georgia. Although a move to her home state felt premature— and a bit presumptuous—I followed my heart, taking a job with a boutique design firm and signing a one-year lease for the cutest one-bedroom apartment in Austin's Warehouse District. Recently, I also made the decision to start taking part-time classes at UT with the ultimate goal of earning a master's in interior design. It was originally Olivia's idea, as she had pointed out how amazing it would be to one day work for myself.

"You could even start your own firm," she'd said to me one weekend on a road trip to Marfa, Texas. "That way you could have people working for *you* when you have a baby."

Although we were nowhere near that stage of our relationship, she'd given me a look when she said it—and I could tell she was picturing the two of us having one together.

Deep down, I could see it, too. Being with Olivia makes less sense than anything I've ever done in my life, but in some ways, that's what lets me know it's real. For once, I'm not living my life for my mother. At the same time, I'm not rebelling against her, either. She simply doesn't factor into my decisions. I've yet to introduce her to Olivia, and I'm in no hurry to do so.

The only opinions that matter to me are those of my two best friends. My *chosen* family. To be clear, I don't feel like I *need* their approval, either, but I very much wanted it. So I was thrilled when Lainey got out of rehab and immediately suggested a "do-over," i.e., that we all—including Olivia—meet up for a few days in New York. We ended up staying at one of Lainey's friend's cabins in the Catskills, and our quiet weekend of hiking and talking by the fire couldn't have gone any better. By the end of it, Tyson and Lainey were almost as smitten with Olivia as I was.

On that same trip, Tyson and Lainey made an announcement of their own. While we were on Capri, and seemingly out of nowhere, the two had developed feelings for each other. They had put those feelings on hold while Lainey was sorting out her life, but they were now ready to explore a potential relationship.

On one level, I was shocked. On another level, I think I had seen it coming. Since Lainey's accident, they were both talking about each other in a much different way than they ever had before. Tyson was less judgmental, and Lainey was more unguarded.

A few weeks before we left for Paris, Tyson made another big announcement. Things were getting more serious with Lainey, and he was going to move to New York and take a job teaching AP Lit at a high school in Brooklyn.

I still can't believe the good fortune of it all. I found the person who could be my soul mate; Lainey found her sister; and Tyson and Lainey found each other. Sometimes it almost seems too good to be true—which scares me. The stakes feel so high, and I can't bear the thought of a breakup causing any sort of rift in the bedrock of our friendship.

But I have come to learn that we can't live our lives in a small, fear-based way. We have to take risks. We have to love big. And we have to have faith in our friendships. They've gotten us this far.

"WHERE ARE WE meeting up, again?" Lainey asks as we finish our training run.

"Hold on—let me check," I say, pulling my phone out of my fanny pack.

The past few mornings, we've met up at Café de Flore near our hotel, but Tyson mentioned another spot this morning and promised to text us after he finished his own (much faster) training run.

"He dropped us a pin. Looks like it's right near the Eiffel Tower. On the Place du Trocadéro?" I say.

"What's that?" she asks.

I shrug and say I guess we'll find out.

By the time we get there, I can see why he chose the meeting spot. The views of the Eiffel Tower are stunning, and the sun, now rising, is forming a bright halo around it. Lainey snaps a selfie of the two of us.

We scan the crowds for Tyson. When we don't immediately find him, I call his phone.

"Come to the fountain," he says, something in his voice sounding cryptic.

My heart skips a beat. Olivia was oddly unavailable last night when I called before bed, her phone going straight to voicemail. I'm wondering if she might be here—and I'm hoping that I am right.

As we approach the fountain, I press Lainey. "Is Olivia in Paris?"

She shrugs and says, "Not that I know of."

She's completely convincing, but I remind myself that Lainey is an actor—and a damn good one. She's yet to get another big break like *The Pigeon Girl,* but she's been getting steady work since rehab.

A moment later, I spot Tyson. And then Olivia.

"She *is* here!" I say, running toward them.

Lainey laughs, running behind me. "Surprise!"

"Oh my goodness!" I say when we reach them. I'm smiling so hard my face hurts. "How long have y'all been planning this?"

"Not as long as I've been planning *this*—" Tyson says. He pulls a piece of paper out of his pocket and hands it to Lainey.

I watch as Lainey scans the page, then looks up in surprise. "Oh, wow!" she says.

"What is it?" I ask.

"It's our pact," she says. "The Summer Pact."

"You saved it?" I ask Tyson.

"Of course I did," Tyson says. "But there's an addendum you might want to read." He points back down at the paper.

As I read over Lainey's shoulder, my eyes drop to the bottom of the page. In Tyson's neat handwriting, there is a new line below our signatures.

I squint and make out four words: *Will you marry me?*

I hear Lainey gasp, and then suddenly Tyson is down on one knee, holding a diamond ring, staring up at her.

"Will you be my best friend *and* my wife?" he asks. "Will you marry me?"

Lainey starts bawling, speechless for one of the first times in her life.

"Yes," she finally says. "Yes, I will!"

Olivia and I are now sobbing, too. We watch as Tyson slides the ring onto Lainey's finger. The sun glints off the simple brilliant-cut diamond.

He stands and gives her a long hug as people around us start to applaud and take photos.

When Tyson finally lets go of her, Lainey looks around, beams at the crowd, and asks complete strangers to please airdrop her any photos or videos.

"And follow me on Instagram! At LaineyLawsonActor!"

The moment is so classically Lainey that I'm now laughing as I cry.

"Here. Let's get one together," Tyson says, throwing one arm around me and the other around his fiancée. "You too, Olivia!"

"Let me get one of the three of you first," she says.

We pose, smiling, before she joins us.

Against all odds, we are a foursome once again. As much as we will always miss Summer, I know that she is with us—and that we wouldn't be here without her.

As strangers continue to snap photos, Lainey holds up her ring and shouts friendly instructions. *Make sure you don't cut off our feet! Or the Eiffel Tower!*

I laugh, hoping that someone captures the perfect shot. Then again, I know that's not what matters. Our lives will never be perfect, nor will the photos we take. What matters is that we are all doing our best. We are showing up for one another, even when things get rough, and against all odds, we are finding our way to happiness.

ACKNOWLEDGMENTS

I am deeply grateful . . .

To Jennifer Hershey, my gifted editor, who not only elevates my writing but also provides unwavering moral support.

To the most incredible publishing team: Kara Welsh, Jennifer Garza, Debbie Aroff, Kim Hovey, Corina Diez, Wendy Wong, Melissa Folds, Katie Horn, Ada Maduka, Loren Noveck, Jo Anne Metsch, Paolo Pepe, and Elena Giavaldi.

To Kate Hardie Patterson, my loyal assistant, who has been by my side for a dozen years, supporting me both professionally and personally.

To Brettne Bloom, my bright light of an agent. Our union truly was *bashert*.

To my original family: Sarah Giffin, the best sister in the entire world; Mary Ann Elgin, my loving mother; and Bill Giffin, my dear ol' dad. I'm so fortunate to have them in my corner.

To Nancy LeCroy Mohler, my college and forever bestie, for her tireless input on every draft, paragraph, and sentence of this novel. I remain so touched by her care and truly can't imagine publishing a book without her.

To Troy Baker for his invaluable contribution and insight into Tyson's character. I don't know anyone with a higher EQ.

To Jennifer New for hosting cozy writing retreats in her New York City apartment. Her thoughtful heart is a gift that keeps on giving.

To Charles and Andrew Vance-Broussard for always showing up and for helping to make my house a home.

To Michelle Fuller, travel advisor extraordinaire, for planning our gorgeous trip to Capri. Book research has never been so fun.

To my extended family and dear friends who have supported me in so many ways over the past year, with special thanks to: Allyson Jacoutot, Julie Portera, Laryn Gardner, Sloane Alford, Jeff MacFarland, Elizabeth Blank, Marc Blucas, Laurie Mallis, Jolie Cunningham, Yvette Gregory, Heather Spires, Lesli Gaither, Amber York, DeAnna Thomas, Katie Moss, Lea Journo, Martha Arias, Ashley Preisinger, Radhika Behl, Anna Walker-Skillman, and Harlan Coben.

To Buddy Blaha for being my partner in raising three of the most compassionate, hard-working, beautiful humans.

Most of all, I am grateful for Edward, George, and Harriet. Being their mother is my proudest achievement and greatest joy.

A final word to my readers, especially those who are struggling: Life is tough. Life is messy. Life can be heartbreakingly cruel. You have helped me through some tough times, and I hope my stories have also brought you a measure of comfort. I care about each and every one of you and wish you endless silver linings.

ABOUT THE AUTHOR

Emily Giffin is the author of eleven internationally best-selling novels: *Something Borrowed, Something Blue, Baby Proof, Love the One You're With, Heart of the Matter, Where We Belong, The One & Only, First Comes Love, All We Ever Wanted, The Lies That Bind,* and *Meant to Be.* She lives in Atlanta with her family and two dogs.

emilygiffin.com

Facebook.com/EmilyGiffinFans

Instagram: @emilygiffinauthor

ABOUT THE TYPE

This book was set in Sabon, a typeface designed by the well-known German typographer Jan Tschichold (1902–74). Sabon's design is based upon the original letter forms of sixteenth-century French type designer Claude Garamond and was created specifically to be used for three sources: foundry type for hand composition, Linotype, and Monotype. Tschichold named his typeface for the famous Frankfurt typefounder Jacques Sabon (c. 1520–80).